THE IMMUNE

DAVID KAZZIE

GRUB CLUB PUBLISHING

ISBN-13: 978-1735010519

❀ Created with Vellum

ACKNOWLEDGMENTS

To Dave Buckley, Matt Phillips, Wes Walker, Scott Weinstein, Kerry Wortzel, Rima Wiggin and others for their valuable input on early drafts of the manuscript.

To Geoffrey O'Neill and James Pickral for their insight on military matters.

To Hiba Mosrie, M.D., for her assistance with medical matters.

All errors are mine alone.

UNRAVELING

BOOK 1

In the middle of the journey of our life I came to myself within a dark wood where the straight way was lost.

DANTE, THE DIVINE COMEDY

∽

1

Miles Chadwick sat in a corner booth of Keens Steakhouse on West 36th Street in Manhattan, waiting for the apocalypse to begin.

A medium-rare filet mignon, accompanied by a side of fresh asparagus, sat in front of him, prepared to fulfill its destiny as his dinner. Chadwick stared absently at the food as if he wasn't quite sure what to do with it. He poked at the plump, crisp stalks of asparagus with his fork, their presentation on his plate reminding him of the gruesome black-and-white Holocaust photographs he'd seen as a schoolboy growing up in Carbondale, Illinois, of bodies stacked together like so much cordwood. That this was the memory flickering in his mind was ironic, given the course his life had taken, given the final answer to his own personal game of *What Do You Want to be When You Grow Up?*

As he sat there, considering this great irony, the smokiness of the charred meat began tickling his nose, which made him think of something even more horrific than the photographs, and it made his stomach flip a little. Because when you got right down to it, the thing he was now a party to was no different than the things he'd seen in those photographs. Had he really thought he was somehow better than that because he wasn't discriminating against this group or that one?

He took a deep breath and looked back at his filet. Maybe looking at it was nauseating him more than eating it would, and besides, he hadn't eaten anything all day, and so he ate every bite, chewing his meat slowly and thoroughly, just in case it might be his karmic comeuppance to choke to death on the day his plan was set into motion.

After cleaning his plate, even taking the time to wipe up the steak's juices with a crusty pumpernickel roll, he sipped his Dalwhinnie – four fingers' worth, because if there had ever been a time for scotch and a lot of it, it was now – and looked out across the wood-paneled dining room, which was packed to the gills tonight.

He first held his gaze on a group of young men in their mid-twenties at a table near the center of the main dining room, laughing like drunken hyenas. There was a wave of energy emanating from the table, a vibe that every one of these men would be getting a lap dance sometime in the next two hours. They were well-dressed and loud, commodities traders or investment bankers, managing the latter-day ritual of simultaneously yelling at one another and checking their smartphones. Empty beer and wine bottles littered the table like fallen soldiers on the pitch of battle, and reinforcements were on the way. If there was one thing Chadwick had learned about fine dining, it was that the amount of money a group spent on food and booze was directly proportional to the amount of noise it was allowed to make at dinner.

At the next table, two elderly couples, dressed for the theater. He couldn't quite make out what they were saying, but he would have bet all the money in his wallet that they were talking about tough times, how things used to be back during the Depression, discussions he hated listening to. Just hearing old people talk made his stomach muscles clench, what with their faux surprise at how fast everything was changing and how they never had anything to eat growing up other than soup rendered from the sweat of their shirts. He wondered what they would have thought about the truly hard times ahead, if any of them were fortunate enough (or unlucky enough, depending on your perspective) to survive. Probably won't be able to impress the young'uns with tales of the Depression and your black-and-white televisions, you old farts.

A third table, a booth just catty corner to him, was the hardest to look at. A man in his early forties, eating with his twin teenage sons. The man wore no wedding band, maybe Dad's weekend with the boys while his ex-wife got on with her life as a single mom. On the one hand, he pegged the father for a douchebag, dropping three hundred bucks on dinner when the boys would've been happy with a twelve-dollar bucket of chicken; on the other, the boys looked like they were having a ball, each of them chowing on porterhouses almost as big as they were. Difficult as it was, Chadwick made himself watch the boys eat their steaks, to make sure he didn't forget what they'd spent so many years working for.

Chadwick wondered if any of them would still be alive a month from now. Unlikely. Very unlikely. But he just didn't know what was going to happen. They had planned and planned and worked and worked, and there was no way to know how things would play out until they just went ahead and did it. There were about a hundred people in the restaurant that night. At least one of them would be naturally immune to the virus. Possibly two, but probably just one. He found himself hoping it would be one of the boys. He watched them dip their steak fries in ranch dressing and drink their cherry Cokes, and he watched their dad let them steal a nip from his tall glass of beer, painfully aware the trio would almost certainly be dead by Labor Day, four weeks from now.

Another wave of nausea washed over him, and he shut his eyes tight, trying to will away the queasiness. He'd known this was coming, and why in God's name he had just eaten a nine-ounce filet was beyond his powers of comprehension. Probably no one in human history had ever felt as much stress as what Miles Chadwick was feeling at this very moment. He gagged, fearful he had confused stomach-liquefying panic with hunger.

His phone began chirping, which just added fuel to his already over-heated heart. One of the elderly foursome threw a nasty look in his direction, clearly unhappy with the technological intrusion. He resisted the nearly overpowering urge to flip her the bird, reminding himself that older folks still had a problem with the wireless phones in public, and besides, she'd be dead by the end of the week, so who cared what she thought?

The phone was a dinosaur, prepaid, purchased with cash at a 7-Eleven, for one use, for this moment only. At the other end of the line was another prepaid wireless phone, also purchased for this one historic telephone call. He struggled to grip the phone, which refused to find purchase in his sweat-slicked hand.

"Yes?" he answered, his voice catching.

Jesus, Chadwick, man up.

He cleared his throat. Then, more forcefully: "Yes?"

He could feel his heart pounding in his ears while he waited for a response.

"It's done."

"You're sure?" Chadwick asked.

"As sure as we're going to be right now. All canisters were deployed without issue or interference."

Reflexively, he touched his left bicep, the site of the vaccine administration one year ago. He would've bet anything that the caller had just done the same thing. Now they'd see if things unfolded as they predicted. Following exposure, an asymptomatic but contagious incubation period of about eight to twelve hours, which would facilitate the spread of the virus, and then another twelve to twenty-four hours for the disease to run its course. The key was the virus' design, Chadwick's engineering, its remarkable communicability and lethality.

"And there were no problems?"

"No problems," the man said. "All operatives reported in on schedule with the appropriate code word. Everything went according to plan. Fucking unbelievable, eh?"

Along with the very special vaccine to the soon-to-be-famous virus, relief coursed through Miles Chadwick's veins. But it wasn't just relief; riding shotgun was a sudden horror at what he had wrought. Part of him, and not a small one, wished he could undo what he had done, wished he had never created the PB-815 virus, impressionable and easily manipulated, like an insecure teenage girl, which he had brainwashed into becoming a ruthless serial killer. It was too much, too extreme, too fucking crazy. He felt cold; a shiver rippled through him.

"You still there?" the caller asked.

"Yes. Sorry."

He was biting his lip so hard that he had drawn blood. The taste of iron filled his mouth like he'd been chewing on a penny. He dabbed his lower lip with a napkin; he looked down at it, noticing that the tiny red spot left behind had taken the shape of a scythe. This he wrote off to his mind playing tricks on him. Still, he didn't want to keep looking at it, the non-symbolic symbol, so he quickly stuffed the napkin into his coat pocket. Scotch, he thought. The scotch would settle him down. He demolished the rest of his drink in one fell swoop.

"Now we wait, right?" the caller said.

"Now we wait," Chadwick confirmed. We wait, Chadwick thought, until nothing happens, or people start dying like flies. One or the other. "We'll meet at the compound in two weeks."

"Enjoy the rest of your summer," the caller said before clicking off the line.

That brought the faintest of smiles to Chadwick's lips, and he immediately felt bad about it because it was disrespectful, making jokes at the expense of the human race.

Chadwick ordered a second scotch and glanced at the boys, each now laying waste to a slice of chocolate pie. Then he turned his attention to the front door, positive that any minute now, a hundred federal agents would swarm in like locusts and arrest him, giving the restaurant's other patrons the winning story at their next get-together. They would charge him with about fifty different violations of the federal antiterrorism statute, and he'd have an all-expense paid trip to the execution chamber at the supermax prison in Florence, Colorado. Wasn't that how it always played out in the movies? The bad guy never got away. Didn't the hero always crack the case at the last minute, saving everyone at the zero hour?

Every shred of doubt about his intellect or ability that he had ever felt in his life drew up into a tsunami of fear and panic and washed through him like a flash flood hitting a barren gulley. How could he have been so stupid, so arrogant, so foolish? Who was he to think that he could alter the course of human history? He thought about all he was trying to undo, thousands of years of human achievement, from the wheel to the computer, from fried Twinkies to bluegrass music, from Harley-Davidson to the moon landing. His plan was too big, too insane, too impossible.

He took another sip of scotch, a long one. Calm down, he whispered to himself. Calm down. He closed his eyes and counted to twenty. Finally, finally, the alcohol started to work its magic, and he felt warmth at his core, spreading out to his extremities, his face, and at long last, his brain. His mind settled, he thought about the plan again, a decade in the making. Its genesis, its infancy, its rocky adolescence, and finally, tonight's debut. He reached into his pocket and pulled out the photo-graph he'd carried for two decades. Ragged on the edges, folded and unfolded so many times that the creases had split. He stared at the picture, and it reminded him why he was doing this, why he'd made it his life's work to make PB-815 all that it could be.

A basic tenet of virology was that viruses could be extremely lethal or extremely communicable, but not both. Thus, a quick-killing virus, the type that became fodder for movies and books and scaring the bejeezus out of people, normally faced one of two fates: either it burned itself out and disappeared because it killed its host too rapidly, before it had a chance to jump to the next one, or it mutated into a less virulent form to ensure the hosts stayed alive long enough to perpetuate the virus' continued survival. See, e.g., the common cold, which ran unchecked around the globe, a big, dumb, happy germ that just wanted everyone to like it. The Labrador retriever of the virus world.

Chadwick believed there was a reason that the Ebolas of the world had stayed put, occasionally rearing their heads to remind humanity that they were still here, but never quite making the big crash into the human race. At their core, these super-hot viruses, like Ebola and Marburg, were programmed to stay hot, and so the price they paid for their deadliness was existence on the fringe. They were viral royalty, not interested in infecting millions or billions at the risk of sacrificing their virulence, satisfied, maybe at some unknowable level, at being the very best with a limited body of work.

But then Chadwick had created PB-815 while working for that private, off-the-books laboratory in southern Nebraska, funded by Leon Gruber, the benefactor who had started the project. Without government oversight to worry about, Chadwick's work progressed quickly. Within two years, he'd developed his masterpiece – a jacked-up virus with the serial-killer drive of Ebola and spliced with the sociability of the commonest of colds. He was fortunate the virus hadn't claimed him along the way. But their tedious, careful, painstaking work had been completed, not just on the virus, but on the vaccine as well, because without the vaccine, a true marvel, PB-815 was useless, a monster that couldn't be controlled, a beast that would turn on its handlers.

And now it was ready. If everything went according to plan, it would spread quickly, so quickly that if the virus indeed did mutate a few weeks from now, it wouldn't matter. Chadwick had made his peace with the fact that there were certain things beyond his control, that no one truly knew how PB-815 would interact with a complex system like the vast tapestry making up the human population. In fact, a very tiny fraction of the population, perhaps less than two percent, would be naturally immune to the virus thanks to a genetic anomaly he'd discovered. Boy, were those folks in for a big surprise.

They had estimated the first wave of infections at about five thousand, five thousand people who would leave tonight's Yankees game with a very special souvenir, and each of whom would infect a dozen or so people before becoming symptomatic themselves, about eight to twelve hours after exposure. Before the first wave began dying about a day from now, they would have spread the virus to about another 60,000 people. Then their virus would truly go viral, up to five million before health officials even got wind of an outbreak, and then that, as they said, would be all she wrote. And he wasn't even counting the supercarriers, the ones who would board airplanes and buses and trains and subways and expose hundreds, if not thousands, of people in one fell swoop, and send the virus to the four points of the compass, aboard the transatlantic flights to London and Paris and Johannesburg, the westbound airliners to Tokyo and Sydney and Beijing, on the morning shuttles to Chicago and Washington and Los Angeles and Houston, cutting any effective quarantine attempts off at the legs.

Miles Chadwick held up his tumbler of scotch and silently toasted the noisy dining room, a eulogy for a world that had ended at Yankee Stadium, during the second of a three-game series between the Bombers and the Red Sox, the teams tied for first place with eight weeks to go in the regular season, the baseball universe in its proper order.

2

Adam Fisher held the letter in his hands, the words lying flat against the page. Standing alone, each word was just that – a word, meaningless without context, a dictionary entry. But strung together in this way, on this sheet of paper bearing the letterhead of the Virginia Board of Medicine, the words joined together into something accusatory, something lethal, something ruinous. He read it again, skimming over the clutter and procedure of the opening paragraph and focusing on the meat, a single sentence near the bottom of the heavy bond paper the Board used in flexing its muscles when summoning its licensees before it.

Specifically, Adam Fisher, M.D., failed to adequately monitor Patient A, who was 39 weeks pregnant, causing the patient's death and the loss of the full-term fetus.

Twenty-six words. Twenty-six words that had chewed their way into the fabric of his life like moths set loose in a musty closet. Twenty-seven, if you counted the M.D., the two letters that meant so much to so many people, the two letters that earned him a spot in Richmond Magazine's list of Most Eligible Bachelors every couple of years, the two letters that had placed him under the jurisdiction of the Board of Medicine since he'd become licensed as a physician sixteen years earlier.

He set the letter down on his blotter and leaned back in his chair. He was in his private office at the Tuckahoe Women's Center, on the campus of the Henrico Doctors' Hospital, a few miles west of downtown Richmond, Virginia. It was early, a little after seven, and the office was still quiet. The day promised a full slate of expectant mommies, menopausal grandmothers, teenage girls embarrassed by their mothers hell-bent on getting them on birth control. Adam hadn't slept since the letter from the Board had arrived in yesterday's mail. Of course, he'd known it was coming since that awful day the previous November. It was like waiting eight months for a punch in the stomach, a punch you knew was going to drop you and take your breath away, but one that you couldn't do anything about.

His gaze drifted up to the large corkboard pinned to his wall, every square inch covered with photographs, the faces of countless babies staring back at him, children he'd shepherded into the world. He'd never planned to start the Baby Board, as it was known in the office, but early in his career, following a patient's difficult but successful delivery, the new mom had sent him a photo of her healthy baby. Not knowing what to do with it, Adam pinned it to the new corkboard, an office accoutrement he hadn't found a use for yet. A week later, another patient saw the picture during her last office visit before delivery, and she too sent a photograph of her newborn. And it grew from there. Not every patient sent in a picture, but many did, and in sixteen years, the board had filled up, getting more and more crowded until it looked like a giant group shot of a baby rave.

Adam started each day with a quick look at his body of work, at the chubby babies, the skinny ones, preemies, late arrivals, the Down Syndrome babies, the healthy babies, black babies, white babies, Asian babies, Latino babies. The oldest, the very first picture on the bulletin board, was in high school now; the newest photo was of a little boy born about three weeks ago. Two of the babies on the wall had since died, one of leukemia at the age of nine, the other in a car accident before her first birthday. Neither mother was his patient anymore; Adam didn't know if it was appropriate to keep those photos up, but he couldn't bear to take them down, and so there they remained. He thought about Patient A again, who'd said at her last appointment that she couldn't wait to send in her picture for the board.

At 7:45, he changed into a spare pair of khakis and button-down oxford he kept at the office and eyed the worn couch in the corner, a holdover from the old apartment he'd lived in during med school. He'd been up for twenty-four hours, but Adam had never needed much sleep, a useful skill for a doctor. It would be more for the brief escape from this new reality of his. He rubbed his eyes, ran his hands against his closely shorn hair, decided against the nap. He sat back down and read the letter again. For the hundredth time? The thousandth? He didn't know.

A knock on his open office door interrupted him, and he felt a burst of heat run up his back, as if someone had caught him looking at Internet porn. He briefly debated stuffing the letter in his desk, but then it would look like he was trying to cover what he was doing, and then it would look like he was admitting he was guilty of the terrible thing the letter was accusing him of, that he had, in fact, failed to adequately monitor Patient A, which, of course, was a euphemism for *killing* Patient A and her unborn baby, who had been doing just fine, thank you very much, until Dr. Adam Fisher had gotten his incompetent hands on them.

During a professional ethics class he'd taken his last year in medical school, one of those weekly classes he frequently skipped, Adam had been required to observe a hearing before the Board of Medicine. It was a *Scared Straight* sort of thing, designed to remind these fledgling doctors that they should avoid the Board offices, unless they'd made the right kind of friends and gotten themselves appointed to the Board itself. Adam couldn't even remember what the respondent, an oncologist (or was it a cardiologist?), had been charged with. He'd gotten there late, a little hungover, and could barely manage to stay awake during the interminable hearing. He remembered very clearly thinking that would never happen to him, feeling a certain detached pity for this poor sap before the Board, four doctors and one chiropractor (a chiropractor – for God's sake, medicine's equivalent of a snake oil salesman!) second-guessing his life's work.

He looked up and saw Joe McCann standing in the doorway. He was a large man, and despite having rounded the turn toward his seventieth birthday, he was still blessed with a shock of thick red hair topping his huge dome. This was his medical practice, now in its fourth decade of serving the Richmond area. He didn't work a full schedule anymore, but he still had his finger on the pulse of what his six physicians were up to.

"Morning," Adam said. He didn't try to put on airs or pretend like nothing was wrong, because Joe would have sniffed it out in a heartbeat. Worse, he would have felt like his intelligence was being insulted, and there was nothing the man hated more.

"How you doing, son?" McCann asked.

So he knew. Of course he knew. Did Adam really think he wouldn't know? McCann had friends everywhere in the medical community, including, but not limited to the Virginia Board of Medicine. Besides, there was nothing secret about the Board's Notice for Adam L. Fisher, M.D., to appear on September 9, some five weeks hence. It was public record, out there for all eternity, so even if Adam was fully exonerated, that Notice would be out there for all to see, a little whisper in the ear of a prospective patient who'd decided to check Adam out, telling her the terrible story of Patient A.

Adam was a little relieved McCann knew. It was out of the way, and Adam was spared the humiliation of having to knock on McCann's door like a kid who'd smashed his neighbor's window with an errant baseball.

Adam took a deep breath and let it out slowly.

"I've been better," Adam said.

"I know, son," McCann said. He addressed each of his three male doctors as son. "We'll get through this. It's a bullshit charge, but you can't let it eat you up like this."

"I'll be OK," Adam said. "The work will keep my mind off it. We're loaded up with Amanda on maternity leave."

McCann closed the door and dropped his big frame down on Adam's couch. He leaned forward, propping his elbows on his knees.

"Here's the thing," McCann said. "I've been thinking about this a lot. I want you to take a little time off so you can deal with this thing. Get your head straight. I have every confidence the Board will clear you, but you're no good to me while you replay every moment of that night every minute of the day."

Adam looked at his boss, his mouth agape.

"Are you firing me?" Adam asked, his voice small. The office felt hot all of a sudden.

"No," McCann said. "Absolutely not. I'll pay your salary until the hearing, and then they'll reprimand you or cut you loose or whatever it is they're going to do, and we can all move on with our lives. Look, I've read the chart. I talked to the nurses on duty. You did every goddamn thing I would've done. Sometimes patients die."

Adam couldn't hold McCann's gaze; he fiddled with the blotter, his fingers peeling up the corner of the August calendar.

"I don't know. I just don't know."

"I've been watching you the last few months," McCann said. "You second-guess yourself. You order unnecessary tests. You scare patients. You're like Chicken Little all of a sudden. You're a good doctor, a goddamn good doctor, but this is no good for you, no good for the patients. Adam. Sometimes they just die."

Adam wanted to argue, shout, beg, plead, bargain, do something, anything to keep working. He dreaded the idea of five empty weeks ahead of him, nothing left to fill the time but his thoughts. But he remained silent. Once Joseph McCann had made up his mind about something, he didn't change it.

"What am I supposed to do for five weeks?"

McCann smiled.

"Whatever you want. Go to Vegas. Go visit your daughter."

The mention of Rachel made his stomach tighten. She was a rising sophomore at CalTech and lived with her mom Nina and stepfather Jerry near San Diego; Adam saw her once or twice a year. He couldn't bear to tell her about this. Their relationship had finally reached a point where they spoke regularly, where he didn't feel like an interloper in her life. This though, he was afraid how she would see him in her eyes. She would see herself in Patient A. She would see her mom, her closest friends, because that's how she thought, how her mind worked. And she would think less of him. This just served to depress him further. Just tack on *Shitty Doctor* alongside his talent as *Absent Father*!

McCann pointed at the letter on Adam's desk. Before continuing, he grimaced and struggled to clear his throat. He coughed twice.

"Are you OK?" Adam asked.

"Yeah," McCann said. "Woke up feeling a little off. Might be coming down with something." He felt around under his neck. "Glands are a bit swollen."

"I can stay and work today," Adam offered. "You wanna go home?"

"Fisher, if I went home every time I felt a little under the weather, I wouldn't be much of a doctor, now would I?" McCann asked.

"You're not gonna let me slide on this little vacation, are you?" McCann winked at him.

"Good one." He rapped twice on the doorjamb before disappearing down the hall, calling back as he ducked into his own office.

"Work on getting that thing out of your life."

HE DROVE HOME SLOWLY, sticking to the city streets, thick with rush-hour traffic headed toward downtown Richmond for another workday under the broiling August sun. This time of year, the traffic was made up of two groups of people - those who'd already been on vacation and were already missing it, and those who'd yet to escape on their summer getaway. Adam turned south on Robinson, rolled by Buddy's Bar & Grill, one of his old med school hangouts, when life had been so much easier. His whole career ahead of him.

Traffic slowed at Robinson and West Grace Street, and Adam coasted to a halt. The oscillating lights of emergency vehicles in the intersection flickered silently in the morning steam. Two paramedics worked to load a stretcher into the ambulance bay, and a police officer directed traffic down a side street. In the middle of the intersection, the mangled remains of a motorcycle and the spider-webbed windshield of a Ford Taurus, parked at a crazy angle.

Adam rolled down his window as he approached the officer. He was stoutly built, his beefy arms straining against the short-sleeve police uniform.

"I'm a doctor," Adam said to the man. "Need any help?"

"Naw, thanks," the officer said. "Car versus motorcycle. Dumbass wasn't wearing a helmet. DOA."

Adam sighed. Callous as his words might have been, the officer was correct that the biker had been a dumbass.

"Sorry to hear it," Adam said.

"Thanks anyway, doc."

Another block south, he turned right onto Floyd Avenue and found a spot just in front of his two-story brownstone. The premier parking spot was, to Adam, a pretty shitty attempt at evening the cosmic scales. Yeah, yeah, so your career is on the line and you just drove by a fatal car crash,

but how about that primo parking spot, big A! Still, if that was all that
the universe was prepared to offer him today, then he would take it.
Maybe, just maybe, this good parking spot was the bloop single trig-
gering a long streak of good fortune.

He checked the mail and made his way up the front walk, past his
small yard, roasted to a burnt orange, the product of another hot, dry,
merciless summer in central Virginia. Maybe the planet was warming,
and maybe they were all roasting themselves one barrel of oil at a time.
Or maybe it was because the world was such an angry place these days,
and a hot, angry planet was just what mankind deserved.

He'd bought the place just after finishing medical school, when he
learned he'd been matched with the Virginia Commonwealth University
Hospital in downtown Richmond for his OB/GYN residency. After a
childhood spent in Culpeper County, a rural stretch of horse farms and
not much else in central Virginia, he'd grown to love city living, in no
small part because his father Jack, an accomplished computer scientist
and giant prick, hated it so much. His house was in a historical neighborhood of brownstones and Victorian-style mansions called the Fan, so
named because of how its half dozen or so main streets fanned out from
a centerpoint near the VCU campus.

He liked its feel, of sitting on his porch and drinking a cold Sam
Adams when he wasn't on call, smoking the occasional cigarette (even
though he was a doctor and, of course, he knew better). In the evenings,
he liked walking around the corner to Pints & Pies and eating pizza
while listening to the local music scene. Sometimes, he'd make the
acquaintance of a young lady, and that would last a few weeks or a few
months, long enough to make him realize she wasn't The One either. He
liked his strange hippie neighbors, the poet on his left, the alternative
fuels guy on his right.

As he let himself in, he took note of how quiet it was. He wasn't here
often on weekday mornings, and so he wasn't especially tuned in to the
neighborhood's weekday rhythms. The whole neighborhood was ghostlike, a shadow of its normal self. He didn't see any joggers or stay-at-
home moms pushing their strollers like he expected. It unnerved him a
little. Quiet mornings in the beach cottage, those were different, when
the lines on the calendar dissolved. The silence spurred him on, urging
him to pack quickly.

He threw clothes and toiletries into an overnight bag. A stack of unread novels stood precariously on his nightstand, books he'd collected during his trips to the various local bookstores, and he imagined himself sitting at the water's edge lost in a long book, his feet buried in the wet, shifting sand. There was something about a long novel that Adam had always found alluring, the way he could disappear into the story and not look up until the tops of his thighs had burned to a crisp. A couple of paperbacks found their way into his bag as well. After packing, he hopped online and suspended his mail service, his newspaper, set up his bills to auto-pay.

Adam leaned back in his chair and scratched his chin, sandpapery with a couple of days of stubble. He thought about calling Rachel, who would be getting ready to head back to campus. He took out his phone and dialed her number, his heart throbbing. As it rang unrequitedly, he wondered, like he always did when he called and no one answered, if she was sitting there in Sunnydale, holding the phone in her hand as his name flashed on the caller ID, deciding whether she should answer the phone.

He was greeted by the phone's prerecorded message, which always made him smile; he once asked her why she didn't leave her own outgoing message on her phone, and she'd said she didn't have time to waste on bullshit like that. Bullshit, she'd said. That was Rachel.

"Hey, Rach," he began, "it's Dad."

He paused, trying to think of something funny to say, but as the seconds ticked by, he became aware of the silence, of the hiss of the open phone line, and how the silence would sound on her end.

"Sorry about that," he said. "Dropped an apple." His cheeks flushed with embarrassment. "Anyway, I'm headed out down to the beach house for a little vacation. I know you're probably busy getting ready for school, but I'd love to hear from you. Give me a call when you get a chance. Bye."

He nearly told her he loved her but decided against it. He hung up.

He started to get out of his chair, but then he sat back down and pulled up the website of an online florist. Daffodils had always been her favorite, and as sensible as she was, she'd always had a soft spot for flowers. He found an arrangement he thought she would like, cursed at the outrageous price - really, seventy-nine bucks for eight flowers and a cheap glass vase? He raced through the order, pausing at the screen asking for a personalized message.

Rach,
I know you'll do great this year.
Love,
Dad
He left it at that.

~

ADAM LEFT Richmond a little after noon. It was about a five-hour trip, taking him south-southeast through tobacco country for about 175 miles before doglegging east toward Wilmington on Interstate 40. It rained lightly, off and on for most of the first half of the drive. Adam passed the time by imagining where each driver was headed.

He stopped once, just east of the I-95/I-40 junction, for fuel and a gas station hot dog, a guilty pleasure he admitted to no one. He ate in the shade of the pump island as the nozzle delivered its payload into his gas tank. The concrete shimmered in the heat, cooking the scraggly weeds poking up through the zig-zaggy cracks here and there across the tarmac. A tired-looking banner strung across the building's façade announced the sale of a $50,000 SuperLotto ticket, and Adam wondered about the type of person who would be swayed to buy a lottery ticket by the display of such an advertisement. The crumpled-up remains of his lunch flew into the wastebasket, he imagined himself burying a three-pointer to bring the Wizards their first NBA title since the 1970s, and he got back on the road.

It was murderously humid, the sky a hard blue, the kind of day that would fire up big thunderheads by dinnertime, scaring the beachgoers off the sand and into their cottages and condos, the ones with any sense anyway. Even on full blast, the air conditioning strained to keep the car cool, and he grew impatient, the little boy in him wondering when the hell they were going to get there already. Traffic was relatively light as he made his way southeast. The southern North Carolina beaches were still a relatively well-kept secret, and the easy access always made for a relaxing start to a vacation.

A little after five, he turned east off Route 17 and rolled past the vegetable stands and crumbling postwar ranch houses toward the coast. A few minutes later, the white causeway leading to the skinny island of Holden Beach arced up in Adam's windshield. To the west, the sky had darkened, a line of purplish clouds with mayhem on the brain. They looked like a giant bruise on the sky, a harbinger of atmospheric violence to come.

He stopped for groceries and supplies at the big store just before the causeway. Might as well get it out of the way, he thought. He bought steaks, chicken, ribs, sausage; he scoured the less-than-impressive produce aisle because after all that meat, he'd need something to keep the plumbing clear, he stocked up on chips and cookies and beer. As he made his way up and down the aisles, grabbing batteries and pancake mix and bacon, magical, delicious bacon, and whatever else his heart desired, his body loosened, his mind decelerated.

His Explorer stocked with groceries, Adam climbed the causeway slowly, taking in the Atlantic Ocean ahead, gray and choppy on this summer afternoon. Humid air wafted through the open windows, the salty brine tickling his nose. He could hear the waves, the sound of the ocean, of this monolithic thing, forever there, and he could feel his blood pressure drop. Once he was on the island, he picked his way past the quaint post office, past the sign announcing TURTLE PATROL THURSDAY NIGHT 7 PM! before turning west along Ocean Boulevard.

Since it was a weekday, not a turnaround day, the traffic was light on the island's main drag, and he covered the remaining miles to his cottage in the blink of an eye. He was careful not to speed, though, because if there was anything the Brunswick County Sheriff's deputies loved doing, it was ticketing speeders, folks who would never come back to contest the charge six weeks later, long after the vacation had ended and they were knee deep in the routine of their everyday lives.

THE HOUSE WAS one of the older ones, a gray, weather-beaten A-frame, right on the beach, built in the 1960s by Adam's grandfather, Donald Fisher, plank by plank. He had died when Adam was five, leaving the house to Adam's father. And because Jack Fisher, a computer scientist by trade, was nothing if not thrifty, Adam had spent many summer vacations and spring breaks and Christmases here as a kid, so many that he began to resent the place, because would it have killed his dad to take him to Disney World or Hawaii or California just one time? Jack Fisher was a difficult man who'd never recovered from the sudden death of Adam's mother, and he used the house as a drinking oasis, a place for him to escape the disappointment that was his life. He brought Adam here because he could let him run on the beach while he sat in a rickety old rocking chair on the deck, drinking can after can of Pabst Blue Ribbon.

As he got older, Adam grew to appreciate Holden more, and when he got his driver's license, he started coming down here on his own and taking care of the place, which was fine by the senior Fisher. Adam taught himself some simple renovations, looked to the neighbors for help when he got stuck on something, and slowly but surely made the place a wellspring of happy memories rather than a cesspool of sour ones.

After turning on the water main at the front of the house and a quick exterior inspection, Adam let himself in, finding the house to be in relatively good shape, if not a little musty. He went from room to room, checking window seals, looking for yellow stains in the ceiling, the telltale sign of water damage, finding none. A few bulbs had burned out since he'd last been here, but otherwise, the place just needed a good airing out.

It took three trips to unload the Explorer, but an hour later, the truck was empty, the supply closet and the pantry fully stocked. The approaching thunderheads had dissolved, leaving behind a checkered sky of clouds and sun. Adam stretched out on one of the weather-beaten Adirondack chairs on the back deck, looking out over the ocean, a cold beer in his hand, a portable cooler stocked with a six-pack next to him. He'd brought a paperback out here with him, the latest Dennis Lehane, but he was content to watch the ocean and the sunbathers dotting the beach like brightly colored hermit crabs scampering across the sand.

He stayed out on the deck all evening, drinking his beer, slapping at the lazy mosquitoes droning around him. For the first time in nearly a year, Patient A seemed very far away.

3

"It's over, Freddie," Richie Matas said. "You understand what I'm saying, right?"

Freddie Briggs was seated on the ridiculous rattan couch in their sunroom, barely aware of his wife Susan's hand at his back, caressing him, trying to calm him down. The room was bright with sunlight, streaming in from the huge plate-glass windows.

"No one will touch you after the positive test," said Richie, his long-time agent, a founding partner of Elite Sports Worldwide and the one who'd been lucky enough to snag Freddie as he was coming out of college a decade ago. "It's over."

Richie paused and then said it again, like a mob hitman putting another bullet in his victim's head to make sure the job had been done. Then Freddie was up off the couch, prowling like a mountain lion, a scary enough vibe emanating from him to encourage his ever-pacing agent to take a seat next to Susan.

"Freddie," Susan was saying, "it's gonna be OK. We're gonna figure this out."

"Didn't I tell you to stay away from that shit?" Richie asked. "They got tests we can't keep up with. Did you know what it was when you took it? We'll file an appeal."

Freddie ignored him, not wanting to discuss it in front of Susan, even though he knew she knew about it. It was one of those things shared between a husband and wife without being shared, disapproved of in non-verbal ways. She hadn't asked about the hypodermic needle or the vial because as any good lawyer would tell you, you never asked the question you didn't want the answer to. Freddie, his hands clenching into fists and unclenching again, peered out the plate-glass window overlooking the backyard, sloping down toward the lake about a hundred yards distant. To the right was Susan's vegetable garden, in full bloom now, exploding in reds and greens and yellows. Beyond that, the acre of land made possible by an NFL career that appeared to have reached its end.

"Those assholes. Those assholes!"

He never thought he'd be the guy to get busted, but there he was, thirty-two years old, trying to make it back from his second reconstructive knee surgery (on the same knee, no less) in three years. He wanted to tell Richie and Susan that the trainer he'd hooked up with in February had told him that they *didn't* test for that substance, which helped him recover from workouts faster, but the truth was that the guy had said that they couldn't test for it. And Freddie just wanted to believe him so badly because the only thing that was going to get him another chance with the league was to make his body as hard and fast and strong as it had ever been. Then they'd pulled him for a random urine screen two weeks ago, just before the camps were about to open, just before he expected to get a call from Richie telling him that it was going to be Chicago or Houston or maybe New York that wanted to bring in the great Freddie Briggs to shore up a defensive line.

And Matas had called, this morning, in fact, saying he was in Smyrna meeting a potential client and that they needed to talk. When he got to the house, there was no indication that there was anything wrong even though he was pacing because he was always pacing. No clue he was planning to tell his most famous client the news he didn't want to hear, the professional athlete's equivalent of finding out the mass was malignant and that there wasn't anything else that could be done.

Freddie picked up an empty rattan chair and swung it around like an Olympic hammer before launching it through the sliding door. The door exploded like a starburst, shards and splinters of glass blowing out onto the composite deck.

"Freddie!"

He left them there, the sunroom silent but for the tinkling of the broken glass, back through the galley kitchen, the office, and through the family room, past his girls Caroline and Heather, sitting on the couch, watching *Tangled*, oblivious to what was going on around them in that way that kids were. He stopped at the front door, his hand on the knob, and debated just sitting with them as they watched their movie, but he couldn't. He couldn't breathe in here.

He climbed into his truck and drove off. He rolled past the huge homes in the subdivision, occupied by doctors and bankers who were good enough neighbors and had long ago gotten used to the idea of the NFL star next door. He wasn't sure where he was going, only sure that he couldn't be inside his house anymore, in front of Richie, in front of Susan, who would be so disappointed in him for cheating because she told him many years ago that she hoped he never thought he would need to do that.

Near the center of town, he turned down Walker Street and into the gravel parking lot of The Ugly Duckling, wedging his mammoth SUV next to a Ford F-150 with the naked-lady mudflaps, super close, almost hoping its owner would give him a hard time for parking so close to his beloved pickup, because it had been a while since Freddie had been in a good fight.

Freddie stamped across the dusty gravel parking lot and burst through the front door, feeling every bit the cliché of a man seeking to drown his sorrows in drink. His size and presence always drew stares, even from people who'd known him for years. He strode up to the long oak bar and asked Sal, the proprietor, for the Wild Turkey. Sal, who had known Freddie since he started patronizing the bar in high school, when he was already bigger, faster, and stronger than every man in Smyrna and could hold his booze better than the gin-blossomest drunk in the place, poured the shot without comment and left the bottle at Freddie's side.

Freddie drained two shots without blinking an eye, thinking back to his first day at the NFL scouting combines, when he'd left the scouts gasping for air with his 40-yard-dash time. It was legendary, adding to the ever-growing mythos of Freddie Briggs, the greatest defensive lineman in a generation.

He glanced around the bar before knocking back his third shot, still feeling like that teenager who'd snuck in here, too young to drink, even though he was a grown man now, married, father of two girls. The Ugly Duckling had been a Smyrna institution since opening its doors in 1985, making its home in the low-slung building with the giant plastic chick on the roof, keeping its little ducky eye on the town. Someone tried stealing it at least once a year.

As was often the case at happy hour, the bar was crowded with regulars, and people normally left him alone, especially lately, with his recent struggles documented in the Atlanta Journal-Constitution. This he had never quite gotten used to, and he wondered how regular people would react if their performance and career struggles were publicly documented on a regular basis.

Struggle. Something unimaginable three years ago, but rapidly becoming part of his everyday, part of his routine. Someone was telling him he couldn't do something, and there was nothing he could do about it. For all his physical gifts, for all his intellect, a combination of brains and brawn that made NFL scouts drool starting his freshman year at LSU and led some sports commentators to call him the next step in human evolution, it was his body that had finally failed him, leaving him washed up at thirty-two.

Six straight years he had made the Pro Bowl, the unquestioned captain and coach of the Atlanta Falcons defense, no matter who bore the title of defensive coordinator. Then on the first Sunday of his seventh season, rushing the Arizona Cardinals quarterback on a sellout blitz, the slow and overmatched left tackle had lost his balance and rolled into Freddie's right knee, planted firmly into the turf, tearing three ligaments and ripping the meniscus clean off. A year of rehabilitation followed, but he'd lost a step, probably more like three steps, in his return season. He blew out the knee again in the year's last game, and that was the end of that. The Falcons cut him, brutally and unceremoniously, a Hall of Fame career now in question. After another year of rehab, he signed on with New England as a backup lineman, but the knee wouldn't cooperate, and the Patriots cut him as well.

It was early August now, training camps in full swing, and he'd spent the last six months in the weight room, running five miles each day, desperate for one more chance to prove he was as good now as he had been during those six magical seasons with the Falcons. He had the skills, the veteran wiliness, and while he wasn't twenty-two anymore, a body that was more than up for the task. But now this positive test, and the four-game suspension that would follow had all but ended his career at the ripe old age of thirty-two. He wondered if it had hit ESPN or Yahoo! Sports yet; if not, it would soon, and then they would call him a cheater. The pride of Smyrna, nothing but a cheater.

He threw back the next shot, his head telling him he should stop now and scoot back home, where Richie and Susan were undoubtedly huddled together, trying to come up with a plan to soften the landing, make him understand that his football days had been numbered from the moment he'd pulled on a jersey for the Smyrna SkyChiefs in the pee-wee league he'd run roughshod over to the point that the other parents demanded to see a birth certificate because no way was that kid five years old. They would tell him a pro football career had a half-life, that there was life after football and he should be thankful he was leaving the game with nothing worse than a couple of bum knees.

He took a deep breath, slightly buzzed now, fully aware of the cliché he'd become – the ex-jock unable to let go of his glory, marinating his sorrows at the local watering hole. The reality was he didn't even need to be here to get drunk; he had a fully stocked bar in their media room, where he'd studied game film. But he couldn't be at the house anymore. Just being inside its walls was suffocating him, as if the oxygen had been sucked clean out of the house.

Freddie became aware of a presence beside him, another bar patron perched atop the cracked vinyl covering the ancient barstool, rotated just so, his right elbow propped up on the bar. From the corner of his eye, Briggs took in his new neighbor, and his heart sank. It was just not going to be his day.

It was Randy Ferguson, Campbell High School's ex-assistant football coach. He'd lost his job a year ago, after he'd been found in the back of his van with a cigar box full of weed and a fifteen-year-old cheerleader in an inappropriate stage of undress. Ferguson had been another one of Smyrna's shining football stars, not the wunderkind Briggs had been, but Division I material nonetheless, an outside chance to make it to the NFL as an offensive lineman. That dream had ended when he'd fractured two vertebrae in his neck during his sophomore season at Alabama, and Ferguson had never quite made his peace with that.

His hand was wrapped around a bottle of Coors Light, sweating condensation, the droplets catching the light from the bar just so. He was taller than Briggs and heavier, although Ferguson's current mass owed more to beer, pizza and cheese fries. Over the years, he'd developed a reputation as a bit of a brawler, but the fights always went one of two ways; he either knocked his opponent down with one swipe of his meaty mitt, or the brawls degenerated into a slow dance to nowhere.

"So, Freddie," Ferguson said, "how's the comeback going?"

Freddie rubbed his eye slowly, cursing his luck. If there had been a list of *Fucking People He Didn't Feel Like Dealing With*, Randy Ferguson would have been near the top of it. And he'd have to just sit here and take it because getting up and walking out would be just what Randy Ferguson would want; it would signify that Ferguson had won some battle in the eternal war between the two men, a war waged exclusively in Ferguson's head. Freddie and Ferguson had passed each other on the ladder to success, and Ferguson had never forgotten it.

"Fine," Freddie said. He poured another shot and threw it back.

"Been seeing you out running," Ferguson said. "Yeah, putting in the miles. But lemme ask you this – ain't training camps already started?"

Ferguson was drunk, talking loudly, his cheeks flushed, and his southern accent even more pronounced than usual. The volume was due in part to the booze, but it was intentional on a certain level, because Ferguson wanted nothing more than for Briggs to crash and burn, for his star to burn out, and he wouldn't have to hear about Freddie Briggs anymore.

Another shot. Freddie's head started to swim a little bit. He hadn't touched alcohol in six months, and it was hitting him harder and faster than he'd expected. He took a deep breath and let it out slowly, scanning the crowd in the mirror mounted behind the rows of bottles standing a vigilant watch. Every single person was watching the confrontation unfolding in front of them; all knew there was no love lost between the two local legends.

"You know they've started," Freddie said. No point in dancing around the issue. Maybe he'd take the wind out of Ferguson's sails, and the loser could get back to drinking himself to death or selling meth to underage girls or whatever it was he did all day.

"But I thought this was the big comeback year," Ferguson said, his observation coated with ice and snark. "Hometown hero makes good!"

"Go fuck yourself," Freddie said, his own voice booming. He poured another shot and held the glass up to Ferguson. "Cheers."

"Go fuck yourself?" he repeated.

Ferguson spun around to face the crowd, his beefy arms spread out theatrically; beer sloshed over the lip of his glass, splashing Freddie's arm.

"Everyone hear that?" Ferguson said. "Smyrna's golden boy has forgotten his manners!"

He turned back to face Freddie, close enough for Freddie to feel Ferguson's beer-soaked breath breaking across his face like a fetid tropical wind.

"Is that it?" Ferguson asked. "Have you forgotten your manners?"

"Not today, Randy," Freddie said, turning back away from his tormentor.

"Oh, I think today is a perfect day for it," Ferguson said, poking two meaty fingers into Freddie's shoulder. "A perfect day to teach you some fuckin' manners."

Freddie refused to look at the man, focusing his gaze on the beer taps in front of him, trying to ignore the growing heat in his belly.

"You listening to me, fuckstick?" Randy said, another poke in Freddie's shoulder, this one more forceful. "Or are you Hall-of-Fame types too good for us regular folk?"

Freddie's right hand, palm open, exploded into Ferguson's sternum, knocking the drunk man off balance. Ferguson toppled over and hit the floor with a huge crash; the floor shook like a minor earthquake had hit the place.

The big man climbed back to his feet, more quickly than Briggs had anticipated, and, perhaps emboldened by the day's consumption of beer, rushed Freddie's right flank like an angry bull rhino. Ferguson connected solidly, and this time, both men sailed to the ground in a heap. Freddie landed first, his left arm extended as Ferguson's mass drove him to the floor. The men rolled around, their arms and legs entwined like giant sequoias tangled together. They crashed into small two-top tables, sending pitchers of beer and glasses to the floor, where they shattered in a tinkling symphony.

The heat in Freddie's belly exploded, like leaking natural gas catching a spark. He could feel the big man tiring; as big as Ferguson was, he was woefully out of shape. His rabbit punches grew exponentially weaker, and Freddie could feel him gasping huge lungfuls of air. Freddie wrapped his good arm around Ferguson's midsection and flipped him over like a side of beef; then he leapt astride Ferguson's midsection and delivered a right cross to the man's face, his big fist slamming down like a pile driver. The punch crashed into Ferguson's nose, squashing it like an overripe tomato. Ferguson grunted as a tincture of blood bloomed outwards from his face, holding its shape, a crimson rose, for an instant, before raining down on his shirt in a messy splatter.

Freddie reared back to deliver another blow when he heard a commotion behind him. A quick turn of his head, some movement in the corner of his eye, and that was when he felt a sharp burning sensation at the back of his neck. His entire body seized up, like his brain had issued his muscles a lockdown order, and that was when the world went dark.

INTERLUDE

FROM SELECTED TWITTER ACCOUNTS

Hashtag #Flu

August 6

1:16 p.m. to 1:18 p.m. Eastern Daylight Time

@RoseLover: Worried about my neighbor. He was c/o #flu symptoms yesterday. Ambulance came today. Hope he's better soon! #bronx #influenza

@AbbyWeinstein: I live in the #Bronx. A LOT of my neighbors are really sick. Maybe #flu?

@NYHotMama: Boss is sick with #flu, got to leave work early! #Booya! #philly

@BigRigger: This #flu's hitting me hard. Scheduled to head out on long haul 2morrow. Wish I could rest up, but gotta work.

@GoYanks55: Feel like sheeeeeit. Thought it was too early for #flu season! LOL!

@LovePS3: Summer school cancelled this afternoon 'cuz Teach is sick with #flu! Hellz to the yeah!

@TomZapata: #Doctors out there? Saw a weird strain of #flu-like illness in Queens last night. hit me w/ @ reply if you've seen it.

@BlogginBobby: RIP, Carl Hubbard. My uncle died today of the #flu. Came out of nowhere.

From CNN's Facebook Page

   August 6

   3:31 p.m. to 3:33 p.m. Eastern Daylight Time

   CNN is tracking a possible outbreak of influenza in the Northeast. Do you or does someone you know have the flu? Leave a comment!

   Thuy Beltran

   My husband got very sick very fast. We are in hospital. He had fever 106 degrees!

   Megan Waddell

   I'm an ER nurse in the Bronx. We were slammed overnight with patients. High fevers, pneumonia-type illness. Multiple deaths. Scared.

   Eric Martin

   I've got a terrible sore throat. I don't feel too hot right now. I've been traveling a lot for work. I always get sick after a long business trip!

   Michael Horton

   I bet the government's behind it! We're all doomed! lol

   Carolyn Mixon

   My brother is a doctor in Philadelphia. He's worried about this outbreak. He won't say much. Any doctors out there?

From the New York Times, Online Edition

   By CLYDE MORGAN

   New York Times Staff Writer

   Posted to nytimes.com @ 11:59 p.m. Eastern Daylight Time on Saturday, August 7

   DEADLY FLU HITTING THE BRONX

   THE BRONX – At least three Bronx-area hospitals are dealing with a deadly flu-like illness that has claimed dozens of lives in the past day, raising concern among New York City medical professionals that a novel and lethal strain of influenza has emerged. Calls to the Bronx Health District and the New York State Health Department earlier this evening were not immediately returned.

   A physician at one of the hospitals, speaking on the condition of anonymity, reported he had never seen anything like it in two decades as a physician.

"We're overwhelmed," the doctor reported. "We just got slammed one morning with patients and it hasn't let up. Young, old, all races, all ethnicities. I've never seen anything like it before in my life. I suspect it's viral, but that's a total guess on my part. We notified the state health department and we're just trying to ride it out, hope it doesn't get worse."

The doctor further reported that the hospital has established a quarantine unit in the facility, as there are some fears in the hospital that the illness is airborne. The doctor confirmed that symptoms of the virus include sore throat, high fever, seizures, and internal bleeding.

"This thing is a monster," he reported. He urged anyone in the New York City area experiencing these symptoms to be examined by a physician.

All three hospitals refused to comment, citing patient privacy concerns.

4

The knocking at the door was firm and insistent, the kind of sharp rapping that said this late-night visitor didn't really want to be knocking on your door at one-thirty in the morning, but they really had a good reason, and if you could help them out *just this one time*, they'd be forever grateful. Adam was awake and nursing a scotch, dressed in a pair of Syracuse University lacrosse shorts. He was watching *Goodfellas* on DVD, about a third of the way through, the scene in which Ray Liotta's character pistol-whips Lorraine Bracco's old boyfriend from her snooty country club.

He set down the scotch and remembered he was shirtless. As he looked for his misplaced shirt, the knocking ceased, and he wondered whether his visitor had simply given up, or perhaps, had decided he was banging on the wrong door.

A few seconds later, the knocking resumed, more frantic this time, as if whomever was out there had seen a gaggle of zombies closing in. Screw it, Adam thought, abandoning his search for the shirt. His guest was just going to have to deal with his pale, mealy upper body. Adam stepped out into the corridor and made his way to the front door. He pressed an eye to the peephole and, in the spill of the yellow porch light, saw a middle-aged woman, her eyes wide with panic, repeatedly running her fingers through her long brown hair. Her lips were pressed tightly together. Adam instantly recognized the look on her face; as a physician, he saw it almost every day in the faces of patients waiting for test results. He opened the door a crack, fairly certain this woman meant him no harm (because no one who wanted to slit your throat in the middle of the night knocked first, right?), but just a crack because you just never knew these days.

Adam opened the door, but she didn't notice. Her head was turned north, and she was tapping a finger against her lips. She wore a pair of green shorts and a grey sweatshirt on this cool night.

When he cleared his throat to let her know he was standing there, she jumped and let out a little scream. When her eyes met Adam's, she planted a hand over her chest and let out a long sigh, as if she'd been holding her breath for a while.

"Oh, thank God you're home," she said. "You're a doctor, right?"

"Yes," Adam said. "How did you-"

"The sticker on your car," she said. "We noticed it the other day."

"Right," Adam said, remembering the hospital-issued Physician parking sticker on the rear bumper of his truck.

"My family and I are staying two doors down," she said. "I'm sorry to bother you so late, but my husband is really, really sick. I called an ambulance, but they said it might be twenty minutes before they can get here. Twenty minutes!"

"I'd be glad to, but I've had a few drinks," Adam said. "You're probably better off waiting for the ambulance."

"Please, I don't care," she said, her hands clenched at her chest, almost in prayer.

"What's the problem?"

"He's burning up, and he's bleeding from the eyes, ears and mouth."

"Sure, sure," Adam said, trying to mask his alarm at the symptoms the woman had just described. "Let me get some clothes on?"

"Oh," the woman said, the question catching her off guard. "Oh. Yes, of course."

Adam slipped back inside the house to get dressed, his juices flowing, his mind on high alert, in a good way. He'd been at the cottage for three days, living a primal existence: eating, drinking, sleeping and shitting. His supplies would last him for at least another week, and so he hadn't had to leave the cottage. He hadn't bothered checking news or e-mail, because quite frankly, he'd started to enjoy not hearing the same stories reheated like leftovers and spun out to the hungry audiences desperate for another salacious detail about this child murder or that political scandal. He'd been drinking a lot, probably more than he should have, but what the hell – everyone was entitled to a bender every now and again, right?

As he pulled on a shirt and sandals, he considered the man's symptoms. Bleeding from one of those orifices wasn't alarming in and of itself, but bleeding from all three was not a good sign. Before exiting his bedroom, he snagged a pair of latex gloves from a box he kept in the closet.

Adam closed the door behind him and followed the woman downstairs. As they made their way up the road, Adam trailed behind a length. It didn't seem appropriate to walk side-by-side on this beach road. That was for husbands and wives, boyfriends and girlfriends, families headed for a day by the ocean.

They walked in silence for another twenty yards, and she turned up a wide driveway leading to a large home, her pace quickening as she slalomed around a Toyota Sequoia parked in the carport. The home was set closer to the water than Adam's cottage, and it provided a spectacular vista of the ocean. The moon was full tonight, a large coin hanging in the inky blackness of space, its shine cutting a long shimmery path across the top of the water. The night was awash in the crash of waves against the beach, just a little bit to their south. By the time they'd made it up to the expansive front deck of the house, she was weeping, her shoulders heaving up and down.

"What's your name?" Adam asked as she swung the screen door open.

"Katie," she said. "Katie Sanders. We're from Annapolis."

"I'm Adam Fisher," he said.

"It's nice to meet you, Dr. Fisher," she said.

"Hey, we're on vacation," he said. "You can call me Adam here."

This earned a smile, Adam was relieved to see. He had no idea what was in store for him on the other side of this door, but things would go a lot more smoothly if Katie Sanders remained calm.

"Sorry for busting in on you like this," Katie said. "I just didn't know what to do. He started getting sick at lunchtime. It seemed like he was just coming down with a cold, and then things just went down from there. I've never seen him so sick. I've never seen anyone so sick."

Adam nodded.

"Let's go on in and have a look."

ADAM KNEW THINGS WERE BAD, possibly even worse than Katie Sanders from Annapolis had feared, as soon as they stepped inside. They were in the kitchen, quiet but clean, bright and awash in fluorescent light. A peninsula-style countertop separated the kitchen from an eat-in area and served as the home base for the array of snacks fueling any good beach vacation. A large bag of potato chips sealed shut with a plastic chip clip that looked like a pair of bright red lips. Two trays of store-bought cookies were stacked at the edge of the counter. A six-pack of bottled water and two bottles of wine.

Despite the home's outwardly cheery appearance, the air was stuffy and rank, the sweet stench of something that has just turned over hanging thickly in the air. He hated the smell, not because it nauseated him (because it didn't), but because it meant he had already lost. He knew the smell from his hospital's intensive care unit, where his patients occasionally ended up and often never left. It was subtle, like a woman's perfume dabbed on the inside of her wrists, easily missed.

It was the smell of death.

"He's over here," Katie said, pointing toward a room around the corner from the kitchen.

Adam crossed through the living room, where two teenagers sat on the floral-print couch. The older one, a girl, had her knees drawn up to her chest and was chewing her nails. Her brother, maybe thirteen, was sitting next to the girl and was staring at his hands. The television was on, tuned to CNN, but the volume was muted.

"These are our kids," Katie said. "Leigh and Chris."

Adam nodded toward them. He didn't see the need to dispense empty pleasantries. They nodded back, in simpatico with Adam's desire to remain silent.

A pathetic moan from the bedroom broke the silence. The girl drew her knees in even more tightly, as if she was trying to make herself disappear, and tears began streaming down her face. The boy sat stone still, his eyes down, his hands folded on his lap.

"Is he going to be okay?" the boy asked, never looking up from his hands.

"I'm here to help," Adam said. He had not answered the boy's question, defaulting instead to a weak platitude that didn't mean a whole hell of a lot. He didn't know what else to say. Maybe something stronger, a potent elixir of encouragement that would have eased these kids' worrying, but he couldn't bring himself to do it.

"Doctor?" she said softly, dipping her head toward the closed bedroom door.

She rapped twice on the door, and called out: "Terry? Honey, I've got a doctor here to see you."

She swung the door in toward the bedroom. From his vantage point at the threshold, Adam could see a figure prone on the bed, buried under about ten blankets. The odor was stronger here, a sourness in the air. Adam pulled on the latex gloves and approached his patient.

"Terry?" Adam said, sitting on the bed next to the man. "I'm Dr. Fisher. Your wife says you're slacking off on the chores, wants me to make sure you're actually sick."

The man did not respond, but it did draw a half-chuckle, half-sob from Katie Sanders. It never ceased to amaze Adam. No matter how dire, how bleak things were, a well-placed joke mocking the crappy situation in which his patients and their loved ones found themselves often bonded them to Adam. It seemed a little phony to Adam, but he could not deny it reinforced the doctor-patient relationship like concrete rebar.

Adam peeled back the blankets far enough to expose the man's face, and a chill ran up his spine when he saw it. Terry Sanders was bright, almost shiny, with fever; Adam could feel the heat radiating from his body, as if he were standing too close to a hot oven. Blood had caked around his nostrils and his ears, and it was trickling from the corners of his mouth. It gave him a horrifying visage. Older blood had dried and caked to a rusty brown on the pillowcases. Adam ran his fingers along the underside of the man's jaw and found the glands to be badly swollen, like the spine of a wet paperback book. His cheeks were sunken, and his eyes were cloudy. The man had clearly developed some sort of infection, but that diagnosis was about as specific as saying that the man was sick.

Without tests, there was no way to know whether the infection was viral, bacterial or fungal. Hell, it could have been a case of severe food poisoning.

"Mr. Sanders?" Adam called out, loudly and firmly. "Can you hear me?"

Terry Sanders was curled up in the fetal position, his face turned upward toward the ceiling. It looked tremendously uncomfortable, but he didn't seem to care, which only underscored the level of misery the man was experiencing. Adam touched the man's forehead with the back of his hand and jerked it away. The man was roasting with fever; Adam would have gambled his medical license on a reading of at least 105 degrees, a terrifying reading for an adult.

"When did you say he started getting sick?" Adam asked as he continued to examine Terry Sanders. He didn't look up at Katie because he didn't want her to see the look of hopelessness he was certain was plastered across his face. To keep himself busy, he checked the man's pulse, which was weak and erratic, like a radio signal from deep space.

"Let me think," she said. "Lunchtime. He mentioned he had a sore throat, chills, that kind of thing. He napped most of the afternoon and evening, and then he started coughing up blood about an hour ago."

Adam did the math. Twelve hours from the onset of flulike symptoms to death's door. He racked his brain, trying to remember what he knew about infectious diseases from medical school and the random conference where he was trying to catch up on his continuing education requirements. This wasn't his specialty.

"Anyone else sick?" he asked.

"I don't think so," she said, her voice growing louder with each successive word. "Is it contagious? What's going on?"

"I'm just asking right now," Adam said. "First things first. We need to try and get his fever down a little. It's not good for it to be this high."

"Why is he so sick? What's wrong with him?"

Adam took a deep breath and let it out slowly.

"I don't know," Adam said. "I need you to get me a wet washcloth. Cool water. Not too cold. We need to bring it down slowly. And some ibuprofen or Tylenol."

"I gave him some Advil an hour ago."

"Jesus," Adam whispered to himself. "Any antibiotics in the house?"

She shook her head.

"The washcloth, then," he said.

Katie Sanders nodded, pressing a tight fist against her lips and closing her eyes. Adam could tell she was trying to keep her wits about her even as her psyche was fracturing like glass. She left the room, leaving Adam alone with Terry Sanders. He could hear a brief discussion in the living room as the children sought a status update on their father.

Adam took in the room while he waited for his putative nurse to return. It was a standard beach cottage bedroom, sparsely furnished with a rarely used chest of drawers and a flat-screen television mounted in the corner. A penciled rendition of a Holden Beach map hung over the bed.

He checked on the patient again, pressing the back of his hand against Terry's cheek. Still scorching hot, like the man was chewing on a lit match. Adam couldn't recall ever encountering a patient with a fever this high. As he pulled his hand back, Terry started seizing, as if his whole body was experiencing a massive internal earthquake. Adam gently rolled him over onto his side and held him there as his body quivered and heaved, flopping around like a fish in the bottom of a boat. It stretched on interminably. In all his years as a physician, Adam had never seen a seizure go on for so long, had never seen one so violent. Finally, mercifully, it ended, leaving Terry Sanders on his back, his eyes open and glassy and staring at the ceiling.

"Terry?" Adam said. Then again, very loudly this time, Adam no longer concerned with whether he might frighten Mrs. Sanders or her children: "Terry?"

No response. Not a twitch.

Terry Sanders was dead.

INTERLUDE

FROM ATC RECORDINGS OF SKYDANCE AIRLINES FLIGHT 337

August 7

8:53 p.m. Pacific Daylight Time

310 Miles South-Southwest of Los Angeles International Airport

L.A. Center – Skydance three-three-seven heavy, we're gonna have EMS out to meet you.

Skydance 337 – Three-three-seven, L.A. Center, it's getting worse.

L.A. Center – Repeat that, three-three-seven heavy.

Skydance 337 – Franks is dead.

L.A. Center – What about Meadows?

Skydance 337 – I feel like shit, Tower.

L.A. Center – Hey, three-three-seven heavy, check your airspeed. What about Meadows?

Skydance 337 – Roger. Meadows is asleep. Can't seem to wake him up.

L.A. Center – Three-three-seven heavy, your airspeed is a little low. How are the passengers?

Skydance 337 – [WHEEZING COUGH] Jesus. Hurts. It's quiet back there. Not sure if that's a bad or good thing.

L.A. Center – You listen, we're gonna take care of you, three-three-seven. You'll be on the ground in forty minutes. But you've got to give me a little gas here. Put the nose down a bit, just a hair.

Skydance 337 – Gonna climb a bit.

L.A. Center – Negative, three-three-seven heavy, negative. Oh, fuck!

Skydance 337 – [WHOOP! WHOOP! STALL WARNING. WHOOP! WHOOP! STALL WARNING.]

L.A. Center – Nose down, three-three-seven.

Skydance 337 – We're stalled, we're stalled! [LONG SPELL OF COUGHING]

L.A. Center – Ease up on the stick, three-three-seven. You're making it worse!

Skydance 337 – [Unintelligible]

L.A. Center – Nose down, Jesus Christ, three-three-seven, nose down.

Skydance 337 – I don't feel good. [Unintelligible]

At 8:55 p.m. PDT on August 7, Skydance Airlines Flight 337, carrying 238 passengers and crew, disappeared from radar.

5

D r. William Ponce thought he'd known what it meant to be truly scared.

He thought he'd been scared when his son Alex, then three, had choked on a chunk of apple, the little boy pawing at his throat, his face turning red and then blue, as if Ponce was being treated to the worst fireworks display of all time, the pyrotechnics show someone might see on his first night in hell. But as awful as it was, the episode had lasted less than twenty seconds, ending when his wife Molly had delivered just the right force of slap to dislodge the malicious chunk of fruit and send it flying across the room. Alex was a typical sixteen-year-old now, having no memory of how close he'd come to dying before his fourth birthday.

And as the chief pathologist for the U.S. Army's Medical Research Institute for Infectious Disease, he was quite familiar with fear – it was part of the job description. He was fifty-five now, having spent nearly two decades at Fort Detrick in Maryland, working alongside some of the most lethal agents known to man. He still remembered popping his Ebola cherry, his first trip inside Biosafety Level 4 now twenty-five years gone by, when he'd participated in the necropsy of a monkey that had died of Ebola Zaire, the most terrifying organism he'd ever encountered (until two days ago, at least). As they'd examined the liquefied tissue inside that poor monkey (and he still thought about that monkey a quarter century later), his heart had pounded at his chest wall like a meth-fueled jackhammer, threatening to fracture him from the inside out, the virus-laden blood seeping out of the ruined corpse as they worked on it. But that had been restrictor plate racing, the fear capped by the spacesuit he wore, the precautions they took, the strict protocols in place to prevent any breach of the integrity of the equipment or the facility.

He remembered all the stupid things he'd once worried about, like tearing his suit inside Level 4, disappointing his new bosses at USAM-RIID, even panicking inside the spacesuit, which occasionally happened to newbies in 4. Every now and again, a rookie would rip off the space helmet inside the hottest of the lab's hot zones because they'd convinced themselves they were suffocating even though subsequent testing showed the oxygen had been moving freely inside the suit.

In his two-plus decades assigned to USAMRIID, he'd never developed spacesuit fever, as they called it, but he did dream about the viruses, big, bright dreams of accidental sticks from needles dripping with Ebola-tainted monkey blood, or taking a face-full of the black vomit that accompanied the end stage of Marburg infection. Then he'd wake up, bathed in sweat but a dozen miles from Level 4, his bedroom quiet but for the gurgle of the fish tank. He didn't even mind the dreams so much; it was, he supposed, his mind's way of letting off steam, relieving the pressure of working in Level 4.

Only now though, as he sipped his coffee alone in USAMRIID's main conference room, a Baltimore Orioles mug clutched in a trembling hand, did he know what it meant to be truly afraid. The difference, he realized on that humid August morning, was that this wasn't a trip inside Level 4 from the safety of the Racal spacesuit, where the fear was of the hypothetical, always a *What If* question. This was something else entirely, a presence, consuming him from the inside out, eating away at his sanity, threatening to destroy his ability to think coherently before he could even attempt to do anything about this mess. It had transcended the hypothetical into the very fucking real. A real American city, population 1.5 million – the Bronx, for Chrissakes! – had become, for all intents and purposes, an open-air Level 4. It was out there *right now*, spreading from person to person, and there was nothing he could do about it.

The twenty-six-inch monitor in front of him, emblazoned with the seal of the President of the United States, flickered briefly and then showed a long view of the White House Situation Room. President Crosby's chair at the head of the table was empty, but every other chair was occupied, their occupants chit-chatting about *This Important Problem* or *That Important Problem.* He recognized some of the faces from their appearances on the various cable and online news outlets, but the only person he knew by name was Kevin Butler, the White House Chief of Staff, seated just to the left of the President's chair. Butler was leafing through a dossier that had been delivered to the White House in a screaming caravan of black Suburbans, hand-carried by the USAMRIID director himself.

Ponce could just make out his reflection on the screen, and it was not a flattering one. He hadn't shaved in two days, and he haired up like a Yeti. The circles under his eyes were dark and getting darker. Exhaustion held him tightly in its grip, but the fear kept him awake, a never-ending electric charge. As he took a deep breath to calm himself, he heard the sound of a door opening; all twelve men and women around the conference table leapt to their feet as President Nathan Crosby swooped into the room.

Crosby cut an impressive figure, well over six feet tall, still handsome despite three rough years in office, his only concession to the advancing years a bit of gray edging up his temples. Ponce didn't like him, thought he was a dipshit, someone who'd cruised into office on a relentless wave of campaign ads blasting his predecessor for what he had been unable to do, not anything Crosby had actually planned to do. Ponce didn't hold politicians in very high esteem to begin with, but this guy, the former governor of Oklahoma, really took the cake with his anti-vaccination stance, his tirades against evolution, his general tolerance for stupidity because Ponce believed stupid people had put Nathan Crosby into office. Not that his predecessor had been any better. When you got right down to it, the country was a bit of a mess, wobbling from one recession to another like a lost child (even though no one wanted to use the word 'depression'). Crosby was up for re-election in November; he was in a statistical dead heat with his scrappy Democratic opponent.

The President leaned over to Butler and whispered something; both men laughed. This made Ponce's blood boil and all but confirmed what he was worried about. They were not taking this outbreak seriously.

"Dr. Ponce?" Butler said. "President Crosby will hear your report now."

"Good morning, Mr. President," Ponce said, clearing his throat. He pressed a button on a small remote, transmitting the three-dimensional scan of the virus to a 50-inch LED screen in the Situation Room, adjacent to the videoconference screen. The virus, which they had code-named Medusa, looked like a long curlicue, not terribly dissimilar to a snake, coiled and ready to strike.

"I wish I had better news, sir," Ponce said. "This is the Medusa virus you see on the monitor, magnified about fifty thousand times. The mortality rate is in excess of ninety-five percent, perhaps even higher. We've got fifty-six confirmed cases. Fifty-one are dead, and the other five are circling the drain."

"How far has the outbreak spread?" Butler asked.

"We're not entirely sure about that," Ponce said. "The CDC is tracking unconfirmed reports of the illness in eleven states, but the epicenter of the outbreak appears to be in the Bronx. Until we can confirm that, probably in the next day or so, the CDC and USAMRIID both recommend quarantining the affected areas. There's still time to limit the loss of life. Anyone infected with the virus probably doesn't feel well enough to travel far."

"Quarantines?" Butler bellowed. "Dr. Ponce, do you have any idea how much of a cluster fuck quarantines will be?"

"But sir-"

"Nearly two million people live in the Bronx alone," Butler said, his voice tinged with annoyance. "People will fucking panic. We can't go around screaming that the sky is falling like happened with the swine flu thing. We have to step carefully here. The President is in a sensitive position."

Oh, shit, Ponce thought, the picture crystallizing in front of him like the virus coming into clear focus under the scope. This wasn't just a matter of them not taking him seriously. They were viewing this outbreak through the prism of politics, the number of votes that this would cost him if he made a misstep. Ponce recalled the H1N1 outbreak back in 2009, which, in the end, had claimed only about 30,000 lives – a blip on the radar as far as pandemics went. But that hadn't been during an election year. Crosby's Democratic challenger had been hammering him as soft, indecisive, a political development along the lines of the Three Little Pigs threatening to blow down the Big Bad Wolf's house. Now, Ponce knew, Crosby was worried that if he overreacted to this outbreak, he'd be a dead man walking come the first Tuesday in November.

"Mr. President," Ponce said, going over Butler's head and directing his plea directly to the big guy, "I can assure you that this is not going to be like the swine flu thing."

It was a calculated risk, a big one; he'd emasculated Kevin Butler (and it had felt pretty good), but he'd pushed all his chips to the center of the table on this hand. If this didn't work, there was nowhere else to go. Ponce kept his gaze squarely on Crosby, but he could sense Butler cooking with anger.

"How is the virus transmitted?" asked Crosby.

"We're working on that, sir," Ponce said. "Direct exposure to blood and bodily fluids, we know that. I'm virtually certain it's airborne, but I don't have confirmation of that yet."

The words were out of Ponce's mouth before he could stop himself. He had intended to fudge the fact, he had intended to lie his ass off about it because it was the right thing to do. Lie about it, lie about it to the President of the United States so they would take him seriously until he could positively confirm something he knew to be true anyway.

"You haven't confirmed this is an airborne strain?" Butler asked, jumping back into the discussion.

Ponce wanted to punch himself in the face for his stupidity; he felt like he was outside his own body, staring down at the big, stupid idiot, the idiot with the M.D. and double doctorates in virology and pathology.

"No, sir, but we will this afternoon at the latest, and I think we need to err on the side of caution given how deadly the infection has proven to be."

Ponce's words hung in the air as his audience considered them.

"These viruses," Crosby said, "they're not typically airborne are they?"

"No, sir," Ponce said, his shoulders sagging.

"These outbreaks burn themselves out, isn't that right?" Crosby asked. "That's why Ebola has never blown up and wiped us out, why it stays in those African villages."

"No one is really sure why-" Ponce offered.

"But they do, right?"

"Yes, sir, but I'm incredibly concerned this may not burn-"

"As am I, Dr. Ponce," Crosby said. "As am I. That's why I want to leave the management of these outbreaks to the local health departments. It's our belief they're in the best position to implement the appropriate protocols to contain the outbreak."

"But sir," Ponce said, again trying to establish a beachhead against the formidable defenses in the room.

"Dr. Ponce," Butler said, finding a second wind, "you're familiar with the phrase, 'the cure is worse than the disease'?"

"Of course."

"We believe a quarantine is premature at this time and in fact could do more harm than good," Butler said. "People will panic. We'll have looting, riots. It'll devastate the economy, and that's not something we can afford right now."

Dr. Ponce couldn't believe his ears. He ran his hands back and forth through his hair, thick and gray and wild, racking his brain for some way to get through to these morons. He was blowing it. This was the most important presentation of his life, and he was absolutely blowing it! With panic replicating in his core like the very virus he was trying to combat, he flipped through the file on the table in front of him, looking for something, anything that might shake these guys up. There, he thought, putting his hands on a photograph in the file.

"Look here," he said, holding the eight-by-ten photograph up to the camera. "Look at this. This is Dr. Amanda Rutledge. She was on staff at the New York City Health Department in the Bronx. Her husband, Peter Rutledge, worked for the Yankees. Three days ago, Mr. Rutledge began showing symptoms of Medusa and died twelve hours later."

The President held up a finger as if he were going to say something, but he remained silent.

"When they opened him up," Ponce continued, "they discovered evidence of tremendous hemorrhaging and organ liquefaction. His lungs were a mess, just totally fucking vaporized."

Yes, he had just dropped the F-bomb to the President of the United States.

"Mr. President, this is the part you need to know, that I need you to understand," Ponce said, as if he were lecturing a kindergartner. He had probably crossed the line over to insubordination, but he didn't care. He could have told President Crosby that Dr. Rutledge's boss, the director of the Bronx district, had died this morning, or he could have told him the two CDC doctors who had traveled to New York were both infected with Medusa and would be dead by lunchtime. He could have told him they'd be burying millions of Americans in the next month, but that seemed too surreal, too much to grasp. Instead, he zoomed in up-close. All politics are local.

"Dr. Rutledge died yesterday, as did her three children, ages nine, eleven and fifteen," Ponce said, his eyes squarely on the President, ignoring everyone else in the room. It no longer mattered what they thought; all he had to do was convince Crosby, the big kahuna. Crosby had two boys of his own, roughly the same age as the elder Rutledge children. If Ponce couldn't penetrate the formidable political armor, perhaps he could get through to the man as a father; it was the last arrow in his quiver.

"They all died horrible, horrific deaths," Ponce said, panicked. "Scared shitless. Begging for their mom, who they didn't even know was dead. Screaming, burning with fever, coughing up blood and lung tissue, bleeding from the eyes and ears until they had seizures, big massive seizures that all but fried their central nervous systems."

For a moment, like a flash of heat lightning in the distance, Ponce thought he saw the tiniest crack in the President's political visage, the ordered and carefully prescribed face of calm and leadership that he showed the world. For a moment, Ponce thought he'd won the man over, that they might have a chance to stop this thing before it got out of control.

Ponce sat stone still, watching the President carefully. Crosby's hands were clenched together in a fist, tapping his lips nervously. Butler leaned in close, whispered something to the President, who nodded.

"Dr. Ponce," Butler said. "At this time, the President is going to leave incident management in the hands of the locals. The President, however, wants hourly reports on the situation, more if the situation warrants."

Dammit, Ponce thought. They'd known all along what they were going to do, and now they could use the CDC's inability to confirm the airborne spread of the virus to massage the crisis so it fit their desired outcome. They couldn't even use the word "outbreak." *Situation*, Butler had called it. *Incident*. Fucking cowards.

"If there's nothing else," Butler said. "Thank you, Dr. Ponce."

Ponce was tongue-tied, a million things he wanted to say screaming through his brain but freezing on the launch pad, getting tangled together like strands of Christmas lights. He mumbled something in reply to Butler, and that was that. The link to the Situation Room was severed, and Ponce found himself looking at the Presidential seal again for a moment, until that, too, vanished.

He stared at the blank television screen for a very long time.

6

A dam sat on his deck, drinking coffee and smoking cigarettes from a crumpled pack he'd found in his car. He didn't smoke often, but the thing with Sanders family had rattled him badly and had been playing on a constant loop in his head for the last three days. A gnawing sensation tickled his gut like a termite chewing away a wooden floor joist, telling him he'd screwed something up again, that he should've handled the situation differently.

As Adam delivered the bad news to Katie Sanders, he could hear water from the cool-not-cold washcloth in her hand dripping onto the carpet in wet squishy plops. She'd become hysterical, collapsing to the floor, wailing and crying. When the ambulance arrived some five minutes later, Adam spoke with the paramedics, told him he was a physician, tried to explain what had happened, even though he wasn't entirely sure what that was. Katie and her two children followed the ambulance in their car as it made its way east on Ocean Boulevard toward the causeway, leaving everything behind as if they'd just gone up the road a piece to hit Island Mini-Golf for nine holes under the oversized gorilla and grab a soft-serve cone. He'd stood on their deck, alone, for nearly an hour before he ambled back to the house, a healthy dose of shock wrapped around him like a beach towel.

Adam fixed himself his third cup of coffee, or maybe it was his fourth, and settled back into the Adirondack chair to watch the sun start its daily journey into the sky. Daybreak started as a glimmer of light, as if the morning gloom had sprung a leak around its bottom edge, before exploding into every corner and crevice, every nook and cranny, jolting the East Coast back to life. The ocean air was already swampy and thick with brine; it was going to be a hell of a hot day.

He found it indescribably and ludicrously sad that this terrible thing had happened to the Sanders during their vacation. As if it would have been any easier on them had Terry been good enough to wait until they'd gotten home to drown on his own blood, after the suntans had faded, after the inevitable seafood feast, its newspapers spread out for the mess left behind by the crab legs and lobster claws and shrimp cocktail.

He thought about all the shit Katie Sanders would be facing upon their return to Paramus or Reading or Timonium or wherever it was she said that they were from, piled on top of her excruciating grief. The phone calls to stunned relatives and friends, the planning of a funeral, preparing for a life without Terry, when her biggest concern had once been that Terry's little bug might put a little crimp in the family's vacation schedule. Unexpected death was brutal in its assault on the lives of the survivors, the permanent rupture of happiness twinned with the cold machinery of death. It was the ultimate inconvenience.

Adam's eyelids drooped. The caffeine and nicotine kept his synapses firing, artificial adrenaline, but he didn't think it was doing much for him, no more good than paddles applied to a non-responsive heart. He felt the exhaustion deep within his core. The stress of the last few days, starting with the letter from the Board of Medicine and capped off with Sanders' death, was getting to him. He staggered to the bedroom and fell asleep almost immediately.

He woke up around two in the afternoon, amazed he'd slept as long as he did. He was on his stomach, his arm pinned underneath his head, and as he rolled over onto his back, he felt the pins and needles as the nerve endings started firing again. After a quick lunch of a peanut butter and banana sandwich, he decided to get down to the beach for a couple of hours. He could feel it calling to him, the sound of the waves crashing on the shore, delivering the coastline an eternal beating, a salve for what ailed him.

As he changed into his trunks, he couldn't help but wonder about his own exposure to whatever pathogen had killed the family's patriarch. But he reminded himself that even if Terry had a communicable disease, he'd probably experienced a rare complication, unique to his particular physiology. It was entirely possible that Terry Sanders died of garden-variety influenza. That he'd just pulled a rotten card, winning the kind of lottery no one wants to win.

He briefly considered driving back to Richmond, but decided against it. Back in Virginia, he'd be stuck in his stuffy house, unable to work, stuck in a no–man's land between clock-punchers and vacationers, alone with nothing but the memories of what had happened here. As the sun brightened the house with a fresh dose of light, he decided to stick it out.

He went back out on the porch and noticed it was a lot cooler than it had been this morning. The deck was dark with wetness, rain that had fallen while he slept. A bright blue sky extended as far as he could see in each direction, the view unclouded with haze, like a clean windshield. He looked out over his railing toward the sea, calm but for the small waves lapping to the shore, the air fresh and clean. Perfect conditions for a run on the beach. As he scanned the oceanfront, trying to decide which direction he'd head, something about the scene started nagging him, like a phantom eyelash digging in his eye.

After a quick change into his running clothes, opting to go barefoot, he made his way out the front door and curled around the side to the beach access. Although Adam had an unobstructed view of the ocean, he didn't have direct access to the beach because of the ridge of protected dunes that his house backed up to. He set out up the wooden sidewalk, down onto the sand, and then turned east along the water's edge.

A minute into his run, just as his muscles had started to loosen up, Adam stopped in ankle-deep surf, the mental eyelash dislodging itself. The beach was virtually deserted. His heart started throbbing, a visceral reaction to a scene that was wrong, all wrong. It was two-thirty on a beautiful August afternoon, and there should have been dozens, no, hundreds of people out here, sunning themselves, splashing in the water, building sand castles, sneaking illegal beers in those little huggies.

There was nobody out here.

The empty beach left Adam disoriented. It was as if his mind was straining to see what should have been there, what he, in his medical practice, would call *within normal limits*. As the unease grew inside him, his eyes bounced from water to sand to the cottages lining the oceanfront and then back to the water. A bit farther down the beach, he saw a group of empty beach chairs, set up in a semi-circle, but no one around them.

The image of Terry Sanders dying in his beach cottage slammed into Adam's head like a drunk running a red light. He looked at the houses up and down the oceanfront, from the small cottages to the big ten-bedroom jobs with wraparound decks on each floor and pictured Terry Sanders in each of those houses, coughing up blood, seizing, his organs frying inside his overheated body.

He picked up a flicker in the corner of his eye, and he turned to face it. Maybe a hundred yards away, two people were walking toward him. From this distance, he couldn't make out their gender, age, or really anything about them at all. Still, it was something. With his heart pounding, he walked, accelerating to a jog before breaking into a full sprint in their direction.

As he approached them, the pair started coming into focus. A heavyset guy, maybe in his mid-forties, a tall, skinny teenager trailing behind him. The older guy wasn't walking as much as he was staggering across the sand like a drunken pirate who'd forgotten where he'd buried his treasure. The boy, trailing behind, didn't seem terribly concerned with the older man's behavior.

"Excuse me?" Adam called out. "Are you guys OK?"

The man stopped and looked at Adam, his mouth opening and closing but not making any sound. He was wearing dark red swim trunks and nothing else, his large gut stretching the waistband of his suit. His arms and legs were deeply tanned, but his chest and neck were fiery red with sunburn. It was quite the contrast, the reddish pink of burnt flesh juxtaposed against the leathery skin of his extremities, brown from years in the sun. That was when Adam noticed the man's mouth was stained red, almost like he'd been eating a cherry snow cone.

"No," Adam heard himself saying, feeling his body go weak. "No. This can't be happening."

His legs buckled, and he dropped to his knees.

Adam and the man stared at each other a bit longer, up until a coughing spasm grabbed the man in its clutches. He doubled over at the knees as his body fought to clear out whatever obstruction was stopping up his lungs. The first spasm ended, giving the guy a chance to catch his breath before a second one exploded, this one far worse than the first. Blood sprayed from his mouth like he'd been shot in the throat, and he dropped to his knees as well. Adam's training took over, and he pushed himself to his feet.

"You," Adam said, pointing at the boy, whose face was blank. "Is this your father?"

The boy nodded vigorously.

"What's your name?"

"Ethan," the boy said. "Ethan DeSilva." He was tall and thin and sported a thick mane of greasy black hair. He was fair-skinned, but his current complexion looked much worse, an almost grayed-out pallor.

"And your dad?"

"Robert DeSilva."

"What's going on?" Adam asked. "How long's he been sick?"

"Since last night I think," Ethan said, stifling his own cough.

Adam helped Robert down to his seat. He looked up at Adam, his eyes virtually pleading for help. Adam ran his fingers along Robert's jawbone and found oversized glands, engaged in a desperate war to fight off a pathogen. Typically, Adam would listen to a patient's chest, but that wasn't necessary here. He could hear the rattling in Robert's chest even over the small waves lapping at the shore.

"Just you two down here at Holden?"

"No," Ethan said. "My mom and two sisters. We're all feeling pretty bad. I've got a fever and chills. An hour ago, he just up and bolted out the front door."

"How far up the beach are you?"

Ethan looked over his shoulder and stared into the distance. When he looked back, his eyes were glossy with tears.

"I don't remember," Ethan said. "I really don't feel very good."

Adam scraped a nail against his chin rhythmically, almost like a metronome.

"My cottage isn't far from here," he said after a minute. "Let's get you guys to the hospital. I'm going to need your help to get your dad there."

It took them twenty minutes to cover the two hundred yards back to Adam's cottage. Robert was unable to stand up on his own, his body ravaged by a series of innard-shredding coughing spells. Ethan was weakening by the minute. He began yelling at children who weren't there, telling them he knew they'd been the ones who'd TP'd his house.

By the time they'd made it back to his driveway, Adam's legs were burning, and sweat had glued his shirt to his chest. Adam deposited his companions at the steps and then stopped to catch his breath and check on his patients. Robert looked like he was clinging to life by the slimmest of threads. He'd coughed and hacked for most of the walk, leaving a trail of bright red blood behind them. Ethan was lucid again, asking for water and wanting to know how far the hospital was.

"Let me grab my keys and get you some water," Adam said. "I won't be long."

Ethan sighed and nodded, seemingly content with the brief respite on the stairs.

As he climbed the stairs to the front door, Adam took a moment to acknowledge his own fear, his own biologically programmed survival instinct. Whatever it was Terry Sanders had died of, whatever it was these two perfectly nice people had, Adam did not want to catch it. His primal self, the one lingering deep in the DNA he shared with his ancestors and their ancestors, wanted to run, wanted to leave these guys to die, and his primal self didn't feel the least bit bad about it. The fear was huge, careening through him like a wrecking ball, and he felt it growing with each passing moment. He let that part of himself have its fantasy, state its case, and then he bottled it up.

When he was in medical school, it had taken him a little while to adjust to the fact that he was going to be frequently exposed to all manner of dread illness. Then, as a first-year resident, doing a rotation in the emergency room one cold December night, he'd experienced every health-care worker's worst nightmare – an errant needle stick in the soft flesh between his left thumb and forefinger while he'd been treating an HIV-positive drug addict. He underwent the prophylactic drug treatment provided to healthcare workers who'd suffered accidental pokes and submitted to HIV tests every four weeks for a year, all of which came back negative.

Shitty as it was, the experience had made him a better physician. He knew what patients were thinking about while waiting for test results to tell them what was causing the headaches, the vaginal bleeding, the abnormal ultrasound. It expanded his reservoir of patience, something he'd been in short supply of in the first part of his residency. And since the needle stick, he'd been able to compartmentalize the fear, lock it away in a place where it couldn't overwhelm him. But he always acknowledged it. He didn't want to get sick. He didn't want to die. He was no different than anyone else. And there were times, like now, where the fear threatened to break free and paralyze him.

If Robert and Ethan had what Sanders had, then Adam had suffered two major exposures. He accepted that he was scared beyond any plane he'd ever imagined and then crammed two tons of ball-shrinking terror into a five-gallon bag. He thought about Rachel and found himself glad that she was three thousand miles away, far away from this, whatever this was.

He refocused his attention on Robert and Ethan. He took the steps two at a time, but it wasn't fast enough. When he reached the bottom of the stairs, Robert was in the throes of a massive seizure, his body flopping around the concrete driveway. Like Terry Sanders, a man he presumably had not known and would never meet, Robert DeSilva died, horribly, virtually alone, and far from home.

"Shit," Adam said to no one. "Shit, shit, shit."

He looked around for Ethan and noticed the boy had disappeared. Christ, Adam thought, where did he go?

"Ethan?" he called out. "Son, are you there?"

He heard a soft moan coming from behind him, deeper into the carport under the house. He edged his way around his car, his heart pounding. A smear of fresh color caught his eye, toward the back corner of the driveway. Adam followed it to the shed where he stored a grill, boogie boards, half-empty paint cans, the byproducts of life of a beach house owner. It was cool and dark here. The boy was sitting cross-legged in the corner, his back against a stack of boogie boards. He looked up at Adam, a sheepish look on his face, as though he'd been caught breaking into the place.

"Ethan, it's me. My name is Adam."

"How's my dad?"

Adam didn't lie to patients, and he was not going to start now. He responded with an almost imperceptible shake of his head. Ethan leaned his head back against an old, cracked boogie board, a faded blue thing stenciled with the words Wave Destroyer in a repeating pattern down the surface of the board. The news didn't seem to affect Ethan one way or another.

"I don't suppose you knew the Sanders family?" Adam asked. "They were staying next door to my house?"

Ethan shook his head.

"We've got to get you to the hospital," Adam said. "Right now."

"What about my mom and sister?"

He coughed, a little thing that got away from him, but Adam could tell this poor kid was now in the end stages of this thing. Blood bubbled out onto the fist he'd tried to use to cut the cough off. Adam found himself thinking about Rachel again; this boy wasn't much younger than her, and that was when the fear began to break through. The box had sprung a leak. He was gripped with the urge to call her right now and tell her to run for the hills until he could get a better handle on what was precisely going on.

"We'll call on the way," Adam said, his spirits lifted by the mere fact that he had a plan to do something. "You know their numbers, right?"

"I think so," Ethan said, carefully examining his bloodstained hand like it was an unusual seashell he'd found on the shore.

"I'm sorry," Adam said. "About your dad."

"Thanks," Ethan said. There wasn't much *oomph* in his response, a testament to how poorly Ethan was obviously feeling. Then: "Am I going to die, too?"

The question buzzed through Adam like a mild electrical shock, but he didn't answer right away. As he considered Ethan's impossible query, he helped the boy into his Explorer and they began making their way toward the causeway. A few miles east, he began to hear a car horn honking in the distance. He welcomed the sound in all its distracting familiarity. It suggested there was still order here on Holden Beach, and it gave him time to construct an appropriate response to Ethan's question.

"Let's get you some help," he said. "We'll be at the hospital soon." Adam stole another glance at Ethan, who was looking absently out at the road ahead of them.

"What's that?" he asked weakly, pointing a thin finger ahead of them.

Adam's gaze followed Ethan's finger east, and he found the source of the car horn as they approached the turn-off to the causeway, which fed back onto the mainland. But it wasn't one car horn. It was many, and it looked like a parking lot had metastasized in the middle of Ocean Boulevard. There were dozens of cars jammed together, all facing east, people honking over one another, no one moving an inch. Adam slowed to a crawl and came to a stop about a hundred yards short of the intersection. Pockets of people milled about here and there, a few smoking cigarettes, most pointing and talking.

"Wait here," Adam said. "I'm going to see what's going on."

Ethan nodded, and Adam alighted from the car, his heart pounding. It was getting hot again, the freshness of the day passing as another juicy air mass settled in on the area. Adam looked south toward water's edge, the ocean gray and lifeless. They were in the downtown area of Holden Beach, as it were, smack in the middle of a strip of real estate offices, ice cream parlors, places hawking cheap beach gear, t-shirts, hermit crabs that would be dead before their new owners made it back to Route 17. It was here vacations began and ended, the gateway from and back to real life.

Up ahead of him, a trio, two men and a woman, had gathered at the front bumper of a Honda minivan with Georgia plates. A bumper sticker on the center of the rear windshield exhorted the DAWGS to GO! The sliding doors were open, and Adam could see two small kids, strapped into their car seats in the dim passenger compartment. Both appeared to be asleep.

"What's going on?" he asked, trying to mask his growing sense of alarm. Try as he might to avoid it, his gaze kept drifting to the interior of the minivan, on the two kids sleeping in their car seats. He wondered what he would see if he drew in for a closer look, whether he'd see blood smeared across their lips like fingerpaint.

The woman and the younger man, both of whom somehow appeared flushed and pale at the same time, bright red cheeks against a backdrop of gray skin, looked at their companion, deferring to the eldest member of the group. He was in his fifties, heavy-set with a graying beard.

"Some kinda accident," the man said. He leaned in close to Adam, conspiratorially, and added: "I got a real mess here. Whole family's sick with something or the other, trying to get them to the hospital up in Shallotte."

Adam ran his fingers through his hair, thinking about Ethan DeSilva, about the empty beach, wondering if this time, the human race had run out of luck. He felt like he was living the beginning of a bad dystopian movie. He'd first felt it on the morning of the September 11 attacks, when a rumor had spread through the hospital that New York City had been nuked. He was busy with a difficult C-section and didn't get the full story until later that morning. He'd been almost relieved to discover that only a few thousand had died, as opposed to a few million, a relief he still felt guilty about more than a decade later. He'd felt it in 2008, when Lehman Brothers went down, and then Bear Stearns, one after another, and the global economy had teetered on the brink of failure and he was ready to walk down to the bank and withdraw every bit he had in cash before it went up in smoke.

"Yeah," Adam said, not knowing what else to say.

"Yeah," the man said with a disturbing hint of resignation in his voice. "My daughter and son-in-law are both sick too. I started running a fever a couple hours ago."

"Excuse me for a minute."

Adam went back to his truck to check on Ethan, out of answers, out of ideas, nearly out of his mind. The boy was slumped over in his seat, unresponsive, the seatbelt straining under Ethan's dead weight. Adam pressed two fingers against the boy's wrist, checking for the radial pulse. It was there, but thready at best.

"Have you seen anything on the news?" Adam asked when he returned to talk to the man.

"You haven't seen the news? All kinds of crazy shit. Hell, I heard one story saying all the New York Yankees had gotten sick and died. Then another story said their charter plane went down after an engine failure."

Adam stared at the man, slack-jawed.

"You're telling me this thing is everywhere?"

The man didn't respond.

Adam hadn't watched television or picked up a newspaper since he'd arrived here nearly a week ago. He pictured this thing burning through city after city, state after state, leaving graveyards in its wake. He remembered a bit of history about the Spanish flu outbreak of 1918, how that strain of influenza had spread around the world in less than a month, in an era when commercial air travel was virtually nonexistent and even automobiles were still considered a luxury item. He shuddered to think how quickly something this virulent could spread across the nation, across the globe, in this day and age. It could kill thousands of people in the blink of an eye. The idea of this kind of outbreak on a large scale threatened to turn his guts to liquid.

While Adam processed this new bit of information, his news source began coughing. It was a protracted affair, yet another incident that again left Adam feeling as helpless as he had ever felt in his life. The cough brought the man to his knees, and Adam stepped forward and placed a hand on his back. The man was baking with fever, a hellish heat that Adam was becoming far too familiar with. As the spell eased up, the man turned to the side to pat his mouth with a handkerchief. Adam appreciated the man's discretion, but there was no hiding what was happening.

Taking the hand Adam offered him, the man struggled back to his feet, one at a time.

A STORM WAS ROLLING in from the west as Adam made his way back to the cottage, having given up on the hospital. A purplish ridge of clouds was easing in, almost like a shroud over the area. Adam turned on his wipers as the fat drops of rain began spattering the salt-crusted wind-shield; he was briefly soothed by the familiar *wip-woop-wip-woop* of the wiper blades slicing across the glass. As the wind freshened, the skies opened up, forcing Adam to let up on the accelerator. He switched on the headlights, but they did little good against the volume of rain unleashed in the monsoon. Within seconds, his visibility had dropped to zero, and so he carefully edged over to the side of the road, more up on the side-walk than not, and stopped in front of an undeveloped expanse of marsh.

As he braked, Ethan's failing body listed toward him, close enough that he could smell a perverse combination of Old Spice and sickness emanating from the boy. Panic surged through him like electrical spikes. More cracks were forming in his box now. He wasn't sure how much more he could take before it ruptured, like the bulkheads on Titanic after its kiss from the iceberg, before the fear got big enough to pull him under. He found himself swallowing frequently, his hands brushing against glands, on high alert for the slightest sign of infection.

Then the seizure hit. Ethan flopped around the passenger seat, his shell of a body spraying blood across the seats, the dashboard, the windshield, as if the pathogen was intent on perpetuating itself in every way possible. He wrapped his arms around the boy and held him close. The seizure was massive, powerful, a magnitude that Adam had never experienced before. It was like a bolt of lightning had dropped from the heavens and struck the boy. Adam held on for the entire duration of the seizure, refusing to let the boy die alone, tears streaming down his cheeks.

When it was over, Adam shifted back into his seat, his arms and neck splattered with blood, as if he'd just finished slaughtering a hog. Ethan was dead. Tears ran silently down Adam's cheeks, the byproduct of a hot stew of anger and fear and sadness fermenting inside him. It was like he was being made to relive that terrible day with Patient A over and over again, on a much bigger stage, the only constant being his total and complete incompetence, his inability to do one single, solitary thing to help these people.

This was off the charts, the kind of thing discussed hypothetically, maybe joked about in the CDC cafeteria. An invisible tidal wave, wiping the cities clean of life, leaving graveyard after graveyard in its viral wake until it burned itself out.

He dug his smartphone out of his pocket and tried accessing the mobile Internet application. As he waited, he noticed the squall was easing up. He checked the screen again, but it remained blank, the page still trying to load. He shifted back into gear and nosed his way back out onto Ocean Boulevard. Water had ponded in the typical lower-lying spots, and he slalomed around those dark, brooding puddles.

Back at the house, he set Ethan's body next to his father's and covered them with a tarp. Then he retreated to his bedroom with a bottle of scotch and a heavy glass tumbler, his initials etched on the side, and, for reasons he couldn't explain, locked the door behind him. A check of his watch told him it was quarter until six, almost time for the news. While he waited, he conducted another systems check. No fever, no sore throat, no nasal congestion, no unusual skin rashes or lesions, and most welcome, no swollen glands.

He started to dial his office but then remembered that it was after business hours.

He dialed Joe McCann's cell phone number.

No answer.

He dialed his friend Mark Zalewski's number.

No answer.

He dialed his old girlfriend Stephanie Hartman's number.

No answer.

He scrolled through his contacts and paused on Rachel's number for five full minutes before he could muster the courage to call her.

He dialed Rachel's number.

No answer.

He put away his phone.

INTERLUDE

BULK E-MAIL SENT TO 3.2 MILLION UNIQUE E-MAIL ADDRESSES

From: CheapMeds@projectblue.com
Date: August 9
To: Unidentified Recipients
Subject: MEDUSA VACCINE

DON'T BE A VICTIM!
MEDUSA IS A DEADLY DISEASE SWEEPING THE WORLD.
BUT YOU CAN KEEP YOUR FAMILY SAFE
100 EZ –SWALLOW TABLETS OF ANTIVIRAL FOR $29.95

DOUBLE MONEY-BACK GUARANTEE

7

"**B**riggs!"

Freddie turned his head toward the voice, coming from the brightly lit corridor, deep in the cinderblock bowels of the Smyrna City Jail. He'd been lying on his back on the thin bedroll, staring at the ceiling, marking time since he'd been arrested three days ago. It had been a Friday afternoon, too late for a bond hearing, and since it was a malicious wounding charge, they wouldn't let him out on his own recognizance. Due to his celebrity, the sheriff had assigned Freddie to an isolation cell, the one in which they stuck the potential suicides, rather than risk a cafeteria riot over the fact that Freddie had played for the Patriots instead of retiring with dignity as a Falcon. The cell had been sanitized of anything an inmate could use to harm himself. No sheets, no metal bed frame. Just bars, concrete, and time.

After coming to, he'd quietly followed the arresting officers (three of them!) out to the police cruiser waiting in the parking lot of the Duckling, the memory of his little bar brawl with Randy Ferguson still fresh in his mind. He shook his head when the officers asked him if he was going to give them any trouble. They all knew who he was, of course, and they appeared terrified, although he wasn't sure if that was because of his celebrity or because they were worried he might try to eat them. No, he hadn't given them any trouble; in fact, he hadn't uttered a word since the last dumb-shit thing he'd said to Ferguson before they'd done their dance. Instead, he kept asking himself the same question, over and over, wondering why he'd let that loser push his buttons the way he had.

He hadn't come up with an answer, and now, with the bond hearing done, it was time to go home and face his family. His heart began pounding, harder and harder as the footsteps drew closer, and he felt a little silly, like a little boy afraid of being punished. He took quick stock of his cell. It was a small cell, about eight-by-eight square, steeped in a pungent stew of urine and sweat and body odor. Pathetic as these environs were, and as happy as he was to be taking his leave of them, they had given him some time to think. About football, about Susan, about the future, about the next step. First, there was going to be hell to pay at home. In a strange bit of irony, nothing drove Susan bat-shit crazier than Freddie's temper. Fine, he thought. It was time to grow up. Time to be a man.

"Briggs?" the man said when he arrived. He was black, tall and thin, his posture and demeanor suggesting a stint in the military. "I'm Captain Allen Freeman. You'll be due in court on August 22 on a charge of disorderly conduct, drunk in public, and malicious wounding."

Richie Matas, Freddie's agent, trailed just behind. Matas looked pale, his thin face drawn tight, like a robe on a cold morning. This struck Briggs as odd. Matas represented a number of athletes, and this was not his first time bailing one of them out of jail. Part of the job description, he'd once commented to Freddie. Freddie stood silently, frozen by embarrassment. It wasn't the first night he'd ever spent in the clink, but it hadn't happened since his freshman year at LSU. Susan had always warned him he'd end up there again if he wasn't careful.

"I owe you one, Richie," Freddie said.

"Listen, Freddie," Matas said. "We need to get you home. Something's wrong with Susan. I drove over this morning to pick her up to come get you, and the girls said she was really sick."

"What the hell are you talking about?" Freddie asked.

Matas was walking quickly, almost jogging up the corridor to the booking area, where Freddie would be able to retrieve his personal belongings. The deputy processed Briggs out of the jail as quickly as he could, which, for Freddie, wasn't nearly quick enough. He and Matas raced back to the car and set out for the Briggs home, in a ritzy development on the north side of Smyrna.

They rode in silence, Richie unwilling or unable to relay any information other than that Susan hadn't looked good. Freddie had tried calling the house, but no one answered. About five miles out, Freddie's cell phone, which was still in his hand after he'd retrieved it from the jail inventory, began ringing.

"Dad?" a tiny voice said.

"Sweetie, it's Daddy, what's wrong?"

"It's Mom," Caroline said. Her words were choked with phlegm, as if she'd been crying.

He pinned the phone against his shoulder and tapped Matas on the right shoulder.

"Hurry up," Freddie said. "Something's wrong."

He put the phone back to his ear and took a deep breath, hoping he could stay calm, for the sake of his hysterical daughter. "What is it, sweetie?"

"She lay down on the couch for a bit, said she was too tired to get upstairs," Caroline said, her voice cracking. "Then she started coughing, and there's blood everywhere." Now each of Heather's words was punctuated with a sobbing heave.

"Caroline, listen to me very carefully. Stay with her," Freddie said. "I'm calling an ambulance."

Freddie killed the line and called 911. Strangely, it took three tries to get through.

The line clicked open, and Freddie started to speak when he was interrupted by a recorded message.

"Thank you for calling the City of Smyrna's Emergency Operations Center. All of our dispatchers are busy assisting other citizens. Please stay on the line, and your call will be taken in the order it was received."

"What the fuck is this shit?" Freddie bellowed, as the message began to replay.

"What?" Matas asked.

Freddie pulled the phone away from his ear and pressed the speakerphone button.

"-on the line, and your call will be taken in the order it was received."

It began to replay again.

"What the hell?" Matas said.

"Put on hold by 911?" Freddie said, looking over at Matas.

Matas shrugged and pushed down on the gas, determined to get them back to the Briggs house as fast as possible. As they hurtled north around Smyrna, they heard the message twice more in its entirety and most of a third time before a dispatcher came on the line.

"911, what is your emergency?" a gruff voice barked at him.

He told the dispatcher what he knew.

"I'll dispatch an EMS crew, sir, but you should be aware we've had an unusually high call volume this morning."

Freddie tried to say something, but the words weren't there. He looked over at Matas, his hands spread apart, unsure of what to do.

"Just send the fucking ambulance!" Matas barked into the phone.

"Thanks," Freddie said, hanging up.

"Fuck it," Matas said. "If the ambulance isn't there, we'll take her ourselves."

Freddie nodded, the panic rising, filling him like a balloon and making it difficult to breathe. Richie Matas, God bless him, pushed down the gas pedal of his rented Audi as far as it would go, determined to make the ten-minute drive home in three. The jail was in the southern part of Smyrna, in a beaten-down industrial area about as far as one could get from the northern suburbs where Freddie and Susan had made their home and still be in Smyrna. Freddie and Susan had bought the six-thousand-square-foot home about a year into his career, after they'd gotten used to the idea of having millions of dollars in the bank, gotten used to the idea of not ever having to worry about money again.

Freddie and Susan had both come up poor, and they'd never forgotten the pain of growing up in Smyrna's trailer parks, which was where they'd first met more than a dozen years earlier. They were scrupulous savers. Freddie loved teasing her for clipping coupons on Sunday mornings, which she said she did to keep her mind off the game, worried sick as she was of watching him end up paralyzed or worse. The house was their sole extravagance. They wanted a place that would be home forever, where they would raise their girls, twelve-year-old Caroline, and Heather, a month shy of her eighth birthday. They wanted a place where they could grow old with the neighbors, where they could take refuge, a sanctuary away from the madness accompanying life as an NFL superstar.

A few minutes later, the turn-off into Freddie's subdivision came into view. As Matas slowed to turn onto the private drive feeding into the subdivision, Freddie heard the ambulance screaming toward him.

"Quick, get up to the guardhouse," he said to Matas.

A moment later, the ambulance appeared in his rearview mirror, screaming its frantic howl. The guard waved them through, and the ambulance rumbled down the wide avenue, now less than a mile from its destination. Matas fell in behind the ambulance, close enough to cross that line from tailgating to drafting, fully flaunting the admonition that he should "Keep Back 500 Feet."

They covered the mile in about forty-five seconds. The ambulance slowed briefly, dipping right into the Briggs' semi-circular driveway, and then came to a halting stop at its midpoint. Matas lagged behind a couple car lengths and met the crew at the ambulance's back door. Two paramedics, a young woman with close-cut blonde hair and a tall heavy-set black guy, got to work unloading their gear. Freddie recognized the man as a teacher at Caroline's school. Mr. Rowe or something like that. He must have been a part-time EMT. Both were wearing powder-blue surgical masks. A handful of neighbors milled about, gathered in small clumps, whispering, pointing.

"Please hurry," Freddie croaked as he met the paramedics.

They ignored him as they unloaded the stretcher and their gear from the back of the truck. As he passed the open doors of the ambulance bay, Freddie realized with horror that four other people were in the back, looking flushed, looking very sick. He put them out of his mind and led them inside. As he made his way down the corridor, he heard Susan coughing, a deep, guttural, hacking cough. He'd never heard anything like it in his life.

"Susan? Girls?"

No response.

"Susan!"

He turned the corner beyond the sunken living room and stepped into the galley-style kitchen, where his shoe slipped out underneath him. His big frame crashed to the floor, and he felt a sharp pain shoot through his right knee. Oh, no, he thought. Thoughts of all the time he'd spent rehabbing the knee came roaring up inside him, followed by a scorching chaser of guilt. He rolled over on his side and started to push himself up on the fresh, bright-red blood slicking the floor. He scampered to his feet, panic engulfing him like fire consuming a house. Freddie heard a female voice behind him, startling him. He'd almost forgotten the paramedics were there.

"Look," the woman paramedic – Gibert, according to the ID card clipped to her breast pocket – was saying. Freddie, panic-stupid now, saw her pointing at something, and he followed her index finger to the back of the kitchen, just beyond the Viking refrigerator.

"What's in there?" Gibert asked, pointing toward a closed door.

"Mudroom," Freddie said as the pair rushed forward, Freddie close behind. "Leave the stretcher out here. It's pretty tight in there."

"Oh shit!" said Rowe, the first one in the door. "In here!"

He slipped into the mudroom behind them, desperate to see her but careful not to interfere with their provision of care. He was a good six inches taller than Rowe, more than a foot clear of Gibert, so he was able to see what was going on. His stomach clenched as he saw the amount of blood splattered on the walls, puddled on the floor. Susan was on her side, curled up into a ball, facing the wall. At first, Freddie thought she was dead, but he saw her shift her right foot, and he felt tears well up in his eyes.

"Aw shit," Rowe said, mostly to himself. "What the hell is this shit?"

"Shut up," Gibert hissed. "Roll her over. We need to get her out of here."

She turned her head to address Freddie. "Sir, is anyone else in the house feeling sick?"

"I don't know. I don't think so."

The girls. Where were the girls? He slipped back down the corridor to the staircase and took the steps two at a time. He was sweating badly, and he could smell a strange odor emanating from his body, a whisky-tinted, fear-coated musk. It felt hot in the house, too hot, even though he could hear the soft, reassuring hiss of the air conditioning blowing through the vents. As he approached the closed door of the media room, he heard a sound that severed his connection with reality. His mind was trapped in a netherworld between the three corners of panic, terror, and anger.

It was a terrible sound. A horrible, ripping sound.

His daughter Caroline was coughing.

INTERLUDE
TRANSCRIPT OF YOUTUBE VIDEO UPLOADED AUGUST 10

3.4 Million Hits Before Video was Removed

Shaky video of parking lot. Image blurs and then is obscured by videographer's hand

"Um, I'm standing about a block north of Turner Field here in Atlanta. That there is the west parking lot of the stadium. There's been a lot of military activity all morning. I don't know… wait, people are unloading from the back of the convoy trucks. I don't know … [COUGHING SPELL] lining them up. [WHEEZY BREATHING] Been hearing rumors of a vaccine. I woke up with it, whatever it is. I feel pretty good overall, maybe I got a mild case or something."

[SOUND OF MACHINE GUN FIRE]

"Holy fucking shit! The soldiers, they just opened up on those poor people! Oh my God, this can't be happening. This can't be happening!"

[WHIMPERS]

"I'm going to try and get a little bit closer."

Video becomes blurry and shaky

"Jesus. [inaudible]. Oh, Jesus, Jesus."

[SOUND OF MACHINE GUN FIRE]

"Oh, shit. I gotta upload this shit."

[SOUND OF COUGHING]

[VIDEO ENDS]

8

"You know, Kevin," Kevin Butler said to his empty office, just a stone's throw from the Oval Office, "you probably should've listened to that guy Ponce."

Then a coughing spell. Hard, ab-shredding coughing.

"No, we should've nuked the Bronx!" he said. Then he laughed.

He took off his dress shirt, leaving him in a white t-shirt and Joseph Abboud pants. He didn't know why he did it. It just seemed like a good idea. When he was done, he sat back down to rest because the simple act of removing his shirt had left him spent. He sat there in his white t-shirt and sweat-soaked Joseph Abboud pants. Or maybe it was piss. He didn't know anymore.

God, he felt like shit.

He cried for a few minutes. Then he stopped because he forgot what he was crying about. Then he remembered he was crying because he was dying, but he didn't start crying again because it required a tincture of effort that he did not currently possess.

He looked at the clock on the mantel. It was three-thirty in the afternoon. He didn't know if his family was alive or dead. He had no idea what day it was, but he didn't really care. All the days had piled up on top of one another, a big car crash of blocks on a calendar. They were all the same day now.

How had he gotten here?

You walked, a little voice called out.

He laughed the manic laugh of a man whose links to reality were breaking, one at a time.

No, not here here. *HERE.*

Oh, HERE.

He thought about the path that had led him *HERE*, about the million tiny decisions he'd made and forgotten, and the million tiny events he'd had no control over, the way those things had braided themselves together into the tapestry that was Kevin Butler's life. He thought he'd figured it out, where it had all begun nearly thirty years ago, an unseasonably warm January morning during his final year of law school at Harvard. Around dawn, he'd been jolted from sleep by a strange noise and had been stunned to see an intruder in his bedroom (his bedroom!), rifling through the drawers of his bureau, looking for God knew what. And only God had known what that man had been looking for, because upon noticing Butler was awake, the burglar had fled the crappy apartment in the crappy neighborhood, never to be seen again.

Butler looked down at his hands, thinking about his law school burglar for the first time in decades, manic-eyed and mangy, so dirty Butler hadn't been able to tell if he was black or white. The experience had convinced him to abandon corporate law and sent him down a much different path, starting as an assistant district attorney in Texas, where he took special joy in prosecuting home invaders, through the state Attorney General's office, to the U.S. Senate, before his old buddy Nathan Crosby, then the governor of Oklahoma, had tapped him to serve as his campaign manager for a presidential run.

The campaign, dismissed in the early days by the pundits as a wild hair, had taken off like wildfire, starting with an unexpectedly strong showing in Iowa, followed by a huge influx of cash to float them through the early primaries. Success begat success, and they'd secured the nomination in Los Angeles that summer, neither of them really believing it was happening until Crosby had taken a concession phone call from the man he'd defeated in the general election, the unpopular Democratic incumbent who'd presided over an economic collapse and had been unable to accomplish just about anything.

When you got right down to it, it had been that anonymous thief who'd shoved Kevin Butler toward his destiny, toward this moment in the White House, struggling (and failing) to deal with the biggest crisis the nation had ever faced. If it hadn't been for that burglar, if he'd rented a different apartment the previous August, if he'd spent the night at his then-girlfriend's place, which he hadn't because they'd had a big fight, if one of a million other things had broken differently, he'd probably have never changed his career track. He'd be a partner at some big firm in D.C. or Chicago or New York, living in some gated community, growing increasingly worried at the widening epidemic.

He didn't know where the President was.

He didn't even know if the man was alive.

His phone rang. It was probably someone very important bearing some very important news that would be very bad, and so he didn't answer it. Ooh, wait, let me guess!

A quarantine broke in Dallas!

No, no, wait! Let me guess! Riots in Des Moines!

Or Army units in Boston are abandoning their posts!

It had all come apart, and he was so, so afraid.

He was burning up now, the sweat pouring off him in rivers.

It had been nearly a week since Medusa had first appeared on their radar. There had been no communication with either the CDC or USAMRIID in at least a day, and he didn't expect any more. Not that they could offer anything more than what they already knew. It was sort of an academic exercise at this point. Under the microscope, the virus bore close resemblance to a snake, similar in structure to the Ebola and Marburg viruses, *blah, blah, blah*. But for all its similarities to those two scary pathogens, plenty scary in their own right, Medusa was different, so achingly and astonishingly different.

The thing that had driven the doctors out of their minds, right up until it killed them, was that they didn't know how it was different. Why was it spreading so rapidly? Why was it airborne? Why was it killing so quickly? Even Ebola Zaire, the deadliest pathogen known to man (until last week, that is), took days to kill its host. They hadn't even had time to figure out where Medusa had come from. And now they would never know! Atlanta was gone. Fort Detrick was gone. Despite all their precautions, Medusa had wiped out both installations.

What surprised Butler the most was how incompetent he'd felt, how foolish, how stupid, and he was one of the ones that was supposed to figure out how they were going to stop this goddamn thing! It had always been a source of amusement that the world often turned on things he said and did and things he told the President to say and do. He still felt like they were playing grownup, like it was Model U.N. or Student Council, and that certainly, the real grownups would swoop in and take over and fix everything. And the fear. He couldn't believe how scared he was.

He stepped out into the hallway outside his office. The lights were on, everything running normally, but it was dead quiet. He'd never heard it so quiet in his three years working here. There was a body in the corridor, one of his staffers, Julie or Donna. He couldn't remember her name. She was single, childless, and had stuck it out here, "managing the crisis," as they had called it. Many others had fled.

He coughed hard, spraying blood across the wall. He poked his head in the office of one of his deputies, but it was empty. Office after office he visited, staggering from one to the next, using the wall to support himself. This one was empty, that one contained a body. It became a bit of a game. Empty Office, 2, Dead Body, 1. Ooh, and now it's tied. Two apiece!

He was getting tired now.

He found a break room and sat at one of the tables. Before him, the vending machines hummed along, the soda ice cold, the snack cakes fresh and moist. And they would stay that way, long after Kevin Butler died. Even if humanity had succeeded in erasing itself from the hard drive, the lights would stay on here. The White House might someday go dark, but it wouldn't be any time soon. Maybe ten years from now. Maybe a hundred.

"OK," he said to no one.

He bowed his head and recited the Lord's Prayer. It felt phony and forced because reciting the Lord's Prayer was pretty fucking vanilla when you got down to it, like you weren't even trying, like you were just going through the motions. Kevin had once fervently believed in God, and the Butlers had been a church-going family, because you didn't become the Chief of Staff to a Republican president without the appropriate set pieces on the stage of your life. Over the years, though, his faith had grown weaker, like a radio station getting farther and farther away with each passing mile, its signal breaking up, heavily laced with static.

"... for thine is the Kingdom, the power and the glory, forever and ever, Amen."

Butler opened his eyes and found a young staffer staring at him. Her nose and mouth, caked with blood. Copies of copies of copies. It started to get old after a while. *I get it, God, I fucked up!* I should've agreed to the quarantine or paid a little more attention to that intelligence briefing about that bioterrorist group in Waco or whatever it was that we missed that had brought us to this point.

"Hi," he thought he said to the young woman, but it actually came out, "Heaaagghhhh!"

The staffer turned and fled down the corridor.

Kevin bought a bag of potato chips and sat back down to eat them. They did not agree with him and he vomited violently on the floor of the break room.

He laid his head down on the table and died at four-thirty that afternoon.

INTERLUDE

FROM THE STATE NEWSPAPER (COLUMBIA, SOUTH
CAROLINA)

EXTRA!
SOUTH CAROLINA SECEDES FROM UNION
WASHINGTON THREATENS NEW REPUBLIC

By SIOBHAN MOON

The State Staff Writer

COLUMBIA (August 13) – Calling the Medusa virus an "unprecedented" threat to its continued existence, the state of South Carolina officially seceded from the United States of America last night for the second time in its history, renaming itself the People's Republic of Columbia and installing former Governor Alan Moran as its new President.

"The people of this brave new nation have spoken," said President Moran, speaking from an undisclosed location. "This towering crisis has forced us to make some difficult decisions, and we believe that we alone hold the key to our survival. The government of the United States has proven itself unable to handle this catastrophe, and we will not stand idly by while my fellow citizens suffer."

The secession became official at 11:18 p.m. last night, when then-Governor Moran placed his signature on the state's Declaration of Secession, which had been passed unanimously in both houses of the South Carolina legislature earlier that evening.

The House of Representatives voted 44-0 in favor of secession, with 80 House members unable to participate due to illness. The South Carolina Senate quickly followed suit, unanimously passing the resolution 14-0, with 32 senators abstaining due to illness.

Moran added that the borders of his nation were closed indefinitely, and that any unauthorized persons attempting to enter Columbia would be dealt with "harshly and swiftly."

The White House reacted angrily, quickly issuing a statement denouncing the secession and threatening military action to preserve the Union.

"The United States does not recognize the so-called 'sovereignty' of the state of South Carolina," the statement said. "This White House is confident the state's action is a legal nullity and has no effect. Furthermore, this Administration considers Governor Moran and his 58 state legislators to be traitors, and they will be held accountable for this ridiculous act. The U.S. does not acknowledge Governor Moran's so-called borders, and any attempt by the state of South Carolina to enforce those borders will be met with force."

The current status of the state's nine military bases was unknown at press time.

According to multiple sources, several other states are considering similar secession resolutions, including Virginia, North Carolina, and Tennessee.

9

A steady rain fell as Adam crossed the James River just south of the Richmond city limits on that Friday evening, the thirteenth of August. Spires of frozen traffic stretched away in either direction along I-95, and in the distance, he counted three fires burning against the backdrop of downtown. The lights of the cityscape shined dully against the twilight, but at least they were still on, a fact that Adam was deeply grateful for. He checked his watch; it was just past seven-thirty. He was drenched, exhausted, and starving. The one thing he was not, to his pure and utter amazement, was sick. Physically, he felt perfectly fine. The country appeared to be crumbling around him under the weight of this invisible conqueror, which had, so far, overlooked him.

And somehow, that made it worse.

The waiting.

It had been one week since he'd first encountered what the media were now calling the Medusa virus, and based on the few bits and pieces he'd been able to cobble together, the virus was burning its way across the globe and order was starting to break down. And Medusa's communicability was like nothing ever seen or studied. After the deaths of the DeSilvas (and he never had found the remaining family members), he'd spent two days on Holden Beach trying to tend to sick vacationers, trying something, anything to keep someone alive. And all he had seen had left him terrified, hopeless, adrift.

He'd tended to the bodies of the DeSilva men the morning after they died. It took an hour, but he finally had gotten them indoors, lying side by side on his kitchen floor, covered with sheets, perhaps a fraction of their dignity preserved. Adam had tackled the senior DeSilva first, a job that had all but wiped him out. Ethan's father had outweighed Adam by fifty pounds, and so Adam had dragged him up the staircase, his arms locked around the big man's chest. One step at a time Adam had taken, his arms and back burning with liquid fire. At one point, just two from the top step, Adam had gotten a little off balance, a little high on the rain-slicked stairs, and he'd nearly lost his purchase; he felt both of them teetering downward, a tumble that Adam feared would leave him as dead as the DeSilvas. He managed to find his seat before he fell forward, slamming his tailbone down against the wet edge of the step. After a quick rest, he finished the job, and he brought Robert to what, unbeknownst to Adam, would in fact become his and his son's final resting place.

Adam made shorter work of Ethan's remains. The boy had been tall but rail-thin, a body that would never fill out. As Adam hoisted him over his shoulder, he felt the boy's smooth cheek rub against his own; it was a face that hadn't seen the edge of a razor yet. Adam was reminded of Ethan's youth, of all the promise that would go unfulfilled, and an immense sadness swept through him. He thought about all the things Ethan DeSilva would never do, never see, and he felt his eyes water like a heavy cloud. Maybe he was being a bit maudlin, because for all Adam knew, Ethan might have grown up to be an embezzler or a drug dealer or child molester, but he didn't want to think about that right now. Whatever possible future may have lain ahead, Ethan DeSilva deserved a better fate than he had gotten.

Standing in his kitchen among dead men, Adam's muscles ached and his legs quivered with exhaustion. He searched for something to say to the DeSilvas, some eloquent benediction to bid them farewell from this world, but he could think of nothing. He clicked his teeth together for a few moments.

"I'm sorry," Adam had finally said, his voice catching.

Sharp swords of guilt and regret buried themselves into Adam's soul, up to the hilt. He wished he could give them a proper funeral, but storing them inside was the best Adam could do. He wasn't planning to stay long anyway – he could simply crank up the air conditioning to help slow the rate of decomposition. For all Adam knew to the contrary, he might be joining these men in death in a day or two anyway. A sudden burst of terror then, like a kick in the stomach, and he found himself trying to imagine the DeSilvas' final moments. How afraid had they been? Did they know the end was near? Could they feel life slipping away, like the taste of something delicious dissolving into nothingness? Was it stinking, bowel-loosening terror? He thought these things, and he couldn't stop himself.

That afternoon, as he'd peered out over the ocean from the Holden Beach pier, he'd met an older Asian woman, on holiday with her family, who, like him, had remained healthy. She spoke very little English, but at some primal level, she grasped that Adam wasn't sick either. She dragged him by the collar of his shirt, all one hundred pounds of her, to her family's beach cottage. Her entire family had come down with it. The first three to fall ill, two adults and a ten-year-old girl, had already died, and the others were deteriorating rapidly. She was hysterical.

And so he waited with the elderly woman, whose name he finally learned was Sang-mi, as her beloved relatives expired, one by one, as her family disintegrated, a great machine failing unexpectedly when only hours before it had been humming along in perfect synergy and harmony.

At the goddamn beach.

He held her hand and cried with her.

Sang-mi had been inconsolable. When Adam went to pull a sheet over the body of her son, who'd been the last one to die, she bolted out the back door and onto the back deck, screaming hysterically. He raced out after her, reaching out to pull her down before she could jump, even grabbing a swatch of fabric from her peach-colored housecoat, but she was fiercely determined to join her departed relatives, and that was precisely what she had done. Sang-mi flung herself from the railing; Adam closed his eyes as she plunged down, a second later, he heard her body hit the roof of their Dodge Durango some fifty feet below, the sharp crunch of the metal skin of the roof crumpling under Sang-mi's weight.

And much like he couldn't leave the DeSilva men alone in the carport, he couldn't leave Sang-mi there, like a fragile bird that had fallen from flight, and so he carried her broken little body back upstairs and laid her to rest with the rest of her family.

He sat there with the dead family and watched the news, and that was when it had hit home for Adam, that this monster was roaming the countryside, all the countrysides, it was everywhere and nowhere, ghostly and very real. Regular programming had been interrupted for round-the-clock news coverage of the epidemic. Outbreaks had been reported in twenty-five states and across the globe. The more he watched, the sicker he felt, hope sluicing away, like tiny grains of sand trickling through an hourglass.

Driving off the island was no longer an option; the traffic jam he'd encountered with Ethan had metastasized into a bizarre still frame of a demolition derby, cars turned every which way, smashed up against one another. So he'd ridden his bike, an old beach cruiser he kept under the house, across the causeway on the morning of the eleventh. He rode all day, stopping only to relieve himself. He made it to Wilmington at dusk, but there was no respite there, just more chaos. Large crowds drifted through the streets, loud and panicky. Automatic gunfire chattered in the twilight. It was too dark to keep riding, so he spent a restless night in an alleyway.

He had to get home.

West of Wilmington, the congestion had eased up some, enough to warrant commandeering a Ford Taurus he found by the side of the road, its driver dead of Medusa. After laying the body on the shoulder, he loaded his bike in the back seat and shoved off, sticking to the back roads cutting through central North Carolina and into Virginia. Even in these rural areas, he saw nothing but chaos. Fires burning, car wrecks, throngs of people migrating on foot, carrying what they could. He listened to the radio for news, but it was confusing and contradictory, and so he had shut it off.

By the following morning, August 13, he was about a hundred miles from home, and he decided to make the rest of the trip on the bike. Dead traffic choked I-95, so he had used the cars as refueling stations, raiding them for snacks and water. Most of the vehicles were abandoned, but many contained the bodies of Medusa victims, their desperate flight from the plague now over.

He called Rachel half a dozen times, but on the few occasions the call went through, he got only her voice mail. Thinking about what was going on around him was too much to contemplate, and so he had simply focused on the road ahead. Terror powered his legs; his mind had shut down, perhaps as an act of self-preservation. He rode past the towns of Emporia and Jarratt and Carson and found things just as fucked up in Virginia as they'd been in North Carolina.

That had brought him here, just north of the bridge spanning the James. Adam curled onto the Broad Street exit, desperate to get home, numb, exhausted. His ass hurt from so many miles on the bike. As he merged onto Broad Street and cycled past the Virginia Commonwealth University Hospital, three gunshots cracked the night air in quick succession, one after the other – POW! POW! POW! A chilling scream followed, a howl so primal that Adam slammed down the bicycle's brakes, almost reflexively. The wheels locked up, but on the wet surface, they continued to slide underneath him; a second later, his weight disrupted the balance of the bike, tipping it over and dumping him onto the blacktop. His body rolled into the curb like a discarded beer bottle.

He lay still for a moment, anxious for reports from his various body parts. Pain buzzed through his body, but he took solace in the fact that he could feel pain everywhere. Carefully, he wiggled all the wiggly parts, starting with his feet and moving upward to his head. It was going to hurt like hell the next day, assuming he lived that long.

There were more people here, pockets of them, wandering the streets, the air buzzing with panicked voices. The tinkle of breaking glass. They were right, the novelists and screenwriters with their depictions of the apocalypse. They'd been so goddamned right. The crowd consisted mostly of young people, some of them engaged in a kind of protest march.

TRUTH NOW! one sign read.

Another: NO MORE LIES!

A third: MEDUSA IS OUR DOOM

He heard a low growl approaching from the east; a moment later, a pair of olive-green military transports pulled up and blocked the intersection at 10th and Broad Street, just a few blocks from the state capitol building.

"Clear the streets and return to your homes," a soldier announced via megaphone. "You are in violation of a military curfew."

Adam's stomach flipped. How was this happening, how was this happening, how was this happening? His feet felt locked in concrete as he watched the protestors ignore the soldiers' mandate. He could hear coughing and sneezing and if they had it, Adam thought, they really didn't have anything to lose by ignoring the soldiers. That made for a very bad combination.

He needed to get out of here.

He was half a block shy of the hospital's emergency room entrance. In the falling darkness, the familiar red lights of an ambulance strobed across the neighboring buildings. Almost instinctively, his feet began shuffling toward the door, the hospital's gravity pulling him in, his life so inextricably tied to medicine and the healing arts that there was no separating him from it, especially in the face of this immense disaster. Hell, maybe he could help out!

The closer he got, the faster he moved. He had to see for himself. One last light of hope flickered deep in his soul, perhaps nothing more than a pilot light, but, with the right spark, could reignite his faith that it wasn't as bad as it seemed, that this outbreak had burned hot and fast but like a falling star scraping the roof of the world, was flaming out, that his colleagues, his brothers and sisters in arms, were bringing their best game in their most desperate hour.

These were the thoughts pinballing around his head as he drew closer to the double doors, and these were the ones that died the most brutal deaths when he saw the words GOODNIGHT MOON grotesquely scribbled on the glass doors in ... Jesus God, was that *blood*? The sliding doors were malfunctioning, opening and closing like a metronome. To his left was the ambulance whose lights he'd seen flashing earlier; one of the bay doors was open, swaying in the rain-freshened breeze. Half a dozen bodies were piled up inside the ambulance bay.

As he drew close enough to see inside the hospital, to see the stretchers scattered about the unit like a child's abandoned toys, the smell hit him like a runaway truck. It was rich and deep, a pungent, gassy smell that all but wrapped its invisible hands around Adam's throat. He recoiled, losing his balance and finding his seat on the wet asphalt behind him. He sat in the puddle, feeling the cold rainwater seeping through his clothes, thinking about Rachel, Rachel, Rachel.

Behind him, back on the street, the protestors were growing louder. At first, he couldn't quite make out their words, a tri-syllabic chant, but as he primed his ears, the words came through loud and clear.

"Fuck you, pigs! FUCK YOU PIGS!"

Over and over they screamed it, louder and louder until the desperate chatter of gunfire exploded and cut the mantra short. Then their screams of protest were replaced by howls of pain and agony. He heard footsteps, and terror stabbed at his core.

"FUCK YOU, PIGS!"

Hide, you moron, hide!

The dark cave of the ambulance bay beckoned him; he didn't want to get in, but he had to. He grabbed the edge of the door and hoisted himself up onto the bumper. Even with the doors open, it was rank and hot, like an ancient evil expelling its hot breath on him. The sound of automatic gunfire erupted again, this time closer, much closer, almost like it was in his head, and he forced himself deeper into the ambulance, toward the back, using the dozen bodies for cover.

It was dark, but not pitch black, and that was horrible in its own way. Silhouettes moving about, soldiers pursuing and cutting down fleeing protestors, the tongues of flame erupting from the muzzles of their heavy guns.

Finally, silence, as the soldiers finished their sweep, leaving Adam alone in the back of that dead ambulance.

Rachel, Rachel, Rachel.

Then the bad thoughts started rushing in, pouring in as if a water main had ruptured. Fear that she wouldn't answer if he called. Fear that she was already gone. Fear that he would never see her again, and he would never get a chance to make right what had gone so terribly wrong.

He had tried to make a go of it with Nina Kershaw, Rachel's mother, when they'd discovered she was pregnant. They'd been on a few dates together, so it wasn't quite a one-night stand that had led to the pregnancy. A couple weeks after the pregnancy test came back positive, they'd ridden down I-64 to Busch Gardens in Williamsburg, about an hour southeast of Richmond, just to get their minds off the very sudden and unexpected detonation of a reality bomb in their lives.

It had been a beautiful September day, the day clear and fresh with just a hint of fall in the air. They ate funnel cakes and chili dogs, and Adam had ridden the Loch Ness Monster; Nina had opted for the less exciting rides in her delicate condition. Toward the end of the day, he'd won her a gigantic stuffed bear at one of the carnival games, a stuffed animal that had stood guard over Rachel's room to this day.

On the drive back to Richmond, they'd held hands. That night, she stayed with him at his apartment, where they made love. They slept until noon, and Adam felt like everything was going to be all right. Maybe things weren't as clean or neat as he once imagined they'd be, but if there was one thing he'd learned in medical school, it was that life wasn't particularly interested in neat and clean. It was dirty and messy and sloppy, and you had to be able to adjust to it, to read the defenses, call the audibles.

And so when she had ended things three months later, there in the parking lot of St. Mary's Hospital, after the twenty-week ultrasound that had told them it was a girl, he felt like he'd been punched in the stomach. He'd missed the signs, the ground shifting underneath him, the chill in the air, the distance growing between them, two tectonic plates drifting apart.

He pulled out his phone, the glow from the screen illuminating the corpses around him. In the top left corner of the bright screen, two bars reflecting signal strength flickered at him. This worried him; he normally got great reception downtown. It was too creepy, too symbolic. Pushing the thought out of his head, he dialed her number, his heart pounding, the blood rushing in his ears.

The phone rang and rang and rang, its buzz as lonely a sound as he had ever heard in his life.

No one answered, and the call rolled into voice mail.

"Rachel, it's Dad," he said, trying to hold his panic down like a runaway steer. "Call me. I'm not sick, but I don't know what's going on. Today is, uh..."

He had no idea what day it was. Urgent requests for information skittered along his neurons, tapping his brain for the information, but the answer was not forthcoming.

"Shit, I don't even know what day it is. Please, chicken wing, call me."

He ended the call and slipped the phone back into his pocket.

Chicken wing. That had been his nickname for her when she was a kid, a skinny mess of arms and legs. It had been years since he'd called her that.

As he retrieved his bike, two camouflaged Army trucks rolled by, headed east on Broad Street.

He had never felt so alone.

THE STORM GREW STRONGER as Adam drew closer to his house, there just near the end of Floyd Avenue. Old oaks and maples dating back to the Civil War swayed in the stiffening wind like angry sentinels. Sheets of rain washed across the blacktop, the throaty ripple of thousands of gallons of water rushing into the city's ancient storm drains audible above the downpour. Lights were still shining in many houses, the rooms bright in the falling gloom; he paused at one bay window and peered inside, cupping his hands around his eyes to sluice away the rain. He hoped, no, he prayed to see signs of life, someone watching television, lingering in front of a bookcase, making dinner. But instead, he saw a middle-aged woman on a couch, curled up under a blanket, the blue light of a television screen flickering against her face. Her eyes were closed. He moved on.

At the last intersection, he saw two people arguing, their arms wild and animated in their accusatory slashes. In the intersection, a Jeep's front quarter panel was smashed to hell, and its assailant, a large Buick sedan, now sported a crumpled front grill. Steam curled from cracked radiators.

Then the larger of the men, a heavyset, balding fellow wearing a black windbreaker, shoved the other man in the chest. The skinnier fellow stumbled backwards, and Adam's face tightened as he sensed, deep in his soul, something extraordinarily bad was about to happen. He slowed to a stop, keeping one foot perched upon the pedal, the high one, just like he'd learned as a kid. He debated making a U-turn, approaching his house via one of the other streets that-

BLAMM!

The sound of the gunshot exploded through the rain, the impact of the bullet spinning the heavyset man's body around before he crashed

to the wet pavement in a heap. Adam's medical training kicked in, and he got off the bike, ready to rush to the man's side to treat the wound. Part of him wanted to be there for him, maybe give him a chance to help someone this week, after the catastrophic few days he'd spent at Holden Beach. But then that, too, was stolen from him, when the shooter stepped forward and fired two more bullets into his victim's face.

"No!" Adam called out.

The shooter looked up in Adam's direction. Their eyes locked, and in that moment, Adam saw the panic and the fear and total disintegration of everything this man might have been yesterday, hell, five minutes ago. He aimed the gun at Adam, who froze. His mind went blank; it didn't seem real, what was happening, as though he might have been watching this scene unfold on television.

Everything became exquisitely clear, down to the fat drops of rain-water forming on the barrel of the gun and then splashing down onto the blacktop to join the thin rivulets flowing across the blacktop. As Adam sat there, straddling his bicycle, the shooter held up a free hand, a defensive posture, as if he were the one facing the barrel of the gun. Then he fired.

The bullet missed by a country mile, but it sent Adam tumbling to the asphalt, pulling the bike down on top of him. His foot became tangled in the spokes of the rear tire and as he attempted to wrestle it free, he noticed the man approaching, his gun up again.

The spike of terror was so sharp Adam gagged; he kept one eye on the armed man and worked to free himself. Why hadn't he just pedaled away? He would've been three blocks away by now.

"Are you sick?" the man was yelling. "Are you sick?"

"No!" Adam called out. "Don't shoot, please don't shoot!"

Adam hoped this would defuse the situation, assure the man he had nothing to fear.

But instead, the man fired again. Adam screamed as that infernal spoke finally released his foot from captivity, but again the man had missed. He was a foot away now, close enough Adam could see the man's flushed cheeks, feel the terrible heat radiating from his rotting body.

"Why aren't you sick?"

The man stood there, unsteady on his feet, as if the street was rippling beneath him, the gun tottering from side to side. He was at point-blank range; there was nowhere for Adam to go.

"Why ... aren't... you... sick?"

Then a coughing spell overcame him, and for a moment, Adam couldn't believe his luck; he stood there, watching Medusa tear this man apart from the inside out. Finally, he made his move. He drove into the man's midsection, shoulder-first, and the pair flopped to the ground in a tangle of arms and legs. Still coughing, the man pawed at Adam's face and head, but he got up a little high, and Adam slid his hand onto the barrel of the gun. Now he had the leverage, and he began pushing the muzzle away from his torso. Next, he went for the trigger, wedging his thumb under the other man's finger into the trigger guard; he felt the skin from his knuckle peel back.

The pain was huge and immediate, like his thumb had been dipped in fire. But he dug deeper, seeking the leverage he needed now that the muzzle was facing the other way.

Dig, dig, dig, dig!

Tears streamed from the corner of his eyes and down into his ears. Every muscle howled with pain and fatigue. He felt congestion fill his nose and throat. As his left thumb continued its quest, Adam used his right arm to block the man's forehead. His lips were peeled back, his teeth flashing and clicking together. No words were exchanged, just a series of painful, desperate, primal grunts from both men.

Now or never, Adam, now or never. Adam pulled hard on the trigger, screaming like a banshee as he did so; the gun roared and bucked between their bodies. Immediately, the man's body went limp and eased down on Adam like a sigh. Adam reacted with a half-gasp, half-scream. As quickly as it had begun, it was over, and Adam was alone on the street, in the middle of this deepening shitstorm.

He staggered to his feet and stumbled in a little semi-circle around the man.

He heard himself howling, a deep, guttural thing of victory, a war cry of sorts, and he could scarcely believe the sound was coming out of his own body. He began shivering, and his stomach heaved.

Ingrained habits died hard, and so he glanced up and down the street for rubberneckers, eyewitnesses, police officers. At a house just catty-corner to him, there was a little girl standing on a covered porch, wearing a bright red dress that was emblazoned with yellow flowers. She stood there holding a stuffed pig, a blank look on her face. As Adam watched her watching him, he could hear in the distance the sounds of sirens and gunfire and shouts and screams. He looked back toward the intersection where this had all started; the two cars were still engaged in their embrace, where, unbeknownst to Adam, they would remain until the rubber tires disintegrated into dust, until the cars' metallic paint had decayed to a rusted orange.

His head hurt.

He sat down.

Right on the street.

Next to the man he'd just killed.

His mind was an empty thing, a blank notebook.

He looked back at the porch, but the little girl was gone, and he didn't know if she'd been there at all or if he'd been hallucinating. He mounted his bike again and pedaled for home. The rain intensified as he drew closer to his house, drowning out everything else. Two minutes later, he braked at his front stoop, hopped off the bike and carried it inside. His clothes were soaked with a thin mixture of blood and rainwater, and he left a trail of pinkish spatter as he climbed up the stairs. He changed into dry clothes and crawled into bed. He turned on the news.

Outbreak, panic, blah, blah, blah.

He slept.

Outside, the rain roared.

INTERLUDE

LEAFLETS AIR-DROPPED OVER MIDWEST & SOUTH AUGUST
15-16

ATTENTION
BY ORDER OF THE U.S. DEPARTMENT OF HOMELAND SECURITY

1. All healthy individuals are ORDERED to immediately report to Busch Stadium, West Entrance, St. Louis, Missouri, United States of America for examination by the Centers for Disease Control and Prevention.

2. You will be provided food, clean water, and shelter, and you will be generously compensated.

3. You will provide a blood sample for use in the development of a vaccine for the Medusa virus.

4. Failure to comply with this directive shall constitute a federal crime pursuant to Title 18 of the United States Code.

Your Country Needs You!

Signed,

Thomas Roberts, Acting Secretary of Homeland Security
Nathan Crosby, President of the United States of America

GOD BLESS AMERICA

10

Captain Sarah Wells wanted a cigarette, but the respirator covering her face, already busy giving her a bad case of claustrophobia, had made that impossible. She would have been happy with just about any distraction, a piece of gum, a goddamn Tootsie Pop would do at this point, anything that would take her mind off her current reality, walking a turn in the week-old Bronx Quarantine on August 15. She double-checked the thick canvas strap of the M4 rifle around her neck, which she hated using because of the way it chafed her skin, and set her hands on the small of her back, trying to break up some of the tightness that had drawn her muscles taut. It felt like someone had been slowly using a handcrank on her back.

Dawn was breaking in the east, the night slowly morphing into a dull grayness. A crescent moon hung low in the lightening sky like a smirk. They were in a mixed commercial/residential district near the Harlem River, fertile ground for the symbiotic relationship between the residents of the brownstones and the shopkeepers whose bodegas dotted the strip. As it had been for hours, it was drizzling, the worst kind of rain, the kind that did nothing to cool you off. Sarah kept hoping the shower would just metastasize into a downpour, perhaps break the padlock of humidity holding the city in its clutches, but the drip-drip-drip just kept on, maddeningly, infuriatingly so, against her standard-issue helmet.

There must have been a hole in her rain poncho, because she could feel rainwater dampening her fatigues, and the cold squishiness of the fabric against her hip. The air stank of smoke and diesel, the smells intensified by the humidity and wrapping around her in a sweaty fog. She was tired, so tired. She'd grabbed a few hours of sleep after dinner, but it had been thin, right at the edge of waking.

Her platoon was stationed on the northeast side of the Third Avenue Bridge in the Bronx, which separated this borough from northern Manhattan. They'd blocked each of the two spurs that ran north into the neighborhood. The canopy had been removed from her truck, to make room for the Browning .50-caliber machine gun mounted in the truck's bed. The gun was a monstrous, serpent-like thing that Sarah could not keep her eyes off, as if it might come to life and swallow her whole. It was one thing to see it overseas, but she could not imagine having to call that thing into service in the Bronx. Yet there it was, its ammunition belts draped over it like a pageant sash. The platoons had set up sawhorses with electronic displays to fill in the gaps, their orange lights blinking disinterestedly. A series of messages cycled through the digital display, leaving no doubt about the Army's purpose here.

Quarantine
No Access
DEADLY FORCE AUTHORIZED

There had been twenty of them on this detail at the beginning, at the top of the southwest spur. They were down to ten now. Eight had fallen ill with Medusa in the first two days and rotated out, and two more had simply bugged out and gone AWOL. Nearly all of the others were now complaining of symptoms, but the battalion commander had told her not to expect any additional relief for ill soldiers. They were just going to have to man up with ibuprofen and NyQuil. Her two other platoons, stationed farther north along the Harlem River, were reporting similar rates of attrition, but the quarantines were holding. Forget the fact that they were holding because almost everyone inside the quarantine zones was dead. Incidental, and not to cloud the success of the objective.

Sarah herself still felt fine physically, experiencing none of the symptoms the others had described. Two were laid up in the covered truck, too sick to man their posts, and honestly, Sarah didn't know what to do for them. It was all they could do to keep the perimeter secure; things inside the quarantine zone were deteriorating by the day, pressure building up like a failing nuclear reactor. The civilians were sick, angry, and spoiling for a fight. The Bronx hospitals were overwhelmed, turning away patients now, and they'd been left to hear the pleading and the begging from the ones still feeling well enough to be up and around.

That she herself was standing here at all was probably prima facie evidence of sheer insanity, but it wasn't like she'd had any choice in the matter. She didn't want to be here, she didn't want to be anywhere in New York, thank you very much. She'd be lying if she said she hadn't thought about running. She could've run, she supposed, like Lowell and Hewitt had, it was something she was sure they'd all considered, but she never would. She would think about her brother, who had died in Afghanistan, and her dad, a retired mailman who never shut up about how proud he was of her, and she couldn't stand to think she had let them down. And she never forgot that she was a female combat soldier, a *black* female combat soldier, one of the few female officers at Fort Dix.

Her dad, a widower, lived in Raleigh. She wondered how he was, what the story was down there. Fresh, reliable news had become scarce in the last twenty-four hours, nothing but platitudes from the battalion commander that the situation was under control. But if that were true, why were they hearing slices of insanity from the locals, the ones inside the quarantine zone who said the outbreak was getting worse, that the quarantines were collapsing, that no one really had any plan to bring this under control? And some of the estimated casualty figures, if they were to be believed, had made Sarah's legs buckle. Ten million dead. Fifty million dead. Tens of millions infected. No cure.

Rolling into the Bronx had been the most bizarre experience of her life. They had come across the Third Avenue Bridge over the Harlem River, one of many Army units sealing off the bridges into and out of the Bronx. She'd felt on edge during the entire rollout, believing the slightest misstep would cut her, and the unease had grown with each passing hour. Her tours in Afghanistan and Iraq, those had been bad enough, but those were the right kind of scary, the kind she'd expected when she'd joined ROTC her freshman year at SUNY-Albany.

From the passenger seat of the Army truck, she had looked over her shoulder into the cargo area, into the respirator-covered faces of her subordinates. Their average age was about twenty, meaning that these men, boys really, were only about one Olympics removed from sprouting their first pubes. Barely boys. Babies. Many of them had still been in diapers when the Twin Towers came down.

"Captain Wells."

The voice startled her. It seemed like hours had passed since anyone had said anything. The platoons had been pacing nonstop, carving grooves into the asphalt, nervously looking at one another as the minutes ticked by. She looked up and saw Private Qureshi jogging toward her, his arm pointed north, into the quarantine zone. He was one of the youngest in the platoon, rail thin, a sweet kid, a good soldier. He was sweating and his cheeks were flushed, but she tried to ignore that.

"Something's going on," he said. "Inside the Q zone."

"What is it?"

"Not sure," he said. "This seems organized." He coughed twice, and Sarah's heart broke. She didn't understand how this could be happening, how this thing was spreading the way it was. They were wearing the masks. The fucking masks!

"You feeling OK?"

"Fine," he said. "Fine."

She could see the panic in his eyes; he finally had the answer to the question she'd asked herself a million times – when was she going to start coughing and roasting with fever, when would the blood start pouring from her nose and ears? If anything, she'd fully expected to be one of the first to get sick, but here she was, more than a week since this thing had blown up, and she still felt fine.

The universe, she did have a sense of humor, didn't she?

She followed Qureshi around the truck, toward the intersection of Lincoln Avenue and Bruckner Boulevard, where they'd established the perimeter. As she came around the front grill of the truck, she saw a crowd forming in a parking lot to the east, swaying back and forth, buzzing with chatter. Two of her soldiers were walking toward the group, their rifles up, trying to wave them off. Within seconds, people were yelling at the troops, getting up in their covered faces, almost as if they'd been waiting for them.

An angry undercurrent rippled through the crowd, the inverse of a happy summer block party. There were hundreds of people, of all colors and ethnicities, milling about. Flushed faces, shirts dark with sweat, eyes hollow and sunken. The sidewalks were narrow and jammed, a stinking, nervous mass of humanity rippling in the virgin light of the morning. She could hear people sniffling, sneezing, coughing, deep, ripping coughs exploding like hidden land mines.

Sarah jumped back in her truck and activated the built-in megaphone.

"Return to your homes," Sarah called out, her amplified voice laced with static and sounding far away, like it was too far away to do any good. "You are interfering with a military quarantine."

This only antagonized the crowd, and the buzz continued to amplify. Replies mingled together to form a loud symphony of anger and frustration. Behind her, she could hear the troops yelling and cussing, the sounds of magazines being locked and loaded.

The soldiers fanned out around the truck, forming a defensive perimeter, their rifles up and pointed at their fellow citizens. Out of the corner of her eye, Sarah saw another throng approaching from the east, via a side street, hidden just so by the bodega on the corner. She didn't like this. It appeared coordinated, as if the locals had decided they'd had just about enough of their party guests and had stayed up all night coming up with a plan to rid themselves of their company. She activated her shoulder mike.

"Echo Three to Echo Base," Sarah said. "We need backup. A large crowd of civilians, possibly turning hostile."

As she waited for a reply, an organized mass of young men, white, black, Asian, Latino, formed on the southwest corner, blocking their continued progress north and drawing the attention of her platoon. Two of her soldiers, the two oldest in the platoon, stepped forward.

"Negative, Echo Three. Good luck," said Lt. Col. Craig Curwood, the commanding officer in the Bronx.

Jesus.

If Echo Base had bigger priorities than a dozen American soldiers trapped by an angry and armed mob, it was going to be a very, very long day.

A gunshot broke her out of her trance, and that was when Captain Sarah Wells knew things had changed forever and irrevocably so.

Without thinking, she dropped prone, the way she had in Kandahar Province and Iraq, in tours and days gone by, the ground knocking the wind out of her. Two feet in front of her, Private First Class Wally Griffin failed to move fast enough. His big body, six-four, 220 pounds of unfulfilled dreams of life as a Division I quarterback at Alabama or Tennessee, some good SEC school, seized up for a moment, just a flash of a second, and then he fell to the ground like he'd dropped through a trap door.

"No, no, no!" Sarah groaned.

From her stomach, Sarah aimed her weapon high and squeezed off two shots. This was by instinct, years of training imprinted on her, almost like a brand. Executed like a computer program, and that was for the best because she had just fired her weapon on U.S. soil, on American citizens, and, the worst part of it was that she was defending herself and her troops. Before the thought could overwhelm her, flood her engine, she slid up to Griffin's side and found him still. There was a small dime-sized hole just over his left eye, and an exit wound the size of a silver dollar at the base of his skull. Blood was pooling underneath him, the dark red liquid staining the asphalt.

As Sarah tended to her dying charge, a burst of small-arms fire erupted near her – from whom, she couldn't tell, and in the end, did it even matter? Howls of agony and terror followed as the 5.56x45mm NATO rounds in her platoon's M4s found targets, thick, heavy thumps as the big rounds slammed into dense flesh, cutting through muscle and bone like teeth into a rare steak. Many scattered at the exchange of gunfire, but some remained, and Sarah was sickened to see the ones that stuck around were armed, intent on continuing this insanity. One of her soldiers, maybe Private Woods, was caught in a no-man's-land, and two unseen gunmen opened up on him, raking his legs with a hail of large-caliber bullets. There was no precision to the attack, just some lunatics unloading their semi-automatic pistols. Woods dropped to the ground, writhing in pain. Two other soldiers lay down fire as they tried to recover their fallen brother.

Back to her shoulder mike. Certainly, Echo Base would want to know about American soldiers engaged in a firefight with American citizens in the fucking Bronx on a Saturday morning, right? They hadn't seem concerned with any of the other status updates she'd called in, but this would be different, she told herself. If not, well, Echo Base could go fuck itself.

"Echo Base, Echo Three is fully engaged," she said, tipping her head toward her shoulder mike, shouting over another staccato M4 burst. "Requesting helicopter support, goddammit!"

This time, Echo Base didn't make her wait long, barely an instant.

"Request denied," came the reply, sounding far away and emotionless. "Echo Three, you are ordered to maintain the quarantine by any means necessary. Acknowledge."

Sarah felt every muscle in her body tighten up like she'd been hit with an electrical current. Around her, the small arms fire was intensifying, almost like a Fourth of July fireworks show reaching its final crescendo. Most of the gunfire was of the M4 variety, the sound as familiar to her as her own voice, but there were still others woven into the fabric of the gunbattle, .38 specials and SIG Sauers from dusty shoeboxes on closet shelves, possibly a MAC-10 in there. Street guns, no match for the military hardware Echo Three was packing.

Any means necessary.

Jesus. So this was for real. Really real. Her mind went blank and she let herself be the soldier she'd trained for more than a decade to become. Not for the first time in her life, she was thankful for her Army training. She was trained to follow orders, and it let her detach from the current reality. Many times, it was the job that had drawn her through the darkest times in her life. She had to believe this terrible order she'd been given, one that would surely haunt her for the rest of her days, however many of them remained, was being issued for the greater good. That thoughtful, careful, deliberate men had examined the situation here and the situation elsewhere and determined that this was the only way.

"Acknowledge, Echo Three."

"By any means necessary," Wells repeated. "Copy that."

"God bless you, Echo Three," came the reply, the voice softer this time, followed by a quick burst of static. Then silence.

This made Sarah's blood run cold, and a hard shiver rippled through her body. Using the helmet-com, she switched the channel over to the platoon's dedicated frequency.

"Echo Three, fall back!" she barked.

After clicking off her communicator, she did a quick recon of their situation. Multiple casualties, multiple itchy trigger fingers and their scared shitless captain. Immediately to her left, four soldiers – Preston Beaumont, Johnny Weekes, Clint Vranian and Faisal Qureshi. Quite a quartet, she thought. All barely out of basic training. The others were scattered around the perimeter of the truck. Just ahead was a side street, an alley more than anything, which cut behind a bodega; she took note of it as a possible escape route in case they needed to get out quickly. That's what it had come to. Planning a possible bugout.

"Our orders are to maintain the quarantine by any means necessary," she said after they had congregated behind the truck.

"Fuck that!" came the deep, bellowing voice of PFC Vinnie Matthews. He'd been sick since midnight. "What the fuck is the point of all this? We're all fucking dead anyway! I fucking quit."

Without thinking about it, Sarah drove the butt of her rifle into Matthews' midsection; when he doubled over, grunting, coughing up blood, she brought up her right knee squarely into his chin. She laid him down gently on the ground and knelt down close to him, his panic-stricken face just inches from her own.

"Don't ever question my orders again," she said softly.

Matthews nodded, his eyes shiny with tears. She eyed him for a moment longer, debating whether she should try and give him a comforting word. She decided against it. They were all in the same sinking boat.

"Anyone else want to fucking quit?" she asked, surveying the faces of her terrified troops.

"We have a fucking job to do," she said when no one replied. "I don't know what the fuck is going on, or how long we're going to be here, but we have to believe our orders are part of some bigger plan to get us out of this shit. Are we clear?"

A gaggle of "Ma'ams" and "Yes ma'ams" followed. She didn't know if they believed what she was saying; she wasn't sure she believed it. But if she didn't *act* like she believed it, she'd lose whatever thread of control she maintained over her platoon.

"All right, let's get back to work."

In the distance, she heard shouts, some English, some Spanish, still others in languages she didn't recognize. Gunshots peppered the air, the smell of smoke and metal intensifying. She peered around the front edge of the truck, back toward the quarantine zone and saw another crowd forming, this one louder and angrier than the first. Pockets of people swarmed the area, people hiding behind parked vehicles, in alleys, behind the buildings. She saw many were armed this time, the mob evolving like a strain of deadly bacteria. Movement along the tops of the buildings near the perimeter caught her eye, and she realized with horror these people were getting ready to launch some kind of offensive against her unit.

"Weekes!" she barked into her communicator. "Looks like we've got movement on the rooftops."

As if on cue, a hail of gunfire rained down on them from above. Sarah and Weekes turned and directed their fire on the rooftop snipers. She fired one burst, and then another, and then another, her M4 growing hot in her hands. Weekes edged around the far side of the truck and came up firing, but the shooter retreated from the edge. Then she turned her attention toward the clusters, crying as she cut down citizen after citizen.

A loud, revving groan caught her attention, and she swung her gaze toward the source of the noise. A large vehicle was accelerating toward the roadblock, coming from the north, possibly a moving van or delivery truck. As it breached the last roadblock-free intersection, hell erupted around Sarah. The street exploded with heavy gunfire. She rotated back around the front of the truck and opened up with her M4, tears streaming down her cheeks, partially from fear, but mostly from sadness, terrible, crushing sadness that her life was probably going to end here, in New York City, everything fucked six ways to Sunday.

"I'll man the gun!" she shouted. Her heavy footsteps twanged against the metal bed of the truck, and within seconds, the air was filled with the terrifying whisper of the .50-caliber gun as its rounds found purchase in the front grill of the truck. The machine gun edged upwards slightly, just a hair, and within a second, a splatter of red splashed against the windshield. But it was too late. The truck's trajectory shifted slightly, as it continued without human control, but it didn't decelerate at all.

"Fall back!" she screamed.

Realizing there was no chance to divert the truck from its homicidal trajectory, Sarah leapt off the machine gun battery; a second later, the truck's grill crashed into the side of Sarah's armored personnel carrier and it careened up Lincoln Avenue toward the bridge. She hit the ground hard and rolled, her body a rag doll against the rain-slickened asphalt. The truck pitched and yawed as it hit the bridge, scraping up against the left guardrail. It overcorrected, sweeping across the other travel lanes before punching through the guardrail on the north side of the bridge. It plunged sixty feet into the dark waters of the Harlem River, piercing the surface with a terrific slap.

The crowd poured into the gap created by the collision like water from a ruptured main, flowing, flowing, flowing. Sarah scampered out of the way, taking cover under the remains of an old Toyota Celica; she lay prone and watched hundreds, thousands of feet slapping the pavement. She activated her shoulder mike.

"Echo Base, Echo Three."

The open line hissed with static.

"Repeat, Echo Base, Echo Three. Third Avenue Bridge quarantine breached. Repeat. Third Avenue Quarantine breached."

More static. No answer.

Sarah watched them stream through, sick, dying, carrying the virus with them into Harlem. When the flow had tapered to a trickle, she crawled out of her hiding spot, her M4 at the ready. But it wasn't needed. The crowd cascaded across the bridge now, people staggering and stumbling over one another like a haunted funhouse version of a picturesque marathon start.

She had failed.

A buzz drew her attention, and she turned her head south, where she saw two low-flying helicopters following the cut of the river, closing fast. Apaches, loaded for bear. Multiple starbursts winked in the low morning gloom as each chopper unleashed four Hellfire missiles upriver. The rockets screamed north and slammed into the Third Avenue bridge superstructure; it disappeared into a cloud of smoke, debris and body parts. As fifteen hundred men, women and children plunged to their deaths alongside the twisted, burning wreckage of the bridge, the screams were so loud, so piercing it made Sarah's head throb.

When it was over, the Apaches dipped their noses low, as if sighing, and continued upriver. A strange silence enveloped everything around her, and Sarah stood there watching the burning rubble and bodies floating in the Harlem River.

INTERLUDE

FROM SELECTED TWITTER ACCOUNTS

Hashtags #Medusa #plague #flu

August 15

9:16 a.m. to 9:17 a.m. Eastern Daylight Time

@NewYorkCity: Quarantines will remain in effect until further notice #Medusa

@LynnSwanson: The hospitals are full here in Topeka. Please spread the word #Medusa #flu

@Andre2K: Bodies stacked up on outskirts of town. Long ditch being dug. #Bozeman #Medusa #cobra

@JavierWriter: I just saw a policeman shoot and kill two looters! #cleveland #medusa #plague

@CarlosDiaz: Todo el mundo en mi edificio está muerto! Tengo una fiebre. #medusa #ayudar

@USHomelandSecurity: A #Medusa vaccine is nearly ready for widespread distribution

@NBCNews: RT @USHomelandSecurity: A #Medusa vaccine is nearly ready for widespread distribution

@TadMcGuire: Sounds of heavy gunfire all night long. So scared. #trustinjesus #medusa

@ErinCollins: here's a pic of the fire at Murfreesboro water tower. No firetrucks!!! #medusa #tennessee

@DesMoinesEmergencyOps: Please mark an X on your front door for body removal #medusa

@VanceBaker22: It is time to make your peace with YOUR LORD! The TIME OF THE RAPTURE IS AT HAND! #medusa

@WorldNews: #Medusa outbreaks reported in London, New Delhi, Tokyo. Mortality exceeding 90 percent in some areas. North Korea reporting no infections.

@PastorJohn: #Medusa is God's judgment on our wicked world! The fag marriages and the homos are to blame!

11

When the end came for his seven-year-old Heather, the last surviving member of his family, Freddie Briggs was holding her hand, sitting on a cold metal chair next to her bed. As she slipped away, he made no attempt to hale a nurse or flag down a doctor or otherwise ignite the engine of modern medicine. Instead, he squeezed her hand and whispered in her ear, knowing from the countless explosions of grief that had rocked the intensive care unit throughout the day that no one was going to do anything, that no one *could* do anything. Everyone in the hospital was stumbling drunk through a surrealistic minefield, the landscape getting smokier with panic and misery with each passing hour.

In her last terrible moments, Heather seized briefly and then her body simply shut down. It was the quickest and least traumatic of the deaths of the three people Freddie loved more than anything in the world. She didn't seem to be in any pain, but wasn't that what they all said? How the hell did anyone know that anyway? She was lying perfectly still, her eyes closed, as they had been for the last six hours. Freddie folded her hands over her heart, brushed her hair, which had been matted down around her face with sweat, out of her eyes, and then sat back in his metal folding chair.

He became very aware of an itch on his neck and scratched it. The relief was huge, the sound of the fingernail scraping the dry patch of skin more soothing than seemed normal. He looked at his watch; it was six-fifteen. A perfectly ordinary time of day, with its own rituals and routines. Dinnertime. The early SportsCenter. Happy hour.

Freddie looked around the room that had become the Briggs family crypt and wondered what the hell good this private hospital room had done for his Susan and Caroline and Heather. Not a goddamn thing. As he thought about the last few days, he felt tears sliding down his cheek, and he wiped them away with the back of his hand.

By the time the ambulance had pulled away from the Briggs house, Susan and Caroline were both symptomatic. Susan had been the sicker of the two, worsening by the minute. Her chest was rising and falling quickly as her body struggled to draw in oxygen. Pale on her healthiest days, Susan's skin had taken on an ashy tone and was stretched taut against her already thin frame, as though it had shrunk and no longer fit. One of the paramedics, the teacher, kept attaching and reattaching a blood-pressure cuff, seemingly unhappy with the results he was getting. As the ambulance rounded a corner, he felt Susan's body heave, and she began coughing, an interminable spasm that didn't subside until they'd made it to the hospital.

Freddie was thrilled they'd been assigned the last available room, and he tried not to think about the fact they'd been afforded that luxury because for the first time in his life, Freddie had used the "Don't you know who I am?" card. As it turned out, the staffer in charge of room assignment had known who he was; she and her husband were huge Falcons fans, hopeful they could afford to get season tickets this year, but it would probably be next year. She had prattled on and on about foot-ball while working to check them in, apparently oblivious to the fact that things were going straight to hell, and Briggs had indulged her only because he had hoped it meant they'd get seen faster.

They probably had gotten seen faster, but in the end it hadn't mattered. Susan died within an hour of checking into the room, despite an exhausted-looking doctor doing his best to keep her airway open. Freddie had begged him to tell him what was going on, how could so many have gotten so sick so fast, what the plan was to treat his family. The man hadn't replied, and after he'd given up his resuscitation efforts, he simply said he was sorry and disappeared from the room. Caroline died two days after they checked in; Heather, the littlest one, fought the hardest, her body standing its ground for days, much longer than virtually anyone else in the unit, but eventually, she too, began to lose her battle.

As Heather deteriorated, Freddie began to realize the din, the frantic shouts of physicians' orders and medications and codes, was nothing more than busy work, a desperate attempt to make it look like there was still order and structure in the hospital, because admitting that there was no order or structure would be like a boxer quitting on his stool in between rounds, throwing the blood- and snot-soaked towel into the middle of the ring. Brief sorties out of the room to get ice or juice or towels or just to see what the hell was going on had told him all he needed to know. So he just sat there with his beloved daughter, feeling oddly empty inside, as if the parts that had made Freddie Briggs Freddie Briggs had been scooped out with a shovel, and he was just the shell left behind.

Freddie sat back down in his chair and let out a long sigh. The machines in the room, a heart monitor and an IV cart, were silent. He hadn't seen a nurse or doctor in about ten hours, not since Caroline had died in his arms earlier that morning, crying and coughing blood and writhing until she'd simply gone limp, a puppet with its strings cut. The doctor, ill himself with Medusa, had stood there, hugging them both, crying and apologizing. After it was over, the doctor had fled the room like it was on fire, shouting garbled nonsense. No one had made a pronouncement of death, no one had signed a death certificate, and no one had come to remove the body.

Her small body was wrapped with a bedsheet, tucked in the corner of their room because Freddie Briggs hadn't had the first fucking clue what, precisely, he was supposed to do with the dead body of one daughter while watching the life drain out of the other.

The dead had been cast wherever there was open space, in some places two on a gurney. And they were the lucky ones. Many had been lined up on the bright, cold tile floors, under sheets and blankets, and they had simply died there, having never received a single second of treatment. The other rooms had been crammed full of patients, haphazardly triaged by the stage of infection. Adherence to universal precautions had long been abandoned; the intensive care unit was covered in blood and all manner of bodily fluids, but no one had bothered to clean it up.

He watched a fly (and there seemed to be a lot of flies buzzing around this evening) land on his daughter's nose, and that was when it finally hit him. His sweet, gentle, serious Heather was gone, like her sister and their mother, leaving him all alone in a world disintegrating around him. Heather had loved her hamster and their two family cats, and since she'd been old enough to understand the concept of veterinary medicine, that's what she'd wanted to do with her life. Never once had she wavered, never once had she talked about becoming a princess or a nurse or a professional soccer player. She bought books about animals by the armful and loved going to the zoo, even though she'd been torn on the whole concept of zoos and whether it was thoughtful conservation or just plain cruel to the animals, and just like that she was dead.

His family was dead.

"My wife is dead," he said to the empty room. "My daughters are dead."

The room remained silent.

He said it again.

"My family is dead."

He turned on the television with the remote control.

Why had he done that?

He didn't know.

The television was tuned to the NBC affiliate, but it was drawing the MSNBC feed for some reason. Onscreen, the words ON THE PHONE: *Lenox Bowman, Byron, MN*, were superimposed over a graphic of a rotary telephone.

"...we're just praying real hard, Megan," a voice was saying, but Freddie tuned the voice out because he didn't want to hear what Lenox Bowman from Byron, Minnesota had to say about anything, thank you very much.

At the top of the screen were the words **NATION IN CRISIS**. At the bottom was the ubiquitous crawl, the ticker relaying undoubtedly important information about wearing facemasks or eating chicken soup and staying in bed or whatever. And that wasn't all. Somehow, the genius producer had managed to slap the number for the Centers for Disease

Control on there as well, and it all swirled together in a miasma of nonsense until he changed the channel.

Modern Family was on.

Much better than Lenox Bowman from Byron, Minnesota!

He watched two episodes. One of them he'd seen before, but the second was new to him. Weird that he'd missed an episode of *Modern Family*! Susan used to DVR it for him, and they'd watch it together before bed. Susan.

He changed the channel again. A nature show talking about the blue-footed booby, and this seemed soothing in its own way, so he left it on. Then he sat back down in his metal chair because he really didn't know what he was supposed to do now. He sat there for another ten minutes. Then he went over to the door and cracked it open, just a sliver, not wanting to draw any attention to himself. If he turned his head just right, he could make out the nurses' station at the center of the floor. Everything was still chaotic, still madness, a giant sewage-like wave of horror washing across the cold tile floors, engulfing all in its path. A tall, skinny man, pacing back and forth in front of the nurses' station, arguing with two nurses inexplicably still on duty. Few were still working, and Freddie didn't know if that was because they'd fled the hospital or if they were now patients themselves. He wondered where his agent Richie was.

The man was shirtless, his chest speckled with blood and Lord knew what else. Freddie heard moaning in other rooms, and of course, the wet, ripping sound of that horrible cough that had become the background music to the disintegration of the hospital. On the far side of the nurses' station, a middle-aged man wearing a perfectly nice Hawaiian shirt was arguing with a doctor about something or the other. He became increasingly animated, and then Freddie watched, stunned, as Hawaiian-Shirt Man plunged a white plastic knife into the doctor's throat.

As blood began spurting from doctor's wounded neck, Freddie slammed the door shut and slid down on his bottom. There just wasn't enough room in his brain to deal with such insanity. He held his huge hands over his ears as the volume ramped up. A shout, then another, and then a gunshot. Freddie heard heavy footsteps race past his door, and that was when he started to wonder why he hadn't come down with it, why he hadn't started coughing up blood and burning with the terrible fever that had taken everything he had ever known and loved. Until now, he hadn't had time to think about it, but now that he did, he felt fine, just fine, and he believed it had been because he had to be there for Susan and Caroline and Heather as they grew sicker and sicker, as they died, and he sure as hell wasn't going to let them die alone.

But now they were gone, and he didn't care about feeling fine. He didn't care about feeling anything because feeling meant thinking about them and the fact that they were dead and gone. How could they be dead? Caroline was supposed to start the seventh grade in two weeks, Heather, the third grade. Susan was a kindergarten teacher and she was about to start getting her classroom ready, one of the things she enjoyed the most about a new school year. He found himself thinking about the glitter and glue sticks and pencil boxes and Back to School Night, which would make Susan so nervous she barely slept the night before, and the classroom's guinea pig, which was now three years old. Or was it four?

Then the most ridiculous thought zoomed through Freddie's head as he sat there on the cold tile floor, in the company of his dead family.

Who was going to feed the guinea pig?

The guinea pig. The guinea pig. He kept thinking about the guinea pig, skittering around its cage in their family room, where Susan kept him during summer vacation. Freddie hadn't spent more than thirty seconds of his life thinking about the goddamn guinea pig, and now it was all he could think about. Chewie the guinea pig, with his pink-rimmed eyes and the light brown spot on his back.

Who was going to feed the guinea pig?

He was crying again, big silent tears streaming down his face. The room seemed very small, as if the walls were closing in around him. He became aware of the smell, the sourness of his own body odor, the rich, gassy smell of decay in the room, and he saw the blood and vomit and the other byproducts of death to which he'd somehow remained oblivious for the past few days. But now it was all coming home, the true reality of what had happened, and he needed to get out of this room right now, right away. Part of him, the responsible family man part of him, told himself to stay right where he was because his place was by his family's side, but its voice was growing weaker and fainter, and he needed to get out of this hospital right now.

He kissed his three girls on their foreheads, and then gently set Susan and Heather's bodies next to Caroline's. He wasn't going to stay here in this house of death, and, he decided, neither was the rest of the Briggs clan. After covering their bodies with a sheet and locking the bedrails, he pushed the bed out of the room, nearly blinded by the tears, almost hoping someone would try and stop him.

No one did, no one even gave him a second look as he wheeled the bed down to the elevators at the far end of the hallway, moving slowly so as not to jostle his precious cargo. The elevator vestibule was dark, empty but for a dead woman and the now-lifeless body of Hawaiian Shirt Man. The floor under his body was shiny with blood.

Freddie wasn't sure if the elevators were working, but the call button lit up like a solitary Christmas light when he pressed it. He considered his next move as the elevator hummed its way to the fourth floor. Home was his final destination; he was going to get his girls home where they belonged, and if that meant he was going to bury them in their backyard, then so be it. He'd be damned if he was going to let them rot here in this hellhole, in this dead place. If he had to carry them the four miles, then that's what he would do.

The familiar *bing* broke him out of his trance, and he prepared to roll the bed into the elevator. As it opened, he changed his mind. Three plague victims were lying on the floor of the elevator, dead or very close to it. One appeared to be a doctor, his white lab coat streaked with blood. He was on his back, his eyes fixed on the ceiling, and he was moaning softly. He either did not notice Freddie's presence or simply paid it no mind. And the smell was what Freddie really noticed, an overpowering stench of raw death that sent Freddie's stomach into revolt. One whiff, and he was doubled over, dry heaving because, since he hadn't eaten in more than a day, there was nothing to bring up. As Freddie struggled to catch his breath, the heaves stealing his ability to breathe, the dying doctor rolled over on his side and flung his arm out across the threshold of the elevator. When the door tried to slide home, it met the doctor's arm and then bounced back open again.

The hell with this, Freddie thought, as his stomach began to settle down. He said a little prayer for his family, asked God for strength for what he was about to do, and then slung Susan's body over his right shoulder, the girls' bodies over his left. The stairwell was just beyond the elevators, and he carried them down the four flights like sacks of flour, taking special care not to bang their bodies against the rails or the walls.

At each landing, he found more of the sick and the dead, bodies sprawled everywhere, and he stepped carefully so as not to trip. He was a little winded by the time he got to the first floor, but his legs were strong. He was thankful for the six months he'd spent running and weightlifting. It hadn't been to make it back to the NFL, he now understood; it had been so he could be strong enough to take his family home one final time.

More chaos greeted him on the first floor of the hospital as he burst out of the stairwell, possibly even more than he'd left behind on the fourth floor. Bodies lined the corridor, stacked one on top of the other like firewood, double-wide in some places, leaving barely enough room for two people to pass each other in the hallway. Here and there, he'd see someone stumbling around, the look of someone who was lost, eyes open but far away. It was warm down here, the air stale and thick with an oppressive stench Freddie couldn't identify, that he didn't particularly want to identify. He spotted one of his neighbors, a pleasant stay-at-home mom named Meg Tinsley, sitting on the floor, weeping. She didn't appear to have seen him, and so he kept on walking, unsure of what the hell he would even say to her.

No one paid him any mind as he staggered through the white corridors, through the emergency department, past the curtained areas and the gurneys. Any semblance of order in the hospital had crumbled like a cookie in a child's hand. The unit was drenched with moans and howls, a terrible soundtrack to this constantly evolving and endless horror show. The main entrance was blocked by an ambulance that had crashed through the doors.

He kept moving, past the ER and into another series of corridors. Panic chewed at his insides like a rat as each of the corridors began to look more and more alike. At a large intersection, where he saw signs directing visitors to cardiology and radiology and physical therapy and other perfectly ordinary hospital destinations, he saw two dead doctors sitting on the floor, backs to the wall; their hands were laced together, dried blood caked on their faces and lab coats. One of the doctors even had a chart set on her lap, God bless her little heart. As he gazed down on these two, he wondered if he would have the courage to stay and treat the sick if he'd found themselves in their shoes. He began to cry because he wouldn't have stayed if he were one of these doctors. He would have fled, he knew it as deeply and as surely as he'd ever known anything in his life.

As he turned left at a bank of elevators, he finally spotted the reassuring red glow of an EXIT sign, and his heart soared. It was bad in here, much worse than he'd ever imagined, and he wanted to get out of here more than he'd ever wanted anything in his life. Part of him couldn't believe how widespread this thing was, but he pushed those thoughts out of his head as he continued his funereal procession. There would be time for that later; right now, his focus was on getting his family home. And besides, what difference did it make how far the disease had spread? His own universe had imploded, taking with it all the galaxies and stars of his soul.

He turned a corner and saw the main foyer ahead of him, but it looked nothing like the one he'd seen when they'd checked into three days ago. It was a dead place, crowded with the bodies of plague victims who had died waiting to be seen. The EXIT sign glowed ominously, a deep warning shade of red. A makeshift wall of sandbags bisected the foyer, and a pair of unmanned machine gun batteries had been mounted there, the turrets pointed in opposite directions. Freddie puzzled over the scene for a moment, trying to ascertain what had happened here, but his head began to swim with confusion. Nothing he'd seen in the last seventy-two hours had made a lick of sense.

The foyer was silent but for the heavy breathing of a National Guardsman curled up in the corner, where the sandbags met the glass wall. At first, Freddie couldn't tell if the man was conscious; then the soldier looked up at him, his M4 rifle pointed squarely at Freddie's chest. He was a young guy, a thin wisp of mustache coloring his upper lip. His name patch identified him as Barousse.

"Not supposed to leave the hospital," Barousse eked out.

"Please leave me alone," Freddie said.

"Quarantine," he said. "The quarantine broke."

"What the fuck is going on out there?" Freddie asked. "What happened?"

"No one-" A spasm of coughing interrupted, and thin, ropy splatters of blood sprayed the soldier's pant legs. Private Barousse wiped his mouth with the back of his gloved hand and examined the residue of his spittle.

"What a Charlie Foxtrot this turned out to be," Barousse said.

"A what?"

"Cluster fuck."

"What happened?" Freddie asked again.

"Not really sure," Barousse said. "Things just fucked up."

He sighed deeply.

"Hey man, do you have a cigarette? I'm sleepy."

He leaned his head back against the glass and closed his eyes. Freddie paused for a moment, sorry he didn't have a cigarette, hoping the soldier didn't intend to enforce the quarantine that no longer existed, and then swung his legs over the sandbag barrier, one at a time. The hospital's main doors slid open, and Freddie stepped out into the bright August afternoon, the sun harsh and merciless. His eyes adjusted to the glare, but slowly, as if they didn't believe what they were seeing, hesitant to report the images back to Freddie's brain.

Two Georgia National Guard trucks were parked in the semi-circular drive at the main entrance; one of them was barely recognizable, its front end a smoldering husk, thin wisps of smoke still drifting from the engine block. The street fronting the hospital was barricaded at both ends by police cruisers, but Freddie couldn't tell if anyone was manning the road-blocks. On the south side of the street was the hospital's main parking lot, where a ring of police cars had set up shop around the perimeter. The parking lot itself was not particularly crowded with cars, as only about half the spots were occupied. The driving lanes, however, were lined with rows of cylindrically shaped objects of varying sizes, shrouded in white. Freddie stared at it for a moment and then froze, his eyes locked on the rows, knowing what he was seeing, but not wanting to accept it. He forced himself to break eye contact and headed north along the street, the image of the shrouds strong and bright in his memory, like marquees on Broadway.

The parking lot had become a mass grave.

INTERLUDE

August 16

    0345 Greenwich Mean Time

    Bekaa Valley, Lebanon

    Unsub: Unknown Subject

    AAN: Ahmad Abu-Nidal, Second-in-Command of Dawn of God

    Translated from Arabic

    TRANSMISSION BEGINS

Unsub: What the hell is going on?

AAN: I do not know. An evil eye is watching down on us. [COUGHING]

Unsub: No way this happened naturally.

AAN: Regardless of how it is happening, it is happening. [WHEEZING, COUGHING]

Unsub: They are going to blame us. You know that, yes?

AAN: Yes, but I do not think it matters.

Unsub: How could it not matter? They will scorch the earth looking for us. Do you know how many have died in America alone?

AAN: Do you know where I am right now? [COUGHING]

Unsub: Don't you dare!

AAN: I am just north of Ain Hirshey. Have you heard of it?

Unsub: No. My God, they'll be on you in a day.

AAN: It's a little village in the mountains. Barely a village, really.

Unsub: And I care about this why?

AAN: Because every single person in this town is dead. The last village, dead. The village before that one. Dead.

Unsub: How does that impact us?

AAN: You fool. This sickness is everywhere. There won't be anyone left to look for us. I've spoken to our comrades in China and Russia and South America, and there it is the same.

Unsub: God is great! The pigs will die.

AAN: [LAUGHTER, FOLLOWED BY COUGHING]

Unsub: What is so funny?

AAN: God might be great, but he is also pissed.

Unsub: God be with you.

AAN: Go to hell.

TRANSMISSION ENDS

INTERLUDE

FROM THE SUICIDE NOTE OF WILLIAM BRADY

Knoxville, TN

Undated

I'm sorry. I'm so sorry. I thought this would be so much different. I used to think an apocalypse would be cool. I liked zombie movies and *The Stand* and those kinds of books and movies and I thought it would be cool to be a survivor. And here I am. I'm a survivor and I didn't get sick and I watched my mom and my four sisters die in the last five days and it was the worst fucking thing you could imagine. And I think I might be the last person alive in this shithole city and I'm not exaggerating. I haven't seen a single living person in I don't know how long and we just went and fucked ourselves pretty good didn't we. And it's so QUIET so GODDAMN QUIET I can hear my fucking heart beating! The smell is getting worse because it's been hot and humid this summer and it gets worse after it rains, oh, Jesus, it gets so much worse. I don't know why I'm writing this at all because no one is ever going to read it but I had some things I wanted to say before I did it. I'm so sorry. I'm so afraid & I don't want to be afraid anymore.

If anyone reads this and wants to know, well, let me just tell you, it was so bad, so bad at the end. Everything just went to hell it was like we were animals worse than animals. Sorry, God. We must've really pissed you off.

fuck you.

12

I t was August 24.

That was according to Adam's watch, which he found himself looking at with increasing frequency. He wore it all the time now, even when he slept, something he'd never done before. He kept the band tight, to the point that it was chafing his skin, but he wanted to feel it close to his body. It was very important to know what time it was, all the time. He would check it and be a little amused to find that time had continued to tick by as it always had, second by second, minute by minute, Medusa victim by Medusa victim. Time was decidedly unconcerned with the affairs of men. Time didn't care. What, was his watch going to stop ticking because the human race had offed itself?

Then he found himself thinking about the Doomsday Clock, that delicious bit of geopolitical commentary in which a bunch of old farts got together each year and passed judgment on how well the human race had behaved itself, their decision reflected in the minute hand of a giant analog clock set to a few minutes before midnight. The closer humanity got to midnight, the story went, the closer it was to extinction. The last time he'd read about it in *Time* or the *Huffington Post* or what-have-you, the clock had been moved forward three minutes, all the way to 11:57 p.m., thanks to a whole shitload of new problems humanity had created for itself. He wondered what time they'd set the Doomsday

Clock to now. Probably two-thirty in the morning. They might even make a little note in their little Diary, if there was such a thing, that not only was it way, way past midnight, but that humanity was stumbling around drunk, vomit on its shirt, looking for a late-night slice of greasy pizza.

Adam was on the couch, his television tuned to ESPN, a bottle of Jack Daniels nestled between his legs. The electricity was still on, and that was one of the few pieces of good news, but he wondered when that bit of luck would run out. Currently, the television cameras were broadcasting from the Bristol, Connecticut studio where they taped Sports-Center – *used* to tape SportsCenter, a little voice squeaked from within – but the place looked abandoned. Someone had left the cameras on and, not surprisingly, no one had been back to turn them off. The camera was still pointed at the unmanned anchor desk. Off camera, from somewhere deep in the studios, Adam could hear someone coughing, nearly retching. Adam couldn't bear to change the channel. He didn't want the person in the studio to be alone. Maybe if he kept watching, that poor bastard, dying alone inside the headquarters of the Worldwide Leader, wouldn't be so alone. It didn't make a whole lot of sense, but it wasn't like there was anything else to do anyway.

He took another nip of the amber-colored whisky. The liquor burned his throat like drain cleaner as it sloshed its way to his stomach. He considered the last week of his life, which in many ways had been the final week of his life, his old life, before he had been birthed through the blood and viscera of a dying mother into this new world on the other side of history.

He got up from the couch and wandered over to the big bay windows looking south onto Floyd Avenue. It was evening, still light out, but long purple shadows had just begun to creep across the street and up the sidewalks, the beginnings of a blanket of twilight on the city. Night filled him with dread now, as it had when he was a boy. A random memory from his childhood began playing in his head, like a song from his iPod set to shuffle. He'd been seven or eight years old, unable to sleep thanks to the shadows cast by a pair of saplings outside his bedroom window, shadows that shimmied in the wind like the bony arms of the undead, plotting and just waiting for little Adam to fall asleep so they could sneak in his window and cut his throat. Adam crawled down the hall, seeking comfort from his father, who had called him a pussy, smacked him across the side of the head and sent him back to bed.

For the first few days he'd been back in Richmond, he was certain he had to be dreaming. There was simply no way that what was happening was actually happening. Even when he'd reported to the hospital for a marathon three-day shift beginning on the fourteenth, during which he'd made two hundred and fifty-six pronouncements of death, and would have made hundreds more if they'd continued keeping track of them, it had to be a dream. When he told them he was on suspension, and the acting chief of medicine had said he wouldn't have cared if Adam had been a rabid raccoon, it had to be a dream. He watched his patients die, then he watched the nurses and doctors die, and by the time he left on the afternoon of the seventeenth, he was one of only a handful of people still alive.

But he had to be dreaming. Soon he would see goats wearing reading glasses or transparent hot-air balloons filled with marshmallow crème and that would be it for this nightmare. Goodbye, crazy-ass subconscious, hello six a.m. and the morning news on the NBC affiliate, Channel 12, with the pretty anchor talking about another homicide down in Gilpin Court or a dog attack on a petite widow out for a stroll with her Bichon frise puppy. The smell of coffee brewing in his coffeemaker. The hiss of the machine followed by the reassuring trickle into the carafe, the pungent aroma of coffee spreading through the house.

But the dream hadn't ended, it had kept right on keeping on, and he sat there, cocooned by the silence, its big brawny embrace squeezing him until he could barely breathe. Then he tried to force the dream's hand, thinking maybe he could declare a jihad against it. At noon on the twenty-first, he wandered out onto his porch wearing nothing but black dress socks and running shoes. Everything about it seemed wrong, and that was what he wanted, standing there with his wang and balls hanging free, he wanted it all to feel wrong because that was what usually pierced the heart of a dream. But there he was, in the big empty summer day, naked as the day he was born. When that didn't work, he jogged down the steps and headed east on Floyd Avenue. As he ran, he heard nothing but the sounds of his ragged, shallow breathing, the thrum of blood whooshing in his ears. On he ran, sweat slicking his body, and he began to cry, his sobs echoing off the houses of his dead neighbors. He ran faster and cried harder, and when he finished the loop around the block, he'd sat on his porch and cried like a baby. He went inside and hadn't been back out since.

Since then, he'd spent much of his time on the couch with his laptop, drinking, eating peanut butter, watching Internet access grow spottier and spottier, the news channels go off the air one by one. One of the last news reports he'd seen was of a nuclear power station in Michigan melting down when the staff had failed to execute the plant's emergency shutdown procedures properly. It was like watching your favorite team get its ass kicked on national television. Except this time, the team was mankind.

Now he had a burning desire to be outside while there was still light. He cracked the front door, just a sliver, and when he was convinced it was safe, he stepped out onto the small concrete porch, his hand gripping the neck of the whisky bottle like a weapon. The air was thick and heavy, the feeling of wearing a sweatshirt on an unexpectedly warm fall day. He lit a cigarette right away, mainly because it made him feel tougher, because it made him feel like he had a grasp on things. You walk down a street and see a guy on his porch smoking a cigarette and drinking Jack from the bottle in the middle of the mother-fucking apocalypse, that is a guy you do not want to mess with, right?

The sounds of summer were huge and everywhere, the cicadas buzzing, the birds chirping. In the distance, he could hear a dog barking. The hum of the overhead power lines in there somewhere. But underneath that was a huge void of silence.

A flicker of movement to his left caught his eye, and he looked over to see a cloud of flies buzzing around a body in his neighbor's yard. It was Jeannette, the poet, lying dead on her perfectly manicured lawn, the grass still a bright, resplendent green. Adam stared at her blankly, the way he might have looked at a painting he didn't quite understand. She was dressed in pajama pants but nothing else; her hair was a tangled mess, and her face was bloated, caked with blood and mucus. He wondered how she'd ended up in her yard, how long she had been out here. Had she crawled outside, sensing the end was near, unwilling to lie for all eternity in a hundred-year-old brownstone?

The scope of what happened crashed down on Adam like a rogue wave and stole his breath away. It was always there, lapping at the shores of his mind, but it was these big waves eroding his sanity like an unprotected sand dune. Had he not lived through it himself, he wouldn't have believed such a catastrophe was even possible, and he was a doctor, a full-fledged, card-carrying man of science. The speed at which the virus overwhelmed everything had been dizzying; it was as if the battle to contain the outbreak had been lost before it had even begun. It was a thousand, no, a million times worse than anything he'd ever imagined. And here he was, standing at the end of history.

A breeze rustled the trees, full and thick with summer foliage, the leaves whispering amid the dying light of the day. Thunder rumbled in the distance, a low guttural drum. Adam looked west and saw a line of black clouds moving in, flashes of lightning laced into them like strobe lighting. It had been dry in Richmond for days; he'd heard faraway thunder each of the past few nights, but the storms had swept around the city, doing their duty elsewhere. The approaching tempest riveted him for a bit, like the passage of time had, because a summer storm right now was exquisite and ordinary all at the same time.

A series of electronic chimes from behind him broke him from his trance, and at first, he thought he'd imagined it. Broken out of a daydream by another daydream. A sure sign of insanity. But a few moments later, he heard the chimes again; it was his iPhone, the sound drifting through the screen door. His goddamn iPhone was chirping inside the house. An e-mail. A text message. Someone had tried to contact him. Rachel. He flung the screen door open, his eyes desperately scanning the house as the door clacked shut behind him.

Where was it? Where was it? He closed his eyes and, a moment later, he remembered he'd dropped it in the basket on the little end table by the front door after one of his many efforts to reach her. He had tried calling, emailing, texting, he had sent her messages through Facebook and Twitter, but he didn't know if anything was getting out.

He brought up the home screen (noticing with some alarm that he had less than a twenty percent charge) and saw the numeral 1 stamped over the telephone icon. After plugging the phone in to charge, he tapped the icon to enter the voicemail module, where he found a single message waiting for him.

Rachel's Cell

August 22

9:42 p.m.

August 22? That had been two days ago. But the message had just landed in his inbox, leading him to the conclusion that it had been hung up in the ether somewhere, and had just managed to make it through the once-impossibly clogged communications lines. Maybe they weren't clogged anymore because there wasn't anyone left to use them.

He tapped the screen again, activating the playback function. Outside, the wind freshened as the storm drew closer. A burst of static, and then:

"Dad?"

Her voice was an atomic blast of light in his darkening world.

"I got your messages," she continued. "All of them showed up on my phone at the same time. I've tried calling you like fifty times."

Adam felt his heart break, an almost palpable sensation of his chest caving in. His daughter needed him, and he hadn't been there. Every decision he'd made in his life since the day Rachel had been born had been just flat out wrong, because they'd added up to put him here, clear across the country from his daughter, where he couldn't do shit for her in her darkest hour of need.

Father of the Year!

"Jesus, I hope you get this," she said. "Mom's dead. Everyone's dead."

Her voice cracked and then she sobbed for a moment. Then she took two deep breaths before continuing. Adam didn't dare move a muscle, didn't even take a breath, lest he somehow fuck up and delete her message.

"It's the 22nd," she continued. "I think. I'm headed up to my stepdad's condo at Tahoe while I try to figure out what to do," she continued. "I'm not sick. I don't think I'm going to catch it. I don't know how. I was hoping it was hereditary. No, that doesn't make sense. Because Mom died. But maybe the immunity passed through you. I still feel fine. Is it bad there? I haven't seen any news in a couple days. But it's so bad here. So fucking bad. Sorry for the F bomb. Everyone is dead."

She was rambling now, and Adam could hear the panic in her voice. She broke down again, but it was softer this time, more measured, more controlled.

"God," she said, her voice trailing away. "I don't even know if you're alive. Please, if you get this, please, please call," she begged. "The power is out here, but I guess the cell towers are still running somehow because I'm still getting a strong signal. I'll leave the phone on as much as I can, charge it with a car adapter. I'll do that until the cell towers go down."

Adam heard the tinkling of glass breaking in the background of the call, and he froze. He waited for her to come back on the line.

But she didn't.

"End of messages," a mechanical female voice said.

Adam played the message again, tears streaming down his face as he listened to her voice a second time. He checked his watch, his trusty Casio, faithfully marking the passing time. If she was still symptom-free two days ago, that meant she'd almost certainly survived multiple exposures to the virus. As best as he could tell, the disease was winding down by then, certainly in any decent-sized population centers. He called her back immediately, but the line wouldn't connect.

Did she share his resistance to the disease? Was it hereditary somehow? Some recessive gene buried deep in the Fisher DNA that had protected them? He told himself to calm down, to look at it clinically, to not get his hopes up. Anything could've happened in the last two days. This set off a huge debate in his subconscious, one that he decided to ignore for the time being. Up front, he set himself to gathering more information, more data, more evidence as to what might have become of her.

He played the message a third time, scouring it for any clues that Rachel might have left about her experience. The power was out in California, not surprising given the energy problems the state had had even before all this. She sounded alone, a single flickering light in a dark and dying world. Heading for Tahoe wasn't the worst idea in the world. Safer than staying in a metro area, but the idea of her by herself out there made his throat tighten with panic.

He had to get to her. Nothing else mattered.

A boom of thunder shook the house, sending Adam's balls into his chest. He slammed the door behind him, locking it, and moved deeper into the house, away from the windows. He ran upstairs as the skies opened up and unleashed a monstrous deluge of rain on the city. The rain was deafening, louder than any storm he'd ever heard before, its sounds amplified, as if Mother Nature was sporting a bullhorn, making sure whomever was left was listening very carefully.

AS THE STORM RAGED OUTSIDE, he spread a large map of the continental United States out on his bed and plotted his course. Richmond was a bit of a gateway town, the nexus of three major interstates – I-95, I-64 and I-85. Whereas I-95 hugged the coastline from Maine to the tip of Florida, and I-85 plunged south into Dixie, I-64 meandered away from the ocean, toward the plains. Interstate 85 was his best bet. Away from the mountains, but digging deep into the heartland before an eventual westward turn on I-40.

He packed slowly, taking his time, carefully going through each room in the house. He filled an emergency kit with medicine, bottled water, canned goods, matches, a rain poncho. Then he packed clothes, toiletries, flashlights, even the photograph of Rachel he kept by his nightstand. From the closet in his bedroom, he retrieved a handgun, a nine-millimeter Glock he'd owned for years, since medical school, when he'd lived in the slums near downtown. It was wrapped in a white hand towel. He thought back to his close call up the street with the man who'd tried to shoot him. The very thought of shooting a gun again made his heart throb, as if his chest were too small to contain it. He'd taken the Glock to the range a few times, but it had been a while. He made a note to fire off a few practice rounds when he was out on the road.

The basement he saved for last, where he got to work dusting off old, rarely used camping gear. The place was dim and dank, and he was glad he'd tucked a flashlight into his pocket. The bulb sizzled and popped when he flicked the switch, and so he worked by the light of the hall corridor upstairs, using the flashlight for pinpoint work. As he picked through the detritus littering his basement, he thought about the origin of his gear, a byproduct of the thing with Stephanie, the outdoorsy one.

She was a third-grade teacher at St. Catherine's School, a friend of a friend. She was nice enough, and they had some good times, but they'd never really clicked, not in the way that said forever. They'd hiked along the Appalachian Trail a few times, and she knew what she was doing, whereas he did not. He ended up buying a thousand bucks worth of camping gear and then decided he needed to break it off. She hadn't seemed all that upset about it. There hadn't been any tears or long talks or anything like that. He saw her out with another guy a few weeks later, and he briefly debated approaching the guy and offering to sell him the tent and the backpack and the GPS tracking device because when was he going to use any of that shit?

And then it hit him that Stephanie was probably dead, and this felt tremendously unfair to Adam, that he was standing here, preparing for the camping trip of a lifetime, and it was only because of Stephanie that he was properly equipped to take it on.

He lugged the tent and the backpack up to the main floor, trying and failing to envision the days and weeks ahead of him. There was no frame of reference for this. For as much as he knew about the world in its new form, he might as well have been dropped on the surface of Mars. But what choice did he have? He had to get to California, to Rachel, because finding her meant he was doing something. Because finding her meant he had some purpose left.

He thought about Patient A, for the first time in days, and it occurred to him that his case before the Board of Medicine had been continued, postponed indefinitely, postponed forever. Patient A was still dead, but, he supposed, so were the nine members of the Board of Medicine. He would never get to tell the story about what happened, clear his name, and then he felt guilty because how could he think about *Something Like That* in the face of *All This*.

The thoughts just kept whizzing by as he inventoried his supplies, and he couldn't stop them, like he was watching train after runaway train race by from a deserted subway platform. Patient A and Natalie, the office receptionist who, inexplicably, had hated Adam from the day he'd joined the practice and basketball practice and his high school basketball coach who had skipped town in the middle of his junior year of high school and losing his virginity to Dena Chamberlain while his dad was passed out on the sofa and his dad, Jack Fisher, his giant prick of a dad who'd gotten off easy, preceding the rest of the world in death by several years, lost in a sailing accident at sea. Little League and the free soda they got at the end of each game. The way they'd fill the cup with a little of each kind of soda, a suicide they'd called it. Going to birthday parties at Chuck E. Cheese's and the feel of warm video game tokens in his hand.

The tears sluiced down his cheeks to the corners of his mouth, and he tasted salt. He wiped his eyes and his face, ran his hands through his hair, and then laughed at himself a little because just who the hell was he cleaning himself up for? He hadn't seen a living soul in days, and he wasn't entirely sure he hadn't hallucinated that little incident. He was looking out his window on the morning of the twenty-second when a man in full cycling gear had ridden by on Floyd, up out of the saddle, hunched over the handlebars like he was leading the peloton at the Tour de France. He raced by, never looking up at Adam, never slowing down as he zoomed west.

Another crash of thunder, this one rattling the windows, and the power died, the residue of the light hanging in the air like a ghostly apparition before it, too, faded away. The basement was plunged into blackness, a darkness so extreme that Adam couldn't see his hand in front of his face. In the black silence, he could feel the blood rushing in his ears, the way the ocean sounded on a dark night.

You just need your eyes to adjust, just give it a minute.

But his eyes didn't adjust, and it remained pitch black, a photo negative, the inverse of light. It felt ten degrees hotter in the room, like someone had started preheating an oven; a drop of sweat traced its way down Adam's flank. He began seeing shadows rippling against the wall, even though he knew he was imagining it, twisted shadows of evil men whispering to each other and rubbing their bony hands in anticipation of a sleepy little boy drifting off, like the ones he had seen through his bedroom window as a child. A bug of panic crawled up his legs.

He bolted for the steps, crashing over a half-filled laundry basket on the way, and raced up the stairs as if he had escaped a portal from some hellish dimension. By the time he burst into the corridor on the first floor, he could barely breathe, the fear lassoing his airway like a cowboy roping a steer. He tried to collect his thoughts, to remind himself what he still needed to pack, but his box had ruptured like the bulkheads on Titanic, and now terror was flooding the hull of the H.M.S. Adam. He'd kept it in for two weeks, but that was over now; every strand of his DNA had sounded the alarm, the one you did not ignore.

He felt his way down the hallway from memory, and mercifully, his keys and phone were still in the basket where he'd left them. As he grabbed his keys, it hit him. His SUV wasn't here. It was still down at Holden Beach. He had no car. He giggled. He couldn't stop himself, and the giggles bloomed into full-blown hysterics. His laughs echoed in the evening gloom, bouncing through the ether, sounding huge and insane. Tears streamed down his cheeks.

Insane. You're going insane, he thought as the giggles faded away.

He grabbed a flashlight and went next door to Jeanette's, the rain soaking his clothes. Her Honda remained parked at the curb, and her body was still lying in the yard, *just another scene from the apocalypse, dontcha know?* Her body had been picked over some by the animals, which really must have been sporting giant woodies with the vast selection of carrion that had suddenly been bestowed upon them. Adam avoided looking at her as he went up to the front door and let himself inside.

The house was a wreck. Clothes, food, the sour stench of something turned over. He stepped gingerly to the kitchen, where he knew she kept her car keys, hoping they were still there. He found them on the counter and then he rushed back outside, down the porch steps, and back to his house before the hot spike of guilt overwhelmed him.

It's OK, he thought. It's an emergency.

He loaded the car as quickly as he could, oblivious to the storm raging around him. When he was done, he ran back inside to change out of his wet clothes. He had to go, go, go! But as he did so, standing there in his wet shorts dripping on his floor, the absurdity of his impatience struck him. Where was he going at this hour, a terrible thunderstorm buffeting the city, the power out? He suspected the going would be tough enough in broad daylight, but to try it now would be just asking for trouble. In the morning, he decided. He would set off in the morning.

By nine o'clock, the storm had pushed off to the east, leaving behind a clear, moonless night. Adam stepped outside to smoke a cigarette. The darkness was total and complete, the city sealed tight in black ink. Sure, Richmond had had its share of storm-related power outages, but those were usually brief, nothing like the immense blackness he now faced, as though the entire city had been shoved inside a body bag and forgotten. No generators hummed, no candles warmed the windows. That was the difference. Blackouts had once been communal affairs, bringing people onto their porches with their Pinot and gin and tonics, their cigarettes and their pipes, laughter peppering the evening air, their jam-packed schedules paused, if only for a little while. This, though, was something else. Unseen back rooms of impromptu parties, where the roaches and spiders and rats scurried about, where evil men lured small children and young women and left forever scars no one could see.

He spent the night on his couch, the gun perched on his chest.

VOID

BOOK 2

How lonely it is going to be now on the Yellow Brick Road.

RAY BOLGER, THE SCARECROW

13

D awn.
    The sun spread its virgin light across the plains, covering up the darkness like a fresh coat of paint. Miles Chadwick was up early, as he usually was, sipping coffee and looking out across the eight-hundred-acre Citadel compound. He kept his office in his living quarters, on the second floor of the main building. Floor-to-wall windows looked west toward the growing fields, which would provide sustenance for their new world, the proverbial bottle for the infant society. It had been a good summer for the crops, and the land was alive, breathing, pulsing. The summer harvest was in full swing, tomatoes, cucumbers, peppers, squash, zucchini coming into the kitchens by the truckload. A pair of tractors was already out, chugging along, preparing the ground for the fall planting season.

He still found it hard to believe they'd made it. They'd executed the plan to perfection. As he did every day, he thought about the first time he'd met Leon Gruber, the German billionaire who'd made all this possible. Gruber was the majority stakeholder in the Penumbra Corporation, a multinational conglomerate with nearly 100,000 employees worldwide. Penumbra had its fingers in a number of pies, most notably transportation, energy, weapons, technology, agriculture, and pharmaceuticals. Starting when he was twenty, Gruber had built the company from the ground up and held more than ninety percent of its shares.

When Gruber approached him, Chadwick had been in Special Pathogens at the Centers for Disease Control and Prevention, passed over for promotion yet again. Gruber approached him at a Wendy's near the CDC and invited him to head up his private lab, dedicated to the study of exotic pathogens. The lab was off the books, with no government oversight to interfere with their work. As he sat there, chewing his spicy chicken sandwich, Chadwick relished the idea of telling his bosses in Special Pathogens to go fuck themselves.

The facility was top notch, the security better than he'd seen at the Centers for Disease Control. He'd never asked where or how Gruber had assembled the Citadel's stock of pathogens, the viruses and bacteria that could lay waste to millions of people; he wasn't sure he wanted to know the answer. He worked there for six months before Gruber told him what he really wanted Chadwick to do.

It had been a good six months, the most productive in Chadwick's career. He was having dinner at Gruber's home on the lake in the northwest corner of the compound, briefing the elderly man on his work. Chadwick believed he was close to developing a vaccine for Ebola Sudan; it wasn't the deadliest of the Ebola strains, but a vaccine would constitute one of modern medicine's great achievements and would be worth billions for Gruber and Chadwick. A huge victory against the tropical viruses that kept health officials around the world awake at night and wondering when one would mutate just right, bust loose like the cartoon Tasmanian devil, and take humanity down with it.

At first, Chadwick thought it had been a hypothetical question.

Could he fashion a virus deadly enough and communicable enough to wipe out the human race?

Enjoying the academic nature of the conversation, Chadwick talked about the challenges inherent in such an endeavor. Balancing virulence with communicability, both of which would have to be at a level unseen in human history. Engineering it so that it wouldn't discriminate against this ethnic group or that age group. Possibly a virus that was constantly mutating so that the human immune system eventually gave out. It would be tough, Chadwick had said, but not impossible.

"So will you do it?" Gruber had asked.

At first, Miles had nearly choked on his meat, laughing. But as he wiped his lips with his napkin, he looked at Gruber and knew the man was most certainly not joking. He didn't know how he knew. He just knew.

In that moment, as the proposal hung there, pure, virginal, a Schrodinger's cat of an idea that had neither been accepted nor rejected, he expected to be filled with horror. But he hadn't been. Saying yes, joining the greatest conspiracy the world had ever known, had seemed so easy, as though he had been meant to do it.

"Yes," Chadwick had said.

"I realize what I'm asking you to do," Gruber said. "But don't think of it as me asking if you to end the world.

"Think of it as my asking you to end climate change.

"Hunger.

"Racism.

"War.

"And for Zoe," Chadwick had said softly, almost unaware that he'd said it. He was almost in a trance, picturing a world that he could control, a world stripped clean of all the evil that had cut its purity like cheap heroin.

"And all the Zoes," Gruber had said, placing his hand on Chadwick's shoulder. He hadn't even realized Gruber had gotten out of his chair, now looming above him. "It's time for the world to evolve, Miles."

Chadwick drank his scotch.

"You knew I'd say yes, didn't you?" he said to Gruber, unable to look the man in the eye.

"I couldn't afford not to know," Gruber said.

And so he had gone all in with Gruber.

Zoe.

Chadwick tried not to think about her because it had been better, less painful, to pack it away deep, rather than think about the meth-addled mugger who had shot his new bride Zoe, six months pregnant, right there at the ATM machine in Atlanta for the forty dollars she had just withdrawn. Twenty-eight years old, a brilliant career ahead of him, and just like that, his life had been turned into a smoking crater. Her killer had never been caught, and Miles took some small measure of comfort in the thought that the virus had almost certainly exacted justice for him and Zoe and their unborn baby. When you got right down to it, the virus had been for *him*.

So he'd worked and worked, creating iteration after iteration, each virus coming up a bit short until finally, he'd developed Medusa (although it hadn't been his name for the virus, he thought it was terribly apropos). Then the gathering of the test subjects, the runaways, the vagrants, the homeless, the ones who had already slipped through the cracks and wouldn't be missed. That last clinical trial was unlike anything he'd ever seen. Aerosol infection of Patient Zero, then exposing her to Patient One for less than *fifteen seconds*, then One to Two, a chain of exposures, and so on through Patient Forty-Four, the virus airborne and moving even before the host developed symptoms. The virus infected every single test subject, and within thirty-six hours of exposure, every single test subject was dead.

But left unchecked, the virus would be the villain of the story Gruber wanted to tell. No, their story needed a hero. And that was where James Rogers, a specialist in nanomedicine from one of Penumbra's subsidiaries, had come in. He used cutting-edge nanotechnology to build the vaccine, the yin to the virus' yang, the light to its dark. They'd been prouder of the vaccine than the virus, using technology to assert dominion over nature, these microscopic machines coded specifically to target and destroy the Medusa virus.

Telling Gruber about each project milestone, recruiting the team to the Citadel, planning the August release, which they had code-named Zero Day, it had all gone off without a hitch. Then about a year before Zero Day, Chadwick received word that Gruber, who was rarely at the compound, had died at the age of eighty-four. Penumbra's general counsel, a man named Dave Buckley, had shown up at the compound bearing the news. He told Chadwick that Gruber's will had bequeathed his privately held fortune to the Citadel entity and left specific instructions that the project was to continue unabated with Chadwick at the helm.

Keens in Manhattan, the night they'd released the virus at Yankee Stadium. After Miles had received the telephone call from Patrick Riccards, his director of security, he'd kept on drinking, the alcohol serving as a restrictor plate for his panic. He'd polished off most of the bottle of Dalwhinnie and woke up the next morning with an exquisite hangover. That afternoon, he caught a flight to Omaha, where he'd left a car, and drove three hours to the Citadel compound. The place had been his home for more than a decade, and he had worked hard to integrate himself with the nearby town of Beatrice, Nebraska, about twenty miles to the east. He was generous with his time and his money, he appeared in town frequently. He was a big believer in the hide-in-plain-sight theory. There was never any local curiosity as to what went on in the compound because people just liked him so damn much. He threw parties, organized toy drives. There was even an annual 5K race for charity. Well, there had been, at least.

He'd waited out the plague at the compound, even dropping into town once the virus popped up in that section of the state. He saw patients in the local emergency room in the first week of the outbreak, before things had just totally collapsed. Even he had been stunned by the pathogen's virulence; he felt close to madness as the dead piled up, in the hospital and urgent care clinic near the center of town, in the churches and houses, from the trailer parks in the southern part of town to the aging Victorian mansions in the east. Although he'd heard about the massive traffic jams in some of the big cities, that hadn't happened in Beatrice because these people had had nowhere else to go. Many of them had never crossed the town limits in their entire lives, rooted to their birthplaces by poverty, family, lack of education, lack of opportunity.

There were one hundred of them at the Citadel now, the chosen ones, handpicked by Chadwick himself. It had been a long, careful process, one that had taken years. None of the men were older than forty-five; the oldest woman was thirty-six. His and Rogers' first recruit had been Charlie Gale, a psychiatrist who'd worked with NASA in screening candidates for a manned mission to Mars. Then the government had all but scrapped the space program, a decision that, as it turned out, had been one of the nails in humanity's coffin. A checkpoint on the highway to extinction. Chadwick had little use for a society that elected to stop learning, to stop exploring. The vast universe beyond the Earth's troposphere, a rich, undiscovered bed of mysteries, and mankind had said, *Nope, we're good!* Together, Rogers, Chadwick and Gale had developed the criteria for membership in the Citadel so they could identify those that would thrive in the new world they were creating. There was no room for error, none whatsoever. Each recruit had to be perfect.

Fifty men. Fifty women. They were doctors, engineers, scientists, botanists, agronomists, survivalists. Single and never married. No children. Rigorous physical examinations. No religious background or participation because the last thing he needed was for humanity's saviors to wipe each other out in a holy war six months later. Even more rigorous psychological evaluations, because these people had to hold up once they executed the plan.

And he didn't even put them through the Citadel screening process until he himself had performed his own thorough background check on each of them. He'd followed each of them for months, studied their habits, their trash, their comings and goings, read their Twitter feeds, subscribed to their public Facebook postings.

There had been hiccups, of course. One bright doctor, an epidemiologist who had looked terrific on paper, quickly figured out what the Citadel was up to. That was as close as the project had come to being exposed, and that was when Chadwick realized how lucky he was to have Patrick Riccards as his head of security. Riccards was ex-CIA, a former covert operative who'd served in Afghanistan. Riccards had sensed a vibe from the kid, nothing more than a hunch. But he'd sniffed him out.

The coffee contained a healthy splash of Bailey's, a little habit he'd picked during the first week of the epidemic, as they'd watched their dark dream come to life. As they watched global news coverage delivered via the satellite linkup, as they'd stayed in contact with their field operatives, his heart was constantly racing, racing, and he found the morning cocktail helped throttle things down a bit. He didn't know why he was so on edge, why he'd been snapping at his senior advisers, even after it became clear they'd executed the plan flawlessly, that the virus had exceeded their wildest expectations. Based on some of the field reports, mortality from Medusa had exceeded ninety-eight percent in many areas.

And the nanovaccine had worked perfectly. This had been their greatest fear. That the vaccine would fail at the critical moment, that someone would break with the virus. But no one did. Three people had developed non-specific symptoms in the first week of the outbreak, incidents that had launched their collective testicles into their collective throats, but they hadn't become ill. One person had experienced a mild heart attack during the epidemic, revealing a previously undiagnosed heart condition, but he had recovered and was on medication.

It was all but over now, and it was time to look ahead. Time to begin the work that would carry him through the rest of his life. A quiet world, a blank canvas on which to paint his masterpiece. A new society in which the population was carefully controlled, in which the planet was given time to heal the scars inflicted upon it by the weighty load of seven billion people. But a world in which they'd have all the freedom they could ever want. A society free of crime, of fear, of hate, of partisanship, of ideology, of extremism, of wants, of hunger. They could recreate society in their image, in his image.

He was still considering his options regarding the unvaccinated survivors of the plague, the ones beyond these walls, the ones who, whether they knew it or not, whether they intended it or not, constituted the biggest threat to his grand vision. Chadwick estimated there were approximately five to seven million survivors in the United States alone. Not today, not next month, probably not even next year. But eventually, they could undo everything they had worked so hard to build. He'd put it off long enough. He had to spend some time coming up with a solution.

Five million survivors.

Taken out of context, the number was huge, overwhelming, the size of the Chinese Army, at least until about two weeks ago, but in truth, the number alone meant nothing. These survivors were scattered all over the place, virtually none of them would know each other, and many of those would go through another weeding out in the coming year, people who were in no position to survive the harsh reality without the modern conveniences they'd all come to depend on. As many as twenty-five percent of the survivors were under the age of eighteen. At least a million, possibly two million, wouldn't make it through the winter. And the North American landmass was enormous. Even before the epidemic, large swaths of the continent were unpopulated. These survivors were just pinpoints scattered across a blank canvas.

The rest of them, though, the ones Professor Darwin would be really impressed with, would become battle-hardened with time. They would adjust, evolve, possibly assemble into a threat, especially if they ever found out the truth about the Citadel. That was their greatest secret, the one that had to be guarded at all costs.

He drained his coffee and looked at his calendar. Chadwick had meetings this morning, meetings all day. There was so much to do, so much to keep track of. First up was Dr. James Rogers, who had been running tests on Citadel women in preparation for the project's second critical phase. Chadwick checked his watch and sighed. It was ten after six. He was already behind schedule. Rogers was due at six, and he was normally early to their meetings. As he waited, the day breaking clear and hot, he poured another cup of coffee, passing on the Bailey's this time.

Rogers knocked on the slightly ajar door just as Chadwick finished stirring in his sugar.

"Come!"

Rogers stepped in the room. The physician was pale, bleary-eyed, his clothes rumpled and disheveled. Highly unusual for the fastidious medical director of the Citadel. It was obvious he hadn't slept. Chadwick went in for a sip of his coffee, his eyes locked on Rogers' face, and ended up with a hefty gulp of the steaming liquid. He felt it scorch his tongue, and wasn't that just a hell of a way to kick off the day? All because he thought he'd seen something in Rogers' face.

"What is it?"

"You're going to want to sit down," Rogers said. He was a tall man, lean, his skin pale from years in the lab. He kept his fine blond hair short, close to the scalp. He was a brilliant pathologist and a pill popper who'd had his license to practice medicine indefinitely suspended.

Chadwick noticed that Rogers had not apologized for his tardiness, which just made Miles even more nervous. He felt the ligaments in his knees loosen, and he nonchalantly grabbed the edge of his desk, lest he collapse from nerves in front of one of his closest advisers.

"What? Is it the virus? Is someone sick?"

"No," Rogers said. "No, it's not that."

He was silent for a moment, picking at his lower lip. He didn't make eye contact with Chadwick, focusing instead on something on Chadwick's desk. Miles followed his gaze to the commemorative baseball on the corner. It had been signed by each member of the St. Louis Cardinals team that had won the 2006 World Series. Looking at the ball twisted something inside him, and he remembered how much he would miss baseball.

"The test results are back," Rogers said. "We've discovered an anomaly."

"What anomaly?"

"In the female subjects," Rogers said.

Annoyance tickled Chadwick like a feather; he hated it when scientists spoke so robotically. Maybe if they'd been a little more approachable, a little more human, maybe none of this would have been necessary. Shortly before the outbreak, Chadwick had read that sixty-one percent of the American population didn't "believe" in evolution. As though it were something you had to believe in. It was like saying you didn't believe that two plus two equaled four. He often wondered who was to blame for such a travesty. Had scientists done their jobs right, maybe the world wouldn't have needed this reboot, this reformatting of its hard drive.

"Jesus, what anomaly? Stop beating around the fucking bush."

Rogers folded his hands together and tapped the fist against his lips, like he didn't want to verbalize his next thought, lined up like a reluctant airplane waiting for takeoff.

Now Chadwick was pissed and scared; a ripple of heat shot up his back.

"We ran anti-mullerian hormone testing on all fifty females," Rogers said. He was still looking at the baseball. "This test checks ovarian reserve."

"I know what it does," Chadwick said sharply.

Rogers ignored him.

"The results were disconcerting."

Chadwick spread out his hands in front of him, as if to say, "And?"

"In each of them, the AMH levels were virtually zero," Rogers said, finally looking up at his boss. "We ran additional tests, FSH in particular, and the results were the same. Complete ovarian failure."

Chadwick sat down and scratched an itch on his palm. That had meant something once, that money was headed your way, right? Good fortune? Well, that was a load of shit because Dr. James Rogers had just dropped an atom bomb in the middle of the Citadel. He felt a big, idiotic grin spreading across his face, and he felt his breath coming in ragged gasps.

"Ovarian failure," Chadwick said softly.

He thought about all the work they had done, the years of sacrifice, the careful, precise planning, and the idea that it had all been for nothing made his stomach flip.

And then, quite unnecessarily, Rogers added: "Miles, all of the women in the Citadel are infertile."

"How is that possible?" Chadwick asked. The question was partially rhetorical, as he already knew the answer. There were only two options.

Either the virus had sterilized the women.

Or the vaccine had.

FIFTEEN MINUTES LATER, Chadwick was in the main conference room with Rogers and his other three top advisers. Rogers and Patrick Riccards, the Citadel's director of security, were engaged in a heated discussion, on their feet, their faces red, like two baboons getting ready to tussle.

Margaret Baker, the director of operations, was in tears, something Chadwick immediately took note of. He wondered if he should cut her some slack. She was thirty-five and hoping to give birth to one of the first Citadel babies, and he could understand her despair. But could he trust such an emotional hair trigger of a woman? He'd never seen the slightest hint of emotion from her, not even a wisp of regret or empathy as Medusa had incinerated the human race. You just never knew with some people.

If the virus was to blame, and every surviving woman on the planet was now infertile, then none of this mattered. This was all window dressing, a really shitty after-party, and they were just the epilogue. Another few decades, and the sun would set on the human race permanently. The Earth would go back to doing whatever it was doing before *Homo sapiens* became the dominant life form, and Chadwick didn't think mother Earth would miss them all that much.

He preferred this scenario because then it meant it wasn't the other scenario. If it wasn't the virus (and he really didn't think it was), that meant it was the vaccine that had done this. Their vaccine. He'd almost been prouder of the vaccine than he'd been of the virus. It had been the ultimate exercise of dominion. In Medusa, he'd created the ultimate weapon, a mechanism to alter all things. But in the vaccine, they'd created something even greater.

If Medusa was the devil, Miles Chadwick had been its God.

And all things served God. Even His fallen angels.

Or so he'd thought.

"Quiet," he said. "Everyone sit down."

He waited while they each found their seats. He was pleased and a little relieved that they responded so quickly. They sat like obedient schoolchildren, their faces open and scared and hopeful all at the same time.

"Up until now, everything has gone to plan," he said. "Better than we imagined. But now we've got our first crisis. Our first real crisis."

He thought of something else to say, but he wasn't sure how it would play. His pulse slowed, like a racecar throttling down, and he thought it ironic that it had taken the end of everything to make him feel like he was in control.

"And, quite possibly, our last crisis," he said casually.

He saw smiles on their faces, even a chuckle from Rogers. The tension seeped out of the room like a deflating balloon. It worked. They wanted leadership, and he was giving it to them. He was in charge.

"We need to find out if the infertility is a side effect of the vaccine," Chadwick said. "We need to bring in an unvaccinated female survivor. And we need one yesterday."

He looked at Patrick, who was already nodding his head, taking notes.

"I've got a team in mind already," he said. "We'll move out in the morning."

"What if it's not a side effect of the vaccine?" Margaret Baker asked stupidly.

Chadwick sniffed, and then let out a slow breath. He reminded himself she wasn't a physician. Rogers, who had been sitting quietly, his head down, focused on his hands, spoke first.

"Then we're all fucked," he said.

14

For months, Sarah Wells had been promising her father that she would come back to Raleigh for a visit, if she could just find the time. On the twenty-sixth of August, she fulfilled that vow. She parked the motorcycle on Eastwood Drive, there next to the mailbox, and secured the helmet on the handlebars, but she didn't dismount the chopper. She stared at the little Cape Cod she'd grown up in. All she had to see was the long grass, rippling in the light afternoon breeze, to know that her father was dead. He'd been religious about cutting the grass, twice a week in the summer, Sundays and Wednesdays, once a week during the winter.

It never crossed her mind that he'd fled when things started going south because that wasn't whom Ernie Wells had been. No, he was in there, no doubt about it, dead now like his wife, like his neighbors, like everyone else she knew. He had stayed and helped and checked on people until he got sick and died. She looked up and down the desolate street, this twisted, nightmarish version of the neighborhood she'd grown up in. Somewhere along the street, a loose shutter clocked against siding, the sound huge in the morning quiet. Next door, over at the Tiricos' house, a cat slinked along the front porch railing.

Sarah swung her left leg over the seat, slung her M4 over her shoulder and walked up to the front door; it was cracked open, and a terrible mustiness tickled her nose. She poked the door open with the muzzle of her rifle, revealing in full color what she knew to be true. There he lay in his recliner, wearing his dungarees as he called them, a white t-shirt (and she ignored the dried blood spatter) and, of course, those suspenders because he'd been a slight man, thin his whole life from his career as a mailman. A blue blanket was bunched up at his feet. On the end table, cold and flu medicines, a half-empty glass of 7-Up. She knew it was 7-Up and not water because there were few ills that Ernie Wells had believed a glass of cold 7-Up could not fix, and she felt the hot tears, stinging her lips as she thought about him sitting here at the end, alone, thinking that maybe one more glass of 7-Up would fix him up.

A horrible feeling swept over her; relief that he was dead. Relieved that her own father was dead. And not just because he would be spared a life in this terrible new world or possibly reunited with his wife, dead two decades now. But because Sarah wouldn't have to face her father and tell him what she had done that terrible day on the Third Avenue Bridge. That she had "followed orders" and massacred civilians, that she had hurt the ones she had sworn to protect. And for what? A quarantine that was obsolete the moment it had been ordered.

It hadn't taken her long to see the folly of the mission. Across the river in a canoe, through the dead streets of Manhattan, block after disease-ravaged block. Everything outside her Q zone had been just as fucked up as it was inside their little cocoon. Her quarantine, and her God-blessed attempt to hold it, had been nothing more than window dressing, something for the bigwigs, for the deciders, to do to make them feel like they were doing something, even as everything spun out of control.

She covered her father with the blanket and went around the house, tidying up. He had been a fastidious man, and she had no idea what she was supposed to do with his body, but she could at least put the house back the way he liked it. Orderly. She cleaned for the rest of the day, until the daylight started to go, until the small of her back ached, and her hands became stiff.

For dinner, she ate some beef stew she found in the pantry, straight from the can. It wasn't great cold, but she'd had worse on her tours of duty.

When she was done, she sat back down on the couch and dug the bottle of tetrabenazine out of her pack. She rolled the amber-colored cylinder between her hands, turning her head just so, the moonlight glinting off the bottle. There were a dozen pills left, her first go around with the medication that would merely manage the disease that would ultimately kill her.

She was such a coward.

She hadn't even been able to tell him about the diagnosis; how had she ever thought she would tell him about what had happened in the Bronx? Four years she'd been living with it, four years since she'd sat in that doctor's office in Olympia, Washington and he'd told her the bad news from behind his desk with his stupid horn-rimmed glasses, that she carried the gene for Huntington's disease. It had killed her mother, and so there was already a fifty percent chance she would get it, and wouldn't you know it, things hadn't broken her way. So here she was, staring death in the face, probably before she turned forty.

Then the plague had come, and she had prayed for death via Medusa, because that killed you quick, and she wouldn't have to suffer for years on end the way her mother had. Two days of fever and internal bleeding and coughing? That was nothing compared to what Karen Wells had endured in the last three years of her life.

But because the universe was a real bitch, I mean, a real Grade-A megabitch, she'd survived the epidemic and she wouldn't be getting an early exit after all, and Huntington's would be waiting for her like it had been all along. She'd been to Iraq and Afghanistan four times; each time, she'd made it home very little physically worse for the wear. The worst injury she'd suffered was a nick in her arm from an IED that had killed six of her fellow soldiers.

Because of course.

And back up in the Bronx, the rest of her platoon had died. She had stayed with them after the thing with the bridge, and she had watched them die, one at a time, punishment for her sins at the bridge. Then she received that bizarre final order from HQ, and when she was done here, she would carry out that order.

Because of course.

She unscrewed the cap and popped the chalky pill into her mouth, where she let it sit for a moment. She could feel it dissolving, the chalky bitterness spreading on her tongue, hitting her gums, and for a moment, she considered spitting it out, and being done with it. No more treatment, no more delaying the inevitable.

But she threw her head back, washing it down with her father's flat 7-Up. It slid down her throat just as smooth as good wine, and she cried.

15

It seemed a little strange to Freddie Briggs that he was even bothering with breakfast, given what he had planned for this morning, but there you go. He couldn't remember the last time he'd skipped his morning meal, and he wasn't going to start now. His mother wouldn't have approved, and he figured he'd better do something she'd have been happy with before the day was out.

And so Freddie Briggs sat on the curb in front of the Cave Spring branch of the Rome Public Library in northwest Georgia, chewing robotically on a Pop-Tart as the day warmed and then blistered before him. He grimaced at the sickly sweet taste, wondering why they hadn't improved their formula in the last two decades. They tasted the same today as they did when he'd first started eating them as a freshman linebacker at LSU, back when he couldn't consume enough calories to keep the weight from falling off.

Well, guess what guys, you've lost your chance!

The library bordered a small park to the east. The smell of wet grass tickled Freddie's nose, and he was back at LSU again, back in the locker room after his very first practice. He closed his eyes as he chewed. Beyond the sweet earthiness of the practice field after a mow, the sour stench of dried sweat hung in his nostrils. The prank the seniors had played on him after that first practice, the heat so immense it felt like you were wrapped in insulation. How gullible he'd been.

"Coach wants a word," the defensive captain, an onyx-skinned cornerback, had told him.

"Really?" Briggs replied. "Coach Hyatt?"

"No, dumbass. Coach Bush. Grad assistant. Said bring your playbook."

"Playbook?"

"Did I fucking stutter?"

Freddie's tongue went numb.

Playbook?

So Freddie had gone looking for Coach Bush, the graduate assistant coach, who, quite frankly, Freddie couldn't even remember meeting, but that didn't mean anything to him. College football was so much bigger and faster than high school had been. He was fast and big, sure, but so was everyone. More coaches, more equipment, more plays, more everything.

And he'd met with Coach Bush, whose office was nothing more than a tiny supply closet (*gotta start somewhere*, Bush had said), and then he told Freddie he'd been cut, that they'd seen everything they needed to see about him in that first sweltering practice, that he might have been a superstar back in Smyrna, but this was Loozy-anna State, goddammit, and his game just wasn't gonna cut it in the ESS-EEE-CEE. Freddie hadn't argued with him because he worried that if he had, he'd break down in tears, and he couldn't have that.

Freddie trudged back to his locker, stepping ever so gingerly, the way a man might when he's been kicked in the nuts. He could feel the stares and he wondered if there were other freshmen meeting with other nameless, faceless graduate assistants in tiny supply closets and learning of a similar fate. They stared at him as he emptied out his locker, which still smelled like the air freshener mounted on the back, so brief had his membership on the squad been.

He made his way for the door, his gear stuffed this way and that in his equipment bag, and had his hand on the handle, the metal cold and sharp, when they burst out laughing at him. He stood there frozen, looking for the will to march out that door with his head high because they could kiss his ass, until he felt the tap on his shoulder. When he turned around, he saw "graduate assistant Coach Bush," who in reality was third-string wide receiver Ricky Bush, a senior who had never seen a single minute of action, had never even dressed for a game, and boy they had gotten him good.

Freddie lifted Bush like he was a sack of potatoes and slammed him against the wall, extinguishing the laughter like he'd yanked a plug from the wall, and he could see the sudden fear in his eyes, and that was when Briggs had known he was stronger and faster than everyone in the room.

And then he'd kissed Bush on the cheek, a loud, juicy one, and the team had roared its approval. That was the last prank he was the target of, but he'd been the engineer of many over the course of the next four years.

Goddamn, those had been some good times.

He wished he could keep his eyes closed forever and live it all over again, from that first game to the national championship the Tigers had won his sophomore year to the defensive player of the year award he'd won his senior year. Instead, he supposed, Coach Billy Hyatt, the AP Coach of the Year, and Ricky Bush, and all the rest were now dead.

His eyes opened, and he was back at the library again.

Ten days on the road. Ten days since he'd buried his girls, three abreast in the backyard, in Susan's flower garden, which she had loved so much. He'd tamped down the last of the dirt on Heather's grave and left Smyrna forever. He would never go home again. It was a dead place. Even Chewie, the guinea pig, had died, probably of thirst.

He had a general sense he was moving west-by-northwest, tracking the sun's path as it crossed the sky. It seemed larger and larger with each passing day, the sunsets growing ever more spectacular, exploding across the sky with oranges and reds. Maybe it was because the air was clearer now, devoid of the exhaust and smoke and pollution of a hundred million cars and smokestacks belching their byproducts into the air. Or maybe it was because of how small and alone he felt in this giant emptiness, which felt bigger with each passing minute.

At first, he'd hoped this walk he'd been on would somehow make it more bearable. That it would somehow drain away the awful reality of what had come to pass. But the pain and the grief continued to stab at him every hour, every minute, every second, like twisting, crippling arthritis.

The decision had been easier than he expected. It had left him skittish with anticipation, which, he decided, was a good sign that he'd made peace with his choice. Wherever his girls were, they were together now. And in just a few minutes, he'd be joining them. He hoped.

He finished his breakfast and, instead of leaving it on the steps, tossed the wrapper in the metal trashcan at the base of the steps. His daughter Heather would have liked that very much. He stood up and dusted off his pants. With a fifty-foot garden hose, tightly spooled, hanging from his beefy shoulder, he crossed the tarmac toward the pickup truck that would be the instrument of his plan. The truck, a shiny red Ford F-150 he'd found abandoned near the library, was parked in a spot by the front door, its keys dangling from the ignition. He opened the door and slid in. He took a deep breath and turned the key over; the pickup's engine roared to life. In the quiet, it sounded like a jet engine.

It was a warm day, but not terribly humid, one of the nicer ones Freddie had seen since he'd left Smyrna. The sky burned a fierce blue, the sky so clear he could see the edge of it blur into the outer ridges of the troposphere. So fragile, this shell separating us from the cold vastness of space, he thought. And how fragile the world had been, far more delicate than any of them had ever thought. The shell separating them from order and chaos, life and death, creation and destruction, had been far thinner than any of them had ever imagined.

He looked up at the sky until his neck began to ache and then returned his attention to the task at hand. One end of the hose went into the Ford's tailpipe, as far as it would go, until he felt resistance. Then he sealed off the gaps in the exhaust pipe with a length of duct tape. The other end of the hose he ran along the side of the truck, through the window, and into the driver's seat. Then he sealed up the gap left by the cracked window with more tape. A quick tug on the hose to confirm that it was well-seated in the pipe, fitted to funnel as much carbon monoxide into the truck as possible.

He felt his excitement growing, like a healthy plant getting the requisite amount of sunshine and water, fed by the fertile thoughts of extinguishing his crippling pain, of leaving behind this terrible world, of maybe, just maybe, being reunited with Susan, Caroline and Heather.

He thought he would be more afraid. But it was being here, in this world, that frightened him and chewed away at his sanity. It was a living nightmare, a twenty-four-hour-a-day hellscape that had begun the moment he'd received that first call from his daughter telling him that Susan was sick. Each successive link in the chain of events had been worse than the previous one. The panic had left him constantly shivering, as though he could never warm up.

The idea had been nagging at him, a splinter in his brain. Try as he might, he couldn't dislodge the splinter, namely because he liked the way it felt. Yeah. That was the fucked-up thing.

He liked the way it felt.

Just another fucked-up thing in a fucked-up world.

He had prayed for God to deliver him wisdom. For an answer. For a plan.

But God hadn't been there to answer. God had abandoned him in this world of the dead.

But then he had seen something that had opened that drawer in his mind, the one housing the soul's self-destruct button. He didn't think he had it in him. Oh, but he did. It was just a matter of the mind receiving the proper authentication codes, the way a submarine commander would wait for an order to launch his ICBMs. It was just a matter of God showing him what he needed to see.

Two nights ago, he'd stopped to make camp at an abandoned peach orchard in west-central Georgia, just near the state line. The sun had been low over the Great Smoky Mountains to the northwest, its rays colliding with the ever-present blue haze circling the peaks like a trendy silk scarf. As his Spaghettios heated up on the small fire, he had scoured the perimeter. Darkness was falling as he finished his sweep, a little faster than he'd expected, a reminder that he was on the back end of summer now. On the east side of the farm, he'd come across a shallow trench, muddy and sloppy on the edges. That little voice in his head had told him to turn tail and scamper back to camp. But he hadn't. He'd shone the trembling flashlight at the center of the pit.

And he so wished he hadn't.

Staring back at him in the full darkness were the lifeless eyes and pasty faces of dozens of plague victims, maybe a hundred total, all of them children. Against the harsh white light of the MagLite, the faces of the lost children floated in time and space, their paleness made ever starker by the dried blood around their noses and mouths. Babies and toddlers and school-aged kids packed together, their bodies lined up neatly. The thing that had haunted him since was that each had been lovingly set down in this mass grave, the only burial they would ever get, with some beloved childhood item tucked under an arm. A tattered Elmo doll here. A Barbie doll there. An over-sized stuffed dog, one possibly won at the county fair, curled up next to the body of an angelic-looking little girl about five years old.

He'd stumbled backwards, tripping over his own feet, dropping the flashlight. His body racked with sobs, he had fled the orchard, leaving behind his tent, his supplies, his dinner still cooking over the little fire. All night he had run as if Satan himself had crawled out of that trench. He finally had slept in a city park, with no tent and no dinner, and dreamt all night about dead children.

When he'd woken up the next morning, his body covered in dew, his mind felt sour, rotten, turned, like curdled milk. There was no sense of relief that the dream was just a dream because he knew there were shallow graves holding the bodies of dead children just like there were houses and churches and hospitals and morgues full of dead children and women and men, young and old.

That was when the idea had first came to him.

No, he wasn't afraid. This thing he was planning, that was the ticket out of all this. He didn't know or care why he'd been spared, for all the good it had done him. Susan and the girls, they'd been given a gift. Called home to God together. The punishment hadn't been dying of the plague. It had been surviving it. Left behind to make his way in this dead world, that was the punishment.

A terrifying thought gripped him.

What if God had forsaken him?

What if God had looked into Freddie's heart and decided that he wasn't worthy, and he thought back to all those times he didn't want to go to church, and, in the Great Faith Ledger of Freddie Briggs' life, he had ended up just a bit in the red.

Stop it. God forgives all. He'll forgive your sorry ass for this.

He waited as the muffler pumped the deadly gas into the car. He wanted the colorless gas to be freely flowing in the cab, filling the passenger compartment, before he got in; it would decrease the likelihood he'd chicken out before it had a chance to carry him away. As the engine purred, he tugged on the hose to make sure it was secure.

He strolled around to the passenger side and sat down on the curb to wait. As good a time as any to pray. The church of his youth, the Smyrna Baptist Church, seemed so far away, in time and space, but it was there he looked for comfort and solace and a reminder that although what he was about to do was a sin, God would forgive him. Truth be told, he didn't think God would be all that surprised to see him.

He found himself wondering if this whole thing had been God's judgment upon man. If so, it had been a hell of a tough one. Guess we really let you down there, eh, big fella?

So this was it. He'd thought about death often, particularly during those last few minutes in the locker room on Sunday afternoons, when he'd wonder if he'd be the first NFL player to die during a game, whether he'd draw the short stick and suffer some catastrophic spinal injury and just die there on the field in front of Susan and Heather and Caroline and millions of Americans watching on television, drinking their Bud Lights and eating spicy chicken wings.

Well, football hadn't been the death of him, and neither had Medusa.

He stood up, his heart pounding, and opened the passenger-side door. The cabin exhaled a puff of warm air, the whisper of a dangerous lover. He had to act quickly, before the carbon monoxide drifted free of its enclosure and dissipated in the morning air. He stepped up on the running board, planted one foot on the floor mat and dropped his girth into the leather seat. As he leaned over to swing the door shut, entombing himself in this metal coffin for all time, he heard a noise.

This froze him. He sat there, his hand on the handle, wondering if he'd imagined it or if he was just wishing he'd imagined it.

Again — a muted, wailing sound, coming from everywhere and nowhere at the same time. A child or a woman. The sound was mournful and pathetic and beautiful at the same time, and he hated it. He wanted it to stop, he wanted it to be erased from his memory banks so he could get back to the business at hand.

Then, a voice to go with the wailing.

"Is someone there?"

Definitely a woman, the voice bearing a timbre of maturity absent from a child's. He tried to pinpoint the location of the voice, but the way acoustics had changed in the last two weeks, it could have been coming from anywhere.

"I'm hurt," the voice said. "Please. I can hear you out there."

"Dammit," he whispered, slamming a massive fist into his thigh. He held the handle tight, fully intent on slamming the door shut on that pathetic voice and this pathetic life and getting on with dying in peace. His brain had its orders, its mandate to constrict the muscles in his massive right arm authenticated. But the treasonous arm refused to budge. It would not close the door.

"Please," she said. "My name's Caroline."

Hearing his late daughter's name aloud launched him from the car like an ejector seat. Behind him, the car continued to idle, and the pent-up carbon monoxide dissipated into the atmosphere. He felt his knees go weak beneath him, and he crumpled to the ground in a puddle. The shakes were back and he felt cold, so cold.

"Where are you?" he called out, his voice booming in the morning air.

"Behind a little restaurant," Caroline called back. Her voice was everywhere, echoing against buildings, across fields and down narrow streets. "I can't move. I think my leg's broken."

"I'll find you," he said. "Just keep talking."

IT TOOK TWENTY MINUTES, but Freddie finally found the woman sitting on the stoop behind Pastrami Dan's, tucked away from the sun under a large black awning. A dozen bottles of water lay strewn at the bottom of the stairs. Her eyes were glassy, and she looked exhausted. Her long red hair was tied back in a ponytail, revealing the fatigue in her ivory face, virtually irradiated with sunburn.

She looked about forty years old. Her light-colored blouse was matted against her torso. Her lower left leg was swollen, a dusky shade of yellow and purple. Freddie had broken enough bones in his day to know her leg was fractured. The good news was that it looked to be a simple fracture. Anything worse, she'd already be dead. But the thing that drew nearly all of Freddie's focus was the noticeable swell in the woman's belly.

Pregnant.

"Please tell me you're real," she said. "Please."

"I'm Freddie," he said, as gently as he could, unable to pull his eyes away from her very large abdomen. A pregnant woman. Until this moment, it had not occurred to him that life would, of course, at least try to go on.

"Caroline Braddock," she said. "Would you mind handing me one of those bottles?"

Freddie grabbed two, warm from the sun, and climbed the steps to the porch, where he handed them to the injured woman. She twisted off the cap and drank down the first in one swoop. After draining it, she sighed contentedly.

"Thank you," she said, the effects of the water replenishment immediately evident on her face.

"What happened?" he asked.

She nodded toward the back door of the deli.

"Found this place a couple days ago," she said, leaning her head back against the railing and twisting the cap loose from the second bottle. "It smells horrible, but there's a ton of bottled water inside. I was pretty pleased with myself, right up until the moment I tripped down these stairs here."

"Did you say this happened a couple days ago?"

She nodded. "Yeah, I've seen two sunrises."

Freddie whistled softly, trying not to think about the dark places Caroline Braddock must have gone as she sat here, crippled, unable to move, forsaken.

"I spent the first day down where you are," she continued, "but it got so hot, I pulled myself up the steps to get some shade. It's a little cooler, but not by much. I was able to carry two bottles of water up with me. That ran out last night."

She patted her belly gently. "This little guy, he's a thirsty one. Anyway, I guess I'd been asleep, and I heard your car start up or something. My lucky day, I guess."

Freddie felt shame coloring his cheeks. Here he'd been, ready to cash it all in, and this woman was fighting and clawing to stay alive. He couldn't imagine the pain she'd felt crawling up those steps, dragging her shattered leg behind her. He suddenly realized that his girls would have been profoundly disappointed in him if he'd sidled up next to them in the afterlife, not by way of the virus, but by his own hand. He felt as stupid as he'd ever felt in his entire life.

"Relax," she said, patting her belly. "I'm not having this baby today."

"I'm sorry," he said. "It just never occurred to me..."

"Well, here we are," she replied.

"When are you due?"

"About a month," she said. "Maybe less. I've kind of lost track."

"So how's that leg?"

She looked down at it.

"Fine, as long as I don't move it," she replied. "I scraped it up good coming down the steps, but I think it's healing."

"Where were you headed?" Freddie asked.

She laughed out loud.

"Headed?" she repeated. "I'm not headed anywhere. I live about ten miles from here."

"I've got a truck up the road a piece," he said. "If you'd like a ride."

Freddie felt her studying him, her green eyes cutting into him like lasers. He had a pretty good idea what she was thinking about. That it had come down to this. To putting her life in the hands of a very large man she did not know versus taking her chances here on the back stoop of Pastrami Dan's. Her whole life turned on this decision. He could see her working it out in her mind, deciding that anything would be better than dying here of thirst or starvation, or perhaps by way of a hungry animal that was getting used to the idea of the places full of rotting food, the people mysteriously absent.

At that moment, he realized how badly he wanted her to say yes, that she did want a ride. He wanted to break down in front of her and tell her that she'd be saving his life, that she already had saved his life, that he was the one owing her the gigantic favor and not the other way around.

"Where are you headed?" she asked finally.

"Honestly?" he said. He ran a hand across his scalp. "I don't know. I just want to keep moving. I need to keep moving. Maybe we can find other survivors. Maybe we can find you a doctor."

A faint smile crept across her face.

"I wish I had something better for you."

"I think I'd be more worried if you had a plan," she said.

"No," he said, thinking about the garden hose snaking its way from the tailpipe into the cabin. Oh, he'd had a plan all right. And not just any plan, but one that would almost certainly have signed Caroline's death warrant.

"I'll go get the car."

He turned to head back up the drive.

"Don't forget about me," she said, her voice quiet. There was a sharp undercurrent of fear just below the surface of her words.

He turned back and looked her squarely in the eyes.

"No," he said as firmly as he could. "I won't forget you."

16

Adam woke up early on the morning of the thirtieth, the day dawning hot and steamy. Last night, exhausted, he had pitched his tent in the middle of the Duke University football field in Durham, North Carolina. He liked its clear lines of sight, which reduced the chance that someone could sneak up on him. Plus, the acoustics made for a lot of echoes, another good early-warning system. The Bermuda grass was starting to go, a little bit shaggier than you'd expect to see on a college football field, but that was true of just about everything these days.

This would be his sixth day on the road; in that time, he had only traveled about two hundred miles, far fewer than he had been hoping to log by now. But this was turning out to be no ordinary road trip, and he'd badly underestimated the impact that the world in its new state would have on him. After that last night on his couch in Richmond, he had started early on the morning of the twenty-fifth, proud of himself for his clarity of thinking. Only a fool would've started such a huge undertaking in the dark, in the middle of a storm.

As he'd driven his neighbor Jeanette's little Honda toward I-195, the local bypass feeding onto the interstate, he'd slalomed around abandoned vehicles and pileups littering the neighborhood roads. At the corner of Belmont and Main, Adam had come across the body of the cyclist he'd seen screaming past his house a few days earlier, lying face-up in the street, his ruined head propped up on the curb, as though he were using it for a pillow. His bicycle was wrapped around a telephone pole, which the cyclist apparently had struck in a last-second attempt to avoid a spilled motorcycle. The curb had cleaved the man's head open after he'd flown over the handlebars, and that had been that.

At Hamilton Street, Adam turned north and found the charred wreckage of an Army truck blocking the on-ramp to I-195, the best inter-state access point for miles. Two soldiers lay dead on the ground near the truck. Adam nervously took one of their machine guns and threw it in the trunk. He had no idea how to use it, and holding it terrified him, but having it in the back of the trunk made him feel better. There was no plug of traffic here, which didn't make any sense, but he'd long since given up trying to make sense of anything. He gave up on the interstates, figuring he'd have to follow the city streets on his way out of town.

He motored west along Grove Avenue, past quaint Cape Cods and boutique shops and trendy restaurants. The streets, littered with branches and leaves felled by the previous night's storm, were silent. No bodies here. No nothing. Then he swung north onto Granite Avenue toward a house he knew well, unable to resist the temptation; he knew he shouldn't check on his med school roommate, Mark Zalewski, and his family, but he was going to anyway. Zalewski, an oncologist, lived in a brick colonial with his wife Ashley and their three kids, two girls and a boy. Adam parked at the curb and left the engine running.

"Mark!" he called out, running up the walk. The houses around him were silent and dark, their blinds pulled tight.

The front door was open, the air rank with the hint of something sour.

"Ashley!"

He was in the foyer now, his breathing shallow and ragged. Nothing moved.

They're dead, you know they're dead.

But he went upstairs anyway. The boy, Parker, was at the top of the steps. He was nine years old and he lay dead in his Spider-Man pajamas. He found the girls, Scarlet and Casey, with their mother in the king-sized bed she'd shared with Mark; Ashley's arms were wrapped around her daughters, as though they'd settled in to watch a movie. Seeing them entwined in death shattered him. Mark was nowhere to be found. Knowing him, he'd gone to help at the hospital and died there. Before leaving, he carried Parker into his parents' bedroom, laid him next to his family, and covered the four of them with the comforter. Then he went back to his car and cried.

At Libbie and Grove, he saw spires of thick black smoke swirling in the early morning sky to the northwest. It reminded him of those awful images from the morning of the 9/11 terror attacks. The stink of burning char filled his nostrils; in the massive quiet, he could hear flames crackling and snapping. It looked like the fire was burning farther west, over toward the hospital. There were a few gas stations in that direction, and it wouldn't have surprised him to discover that one had gone up in flames. It was unnerving to think that this fire would burn, and it would burn, and it would burn, and no one would be coming to put it out.

The further he edged away from home, the more real it became. Everything was gone. He felt tiny, nothing more than a speck of dust fluttering through this gigantic nothingness. Nothing could've prepared him for the staggering shock of mile after mile of emptiness. Roads that were normally bustling with shoppers and delivery drivers and salespeople and stay-at-home moms were eerily quiet that Wednesday morning, August 25. Even the chaos he'd encountered coming home from Holden Beach, when mankind was still fighting, still scratching, still clawing to stay alive, was better than this.

After crossing the James River, he followed U.S. 60 east for a while, past shopping malls and car dealerships and chain restaurants and self-storage facilities. Images of a life lived here popped in his head like camera flashes. The animal shelter from which he'd adopted a lab mix puppy, dead from cancer five years now. The Korean barbecue restaurant he came to with his buddies every once in a while. Then he looped south on to Route 10 and followed it until he finally found an access point onto Interstate 85. That too, had been a difficult row to hoe, the highway peppered with traffic accidents, lanes blocked by military checkpoints in places that made no sense at all, as though the soldiers had been riding along and decided what the hell, this was as good a place as any for a checkpoint. It made Adam feel bad, that humanity hadn't been able to answer the bell, that for all its spirit, it hadn't been enough, and it was left to roll up checkpoints in rural Dinwiddie County. He averaged about forty miles a day, sleeping in his car, living off the rations he'd packed. He took frequent breaks, stopping every afternoon at two o'clock to call Rachel (unsuccessfully so far), and just trying to get his goddamn bearings. The nights were horrible, his sleep fractured by nightmares, photo negatives of all the bad dreams he'd ever had, the terror now grounded not in the fear that the dream was real but that it wasn't because nothing his dream machine had been able to conjure up had matched the broken world waiting for him each morning.

And that was how it had gone until he made it to Durham on the afternoon of the twenty-ninth, when the traffic had become overwhelming, and he'd had to abandon the vehicle at the interchange joining I-85 and U.S. 70. He packed what he could into the backpack, making sure he had Rachel's picture, and began walking. He made it to the Durham city limits as the sun began to drop, and he capped that night with a can of cold ravioli, too freaked out to even start a campfire.

He stepped out of his tent into the morning glare, needing to pee and hungry. He took care of the former need in the corner of the field, behind the end zone, and was about to address the latter when the fox struck. It snuck up on him just as he was digging through his bag for a Pop-Tart. It was a red fox, not full grown, little more than a blur that morning. Its razor sharp teeth clamped down on his wrist before he even got a clear look at it. A huge gasp of pain and shock boomed from him, and he instinctively jerked his arm around, flinging the animal loose as he scampered to his feet. It landed on its back a few feet away and then rolled back upright. Its head twitched once, twice, and then a third time. A stagger to the left before launching another attack on Adam. This time, he danced to his right, narrowly avoiding another full bite, but its teeth scraped against his leg.

Another howl of pain.

He pirouetted around to find himself looking at the fox's backside; the animal was twitching again and staring off toward the stands, as though it had forgotten what it was doing. Adam reared back and delivered a swift kick to the animal's haunches, and its rear leg snapped like a dry twig. The fox hissed and hobbled toward the sideline on three legs, keeping an eye on Adam. Then it lunged again, stumbling as it did so, its two front paws tangling together before it crashed back down. As it struggled back to its feet, Adam kicked it in the head, cracking its skull. It whimpered and went down hard. He stomped its head a second time, turning the fox's small head into a bag of broken pottery.

It was over. His legs turned to jelly, and he dropped back onto his butt. He checked his wounds; there were three raised welts on the calf of his leg where the fox's teeth had scratched him, but the skin was intact. The arm, however, was a different story. Blood seeped from the puncture wounds in his wrist and had smeared his forearm.

But the wounds themselves were the least of his concerns.

The way the fox had attacked. The bizarre twitching of its head. And how it had resumed its assault even after its leg had been broken. He clambered to his feet, dizzy. His mouth watered, but not in a good way, not in a way that suggested he was smelling a couple of ribeyes on the grill. He felt hot, very hot, like he'd spiked a fever. His dinner from the night before, meager as it was, came up all at once, in a rush; he bent over, his hands on his knees, swaying in the morning humidity. The sound of his heaves echoed off the bleachers.

His rational mind made the connection that his primal self already had.

Rabies. Rabies.

He'd just been bitten by a rabid fox.

He needed a vaccine, and he needed one now.

HE VISITED hospitals and urgent care clinics and pharmacies for three days but could not find any vaccine at all. Why that was, he did not know. Maybe in the last days of the plague, people had begun injecting themselves with anything they could find in a desperate, futile attempt to fight off Medusa. He didn't sleep, stumbling here and there looking for the only thing between him and certain awful death. At dark on the third day, he broke into a little bungalow in a quiet neighborhood on the north side of Durham. The bodies of an elderly couple were in the master bedroom, but otherwise, the house was clear, dark but for the shine of his flashlight. He found a bathroom and washed out the wound with soap and a bottle of water from the dead refrigerator.

When he was done, he sat down on the living room couch, amid the photo albums and unfinished crochet and piles of newspapers. The fear inside him was huge, even worse than when he'd been stuck with the HIV-contaminated needle. Statistically speaking, the risk from the needle stick had been extremely low, especially after the prophylactic treatment. But this. This was Medusa fear. What it must have felt like to come down with it, what it must have been to wait for the inevitable, bloody, painful end.

Now that the rabies virus was almost certainly inside him, the disease could present at any time. And once symptoms appeared, that would be it. He would die. His wrist throbbed, and he could almost hear the virus coursing through his veins. The bleeding had stopped and the wound was healing nicely, but without the vaccine, it wouldn't matter. Without the shots, sometime in the next week or next month or next year, he'd develop a cough, some numbness at the wound site, and then his brain would begin to swell and he'd develop a fear of water and then he would die a horrible, horrible death.

This was what it was like.

This is what it had been like for the rest of the world. As if death had wanted him all along. There was no escaping destiny, after all. That's what destiny was.

Right on, old chap. Missed you with Medusa. Will be coming back 'round with something else for you soon.

He was too scared to sleep.

He stayed up all night flipping through the dead couple's photo albums. He didn't know why they were out from their slot on the bookshelf; perhaps the couple had been walking down memory lane when Medusa had found this little house. They were pictures of a lifetime together, black and white wedding photographs, color pictures with that weird yellowish hue, then sweeping through the last three decades of weddings and graduations and Christmas parties and dogs and cats and fish and hamsters. Mr. Whatever-his-name-was checking out a dog on an examining table. He looked at more pictures, more and more, until he dozed and dreamed about this family and their life clicking by like a slide show, a frame at a time. As he slept, a realization flared inside his brain, exploding like a mushroom cloud, shooting him out of slumber.

The man had been a veterinarian.

Rabies.

He raced through the house, rummaging through papers and files until he found in an antique desk a business card emblazoned with the logo of the Phillips Veterinary Clinic. Mosrie Drive in Durham. He strapped on his backpack and sprinted through the dead neighborhood, following the streets out to a main artery. As dawn broke over the city, he stopped at a gas station for a map and found Mosrie Drive not a mile away.

The morning air was steamy and hot; on display around him were more scenes from the last days. Adam saw the body of a young soldier, his hands holding his rotted intestines, chewed free of his body by some heavy-caliber weapon. A black crow was perched on the man's thigh, chewing on his entrails. A turn of his head, this way or that, uncovered more visual horrors. An attractive young woman with a crowbar thrust through her neck. The head and upper torso of a middle-aged man, notably separated from his legs a few yards away. Abandoned police cruisers. A North Carolina National Guard personnel carrier. A Channel 11 news van, its satellite dish still telescoping into the sky like an alien paw. Quiet. Quiet.

The veterinary clinic was housed in a small brick building next to a Hardee's. Adam stood astride the bike, breathing hard, waiting for his heart to slow down. The terror was moon-sized now, orbiting him, threatening to fracture him. He pulled the gun from his backpack and approached the door slowly. A handwritten note on the door read *CLOSED UNTIL FURTHER NOTICE.* He double-checked his flashlight and his gun. The clip was full, and he had one in the chamber.

He went inside, and the door swung shut behind him.

Weak sunbeams streamed through the large windows into the reception area, catching dust and other particulate matter floating in the ether. His heart slammed against his ribcage as though it wanted out of not just Adam's body but out of this dead place entirely. He pictured a cartoon heart scampering down the hallway, using its ventricles like legs. Maybe the rabies was already driving him insane.

He found the medication cabinet in the back, near the kennels, which were full of dead cats and dogs. He checked each kennel, one at a time, hoping that maybe there was one industrious pooch who'd hung on and could join Adam on the road. But there wasn't; there was just more death. He hoped the animals hadn't died of Medusa; it was hard to imagine a world without dogs. He rifled through bottles and vials, antibiotics and emetics and pain pills, chicken- flavored this or that, and then he found it on a shelf. A five-dose package of human rabies vaccine. A dose of immune globulin and four doses of the vaccine itself. He grabbed it along with some syringes and hustled back outside, thanking his lucky stars. It had been illegal for a vet to house or administer human rabies vaccine.

Tears filled his eyes as he read the instructions inside the shrink-wrap. He was supposed to have taken the first dose on the day of the bite, but there was nothing that could be done about that now. He injected the globulin and first dose of vaccine and prayed that he'd done it in time. The other three doses would follow in three, seven and fourteen days. All he could do was hope and pray. Pray that he wasn't left to die of perhaps the one disease even deadlier than Medusa.

The tears burst forth, and he cried, sitting there on the curb outside the Phillips Veterinary Clinic.

"Are you okay?"

The voice startled him so badly he gasped. He couldn't remember the last time he'd heard a human voice. He opened his eyes and saw an attractive young black woman wearing an urban camouflage uniform and holding a gun on him.

He stared at her, debating whether she was really there or if he was hallucinating.

"You gonna freak out on me here?" she asked.

He felt his jaw moving, but no words would come out.

"I'm going to count to ten," she said, "and then I'm going to head on down the road."

Then more quietly: "Jesus, can I not catch a break?"

"No," Adam said. "I'm fine."

"What's with the needles?" she asked. "No hospitals if you O.D."

Adam glanced down at the paraphernalia around him and smiled.

"Oh, no. It's not that. I got bitten by a rabid fox a few days ago," he said, pointing to the bite marks on his arm. "I finally found some vaccine for it."

He watched her watch him, staring at him with her fierce green eyes, as though she was trying to decide whether to believe him.

"My name is Adam."

~

THE DAY BRIGHTENED AROUND HIM, the morning cloud cover pushing off to the east. As they stood there in the parking lot, he felt very small, very alone.

"Adam Fisher," he said again, extending his hand.

Her eyes narrowed as she considered his offer of goodwill. His outstretched hand hung there in the void, suspended, frozen in time.

"Relax, you can't catch rabies from me."

It was just the right thing at the right time, and a smile broke across her face. It lassoed them together, keeping the quickly widening gulf between them from getting any bigger. She took his hand and returned the shake.

"Captain Sarah Wells," she replied. "U.S. Army."

They fell into a brief silence.

"Sounds silly, doesn't it?" she asked.

"What's that?"

"Captain Sarah Wells," she said again, this time in a mocking tone. "I don't even know why I said that."

"You're not going to kill me, are you?" he said.

"For now."

Adam allowed a hint of a smile to trace its way across his face.

"That's good," he said. "Comic relief. We could use some of that."

She smiled back, but it was all wrong. A beautiful rock with creepy-crawlies underneath when you lifted it up.

"So we're in a hell of a bad way here, huh?" she said.

She hitched her rifle onto her shoulder and leaned against a pickup truck in the parking lot of the clinic.

"Yeah," Adam said.

"Lately, I'll forget what's happened," she said. "I'll be doing something, eating dinner, whatever, and it'll seem like it's something I've been doing forever. Then I'll see something. A body. A pileup. And it all comes back. You know what I'm saying?"

Adam nodded.

"Anyway, I'm headed to St. Louis," she said.

"What's in St. Louis?"

She removed a pack of cigarettes from her breast pocket and lit one.

She took a long drag; twin plumes of smoke streamed from her nostrils. "Smoke?"

"No thanks."

She tucked the pack away.

"I was in New York when it went down," she said. "The Bronx. Couple of days before everything collapsed, we got an order from on high. Said the CDC had set up a testing facility in St. Louis and that anyone still healthy should head there for testing."

"Why St. Louis?"

"Beats the hell out of me. Anyway, I didn't realize how bad it was until I got out of New York. I was kind of hoping it was burning itself out the farther from ground zero it got."

"It's everywhere."

She flicked a peg of ash onto the ground.

"Yeah, that's what I'm figuring out. God damn."

He expected her to tear up then, but she didn't. She smoked the cigarette in silence, down to the nub, and then she crushed it under her boot.

"Is the St. Louis thing for real?"

"No idea. But I've got to find out for myself. This might be the last thing I do as Captain Sarah Wells, U.S. Army, so I plan to see it through to the end. Probably a wild-goose chase. But I've got to do it."

St. Louis.

"Anyway, what about you?"

"Got my own wild-goose chase."

"Care to share?"

He was struck by how forward she was and found himself a bit reluctant to talk about Rachel. He was afraid that if he verbalized it, it would sound far crazier than when it was just him thinking about it. Part of what kept him going was that it didn't seem crazy to think she was still out there, still alive.

"Got a message from my daughter in California," he said. "About a week ago."

Sarah scrunched up her face and tilted her face to the sky as she worked out the timing in her head.

"And she was still alive?"

"Said she was headed to her stepdad's condo in Lake Tahoe."

The conversation petered out, and they stood there in the August sunshine, an awkward silence pushing a wedge between them. Adam didn't know what to say. He really just wanted to get back on the road.

"Can I make a suggestion?" she asked.

"Sure."

"Let's team up," she said. "Head west together until we get to St. Louis."

Adam scratched his face as he considered her proposal.

"Look," she said, "someone needed to say it. It's goddamn dangerous out here. People are gonna have to start working together."

Adam tried to analyze the dilemma rationally. But as he did so, he felt his eyes droop, and it made him realize how hard it had been by himself. He couldn't remember the last time he'd gotten a decent night's sleep, which had made getting by in this world that much tougher. But was this the right person to team up with? Would it jeopardize his own quest? There was no way to know when or if their interests would diverge, and how they would handle such a development. And then he thought about the fox and how it had snuck up on him with no warning and how next time it might be someone slicing his throat while he slept because there was no one to stop that from happening anymore.

"OK."

17

At first, Erin Thompson had been relieved when they'd found her wandering across I-235, about sixty miles west of her home in Des Moines. Her fair skin had burned in the merciless Iowa sun, healed and then burned again, leaving behind a ragged quilt of newborn pink skin against sun-scorched ivory. She was starving and dehydrated, but she'd barely noticed, having devolved into a borderline catatonic state in the wake of the plague.

Erin and her husband, a pastor named William Thompson, had been living with their twin four-year-old boys in the small two-bedroom ranch subsidized by the First Presbyterian Church in Des Moines when the plague had hit. Jason, her youngest by eight minutes, had succumbed first, on August 13; his brother Billy had followed on August 14. By then, the pastor himself was gravely ill, and Erin had been absolutely out of her mind with grief. Willie had tried to soothe her, even when he'd been in Medusa's death grip, assuring her that it was all part of God's plan, that He was bringing them all home.

And when they were all dead, all laid up in their beds because she didn't know what to do with them, and they'd long since stopped responding to emergency calls, she sat there with Willie's body, cursing him for leaving her here, unsaved, while the three people she'd loved best, whom she'd given her life for, were rollicking with Jesus. And when she didn't get sick, she hated God, she hated Willie, she hated everyone and everything and she believed she had been forsaken. Apparently it hadn't been enough to be a doting mother and loving wife, giving up her career as a schoolteacher to do her duty as a Christian homemaker, even going through marriage counseling with Willie after she'd found those e-mails he'd exchanged with their nineteen-year-old neighbor, who, along with her three brothers, mother and abusive stepfather, were now dead, like everyone else she'd ever known.

She stayed in the house for another week, barely eating or sleeping, consuming just enough to stay alive. She drank from the tap, neither knowing nor caring whether the water was safe to drink. One day, she wandered the three blocks to their church, where she found it full of the dead. People who had come seeking salvation, relief, cure, something and received nothing but a nice hot cup of *Fuck Off*. The hours slipped by in a foggy haze as sounds and screams from only God knew where peppered the night and the day. The power didn't go out in her neighborhood until August 22, and so as long as she kept the doors closed, the smell didn't get too bad. Not that you could really escape it anyway. She'd cracked the windows one morning to circulate some fresh air, but then the smell hit her, the thick, rich, dead smell barreling through like an invisible and angry presence. Then the power had gone out and the smell was everywhere.

With barely a thought in her head, she packed Willie's backpack with clean underwear, her Bible, and some beef jerky and hit the road on the morning of August 24. Like many other survivors, she left her home because she simply couldn't stay there any longer. She didn't know where she was going, or what she would do with the rest of her days. She was only thirty years old, and the prospect of another five decades in this dead world loomed larger with each passing day.

Her plan had been to take Willie's ancient Camry, but she abandoned that idea after she put the car in drive rather than reverse and placed the front end squarely into their garage door. Embarrassment and shame flooded through her as she climbed out, fully expecting to see her neighbors poking their heads out of their front doors to see what the hell all the racket was. But there was no sound other than the ticking of the engine and the hiss of the cracked radiator. She stared at the crumpled garage door, behind which was the accumulated detritus of eight years of marriage, the garage Willie had been talking about cleaning the same weekend he'd gotten sick.

So she'd left the car there, buried in the garage of a house she would never see again, and walked east. A week on the road, with no destination in mind, no plan, no nothing at all, had driven her close to madness. Outside Windsor City, she'd been approached by two middle-aged women who'd asked her to join them. "Strength in numbers," they'd said, but she hadn't even acknowledged them, she'd barely even looked at them, and now that she thought about it, they'd made hay pretty quickly away from her.

But she hadn't gone with them, and so she was by herself when the black Suburban had pulled up alongside her along I-235 right about the time the sun was at its highest, roasting and broiling. Until the door had swung open and she'd felt the chilly air spill out of the passenger compartment, she didn't really care whether she lived or died. But it felt so good, even with the furnace of the Iowa sun beating down her neck, and she wanted more of it.

The tinted window slid down, revealing the face of ... an angel? Maybe she *was* dying, Erin had thought, somewhat hopefully, and this was how God was sending for her. A black SUV. A fresh face there in the window, young, her thick brown curls tied back in a ponytail, studying her, perhaps even pitying her.

"Oh, sweetie," the woman had said, clapping a hand to her mouth as though she couldn't quite believe what she was seeing. This poor wretch.

The woman disappeared from view for a moment, and behind her, Erin saw a man at the wheel, facing forward, smoking a cigarette. When the woman re-appeared she had a bottle of water in her hand, the condensation glistening in the afternoon sun. Erin stared at it the way a pyromaniac might stare at fire.

"You thirsty?"

She held the bottle out for Erin, who approached the car like a frightened puppy being offered a treat. Erin took the bottle and drank it down in one fell swoop, unaware of how severely dehydrated she was.

"I'm sorry, but do you have some more?" she croaked out, the words slurred and muffled behind cracked, sunburned lips.

"Sure," the woman said. "Why don't you come with us? You look like you need a break."

Erin found herself nodding without the slightest reservation. They had cold water. What other treasures might they have?

The doors unlocked with a decisive *ker-chunk*, and she climbed in. A delicious chill rippled across her body as she settled into the cool leather backseat.

"What's your name, honey?"

"Erin."

She yawned.

"You just rest," the woman had said.

She fell asleep almost immediately, the promise of cold water, endless bottles of cold water lulling her to the deepest sleep she'd had in days. How easy it had been to lure her in, no different than a gullible child lured by promises of delicious candy and lost puppies.

And maybe, she thought to herself two days later, strapped to this examining table, it would have occurred to her that she could've found plenty of water on her own, that she hadn't had to let it devolve to such a state. If any of these things had occurred to her during her self-imposed death march, she might still be out there, pulling herself together.

Or maybe they'd been her only hope.

She just didn't know. No one spoke to her or explained to her what she was doing here. At first, she had thought that these had been government health officials rounding up healthy people for testing. But when they'd etched the inside of her wrist with that strange tattoo, she quickly realized that this was something else entirely. No one wore protective suits, and there was none of that urgency she saw in those last terrible days, on the street, in the hospitals, on the news.

They were in a brightly lit antiseptic room, which resembled one of the examination rooms in the urgent care clinic she'd once frequented with the boys, as they'd negotiated the rough-and-tumble world of ear infections and croup and impetigo. The long counter was stocked with bottles of hand sanitizer, cotton balls and the various and sundry items one might expect to find in a doctor's office. But the walls were bare, bearing none of the full-colored glossies with an artistic rendering of the human heart or the inner ear canal. She wore a paper-thin hospital gown and nothing else. It was itchy and barely reached all the way around her waist. Her feet were in stirrups, restrained, leaving her exposed and about as modest as a porn star waiting for the cameras to roll.

Footsteps clicking along the tile floor drew her attention. She looked over to see the woman from the SUV approaching her, but with far less mirth on her face. A small medical kit was tucked under her arm, which she set down on the metal tray mounted to her hospital bed.

Erin smiled at her, but she did not get one in reply.

"So what's this all about?" she asked in as brave a voice as she could muster.

Still the woman didn't speak. She tied a tourniquet around Erin's arm and promptly drew three vials of blood. The vials were labeled and went into a plastic tube rack. Then the woman snapped on a pair of latex gloves, retrieved a speculum from the bag and set up shop between Erin's legs. Instinctively, Erin tried snapping her legs shut, but to no avail; the restraints held them fast.

"Hey, what the hell is going on here?" Erin barked. "Don't you touch me!"

Her pleas fell on deaf ears, and she felt a strong pinch as the speculum opened her up. She looked at the ceiling and bit down hard on her lip, hard enough that she tasted blood. She tried telling herself this was no different than her routine visit to her OB/GYN, with the super-friendly Dr. Brady, a young doctor who'd been about the same age as Erin. Her daughter had been about the same age as Erin's twins.

(ALL DEAD NOW ALL DEAD NOW)

But she couldn't. This felt bad, very bad, and she felt shame for letting herself be hoodwinked by the promise of fresh water and food and a nice place to lay her head. She squirmed and twisted; hot tears ran down her cheeks. The long cotton swab entered her, scraping at her insides, and she felt her breath coming in ragged gasps.

She closed her eyes and thought about her sons, her sweet, sweet boys who had loved Thomas the Tank Engine and Lightning McQueen and now lay dead in their bedrooms. Jesus God, why hadn't she buried them? Did she think they were going to bury themselves? And it all came to her, all at once, that her little boys were dead and gone and she would never again see them in this lifetime. The sobs exploded from her, so ferociously that the woman examining her scampered backward half a dozen steps. As she lay there, weeping, all she could hope was that one day they would be reunited in heaven.

Then a terrible thought broke loose in her mind, a runaway meteor breaking free of its asteroid field, and turned her veins to ice; the horror of it was so deep, so profound, that she began to shiver.

What if she were dead and this was hell?

The sobs evolved into howls now, as though the woman were murdering her.

"We're all done here," she said.

She packed away the swab sample and the vials of blood and fled the room like it was possessed by all the demons of hell.

Erin continued wailing as the idea took deeper root in her mind and continued to flower. The more she thought about it, the less far-fetched it seemed. What was more likely, that she had somehow miraculously survived a global plague, the mother-loving apocalypse, that she had really hailed from the very deepest end of the gene pool? Or that she was now facing the thing that she had feared above all else?

Damnation.

A lesson from a college class came roaring back to her. Her freshman year at Iowa State, she had taken philosophy, during which they had studied the principle of Occam's Razor, which posited that all things being equal, the simplest explanation was usually the correct one. No, she thought, that couldn't be. Hell was a place of fire and brimstone and eternal pain.

Fire and brimstone. Fire and brimstone?

What had been more fiery than the Medusa virus, burning its way through humanity like a candle left near a musty old curtain? And what judgment could have been worse than watching your sons, the very lights of your life, die before your eyes within hours of each other, with no way to help them, with no one there to help them? Rattled with fear, bleeding from every orifice, screaming for their mommy, who could do nothing for them but watch them die. And now left here with no one and nothing but her thoughts, free to replay the last two weeks until she died or went insane.

Her mind went blank, as though a circuit breaker had flipped. Her gown was rucked up to her hips, leaving her naked from the waist down, but she didn't care. When the man came back for her, she didn't care when he eyed her leeringly, she wouldn't have cared if he'd climbed up on top of her and had his way with her.

He yanked her gown back down and took her back to the dorms.

18

After joining forces, Adam and Sarah commandeered an old Acura, but Durham's westbound points of egress, including Interstate 40, Route 147 and Route 70, had been blocked either by traffic or military vehicles. They had burned the rest of that day trying to find another way out, to no avail. By the time they realized that they'd need to walk or bike out of town, the day was shot, so they spent the evening gathering supplies. That night, they slept in adjoining rooms of a Holiday Inn, and the next morning brought with it two choices: hoof it or bikes. Sarah had offered up her chopper, with Adam riding pillion, but he'd declined.

"Two types of motorcycle riders," he'd said. "Those who've crashed and those who will crash."

Sarah didn't push the issue.

They'd broken into a large sporting goods store in Durham, where they geared up for a long bike ride. Adam had needed to start from scratch, having left much of his gear behind during his desperate search for the rabies vaccine. So when they left the store two hours later, both were outfitted with backpacks, tents, sleeping bags, water bottles, energy bars, ponchos, waterproof matches, compasses, hunting knives, a GPS transmitter/receiver, and flashlights. They also stopped in a drug store and stocked up on toiletries. It was surreal for Adam. Simply taking the stuff had felt so foreign; he kept waiting for the police to swoop in and arrest them for shoplifting. But, of course, none did, and they pedaled out of Durham around noon on August 31.

Adam was hopeful that they'd be able to trade up to something with an internal combustion engine a little ways up the road, but they never found more than a few miles of highway that wasn't blocked those first couple of days in September. So they stayed on their bikes. The slow pace was maddening, but there was nothing Adam could do about it. Moreover, it limited the stock of supplies that they could carry at any given time, necessitating more frequent stops.

As they rode, Adam tracked the landscape passing by; he realized he was looking for some sign that the world had changed, that things looked fundamentally different. But the truth was that it all looked about the same. A grain silo rose up before him, growing larger as they drew closer, and then receding behind them until it was gone from view. A Target distribution center. A salvage yard. These things looked exactly the same. They saw no one, the countryside hauntingly empty.

The early afternoon of September 3 brought them to Kernersville, North Carolina, about seventy miles west of Durham. They ate lunch on the playground of the Kernersville Elementary School. There had been little chit-chat between them since their union, only what was necessary to keep the expedition moving westward. This, Adam supposed, was shock. Didn't matter who you were, what you'd done before, you didn't watch the world die without a little piece of you going with it.

After lunch, Sarah studied their map while Adam administered the second dose of his rabies vaccine. So far, so good in that department. The bites themselves had nearly healed and he'd seen no evidence of any strange new symptoms. The fear was still there, as though hermetically sealed, ensuring it would never decay or yellow or soften at the edges. He wasn't sure he wanted it to fade away. It was important he remember what happened. That he remember how far off the reservation they were.

He got up and walked around, the late summer heat pressing down on him. The trees full and green, a few leaves on the branch tips just starting to turn. The incessant buzz of cicadas. He touched each piece of playground equipment, feeling the heat absorbed deep in the wood, and it made him sad to think how there were no children here. Behind him,

Sarah lit a cigarette, and while she smoked, he checked his iPhone for messages. The dreaded No Service icon flashed in the top left corner of the screen. It had been days since he'd pulled a signal; he figured the cell towers had finally gone down.

Sarah was crushing the cigarette under her boot when he made his way back to her.

"There aren't a lot of population centers west of here," she said. "It might be worth trying to snag a car this afternoon."

This perked Adam's spirits. He couldn't believe how little progress he'd made since leaving Richmond, and this was welcome news indeed. He needed a win, badly. The vehicles left in the parking lot were their first target, but they were all locked or missing their keys. They rode into the center of town and stumbled across a Jeep dealership. A few minutes of trial and error finally resulted in a hit – the keys to a new Jeep Grand Cherokee, just a few miles on the odometer and fully gassed. As they loaded their gear into the cargo area, Sarah tapped him on the shoulder. When he looked up, she tipped her head toward the main road. He looked up to see a car quietly approaching from the north. Behind him, he could hear Sarah readying her M4. His heart pounded.

A rotund middle-aged man jumped out of the car and sprinted toward them, his arms flailing about his head. He was wearing a nice pair of dress pants, but he was shirtless and in bare feet; his shoulders and face were badly sunburned. Adam did not think the man was much in his right mind.

"They're here!" he yelled as he drew toward them. "They're here!"

"Whoa, whoa!" Sarah said, stepping out from behind Adam, making sure her machine gun was visible to all. "Take it easy, big guy!"

"They're here!" he said again. "They're here now!"

The man was becoming hysterical, his face cycling through about eight different shades of red. A bubble of mucus inflated from his left nostril as he repeated his warning again and again.

"They're here!" he yelled again, dancing in place, almost as if he had to go to the bathroom.

Adam glanced at Sarah, who just shrugged her shoulders.

"They're here," he said again, sinking to the ground. "They're here to kill us all."

Then he was curled up into the fetal position, bawling, howling, as though Adam and Sarah were ritualistically disemboweling him rather than simply watching him. Adam knelt down next to him.

"You OK, buddy? Who's here?"

He continued to howl.

"Let's calm down a little," Adam said. "You're safe."

Howls. Screeches.

Adam tried consoling the man for another fifteen minutes, but he simply could not reach him. He patted him on the shoulder. Nothing. He asked him for his name. Nothing. Every minute or so, he'd call out his warning and then retreat back into his catatonic state.

"Adam," Sarah said.

"What?"

"We need to get moving."

Adam dropped his chin.

"I know."

"Hey buddy," Adam said to the man. "We're gonna hit the road. You're welcome to join us."

"Here," the man said. "Here now."

"I can't leave him here," Adam said. "He needs help. Help me lift him in the car. He just needs some rest."

"You sure?" Sarah asked.

"We'll keep an eye on him. Grab his legs."

Adam slid his arms underneath the man's underarms while Sarah hooked hers around his legs. As they lifted him off the ground, the man bucked like a bronco. A runaway fist clocked Adam's ribcage, and the man was up and running and flailing about again.

"They're here!"

He ran back to his car and climbed onto the hood, where he continued his sermon, this time in earnest.

"THEY'RE HERE!"

Adam's head hurt.

"Let's go," he said to Sarah.

Sarah took the first shift and guided them back toward the interstate, the shouter's pleas booming in the giant stillness.

"They're here!"

They were two miles up the road before the man's voice faded away. Adam wondered what would become of him and those like him. How many people were out there right now, falling apart, unable to cope with the enormity of what had happened these last few weeks?

In the ordinary quiet of the car, things seemed almost normal. The air conditioning worked. An album by a band called the *Tattered Remnants* spun in the compact disc player. Just another road trip along a forgotten stretch of highway. Again, chit-chat was kept to a minimum, the experience at the dealership unnerving them both.

Fortunately, as Sarah had predicted, the roads northwest of Kernersville were clear. They drove deep into the wilds of North Carolina, toward the mountains. Adam's unease grew as evening approached, the sun tracing its eternal route through the sky, inching its way toward the horizon. He was still having a hard time at night, when the panic would rush through him as darkness spread across the landscape. It was almost palpable; watching the sun dip toward the horizon was like having his head pushed underwater, unable to breach the surface. He'd find himself clinging to the last bit of light as it leaked from the sky, almost willing it to freeze in place. This new world was crappy enough in the late-summer sunshine. Nighttime in a world of the lost was almost more than he could bear.

"Storm's coming," Sarah said.

Adam glanced up at a ridge of purplish clouds stretching toward the horizon. A storm. He'd loved thunderstorms once upon a time, but now it was just another thing to worry about.

"We may want to think about finding real shelter tonight," she said.

Adam's pulse quickened as Sarah pulled onto the shoulder. Finding shelter was something new. Something different. And anything different in this new world could be bad. Deadly, even. Adam looked down at his lap as Sarah studied the map from the glove compartment.

"This next town looks like our best bet for tonight. We can stock up on supplies."

"Oh, shit, we forgot to get them in Kernersville," Adam said.

"I know," Sarah said. "That scene with that guy just freaked me out."

They curled off the interstate and passed an empty park to their left, the susurration of the tall grasses audible in the giant emptiness. Just beyond, a large sign welcomed them to Walkertown.

"There's a little market up ahead," Sarah said.

Sarah pulled into the parking lot of Hall's Grocery and shut off the engine, which ticked and hissed as it cooled, the sound huge, almost embarrassingly so.

"You wait here," she said. "I'll get us something to eat."

"You shouldn't go alone," he said. "It may not be safe."

She patted her M4 rifle. "I won't be alone. Besides, you can keep a lookout."

She got out of the car, stretched, and went inside.

While she gathered their dinner, Adam fiddled with the vehicle's satellite radio hookup, edging his way across the spectrum, earning nothing but mild static for his efforts. He'd subscribed to the service himself, passing the time behind the wheel with the Bob Dylan channel, the '90s channel, Howard Stern.

Was Howard Stern dead?

That was a weird thought to have.

He took big, shallow gulps of air, sweet evening air, and he had to laugh at himself. He was still giggling a little when Sarah emerged from the store, a sack of groceries tucked under her arm.

"Something funny?" she asked.

"Just laughing at our little predicament here," he said. "Because this is some crazy shit we are dealing with."

This earned him a thin smile, but nothing more. As she stood there, smiling her thin smile, shockingly unfazed by the disaster, a bolt of anger swept through him.

"How are you so calm?" he snapped.

"What are you talking about?"

"We're standing in a worldwide graveyard, and you don't seem the least bit put out. How is that?"

The smile disappeared.

"I don't know what you're talking about," she said.

"Everyone you and I have ever known is dead! You get that? Dead!"

A sneer of disgust curled up on her face.

"Oh, I get it all right," she snapped back. "More than you'll ever know."

"What's that supposed to mean?"

"None of your goddamned business. Do you want to eat or not?"

The fight went right out of him, a balloon floating away from a child's hand.

"What the hell."

She sat down on the curb as the day's last light ebbed out of the sky. Adam switched on the headlights, bathing the storefront with a harsh white glow. Inelegant, perhaps, but better than the dark. Way better than that. He sat down next to her, quiet, as she picked through the paper bag, emblazoned with the Hall's Grocery logo. She handed him a can of spaghetti, a kid-sized cup of applesauce, a pack of Oreos and a lukewarm bottle of beer. He studied the label, AMB Pale Ale, a brand he didn't recognize.

"Sorry the beer's not cold," she said.

"Drank my share of warm beer," he said.

He twisted the cap off, priming his ears for the hiss of carbonation as the seal was broken. They clinked bottles, and he took a long pull. It was shit beer, truly wretched stuff only a college freshman could love, but it was still beer.

Sarah belched, loudly, and set the bottle down next to her.

"You'll forgive the lady."

"Sure."

He rolled the can of spaghetti between his hands, taking comfort in the weight. Sarah popped open her can and dug in with a plastic spoon. The tangy aroma of the tomato sauce tickled his nose, but not in a particularly good way, and he decided to pass on the pasta course.

"You need to eat," she said. "Keep your strength up."

"Think I'll pass tonight," he said, patting his midsection. "Watching my weight."

The joke fell flat, and she continued to eat her spaghetti.

Eventually, he ate the applesauce and the Oreos and then washed it down with the rest of his beer. When he was done, he got up and began stuffing the remains of his dinner into the trashcan posted at the front door. Then he stopped, his hand holding the heavy plastic flap open.

"God dammit, I'm such an idiot," he muttered.

"What?"

He wasn't even listening now, as he stewed in his juices, marinating in the annoyance of his cleaving to the old ways, dumping his trash as though the county sanitation department would be along in the morning to empty the cans out.

"This fucking shit!" He tipped the can over, sending it clattering onto the concrete walkway in front of the store. The lid came loose, and a coil of hot, stinking garbage oozed out, waiting for a garbage truck that would never come. Adam picked up the lid and flung it into the door, shattering it into a million pieces. The tinkling of fracturing glass echoed through the parking lot, and he stood there, watching the shards rain down onto the sidewalk in front of the store.

"Feel better?" she asked.

He stood there, his hands on his hips, his breath coming in ragged gasps. He felt his legs buckle, and he dropped to his knees, shivering, sweating. His heart thrummed, and his breath was catching in his midsection. His stomach hurt. Maybe he needed to go to the bathroom. Hell, maybe he was finally dying of Medusa.

He felt Sarah's hand on his back.

"Hey," she said softly. "Hey. It's going to be OK."

He rolled back onto his seat and pulled his knees to his chest. Hot jets of shame flooded through him, falling apart like this in front of this woman. Come on, Fisher. Come *on*.

He looked into her eyes. They were clear, calm, flat hunter-green pools. No hint of panic, no indication she was unable to handle this pitch the universe had uncorked at them. That's what it was about her. A preternatural calm. Where did it come from?

"I'm gonna run inside the store for a minute," Adam said. "Want anything?"

She shook her head.

Adam stepped inside the store. It was dark and humid. He shone the flashlight across the aisles, across the rack of postcards, the dead cooler full of soft drinks, the weekly newspaper stacked at the front so out of date that the headline read *Early Start to Flu Season*. He opened his wallet and withdrew all the cash inside, some sixty dollars. He left it on the counter and weighted it down with the collection jar. He didn't know why he did it. It was a horribly futile gesture, he knew that, but it made him feel better all the same. Maybe he'd eventually get used to the fact that everything, everywhere was simply there for the taking. But it still seemed wrong.

"Want to talk about it?" she asked when he got back outside.

He looked back and saw her watching him, maybe studying him.

"I don't even know what to say," he said. "I mean, I want to say something, I feel like I should say something, but nothing comes out.

"I mean, what the hell is this?" he said, spreading his arms wide, feeling it all pour out of him, like his sanity had been inside a cup that had tipped over. The scale of it, the everything-ness of it, had pushed and pushed and pushed down on him, the pressure growing like air in a balloon.

She got up and brushed her hands on her pants.

"What's the first thing that comes to mind?" he asked.

She looked up at the sky and let out a long sigh.

"I guess I can't help but wonder what the hell happened."

"Fair enough," he said. "If it makes you feel better, I'm a doctor, and I don't have the first damn clue."

"A doctor? Not sure if that makes me feel better or worse."

He supposed he could understand; if a doctor couldn't explain what happened, that was a pretty sorry state of affairs.

"Can I ask you a question?" Adam said.

"Sure."

"Did you ever feel sick? Did you ever experience any symptoms of Medusa?"

Her eyebrows popped up.

"Now that you mention it, no, I didn't," she said. "I kept imagining it, that I was coming down with it, but I never did."

"Me either," Adam replied. "Now it's possible that we did experience symptoms but that they were so minor that we didn't notice them."

"Is that important?"

"At this point, probably not," he said. "I'm not a virologist or infectious disease specialist, so this isn't really my area of expertise. But I'd love to know why we survived."

"I came through Philly, Baltimore, and D.C. before I made it to Raleigh," she said. "Barely saw a living soul. Heard folks. Voices carrying on the wind and whatnot. You were the first person I'd talked to in a week."

The image of the crowded northeast corridor emptied out made Adam's head spin. The virus would've spread fast, so fast, there.

"What kind of doctor are you?"

"OB/GYN."

"Babies."

"Yep."

She became silent, eyeing Adam, more looking through him than she was at him.

"Will babies get it?"

It was an important question, possibly the most important question of all, and he was disgusted with himself for not considering it. Pregnant women out there in the big empty. There was no way to know whether a fetus would survive its mother's exposure to the virus. And if the baby did survive to delivery, there was no way to know if she'd survive outside the womb. Adam just didn't know enough about how Medusa worked.

"Will they?" she asked again.

"I don't know," he said. "I really don't know."

"Aren't you the big party pooper?"

"I guess," he said. "I feel stupid that it hadn't crossed my mind."

"Maybe you didn't want it to cross your mind."

"Maybe."

"Well, Doctor, here's another question."

"Shoot."

"Why *are* we still here? Why were we spared?"

"Luck. Genetics. No virus is one hundred percent fatal. Well, maybe rabies is."

"What about God?"

This took him by surprise. It was the first time he'd even considered the theological implications of what had happened. He didn't like the fact that he was being sloppy and careless in his thinking.

"What do you mean?"

"What if this was God's judgment?"

He stood there, unsure of how to answer.

"You believe in God?"

When he didn't answer, she smiled.

"Look, I know that's probably getting a little personal, but I think we can do away with societal niceties for now, don't you?"

She was right.

"Some doctors can reconcile their faith with science," he said. "I never could. I've read the Bible. I minored in comparative religion in college. It never took. I'm sorry."

"Why're you sorry?"

He laughed softly.

"I don't even know. It feels like I should be sorry about something. What about you?"

"I used to believe in God," she said. "Once upon a time. I don't know anymore."

"Well, if there is a God, He spared you, right?"

"Maybe we weren't the ones who were spared."

He hadn't thought of it that way. The idea she'd been left behind by her God must have been a terrifying one indeed. It was a hard thing to process, even if it was a concept he didn't buy into himself. He didn't think the Bible was anything more than a fairy tale, written and massaged through the centuries by history's winners. And she had a point. Maybe they had drawn the short straw.

"Why don't we change the subject," she said once the silence had begun to metastasize into awkwardness.

"Good idea."

"How far is it to St. Louis?"

She studied her map for a moment, chewing her lower lip as she did so. He watched her, and he found himself staring into her green eyes again. As he did so, his breathing slowed, and his heart decelerated.

"About six hundred more miles."

"Jesus. It's taken us three days just to get this far."

"Well, we have to stop thinking like we used to," she said. "We can't assume we'll always be able to drive every mile from here to St. Louis."

"I guess you're right," Adam said.

"You sure you don't want me to teach you to ride a chopper?"

"I'm sure."

They were quiet a moment.

"You really think there's anything in St. Louis?"

Her face darkened.

"No, probably not," she said, her eyes cutting away from his. "But I gotta do it. Who knows? Maybe we'll get lucky. Maybe they have roast turkey and mashed potatoes."

"Chocolate milk?"

"Chocolate milk for you," she said. "Icy cold chocolate milk."

It was full dark now. Adam got up and stepped clear of the headlights' glow, into the inky darkness of the night. As he gazed across the undulating hills, the blackness stretched on forever. He tilted his head skyward and saw a blanket of stars twinkling in the night, a handful of diamonds tossed against black velvet.

He was glad to be alive. He was glad they'd teamed up (*those eyes, those green eyes!*). Standing here, watching the world continue to spin on, the way it always had, made it a little easier to believe that Rachel was still alive out there, maybe looking up at the same sky. He pretended it wasn't three hours earlier in California, where sunset was still hours away, and imagined she was looking at these same stars. Maybe she'd met up with other survivors, maybe she wasn't alone, questioning her sanity, wondering what the hell had been the point of surviving.

An hour later, they were camped out in the gymnasium of a local elementary school, listening to the hard rain thrum the roof, deep, throaty booms of thunder rolling through the ether. He tried not to think about Sarah, over there in her own sleeping bag, about her eyes, about her calm. But he thought about her until he fell asleep.

19

G od, he was thirsty.

Yesterday, the thirst had started as a little gumminess of the lips, a little stickiness in the mouth, that realization that it was already afternoon and you hadn't had a glass of water all day. Easily fixed in the old days. You just plopped your glass under the tap, and voila, thirst quenched. But it wasn't the old days. Now Freddie's mouth was dry, an old cotton ball. His eyes itched like hell, and his piss smelled metallic.

They'd run out of water two days ago, and they hadn't been able to find any since. They were in the kitchen of a Taco Bell on the morning of September 6, just outside Murfreesboro, Tennessee, testing yet another kitchen faucet, befuddled by the lack of running water. This was the fourth different faucet they'd tried that day, and so far, all the taps had withheld their bounty.

Freddie held his breath as Caroline, leaning on her crutch, opened the spigot.

Rat-tat-tat-tat-tat.

The deathly rattle of dry pipes.

She shut the faucet and looked up at Freddie.

His stomach clenched with frustration.

"Dammit," he said. "Maybe it's because the power is out everywhere."

"No," Caroline said. "The electric pumps just move the water from the source to the treatment plants and then into the reservoir. But from there, it's mostly gravity pushing the water from the tower through the pipes. So the water should be running as long as there's water in the tower."

"Maybe the tower is empty," Freddie said.

Caroline rubbed a finger along a dry lip.

"Maybe," she said. "If we could just find some bottled water."

They'd been on their way to St. Louis when the water issue popped up, angling northwest through the Tennessee Valley, placing all their hopes into the government flier they'd found flipping through the deserted streets of Chattanooga. Caroline had latched onto the idea like a talisman. As her due date drew closer on the horizon, she was becoming increasingly desperate to see a doctor. Freddie hadn't been crazy about St. Louis, which, at best, would be a chaotic, confusing mess, and at worst, a hot, stinking graveyard like every other town they'd passed through.

But he went along with the plan because it gave them a goal to shoot for – even if this journey wasn't draining the emotional abscess that had formed in the wake of the plague. And besides, he thought they'd be safe because an NFL linebacker, even one who couldn't make a roster this year, was still a terrifying physical specimen for the average person. If nothing else, any troublemakers or ne'er-do-wells would probably not want to chance it, move onto someone they could rob or murder without too much effort. Not even post-apocalyptic highwaymen wanted to deal with hassle. But he would do it for her. Besides, he didn't relish the idea of delivering Caroline's baby by himself.

They were still traveling in the pickup truck that Freddie had intended to die in. Occasionally, they'd hit an unplayable lie, a stretch of highway that was just too clogged with dead traffic, and they have to backtrack and find another way. But there was no choice – her broken leg didn't leave them any other options. And the truth was, it was safer this way. As the days passed, Freddie had become increasingly conscious of the fact that while it had killed a lot of people, Medusa hadn't killed everyone. A few days earlier, they'd come across a dead backpacker along I-24, his throat slit from ear to ear. A harsh reminder that he and Caroline weren't alone in this shitty new world.

After striking out in the Taco Bell, they went back outside and set off again, bouncing from home to business to restaurant, looking for any water at all. In one law office, they found the office water cooler about one-eighth full, but a thin layer of algae had formed along the surface. They hit two grocery stores that day, but the shelves had been stripped clean of bottled water, soda, and juice.

Then they had turned their attention back toward the homes, ignoring the taps, the thirst deepening, digging down into their minds. Freddie's panic began roiling like a pot of water forgotten on a hot stove. Caroline was right, he thought. They'd find a stash of bottled water soon enough. But a search of two dozen homes had turned up nothing. Plenty of food stocked away, enough canned goods to keep them fed for months, if not years.

But the water.

It made sense, he supposed. Once the distribution networks collapsed, there would've been no more deliveries here; whatever bottled water was still on the shelves probably would've been snapped up in a hurry. In fact, people might have drunk the bottled water even when the taps were still running.

They found a twelve pack of Mountain Dew at one house, which they'd drunk greedily, but that was just robbing Peter to pay Paul. The soda provided a brief respite from the dry mouth, but the thirst returned within a couple of hours and in greater force. The sugar would dehydrate them even faster than before, putting the discovery of water at even more of a premium.

"How is this possible?" Freddie had blurted out as day began to soften into twilight, his anxiety rising. He was annoyed with himself. They should've abandoned Murfreesboro and pressed ahead; certainly they would've found water a little farther up the road. But now they were committed. He was exhausted, and his mind was cloudy from dehydration. Wouldn't that be something, he thought. To die of thirst in a land obsessed with bottled water.

At dusk on September 8, they came across a gated community in the western suburbs of town. Freddie inched his way into the neighborhood, guiding the pickup around a *de facto* roadblock of luxury sedans and sport utility vehicles. Perhaps the residents' last-ditch attempt to quarantine themselves from the world disintegrating around them.

He didn't relish the idea of conducting a house-to-house search in the dark, but he couldn't wait. Caroline was badly dehydrated, and the truck was nearly out of gas. He didn't know how long it would take to find the keys for another gassed-up vehicle, and he wasn't sure they had the time to spare.

A wide road bisected the subdivision, which was not unlike Wyndham, where Freddie had lived with his girls. God, he missed them terribly. If only there were an antibiotic to snuff out grief. His sleep came in fits and starts, and the same dream tormented him nightly, over and over, his daughter's last moments in that stinking, sweat-stained, blood-soaked hospital bed.

Large colonials lined the avenue, huge sprawling homes on at least half an acre each. The once well-manicured lawns had started to unravel, reverting to their natural state. For all the time and effort and money pumped into landscaping, the average American lawn was in a goddamn big hurry to let itself go.

He stopped at the first house on his right, dark and foreboding. The moon was full tonight, thank God for that, spreading out a luminous silver blanket across the land.

"Where are we?" Caroline said, startling him. He thought she'd been asleep.

"Gonna try and find some water," he replied. "Wait here."

"Can't this wait until morning?"

Her eyes were sunken and dry, which was all the answer he needed. He was unsure if she was the one who was afraid, or if she could smell the fear on him and was trying to spare him. He did want to wait until morning, he was goddamn sure about that.

"You need water," he said. "It can't wait any longer."

A full-body shiver rippled through her, despite the late-evening heat.

"Wait here," he said again. "If you need help, honk the horn."

"OK," she replied softly.

He smiled at her in the dark and stepped out of the car.

THE WINDOWS WERE DARK, the blinds shut tight. At the top of the porch steps, he paused and held his breath, listening for something, anything.

Nothing. The doorknob held fast when he jiggled it, so he used the flash-light to break the decorative window flanking the side of the door. After clearing the stubborn shards of glass clinging to the window frame, he reached inside the gaping darkness and unlocked the door.

The house was warm, stifling, and a sour smell permeated the air. Before penetrating deeper into the house, he propped the door open to let in some fresh air. He swept the flashlight in a semi-circle around him, the white cylinder of light washing across the relics of a life once lived here.

His breath caught as the beam landed on a figure lying prone on a settee, an antique, high-backed thing in the formal living room. The figure, a woman, did not move as he drew closer. Just another plague victim. The body was bloated, her face swollen and clotted with dried blood. Freddie muttered a small prayer for this poor woman, who'd died on this couch, this really uncomfortable looking couch, and kept moving.

Two more bodies in the family room – an adult male in a recliner, a teenaged girl on the sofa. The man was still holding the remote control in his hand. Onto the kitchen, where Freddie found himself mesmerized by the family corkboard, mounted on the expensive stainless steel refrig-erator. A reminder card for Steven's dentist appointment on September 14. Two tickets to the Titans-Steelers game the last Sunday in September. A picture of the family with a puppy; the photo had been date-stamped July 28, shortly before the virus had introduced itself to everyone. Freddie found himself priming his ears for the sounds or whimpers of a hungry puppy, but he heard nothing. Tears welled up in Freddie's eyes; somehow, these vestiges of the old world were harder to look at than the bodies dotting the wasted American landscape. This was what they had lost. The different threads of every different human fiber, from every race and ethnicity and creed that wove together to make the American quilt.

He opened the refrigerator, which expelled a warm puff of sour air, the breath of a ghost. Rotten vegetables and moldy cheese. Stale bread. A half-drunk bottle of wine, missing its cork. But no water. There was a staircase at the edge of the house. As he made his way downstairs, the flashlight slipped in his hands, and he caught it, just barely. He paused to wipe his sweaty palms on his pants. All of a sudden, he could feel his heart pounding in his ribs, the blood rushing in his ears. He was terrified of everything, all at once, of the dark, of not finding any water, of Caroline dying on his watch, of wandering the God-forsaken hellscape America had become for months or years with each second ticking by like an eternity.

He carefully negotiated the basement, spotlighting each step he took. The cone of light bounced across a water heater, a high-efficiency washer and dryer, a foosball table, items that would never be used again. The place was a wreck, looked like a bomb had gone off. A sweep of the flashlight revealed blood spatter everywhere. Filthy clothes reeking of human waste sat in haphazard piles.

Then: victory. Atop a workbench, a case of bottled water. He burst into tears upon seeing it, weeping as he brushed his fingers against the still-intact shrink wrap. The plastic crackled under his thumb. He hoisted the case onto his shoulder and made his way back to the stairs.

He was halfway up the steps when he heard the truck's horn blow.

No, not just blow.

Blast.

He raced up the stairs and burst out into the dark front yard without a plan or a thought in his head other than a singular focus on protecting Caroline. A puddle of shattered glass pooled on the asphalt. The passenger door of their truck hung open limply like the broken wing of a bird; the car's interior light glowed with a sickly yellow hue, revealing its terrible secret.

Caroline was gone.

FREDDIE STOOD UNMOVING, not breathing, trying to process the scene in front of him. A sound to his right. A *scritch-scratch* sound, perhaps of something being dragged, and he recognized it as Caroline's pack on the ground, a sound he'd learned in their time on the road together. Her leg was still weeks from healing. Someone was carrying her into the night, her pack dragging behind her.

He set the case of water on the front seat and eased into the darkness, cursing it and thankful for it at the same time, nimbly carrying his massive bulk down the street, the way that had been praised and watched slack-jawed during all those Sundays on the gridiron. His eyes darted from point to point, target to target, looking for any clue as to Caroline's whereabouts. Whoever had snatched her couldn't have gotten more than a thirty-second head start and now bore the burden of carrying an injured prisoner.

Stay calm, he told himself. Stay calm.

The roar of an engine shattered the silence, and ahead, maybe thirty yards, he saw a large vehicle, lit up like a Christmas tree, its headlights shining brightly in Freddie's face. Silhouetted against the stark white cylinders of light was a figure, stumbling along, the outline of a body slung over his shoulder. Freddie could just make out Caroline's pack dragging along the street.

If they got to the car, he'd lose her. He broke into a run, a full-throated sprint, chewing up the distance between him and his target like a lion closing in on an injured zebra. But it wasn't exactly like that, not really. The kidnapper held all the cards. And as if Caroline's captor had read his mind, he stopped and slowly swung around to face a rapidly closing Freddie.

"Take another step, and I'll kill her," the man called out. He said it matter-of-factly, without a hint of emotion or bravado, with a coolness that told Freddie that he would do exactly as he promised.

Freddie stopped on a dime, his knee aching. He was drenched in sweat, and his shirt clinging to him uncomfortably in the Tennessee night. Standing in the harsh blast of the car's high beams, how terribly exposed he was.

"She's hurt," Freddie said. "She'll just slow you down. And she's pregnant."

From the corner of his eye, just over the man's shoulder, he saw movement in the car. Time lost all meaning as he stared down his adversary, wondering if the sudden report of gunfire would be the last thing he'd hear in this world.

Why hadn't they fired?

The man shifted his weight from one foot to the other, and Freddie realized he was tiring from carrying Caroline over his shoulder. She hadn't made a sound, and Freddie wondered if she was still conscious. A few moments later, the man crouched down and lowered Caroline to the ground; instinctively, Freddie crouched with him. It seemed terribly important to mirror his opponent's maneuvers. She curled up in the fetal position, one arm protecting her abdomen, the second shielding her head.

A hiss from the car. It sounded like the second person was trying to communicate with his confederate.

"Huh?"

"MOVE!"

It hit Freddie like a bolt of lightning. The shooter hadn't fired because Caroline's captor was in his line of sight. As the man tried to process the order, Freddie made a break for them, hoping that he'd get there in time. A second later, a second too late, the man ducked out of the way, clearing the way for a barrage.

The shotgun roared, its tongue of flame bright and red in the darkness behind the sweep of the headlights. The round missed badly. As Freddie drew closer, the man pivoted just so in a vain attempt to escape Freddie's assault. Just ahead, Freddie heard the shooter fumbling with the shotgun, the clack of the barrel as he hurried to reload.

Body on body. The heavy, violent thwack of flesh on flesh, and Freddie was reminded of the big sacks, the big tackles, the terrifying and dizzying collisions of a sporting life gone by. He wrapped his big arms around his target and drove him into the blacktop with every ounce of his 265 pounds. Freddie felt the man's ribs break, a sensation that hit him in all the right places, lighting up his dopamine receptors.

It felt *good.*

The man whimpered underneath him, his body wrecked, but Freddie wasn't done. He felt alive, free, ready to act after weeks of reacting to the ladles of shit the world had been serving. He grabbed the man's ears, lifted his head off the asphalt and smashed it back down against the ground. The man's skull caved in like a watermelon, and he lay still.

But Freddie wasn't done.

No, not by a long shot.

Not at all.

These men had debts to pay now, debts owed to a society gone away, to see that even if the world lay dead in the gutter, justice would live on.

The shooter continued to struggle with the shotgun; Freddie could hear him whimpering as he seemed to grasp the collapse of their plan, wondering how things could have gotten away from them so quickly.

"Nnnnnh," the guy was muttering.

Freddie wasn't even rushing anymore. He felt strong, easy, fluid. Six more steps brought him to the window, where he found his erstwhile assassin, still unable to load the shotgun. He was young, perhaps in his mid-twenties, his face still bearing the scars of recently healed acne. His hair was long, tied back in a sloppy ponytail. Tendrils of hair bounced loosely like broken springs.

He looked up at Freddie with wide, terrified eyes, Freddie's bulk and mass before him a monster from a child's bedtime story. Freddie simply stared back at him, unfeeling and uncaring. The man's fear had no more effect on him than a fly landing on his arm. He pulled him clear of the vehicle by the ponytail; the shotgun clattered to the ground, and his prisoner flailed his arms about as his body crashed to the ground in a heap. Freddie ripped the man's ponytail from his head, pulling it free in a messy clump. The man howled. Freddie retrieved the shotgun and loaded in its recalcitrant shells. When he was done, he placed the barrel of the gun under the bandit's chin.

"Please! I'm so sorry," the guy pleaded. His breaths came in shallow, ragged gasps.

"I'm sure you are," he said.

It wasn't anger or fear or even hate bubbling inside Freddie just then, as he eyed the skinny waste of space before him. It was disgust. The way one might look at a clump of dogshit on a well-manicured lawn. And what did you do with dogshit? You didn't leave it there to spoil the lawn, did you, to infect it with its parasites and bacteria? No, you got yourself a shovel and a bag and you cleaned it right up.

"Freddie."

The voice startled him. He looked back to see Caroline, who'd pushed herself up into a seated position. She'd propped herself on one arm, the other covering her abdomen.

"You OK?" he asked.

"I'll be fine. You?"

He didn't reply, because he knew damn well she wasn't asking about his physical well-being.

"Why don't we get going?" she said. It wasn't a question as much as an order.

The guy's eyes swung sharply toward Caroline, so hard they could have rocketed out the side of his head, as he sensed that perhaps he had a savior.

"And let him pull this stunt on someone else?"

"I think he's learned his lesson. Didn't you?"

He nodded vigorously, as if to underscore the fact he had most certainly learned his lesson, that he was a very, very good student who had paid very, very close attention to the teacher.

But Freddie wasn't even listening. He looked deep into the man's eyes, unsure of what he was looking for, not even aware if he would recognize it if it were there. Everything, Caroline, his grief, the stickiness of the late-summer night, fell away around him, as he zeroed in on the warmth of the shotgun's barrel in his left palm, the stiffness of the trigger under his index finger as he flexed it just so. It had felt good, killing the other guy, a scratch scratched, one that had been nagging him for so long.

"Freddie," she said again, this time with a little more heft in her voice.

"It's a shitty world out there."

The sound of his voice startled him.

"This will just make it shittier," she said.

He pulled the trigger.

20

They made good time after Walkertown, first cutting along Highway 66 and then continuing along Route 52 through the heart of northwest North Carolina. These roads, undoubtedly just as clear after the plague as they'd been before, made things seem almost normal. They passed through Mt. Airy, the sign at the town limits touting its heritage as the birthplace of Andy Griffith. Then they were in Virginia again, the extreme southwest tip that he had never visited. Adam couldn't help but laugh a little, that after all that time on the road, he was back in Virginia. A bit farther north, they looped onto I-77, and that was when they really started chewing up the miles.

Interstate 77 took them past Hillsville, Austinville, and Max Meadows, all lovely little towns, each as quiet and empty as the others. In Hillsville, they'd stopped and looked around, but they saw no one and heard nothing but the birds. A pack of dogs, looking mighty thin and hungry, had rolled up on them there on Main Street, sending them scurrying for the safety of the car. Then they were in the Jefferson National Forest, and it was here, for the first time since the plague had swept the globe, that Adam felt that his heart rate had dipped back below a hundred beats per minute.

He felt his ears pop a little as the Jeep climbed into the pass. Around them rose up every conceivable species of tree, pines and oaks and maples, thick green fingers reaching up into the sky. Adam rolled down his window, taking in the fresh air. He pulled onto one of the scenic overlooks carved out of the highway and got out of the car. To the north was a spectacular vista, a shimmering lake and a copse of enormous trees that appeared to have taken the passing of mankind in stride.

"Been a while since the world smelled this good," he said.

They spent the night there, opting to sleep in the car because Adam knew that black bears and bobcats roamed these woods. Adam slept deeply, as soundly as he'd slept since it all went down. The quiet was almost otherworldly, as though even the forest itself was paying mankind its last respects.

"How are we on gas?" she asked as they prepared to set off that morning, a warm fog lining the edges of the road.

"Not bad," Adam said. "I think we've got enough to make it to Lexington."

She laughed. "You're dreaming."

"Oh, really?" Adam said. "Care to make it interesting?"

"Fifty bucks says we don't make it to Lexington."

Another eight hours on the road left them running on fumes on the late afternoon of September 5. The Jeep ran dry on the outskirts of Lexington, Kentucky, hitching once, then twice, before quitting for good.

"You owe me fifty bucks," Sarah said as they began unloading their gear from the back of the Jeep. Most of the food and all the water was gone, a victim of the long trek through the wilderness of North Carolina and Virginia.

"No way," Adam said. "The bet was that we had enough gas to make it to Lexington. We are in Lexington."

"Oh, I beg to differ," she said. "We haven't reached the city limits. We may be near Lexington, but we are most certainly not in Lexington. And this Jeep is out of gas."

"Whoa, we never said anything about the city limits."

"You welching on a bet, Fisher?"

He dropped his jaw in mock horror. "I never welch on a bet. But I'm a little short on cash. You think you can give me until next Friday?"

"Have it tomorrow," she said. "Or I'll have your legs broken."

Adam laughed at the absurdity of it all, at the way the world was now, the way that fifty dollars in cash would be better used as kindling for a campfire. He was still laughing as they made their way into town on foot.

It was becoming routine now; as they approached a new town or city, they tied bandannas around their mouths and noses to block the smell, even if just a little bit. The smell was what reminded them how deeply and how widely Medusa had cut them. It was what reminded them that in all those houses and apartment complexes and hospitals and nursing homes were the rotting bodies of countless millions, tens of millions, hundreds of millions of Americans. Someone's daughter or boyfriend or Nana. Now just a smell.

It was this thought occupying his mind as they trekked west along Interstate 64 into the city proper. There was a decent amount of stalled traffic in the eastbound lanes, headed out of the city, but the inbound lanes were mostly empty. That didn't surprise him, since there wasn't a whole hell of a lot behind them. They followed the exit off I-64 down to the main artery through town.

There was a new shopping development at the edge of town, anchored by a series of big box stores. A Kroger, a Home Depot and a Target, all lined up like sentries. The parking lot was mostly deserted, but there were a few cars scattered about like a giant's forgotten toys.

"Hopefully this place hasn't been too badly picked over," Sarah said. "I'm hungry."

She checked her clip as they approached the entrance of the grocery store, always vigilant, as was her wont. Nothing escaped her, Adam had learned, and nothing rattled her. Either that or she had one hell of a poker face.

The doors had been shattered, leaving a puddle of glass bits on the sidewalk. A pungent smell wafted from inside, but it was different than the stench of human decay they'd become so used to. It was chokingly humid, pressing down on them like molten lead. He followed Sarah inside; it was a big store, and there was no way to know if anyone else was inside. They went aisle by aisle, starting in the produce section. The sight of hundreds of pounds of fruits and vegetables decaying in the bright and cheery produce bins was nearly as repulsive as any rotting corpse they'd seen on the road. Rancid juices from the burst skins had puddled on the floor and dried to a sticky residue. Adam had to stifle his gag reflex as they continued through the store.

They saw no one in the first eight aisles. On the ninth aisle, CHIPS/PEANUTS/SNACKS, Sarah held up a fist and motioned around a rack of potato chips, stopping Adam in his tracks. He peeked around the end cap and saw a boy, maybe thirteen or fourteen years old, sitting cross-legged in the middle of the aisle, eating from a bag of Cheetos. He either hadn't heard them or didn't care that he had visitors. His hands and face were caked in orange dust. He was shirtless, wearing mesh shorts and flip-flops. His chest and arms were pockmarked with mosquito bites.

"Hi," Sarah said.

The boy glanced up at them. Then he went back to eating his Cheetos.

"You OK?" Adam asked, worried that they were about to repeat the scene from the Jeep dealership back in Kernersville.

The boy looked up at them again. Then he started crying. As Adam knelt next to him, the boy threw his arms around Adam's shoulders and hugged him tightly. He cried for fifteen minutes, never stopping, not once, never letting go while Adam soothed him. Finally, the crying began to subside, replaced by a series of long, deep breaths.

"What's your name?" Adam asked.

"Max," the boy said. "Max Gilmartin."

The boy's story was his own but not terribly dissimilar to theirs. Tales of surviving the plague were like snowflakes - no two exactly the same, but take just a step back, and they all looked identical: the news stories from the East Coast, and the virus crashing into Lexington like a runaway freight train, then the scenes from your average Saturday after-noon disaster flick playing out *ad nauseam*. He told his tale in one fell swoop, there in the chip aisle, his hand clamped around Adam's elbow as though afraid they might leave him there.

Max and his mom, who'd cleaned rooms at a local motel, had been living in a crumbling apartment complex on the south side of town when the outbreak began. Things had gone downhill in a hurry in Lexington's lower income areas, where people were packed together like rats, where it was hard enough to get medical treatment in summer, when cold and flu season had bottomed out for the year. His mom had died on August 20, and he had no other family nearby, leaving Max to fend for himself for the last two weeks. Since then, he'd been wandering about town, raiding grocery stores and residences for food, sleeping here and there, wondering what the hell he was supposed to do.

When Adam asked him if he wanted to join them, he started crying again.

"Can I bring my Cheetos?" he asked.

Adam smiled.

"Of course," Adam said.

He looked to Sarah for her approval.

She nodded.

"I like Cheetos, too," she said. "But you know what I really like?"

Max shook his head.

"Bubble gum," she said. "You grab the Cheetos, and I'll grab the gum."

IT TOOK them four days and a trying combination of walking and driving, but the trio finally hit the outskirts of St. Louis shortly after noon on September 9. They'd managed the last hundred miles in an Explorer, similar to the one Adam had left back in Holden Beach. The city's skyscrapers were foreboding monoliths, silent giants in the noonday glare. Quilts of middle-class neighborhoods stretched away to the north and south, looking perfectly ordinary on this September day.

They'd been on the road since first light, all of them anxious, perhaps even a little hopeful that the rally point was really there. There had been traffic, even a few pileups to negotiate, but each time, they'd been able to work their way around them. Karma, baby, Adam thought. But as they got closer to St. Louis, the absence of any human activity had him worried that they weren't going to find anything here either.

He and Sarah exchanged glances, their eyebrows raised.

"What's wrong?" Max asked breathlessly from the backseat. "Is something wrong?"

Adam took a deep breath and let it out slowly. He had to remind himself that the kid was lost, adrift, looking for meaning in every word, every look. It was important to him that Adam and Sarah know the score.

"No," he said as gently as he could.

These empty lanes told him no one else was headed for the supposed rally point, that this centerpiece of the Midwest, the gateway to the western states, was as dead as everything they'd seen to the east. The city's residents had tried to flee while they could, for all the good it had done them, and this was the residue left behind. Now Adam had all the information, all the pieces of the puzzle he needed to know that the disaster had been as complete as he had feared. Rachel's report from the West Coast, combined with his own observations on his westward trek gave him the nationwide perspective he'd been simultaneously hoping for and dreading. He realized he'd been hoping that the virus had mutated along the way to a less virulent form, something to help it keep moving and sparing certain parts of the country. But, to steal an analogy from the now defunct world of sports, the Medusa virus had elected to run up the score.

Not very sportsmanlike.

"Where's the rally point?" Adam asked.

"Supposed to be at Busch Stadium."

"Any idea where that is?"

"Not really."

"Think the GPS still works?" Max asked, pointing at the in-dash navigation screen.

"You know what? I bet it would."

Since the GPS wouldn't operate while the car was in motion, Adam drew to a stop in the breakdown lane and punched in the information into the touch screen. They sat silently as the computer processed the request, and when the female voice asked if she could program a route for them to Busch Stadium from their current location just as sweet and pleasant and unoffensive as could be, Sarah burst out laughing. Adam quickly followed, and before you knew it, the three of them were rolling.

"She seems chipper," Sarah said.

"No skin off her back, I guess," Adam said.

They laughed as they continued toward the city proper, through the slums in the east, once notorious in the magazines and Sunday newspaper features as one of the worst neighborhoods in the country but now on the same footing with all the rest. The buildings and cars looked small from this far away, like child's toys left behind on a playground.

A quarter hour later, the Mississippi River came up on them, wide and glassy that afternoon, lazily snaking its way through the heart of America. Adam, who'd never seen it in person, tried focusing on the road, but the river pulled on his gaze time and again. Boats, resembling toys from this distance, rocked in the still waters downriver.

"I just had the most random thought," Adam said.

"What?"

"Is there anyone on the International Space Station? What about a Navy ship or submarine out in the Atlantic? Or an oil rig down in the Gulf?"

"Jesus," Sarah said. "I hadn't thought about that."

"I don't understand," Max said.

"There could be people in all those places," Adam said. "People who weren't exposed to the virus. They could still be healthy. They might be out there right now, wondering what to do."

"What would happen to them if they came back?"

"I don't know," he said. "I really don't know. I don't know if we're carrying the virus inside our bodies. I don't know if it's lurking somewhere or if it burned off. Or if it's mutated."

His mind drifted to the world they'd be facing, and it was more than he could process. Traffic on the river itself would be nonexistent in the coming weeks and months, giving the river a chance to repair the environmental damage it had suffered in the last few centuries. Strange thoughts. Strange days.

"Look," Max said, pointing ahead.

They were approaching an overpass, atop which Adam could make out two figures staring out down across the highway.

"Holy shit!" Max exclaimed. "He's got a gun!"

Adam cocked his head for a better view and could just make out the glint of gunmetal in the sunshine. A round slammed into the concrete about twenty yards away, the report of the gun echoing off the automobile graveyard surrounding them.

"Jesus H. Christ!"

He yanked the wheel to the right.

"Stay calm," Sarah barked. "How's the road ahead look?"

Adam tore his gaze away from the overpass and peered down the highway. The dead traffic had thickened here like trans fats clogging an artery. He decelerated and slalomed his way around the abandoned vehicles. Another few seconds brought them directly under the overpass, just as the shooter prepared to fire.

"It's getting a little crowded here," he said, as a second shot shattered the windshield of an abandoned box truck in the eastbound lanes.

"He's firing blind," she said, a steely conviction in her voice. "He's not a good shot. Just take the next exit and drop down into the city."

Another shot exploded behind them, followed by a loud pop; the car shimmied underneath him and fishtailed.

"We blew a tire, we blew a tire!"

"Shows how much I know," Sarah muttered.

He eased off the gas and steadied the steering wheel until the car rolled to a stop in the middle of the freeway, not far from the exit ramp.

Then another shotgun blast.

"We're gonna have to run for it," Adam said, hoping he was covering the panic he was feeling.

"Max, swing your door open, but stay in the car."

"I don't wanna get out of the car."

He was ramrod still, his eyes shut tight, his hand clenched into little chubby fists.

"Max, it'll be OK. We're up against the jersey wall. We're gonna stay low, and the door will shield us. Max. We can't stay here. I'll make sure you're safe.

"Give me your hand," Adam said, reaching toward the kid.

Max shook his head violently, like a child refusing his medicine.

"Max," Adam said, his voice dropping in volume. "We're going to do this together."

Slowly, the boy slid his hand into Adam's; it was cold and clammy.

"Now with your other hand, swing the door open."

Max swung the door open. The edge caught the jersey wall, making a nails-on-chalkboard screech. Adam retrieved his gun from the console and nodded toward Sarah, who slipped out onto the shoulder with her M4 slung across her back. Max scurried over the center console and followed Sarah out the door. As Adam brought up the rear, a shell shattered the rear windshield. Max screamed.

"Stay low, stay low!" Sarah hissed. She squeezed off a burst at the overpass. The roar of the machine gun fractured the morning, its chatter making everything seem harder and more real. The shooter ducked below the railing, pushed back by the threat of Sarah's heavy gun. Sarah kept the gun trained on his position, and when he reappeared, she took his head off with a short burst from the M4.

They hugged the wall as they scampered east; Adam crab-walked, keeping an eye on the road behind him, listening for footfalls, the click of more shells being chambered. He didn't know if there was one potential killer or three or twenty.

He glanced up the road and saw the exit ramp fifty yards off. More gunfire peppered the afternoon air. Sarah waved Adam and Max past her. Then, using a shiny Lexus coupe for cover, she rose up and fired a burst from the M4 at the second shooter. Adam paused, Max's hand sweaty and tight in his own. Then he shimmied up next to Sarah and drew his gun.

"What the hell are you doing?"

"Helping," he said, although it came out more as a question.

"You ever seen combat?"

"No," he said.

"Get him the hell out of here," she said, nodding toward Max. "I'll meet you at the bottom of the next exit. Go!"

Adam pressed the butt of the gun to his forehead, his teeth clenched. Back toward the overpass, an angry voice bit into the air.

"Go!"

As he turned back toward Max, he spotted a figured closing in from the east, also sliding down along the jersey wall.

"Sarah!"

She swung her attention toward Adam as he gestured wildly to the east. Then she slipped around the front of the Lexus, staying low but leaving herself very exposed.

Adam fumbled with the gun, but it was slippery in his sweaty hands, which were moving in slow motion. The figure drew closer, but Adam still couldn't make the gun work. He might as well have been trying to defend himself and Max with a jar of peanut butter.

Then a stitch of gunfire slammed the man against the wall, and he slid to the asphalt, quite dead. Blood smeared the wall where his body had impacted it. Sarah emerged from between two cars in that lane, her gun still trained on the man.

She slid his gun away from his body with her foot, and Adam exhaled.

21

They made it unmolested to the bottom of the exit ramp and onto 4th Street, which ran north through the stadium area. Adam's heart continued to race in the wake of the little skirmish at the overpass, and he was having a hard time concentrating. He'd known such a thing was possible, even likely, as the world drifted away from the shoreline of civilization, but it had been so harsh and vivid and sudden that he'd barely been able to react. Why had it happened? To what end? The more he thought about it, the more he worried he wouldn't be long for a world like this. How Sarah had done it, he'd never know. She'd say it was her years of training that had kicked in, muscle memory, but it was more than that. It was something he didn't think he had.

"Look at all the bodies," Max whispered as they made their way north.

Max was right. There appeared to be an unusually high concentration of victims here.

"Adam," Sarah said. "Look over to your left."

Adam turned his head and saw Busch Stadium rising in the shimmering afternoon sun. Not twelve months earlier, this place had hosted the National League Championship Series, which the hometown Cardinals had lost in five games to the Washington Nationals. It was hard not to overlay his memories of baseball on top of the empty shell that lay before them.

They were on the stadium's east side now, cutting in between the stadium and the Gateway Arch Park to their right. Adam didn't know what they were supposed to be looking for, but it looked a lot like everything else they had seen. They passed a parking lot full of abandoned military vehicles. At the corner of 4th and Clarke, sandbags and a machine-gun battery.

"See anything?" he asked.

Sarah held her M4 tight.

"Let's find the main entrance," she said. "Stay close."

Dread crawled up Adam's back like a snake.

"There's no one here," Adam said. "We should get out of here."

"I've got my orders."

Adam held his tongue. There'd be no arguing with her. She had her orders.

They proceeded west on Clarke Street, moving slowly, their backs to one another to give them a 360-degree sweep of the area. As they fell into a rhythm, the silence engulfed them like a heavy blanket. They heard nothing and saw no one as they drew closer to the stadium's main entrance. The stench was horrific, deeper and stronger than Adam had smelled yet. Weeks of immeasurable human decomposition was finally peaking.

Sawhorses lined the front entrance of the stadium, but there was no one guarding them. Bodies of soldiers, some wearing gas masks, littered the concourse. The trio passed under the black metal arches, gleaming in the afternoon sun, up the ramp and into the bowels of the stadium. Shuttered concession stands and a dark souvenir store greeted them as they moved along the outer concourse. There were hundreds of bodies in here. Adam felt Max press his body up against him.

Then they were in the bleachers, staring out across the empty field, this dead cathedral to America. Thousands of bodies were scattered through the stands, their empty, bloated faces staring at them, waiting for a game that would never begin. The outfield grass had grown long and rippled in the afternoon breeze, but the infield was still groomed, the white lines marking the baselines still pristine. Tents bearing the logo of the Federal Emergency Management Administration lined the warning track, but they, too, were abandoned, silent. A few crows and vultures here and there, pecking at the remains.

"I just had to be sure," Sarah said, as they descended the steps.

"We should check the tents for supplies," Adam said.

A burst of birdcall above them, and Adam looked up to see the sky darken with hundreds of blackbirds swirling about like a cloud. They flew lazily, in circles, as though the offerings of carrion were so vast, so varied, they didn't know where to begin. A lifetime of dining on squirrels and field mice had been replaced with the greatest buffet line they'd ever seen.

As he watched the birds, his stomach swirled, the dead stadium a gut punch, more than he cared to admit. It had represented the last best chance that humanity still had a pulse, faint as it might have been, and seeing that it was gone left him dizzy. There was nothing. You expect something bad to happen, but there's still that tiny sliver of hope, stuck in your mind like a splinter, that it might still go the other way. But then the bad thing happens, and you're looking at it, and it's just as bad as you feared and there's nothing you can do. They stood there for a full ten minutes, long enough to feel the sun's rays grow uncomfortably warm on their necks and arms.

"Max, you ever been on a major league field before?" Adam asked.

"Uh, no."

"Follow me."

"What are you doing?" Sarah asked.

"Just taking a little break," Adam replied. "Ten, fifteen minutes."

"We should probably get a move on," Sarah said.

"I can't right now," Adam said. "I just need a break."

They found bats and balls and gloves in the Cardinals dugout. Adam threw fat batting practice pitches to Max, who had a nice, natural swing and even put a couple into the outfield. Around them, the empty faces of the dead watched them play baseball. Maybe this wasn't the wisest use of their time, Adam realized, but he didn't care. Rachel, if she was even still alive, was two thousand miles away, and what the hell, he might as well throw a little batting practice.

As he reared back to fire another pitch in toward the plate, Adam froze suddenly. Just over Sarah's shoulder, an enormous man was approaching them, carrying in his arms a wisp of a woman.

"Hey!" he barked. "This the testing center?"

Sarah turned to face the newcomers, her machine gun raised up and ready for business.

"Don't move!" Sarah called out.

"She needs help," the man said, dipping his chin toward his human cargo.

Then the man froze and took in the full scope of the scene before him. His head rotated from one side to the other.

Sarah looked over at Adam, who nodded toward her.

"It might be a trap."

"No!" the woman called out. "I'm pregnant!"

The news galvanized Adam like a shot of adrenaline to the heart. Pregnant. He got a good look at her swollen belly. At least thirty-five weeks along, Adam surmised. Close to full term, close to finding out up close and personal and that pretty goddamn soon whether babies were immune to the Medusa virus.

"It's OK," Max called out, holding his hands up high. "He's a doctor."

"Oh, my God, are you for real?" she said, bursting into tears.

The man looked down at the woman and whispered something to her; she nodded and squeezed his shoulder. He took her down into the dugout and propped her up on the bench. A makeshift splint framed her right leg.

Images of babies dying of Medusa flooded Adam's brain, and he didn't want to be anywhere near this woman. He didn't want them to know he was a doctor. He didn't want to be the one who couldn't do anything for her. What was he going to do, perform a C-section there in the dugout with some plastic cutlery?

They waited.

Finally, Adam followed them down the steps to the dugout and took a knee next to her. The floor was still sticky with tobacco dip and sunflower seed shells.

"You really a doctor?" she asked.

He chewed on his lower lip; he could just lie and say the kid had been making it up, and maybe Sarah would go along with him because she would understand he had some reason for doing so. But in the end, he couldn't.

"Yes."

He saw a big smile spread across the woman's face, and she gently placed her hands on her abdomen.

"Don't suppose you're an OB?"

"I am in fact an OB."

"Jesus. I guess this is my lucky day. Are you a good one?"

"Best in the city."

She laughed and broke into tears simultaneously.

He was glad they'd shared the joke. Humor was humanity's great glue, yoking people together for thousands of years. That was something, he thought, as he drew closer, keeping one eye on her massive companion.

"When are you due?" he asked.

A breeze rustled through the shadowy dugout, cooling them.

"September twenty-fifth."

"How's the pregnancy been?"

"Pretty uneventful," she said.

"Baby been active?"

She nodded.

"Rome burned, and he kept right on kicking," she said.

"It's a boy?"

"Yeah."

"Well, the kicking's good," Adam said. "Real good."

He pointed at her belly and held up his hands. "Do you mind if I examine your stomach?"

"Go ahead."

"You mind lifting up your shirt for me?" he asked, wanting her to be the one to expose her belly. "Just halfway so I can get a look at your stomach."

He gently palpated her stomach, feeling for the head. A moment later, he felt the baby squirm and roll, twisting away from his manipulations.

"Any allergies?"

"No."

"I'd feel more comfortable with an ultrasound machine, but things seem right on track. I'd say another couple weeks."

Her face lit up, and her eyes were wet with tears.

"Thank God," she said. "I haven't seen a doctor since July."

"Well, let's hope your luck holds out."

"Will you deliver the baby?"

There was no way around it. In this new paradigm, not doing his job would put her life in danger. Too many things could go wrong. People thought that delivering babies was a simple matter, and maybe in the grand scheme of things, across the giant sample size that had been humanity, it had been. Most babies and mothers survived their delivery. Most. But this woman would be playing against a stacked deck. It wasn't going to be easy for her with that broken leg, even with another two weeks of healing.

"Of course," he said. "I don't know how many obstetricians are running around these days. I can't promise you everything modern medicine could have delivered two months ago, but we'll do our best."

She reached out and squeezed his hand.

"Thank you," she said, tears in her eyes. "It's been a while since I've heard any good news."

Her eyes narrowed, and her face turned to stone. He knew what was coming, and he began working on an answer before the words were out of her mouth.

"Will the baby catch it?"

"You don't beat around the bush, do you?"

She gave him a wan smile.

"I'm not going to lie to you," he said. "I really don't know."

He searched for something to say, but anything else would have been superfluous, the wilted lettuce lying alongside the entree.

The thin smile disappeared.

"At least you're honest."

"We're probably past the point of lying to make each other feel better," Adam said. "Let's move on. How's the leg feeling?"

"I guess it's healing. Itches like hell."

"That's the bone stitching back together. Mind if I take a look?"

"Think we're getting to know each other pretty well, Doctor.... Oh my God, I don't even know your name."

"It's Dr. Fisher," he said. "But you can call me Adam."

"I think I'll stick with Dr. Fisher," she said. "At least until the baby comes."

"Fair enough."

"My name's Caroline," she said.

"Caroline, I'm sorry we're meeting under these crappy circumstances."

He examined the splint carefully, not wanting to jiggle the leg. There was a dull yellow bruise about the size of a silver dollar about midway between the kneecap and the ankle, and the flesh was slightly swollen.

"When did this happen?" he asked.

"About ten days ago."

"How?"

"Fell down some stairs," she said. "I guess I was lucky I didn't fall on my stomach."

"How's the pain?" he asked.

"It comes and goes," she said. "It seems to be getting better."

"Well, given the circumstances, I think you're doing pretty well. You let me know if he stops kicking."

He gazed up at her companion, who'd been watching him like a hawk, and extended a hand. He was enormous, an amazing physical specimen. A purple and gold LSU t-shirt was drawn tight against his massive chest. His biceps were cut like diamonds.

"Adam Fisher."

The man returned the shake, Adam's hand virtually getting lost in his paw.

"Fred Briggs."

Strangely, the name rang a bell for Adam, but he didn't know why. Certainly, he'd remember having met a guy this big, this imposing.

"So there's nothing here?" the man asked. He glanced over his shoulder and saw Sarah had joined them in the dugout; her M4 was still out, but much to Adam's relief, she had lowered the muzzle.

Freddie looked over at her, wiped a hand over his scalp, which was shiny with sweat.

"No," Adam replied. "Whatever was supposed to be here, it didn't happen."

A gunshot in the distance cracked the silence.

"We're headed for California," Adam said. "It's safer out on the roads than in the big cities. At the very least, it doesn't smell as bad."

"Why there?" Freddie asked.

"My daughter might still be alive out there," Adam said. "Had to give it a shot."

"You think the immunity is hereditary?" Caroline asked, her voice spiced with hope.

Adam weighed his response carefully.

"I really don't know," he said. "If she's still alive, it's possible there's a genetic component to it. I don't know if there are any other cases where a parent and child both survived."

"My kids weren't immune," Freddie said darkly. "They died just the same."

"Oh, Freddie," Caroline began, "I'm sorry. I'm so sorry. I didn't mean..."

He stomped up the dugout steps and toward the infield.

"What's his story?" Adam asked when they were alone.

"God, I've been such a pain in the ass," she said to Adam and Sarah. "I've been so worried about the baby and this damn leg that it never occurred to me to even ask about his family."

"Don't beat yourself up." Sarah said. "I'll talk to him."

Adam watched her follow Freddie, who had drifted over toward the concourse.

"Is this guy OK?" Adam asked.

"I know he's rough," Caroline said. "But he saved my life. Twice. I can't judge him."

Adam didn't know how to process that, so he let it slide for now.

"So what do you think about taking a little road trip?" he asked. "Free medical care the whole way. No co-pays."

"That is pretty tempting," she said, a smile spreading across her face. "I still can't believe you're a doctor."

He held up an index finger.

"Hang on."

He extracted his wallet from his back pocket.

"Still carrying your wallet?"

"Old habits die hard," he replied as he thumbed through the Visa card, the driver's license, the membership card from Sam's Club. A wave of nostalgia, a strong one, swept through him, as he thought back to the last time he'd swiped his debit card for a Starbucks coffee, the last time he'd run into a grocery store to grab a few things.

"Here."

He held out his Physician's ID card issued to him by the Virginia Commonwealth University Hospital. She waved him off, but he kept the card out, pinched between the index and middle fingers of his right hand. Finally, she took it from him and gave it a once-over.

"So there it is," she said.

"There it is."

Caroline burst into tears; she held a hand over her mouth and took several deep breaths, but she couldn't stop crying.

"It'll be OK," he said.

Even though he really didn't know that.

Gunfire peppered the afternoon again, this burst closer than the first.

"We need to get on the road," he said.

"OK," she said. "I'll come with you."

"You think your friend will join us?"

"Yeah," she said. "Yeah, I think he will. He's been so good to me. I don't know why. I've been shitty to him. Like I said, he saved me."

She paused, and her eyes welled with tears.

"It's been hard out there," she said softly.

"I'm glad you're coming with us," he said. "I think there's strength in numbers. Look, I don't know if my daughter is still alive. Maybe it's a pipe dream. But it gives me something to work towards."

Freddie resisted at first, but when he saw there would be no changing Caroline's mind, he dropped his objection to the two groups joining forces as a quintet. Adam still wasn't sure about him. He was wound tight, like old nitroglycerin. But despite his own personal loss, he'd been looking out for this woman he hadn't ever met before a month ago, putting aside any wishes or thoughts or wants or even needs for her benefit. That had to be worth something.

Freddie went to retrieve their vehicle while Sarah and Adam scoured the FEMA tents for supplies. It proved to be a bonanza. They found several cases of bottled water and dozens of MREs. Toilet paper. After loading the new supplies, they were off, winding their way back toward Interstate 64. By late afternoon, the city was behind them, the pickup truck chewing up highway as they headed west. In a couple of spots where the traffic was too snarled to negotiate, they had to double back and detour off the interstate, but there was a well-maintained access road paralleling the main highway.

Adam didn't know what to think, what to feel. He rolled down the window and propped his elbow on the door as Freddie slalomed around the dead traffic. Finding Caroline and Freddie, that had to mean something, right? What were the odds this pregnant woman, a few weeks from delivery, stumbles across likely one of the few surviving obstetricians in the country?

He was glad they found her, as much for him as for her.

He *was* a good doctor, as his boss Joe McCann had said that day, the morning he'd suspended him. The Baby Wall had been a testament to that. He could see their faces, their beautiful, innocent faces and he couldn't help but wonder if a single child from that wall was still alive. A flashback to the office, Joe mentioning offhand that he hadn't been feeling well that morning. Jesus, he thought, his skin crawling. Had Joe already been sick with Medusa? He'd probably seen a dozen patients in the office, countless more at the hospital, before he'd become too sick to continue.

This made Adam's insides clench with sadness, but at the same time, he was glad to be alive. He wasn't ready to die. How glad he was that there was a good chance that Rachel was still alive. That Caroline and her baby wouldn't have to do it alone.

He glanced back at Max, who had fallen asleep on Sarah's shoulder. For the first time since they'd met, his young face looked its actual age. It was smooth and unlined, as though all the stress and panic bunched up on his face had drained away like heavy rains into a storm drain. Caroline napped too.

The sun was warm on his elbow as the St. Louis metro area shrank rapidly in the mirrors, the urban terrain morphing into the western suburbs and far western exurbs. Ahead, the road was wide and open and clear, the air fragrant with the smell of rain. Dark clouds to the west portended afternoon thunderstorms.

They were in a hell of a pickle, he knew that. Each and every safety net all of them had depended on for decades was gone forever. Things could get bad in a hurry, as the thunderheads up the road well proved. The lightning flashed and the thunder rumbled gutturally in the distance, and he hoped it wasn't an omen of things to come.

22

It was slow going west of St. Louis. Even when the roads had been clear, it was becoming increasingly uncomfortable for Caroline to travel, necessitating frequent breaks along the way. They used these breaks to scout for supplies, which required constant replenishment. Sarah took these opportunities to restock her chewing gum and Max's supply of Cheetos, which he ate nonstop. They probably couldn't let that go on forever, but for now, it seemed like it was OK. Caroline got in on the act as well, requesting ready-to-eat pepperoni. Adam loaded up on chocolate bars. Nothing for Freddie, though, which irritated Sarah to no end.

"Are you sure?" Sarah had asked, as she'd headed out on a supply run one afternoon. "Anything you want. My treat."

"Nothing for me," he'd said.

Jerk.

Approaching Kansas City on the morning of September 13, they'd encountered the worst traffic jam they'd seen since leaving St. Louis. Salina, about 180 miles to the west, had been their target that day, but the gridlock in Kansas City had forced them to abandon Freddie's truck, which, in turn, had created the problem of transporting a still-immobile Caroline. They'd spent much of the day looking for a wheelchair for her, and by the time they'd found one in a small hospital on the north side of town, the day was shot. On the plus side, Adam had assembled a bag of medical supplies he'd need on hand for Caroline's delivery.

So at dusk on the thirteenth, they'd set up shop near a heavy truck dealership just west of Kansas City. Beyond the dealership was a grassy plain stretching north to the horizon. Sarah and Adam checked the building, made sure it was clear. It was, and as an added bonus, it had running water and showers. The water was cold, ice cold, but that was fine with them. Sarah had stood under the water until she was shivering, until she'd scrubbed days of grime and grit from her body. She scrubbed until her skin was pink, until the smell of the soap seemed entwined with her DNA.

Freddie and Adam got to work making dinner while Sarah and Max conducted a sweep of the camp.

"How come we never stay in houses?" Max asked as they walked the perimeter.

"Well, Adam said it would be best if we stayed away from the cities and towns," she said. "Things aren't exactly very clean."

"Because of all the bodies, right?"

"Yeah. Because of the bodies."

"Can I tell you something?" Max asked.

"Sure, sweetie," she said as her eyes swept the desolate plains before them.

"I used to think the apocalypse would be cool," he said.

She smiled.

"It's not what you thought, huh?"

"I always thought it would be zombies," he said. Then, his voice softening: "Thought I'd be really good at killing zombies. I used to play this game called *Dead Men Walking* all the time. I feel so stupid. No, it hasn't been what I thought. It's been horrible."

"Know what?" Sarah said, softly.

"What?"

"You weren't the only person who thought like that," she said. "I knew some grownups who thought it would be cool for the world to end. Even some soldiers."

"Are any of them still alive?"

She smiled at him.

"No."

"Why do people think like that? Did they think it would be fun to watch everyone they know die? Did they think it would be fun to not know if you'd have enough food and water?"

"I don't know, sweetie," she said. "I think some people who weren't happy about-"

"Sarah!" he hissed, pointing toward something. "Look!"

Sarah followed the point of his finger toward a figure lying on the ground. The man was as dead as he could be, lying in a thick pool of rust-colored blood. Most of his head was missing, the result of its encounter with a large-caliber bullet. He was young, late teens, twenty at the most. He wore cargo shorts and a long-sleeve t-shirt, both were dark with blood stains.

Max screamed, the howl piercing the late-afternoon stillness, high-pitched, thin, a throwback to the pre-pubescent boy he'd been not too long ago. Sarah pulled Max close to her and clapped her left hand against his mouth. Then she unslung her M4 from her shoulder.

"Shhh."

The scream died in his throat, and he pressed up against her. Sarah scanned the area, keeping her finger tight on the trigger, but she detected no movement. Her head continued rotating in the silence. The tendons in her neck strained and popped as she did so. She could feel Max's hot tears plopping on her arm, his whole body quivering with fear.

The second body was about fifty feet distant, the clothes soaked in blood. And beyond that, a third body. And a fourth. All butchered.

"THEY'RE ALL MEN," Sarah said after she'd conducted a quick search of the camp.

The wind had kicked up, the polyester skins of the tents flapping in the afternoon breeze. The tents had been arranged in a half-moon shape at the base of a hill, in the shade of a line of pines.

"So?" Freddie said.

"But there were at least two women with them."

"How do you figure?" Adam asked.

She waved him over with her right hand and led him from tent to tent.

"Four bodies, but there are six sleeping bags."

"How do you know there were women here?"

She cocked her head at him. Jesus, men could be so dense.

"Come here," she said. "Poke your head in this tent and take a whiff."

Adam complied with her request.

"You smell that?"

"What am I smelling for?"

"Jesus. Perfume."

"Oh yeah, now I smell it."

"Eternity," she said. "Calvin Klein. I used to wear it."

There were two backpacks in this tent, one containing women's clothing and other female personal effects. A wallet, black, leather and worn good, was tucked inside the pack. The driver's license inside had belonged to Patricia Williams, a resident of Indianapolis. The photograph hadn't done her much justice, if there was any to be done. Her hair was stringy, and a leathery face made her look ten years older than she was. But she seemed like a nice enough woman, certainly better than those who had unleashed the carnage in her camp.

"What happened?" Max asked, still rattled by the gruesomeness of the scene.

Sarah chewed on her lip as she thought about how to respond. On the one hand, Max was still a boy, still negotiating that shaky rope bridge between adolescence and manhood. On the other hand, circumstances now dictated he was going to have to grow up a lot faster than he might have otherwise. Sugarcoating things might backfire, make him feel like the world was safer than it really was. And it could seem safe now, what with going a day or two without even sniffing another human being. The sooner he understood the way the world worked, the better.

"I think the women in this camp were taken," she said.

"Taken?" Caroline repeated. "Taken where?"

Sarah shook her head, not wanting to give a voice to her darkest thoughts, about where these two women were right now, what they were enduring.

"Hey, look at this," Caroline called out.

Sarah followed Caroline's gaze, which was fixed on the side of a tent. A strange bit of graffiti had been spray-painted in black across the side of the tent. A silhouette of a large bird against an unidentifiable backdrop.

Max thought the image looked like a set of sharp, pointy teeth, whereas Adam posited a roaring fire.

"Like a phoenix?" Freddie offered.

"Possibly."

Sarah felt a chill ripple through her. Bad enough they were traipsing through a human wasteland, eating canned goods, no idea what the future held for any of them. The dirt on the grave of the world still fresh, and already they're dealing with some kind of roaming death squad? This kind of thing was for shitty cable movies on Saturday afternoons.

She glanced at Adam, his arms crossed against his chest, his middle finger tapping against his bicep like a metronome. It was a pose she'd noticed him assume when he was deep in thought. The others had begun looking to him as the leader, even if Freddie had done so reluctantly. Guilt coursed through her, but that didn't mean she was sorry to transfer the weight of leadership to someone else's shoulders. It was the logical choice. Freddie was fixated on Caroline, who herself was busy with the business of healing and being pregnant. And she was a foot soldier. She took orders. Besides, who wanted to take orders from someone with a death wish? She glanced at Adam again.

Her conversation with Max replayed in her head. She hadn't been entirely honest with the boy. Yes, she had known soldiers who'd wished for an apocalypse. But she'd left out the part that she'd been one of them. It was so goddamn unfair, to know you were already dying at the age of thirty. To hear others talk about the future, about families, about careers, about this or that, when she was staring a death sentence in the face, it was enough to make anyone a little cuckoo. But the universe had seemed hell-bent on making her face her destiny, even as it had wiped the world clean of all those she'd once envied, the ones who had justifiably thought they had decades ahead of them, long, fruitful, more-or-less happy lives, those that now lay dead like abandoned toys.

THEY CAMPED six miles up the road. Adam had hoped to get farther, but the group was exhausted, and Caroline had been complaining of severe back pain. It was an undeveloped parcel of land, clear-cut, easy to patrol. A pair of bulldozers sat at the edge of the property, waiting for drivers who would never be coming back to work. A large billboard reading *8 Acres Available NOW – Call Agent Bernice Sim!* stood at the edge of the tract.

Dinner was eaten in silence. No one wanted to cook, so they settled on protein bars and Gatorade. The discovery of the bodies had drained away what little life their merry little band had. Caroline was asleep within minutes of dinner's end, and Max joined her moments later. After dinner, Adam administered the last of the series of rabies shots. Well, he thought, as he depressed the plunger into his arm. That was that. The vaccine would either work or it wouldn't.

"We'll keep two on the perimeter all night," Adam said with as much authority as he could muster. "We'll stagger the shifts so that each of us can get a little sleep. Freddie, you stay here with these two."

Freddie nodded, the look in his eye of someone who had no intention of sleeping, and Adam and Sarah set out on the first shift. She gave him some pointers about using the gun as they circled the camp, but eventually, the conversation drifted off into silence. They walked quietly for a while. In the shadow of what they'd found earlier, everything seemed petty right now.

"Ask you a question?" Sarah asked.

"Sure."

"Let's say we find your daughter."

"Rachel."

"Right, Rachel. Say we find her."

"We'll find her!"

"Okay. But what then?"

"What do you mean?"

"What next?" she asked. "How do you spend the rest of your days?"

"I guess we do what anyone else left will do. Join up with other survivors. Find a safe place to live. Clean water. Food. I don't know. Maybe write a book."

She laughed at that, a light, infectious laugh that danced across the space between them and for a moment made him forget all the problems surrounding them, a broken world shattered into a million pieces. He glanced over at her, and saw a wide smile on her face. She wasn't looking at him, she wasn't really looking at anything. She just seemed to be enjoying the fact that she was enjoying something.

She ran a hand through her hair, tugging on the end of her jet-black locks, and a flash of sadness flickered across her face. She flipped her ponytail behind her back with authority, as though she'd caught herself engaging in childish thoughts, and the time for that was over.

"What?" he asked.

She shrugged.

"This might be the way things are for a while. We're gonna have to be extra careful."

"I realize that," he said.

"And, you know..." she said, her voice softening. "I just think it's important to stay realistic about what we're doing."

She doesn't think we'll ever find her.

They stood perfectly still, their eyes locking in the late-summer night. The silence was overwhelming, crushing, almost suffocating. Humanity's very existence had sported an ambient noise, a kind of radio static buzzing at the lowest threshold of one's attention, but now, with mankind scrubbed away like a chalkboard at the end of the school day, it was gone.

The look on his face must have given him away, told her he was bruising for an argument about it, readying his catalog of reasons why she was still alive, because she fell silent and resumed their patrol around the camp. He bit his tongue because he didn't want to make an impassioned argument totally devoid of objectivity only to realize a month from now that Sarah had been right all along, that Rachel was gone, vanished into the ether. Her surviving the plague was just one piece of the puzzle and that alone didn't mean he'd ever find her. Even if he made it to Tahoe in the next couple weeks, that didn't mean she would still be there. For all Rachel knew, he had died in the plague. And their link, the cell phones, was gone. Although he'd managed to charge his phone using a car adapter, it had been a week since he'd been able to draw any signal at all, rendering the device a useless brick.

These thoughts swirled about as Sarah continued her patrol, her head sweeping from side to side, using a flashlight to blow away the darkness. There was a hint of a chill in the air, nothing fierce really, but a coolness they hadn't felt yet in their time on the road. He didn't know much about this part of the country, particularly its late-summer weather patterns, and so he reminded himself they needed to start thinking about properly outfitting themselves for the elements.

He fell in step beside Sarah again.

"What do you think you'll miss the most?" she asked. "From before, I mean. Something you took for granted."

He thought about this for a moment, searching his memory banks for the things that had made the old world his own.

"There was a little barbecue place around the corner from where I lived," he said. "Ralph's, it was called. Made the best pulled pork sandwich I've ever had. They had this hot pepper vinegar. I probably ate there two, three times a week. Bring it home after work, sit on the couch. Slap your momma good."

"Excuse me?"

"You never heard that? Something so good it makes you want to slap your own mother?"

"Can't say that I have."

He looked at her and saw her smiling wistfully at his anecdote. Stupid as it was, he could see himself, weary after a long day at work, carrying a bag of greasy food into his house, plopping down at his old coffee table, eating his dinner while watching episodes of *Family Guy* he'd saved on his DVR. Now that he thought about it, he couldn't even remember the last time he had done it, and that pissed him off. Never had it been more apparent that he hadn't enjoyed the little things than in the face of their total disappearance.

"You?" he asked.

"Christmas," she said. "Christmas lights. I know people complained about how commercial everything had gotten, but it didn't bother me. I loved the sweaters and the decorations and the smell of Christmas dinner. I think being on duty a lot at Christmas made it easier to really like it. They tried to go all out for us when we were overseas."

"Well, I don't think commercialism at Christmas is going to be a problem this year."

"No. No, I guess not."

Her eyes shone in the moonlight, and he became conscious of how close they were standing. She was almost as tall as he was, maybe an inch shorter, and it was easy to stand there looking into her eyes, watching her chew on the corner of her lower lip when she was thinking about something, as he'd seen her do several times.

"Yeah," she said. "I think Christmas is the thing I will miss the most."

Adam leaned in and kissed her gently. Her lips tasted like the peppermint gum she chewed constantly. Every nerve ending in his body lit up, the kiss feeling new and fresh and yet like something he'd done a million times before. She leaned in, sliding her hand around the back of his head, their bodies pressed against one another, full of racing heat in a cold world of the lost and the dead, but she suddenly pulled away.

"I'm sorry," she said. "I can't."

"I, uh…" He started to say he was sorry, but that would have been a lie. He wasn't sorry.

"I, um…" she began, brushing her lips with a fingertip. "Maybe we split up for the rest of the shift."

He cleared his throat.

She looked down at her watch.

"Freddie's due to come on in an hour," she said. "I'm pretty wired, so you take the next break, and I'll take the one after that."

"You sure?"

"Yeah," she said.

He circled the perimeter for another hour, savoring the taste of her lips on his own, feeling somewhat stupid. Good job, Adam.

Freddie was awake when he went back to camp, sitting in the cone of light spilled by the LED lantern. Caroline and Max slept just beyond the shadows.

"You get some rest?" he asked the big man.

He nodded slowly, barely making eye contact with Adam. Adam unrolled his sleeping bag and slid in, feeling that anticipation of a good night's rest earned after a hard day.

"Are you OK?" he asked, propping himself up on his elbow.

"Fine," Freddie replied. He stood up and dusted off his legs. "Gun?"

Adam paused ever so slightly at the request, not long enough that Freddie noticed, but long enough that Adam wondered why he had done it at all. He handed the gun over to Freddie, the barrel pointing toward the ground like Sarah had taught them.

A yawn escaped Adam as Freddie joined Sarah on the watch. The two chatted briefly and then took up opposite positions on the imaginary circle surrounding the camp. After they fell into their respective patrols, Adam lay on his back and looked skyward. The stars were bright, burning their ancient fire millions of light years away, totally indifferent to the cataclysm that had enveloped this blue-green rock.

This is it now, he thought. This is the way things are. His little house on Floyd Avenue was empty, surrounded by other empty houses. The sidewalks were quiet, the bars and restaurants dark and stuffy and hot. School wouldn't be starting up this fall, no groan of yellow buses chugging through the neighborhoods. There would be no college football. No Halloween parties or pumpkin-spiced coffee or mall Christmas displays two months before anyone was ready to see them. It was all gone.

He was tired, but sleep wouldn't come. As much as Sarah's rejection had stung, it wasn't her she was thinking of. Instead, he found his thoughts swirling around Freddie Briggs. He still hadn't said much to anyone but Caroline; his devotion to her was nothing short of evangelical, the way a man might cleave to God after a miraculous experience. Adam didn't know if it was powered by love, dominance, obsession, duty, or some combination of the four. He seemed like a decent man, but Adam had been hoping they'd have made a deeper connection by now. They'd been on the road for days, and Adam knew nothing about him other than his name and that Caroline trusted him.

He lay awake for hours, thinking about the way he'd paused when Freddie had asked for the gun.

23

A few minutes before eight in the morning, Miles Chadwick entered the communal area of the *de facto* women's dormitory in the northwest corner of the compound. Tucked under his arm were the dossiers on the twelve women his hunting parties had rounded up in the previous week. Several cups of coffee sloshed around his stomach, but they had done little for the gumminess in his eyes. Sleep had eluded him again, as it had since they'd confirmed that Citadel women were infertile. He probably needed to try a sleeping pill, as he could feel the cloudiness increasing in his thinking process, an approaching cold front in his mind. He needed to be sharp, to make sure these women understood what their new roles were.

Twelve women.

He'd been hoping for twice that number, but the Citadel was, in some ways, a victim of its own morbid success. It had taken a lot longer than he'd anticipated to round up these twelve, let alone the two dozen he was hoping for, and they'd had to range out much farther from the compound. It was just more evidence of the totality of Medusa's work. Already, the hunting parties had drifted as far east as Illinois, north to Sioux Falls. Wichita to the south, west to the Nebraska/Colorado border. Some days, they wouldn't see a single survivor.

His orders had been simple. Find women of childbearing age and bring them back. Kill everyone else. This served to begin thinning the ranks of potential threats to the Citadel, albeit slowly, but then again, Rome hadn't been built in a day either. Ordering these executions pricked him with guilt, needling at him like a paper cut. Strange, really, given the fact he was guilty of murdering billions of people, but ordering the executions of Medusa survivors had seemed particularly barbaric to Chadwick. Simply by not succumbing to the virus, these folks had managed the nearly impossible, and here he was, having them murdered for the effort. Part of him wanted to bring them all in, part of the new regime building a new world from the ashes.

But he couldn't do that.

Control.

Everything had to be carefully controlled, especially in these early months and years. The future would depend on what they did now, the steps they took now. And introducing too many variables too soon could threaten everything.

Plus, there was the matter of protecting the Citadel's darkest secret.

He turned his thoughts back to their new captives.

The directive to capture women of child-bearing years had been, of course, open to some interpretation, and so the hunting parties had snared two young teenage girls in their patrols. Initially, Chadwick had not known what to do with them, but eventually, he'd had them blindfolded and dropped off a hundred miles away. So desperate for test subjects had he been that he had overlooked the potential benefit of bringing children into the Citadel fold. Maybe they'd start bringing in children in a few weeks. That it hadn't been discussed in the planning sessions of the Citadel high command made him feel a little stupid, and it made him think worriedly about what else they might have forgotten.

Because, as it turned out, it *had* been the vaccine that had rendered the original fifty women of the Citadel infertile. These twelve women were fertile, although one had had a pre-plague hysterectomy, and thus was of no use to Chadwick. He was still trying to decide what to do with her.

They were holding the women in a converted warehouse, which they had retrofitted with cheap walls to give them each their own room. Security at the warehouse was high, and he'd sedated the women. It wasn't the Waldorf-Astoria, but then again, these women were not guests here.

It was important he reminded them of that, if only subtly. Quite frankly, these women were the Citadel's most important asset, whether they knew it or not, whether they wanted to admit it or not. But that meant expanding their footprint sooner than they had anticipated.

It was these women that would help usher in a new generation.

For the most part, they hadn't been too much trouble. Most were still in shock, either because of the cataclysm itself or by the manner in which they'd been taken. Some seemed happy to be here, enjoying the Citadel's hospitality, not asking any questions. And a couple of the women worried him.

It was the first time he'd seen all his new recruits assembled together. Several were crying softly. Eight Caucasian, two blacks, one Asian, one Latino. A fairly representative cross-section of the American female population before the epidemic. Their average age was thirty-four. All but one was under the age of forty, which he was particularly happy about. All had at least six or seven good years of fertility ahead of them, and Chadwick intended to take full advantage of every one of those. Two had refused to identify themselves, which annoyed him, but he really couldn't do anything about that. He needed them, and so they didn't realize the power they wielded. Yet. He needed to make sure they never figured that out. He wondered if any of them had figured out he was the one responsible for the end of the world.

He thumbed through each of the folders, scanning the names.

Marilyn Tate, 27 years old. Denver, Colorado.

Julie Micco, 37. Sioux City, Iowa.

Unidentified Caucasian woman, Mid-20s.

Nadia Obeid, 34. Stillwater, Oklahoma. *(hysterectomy)*

Erin Thompson, 30. Des Moines, Iowa.

Robin Cobos, 33. Springfield, Missouri.

Patricia Williams, 44. Indianapolis, Indiana.

Sharee Hawkins, 34. Enid, Oklahoma.

Latasha Gilman, 28. Lincoln. Nebraska.

Kimberly Lockwood, 29. Sioux Falls, South Dakota.

Sasha Goodell, 34, St. Louis, Missouri.

Unidentified Chinese woman, Late 30s.

They were seated in a semi-circle in metal folding chairs, as though they were about to begin a group therapy session. Taking no chances,

Chadwick had their ankles and wrists bound with zip ties, and two of his most trusted advisors patrolled the room with machine guns. He hadn't sedated them this morning, as he wanted them awake and alert. None of the women spoke.

He sat down in the empty chair and crossed one leg over the other.

"Good morning," he said, smiling broadly. "My name is Dr. Chadwick. I want to welcome you all to the Citadel."

"Where are we?" moaned one of them, her voice caked in sobs.

"Patricia, is it?"

She nodded, wiping her freely running nose with her bound wrists.

"This is your new home."

A stream of angry Chinese spewed from the Asian woman. She spoke no English, but tone was nothing if not universal. This triggered outbursts from the others, and Chadwick let them vent. Cutting them off would serve no purpose. Letting them get their say in would make them feel included, as though their opinion mattered. It didn't, of course, but they didn't need to know that.

The invective continued for another minute and then began to tail off.

"I'm happy to hear from each of you," he said. "But let's do this in a civilized manner. Ms. Williams, you were asking where we were."

She nodded. Patricia Williams was a short, slightly overweight woman with brown hair. When they found her, she'd been traveling with four men and an older woman; the group had not put up much of a fight. It would have been easy to attribute her forward question to a streak of self-confidence, but Chadwick didn't think that was the case. She struck him as impulsive, her mouth guided by sheer terror. She was a wonderful physical specimen for her age, her fertility tests belying a woman fifteen years younger.

"We're in a safe place," he said.

"What is this place?" asked Latasha Gilman.

"We're a group of scientists and engineers and doctors," he said. "This was a government installation. We're trying to build a completely self-sufficient society, off the grid. At least, we were trying to, before the outbreak."

"Why did you kill my friends?"

"My men felt like their lives were in danger."

Someone let loose a sarcastic laugh.

"How can so many of you still be alive?"

He paused for a moment, to maximize the dramatic effect of his response to the question.

"We had a vaccine."

Murmurs first, and then explosions, as he expected. A few broke down in tears.

"A vaccine?"

"You've gotta be kidding me!"

"They said there was no vaccine!"

He let them run for a bit and then used his hands to calm them down, a conductor in his finest performance. The room was silent but for the continued weeping, as the women imagined what might have been. Children, husbands, sisters, brothers, all cut down when a simple shot in the arm might have saved them.

"There was a vaccine," he said. "Our government knew what this disease was."

"Why didn't they start mass vaccinations?" asked the unidentified white woman.

"They did," he lied. "On the east coast. Vaccinations had begun in New York and Boston, but the virus moved too quickly. I don't think they realized how quickly the disease would spread or how deadly it would be."

"How did you have the vaccine?" she asked.

"We have a number of vaccines here," Chadwick said, eyeing the woman carefully. "As I said, this installation was designed to be self-sufficient."

"How did you know to use that particular vaccine?" she asked. She was a pretty girl, a little heavyset perhaps. She wore glasses and kept her long brown hair tied in a ponytail.

"We did get lucky in that respect," he said, smiling at the question. "My medical director had some close friends at the Centers for Disease Control. They told him what was going on, that they knew they wouldn't be able to vaccinate enough people in time. That was in the middle of the first week of the outbreak. We began vaccinating everyone immediately and we simply had to hope the vaccine would take. We're in the middle of nowhere, no one coming in or out, so that bought us a little time. We circled the wagons, pulled up the drawbridge, and hoped for the best. Ten days later, our blood tests showed we all had antibodies to Medusa, and no one got sick. Just like you, the people here lost all their families, all their friends back home."

"Lucky you," the girl said, one eyebrow raised. Chadwick felt naked, exposed, as the girl looked at him, looked *through* him. He felt goosebumps erupt along his arms, but he held her gaze, intent on not being the first one to look away.

"No, my dear," Chadwick replied after she broke her gaze. "Lucky you. All of you. Immune to the greatest scourge that mankind has ever seen. All of you are miracles of evolution. Nature chose you to represent our species going forward."

"What do you want with us?" she asked, seemingly unimpressed with his praise of her DNA.

"Quite simply, we're trying to rebuild," he said. "This thing, it all but wiped us out. We've decided we need to start sooner than later if we don't want mankind to just fade away. It means working together, joining forces. It's a big world out there. If we leave it to chance, we may never get our old way of life back. People will start to forget that we were once a great society, a great country."

"What if we want to leave?" Latasha Gilman asked.

"That's not going to be an option right now," he said as gently, as paternally, but as firmly as he could. There could be no misunderstanding about this. "Besides, you're much safer here than you are in the outside world."

The room fell silent for a moment. A chair creaked as one of the women shifted in her seat. He looked upon each woman in turn, holding each gaze like he was turning a key in a lock. Faces fell, jaws tightened, even more tears were shed, but this was quieter, more whimpering than weeping.

"Make no mistake, you will be cared for here," he said. "You have no idea how important you are."

He became acutely aware of the bespectacled girl eyeing him. Again, sweat trailed down the sides of his body. His voice began to crack.

"Thank you ladies. We'll be seeing a lot more of each other very soon. In the meantime, please enjoy your stay."

24

Adam spotted the UPS truck by the side of the road shortly before noon on September 18. They'd been walking along I-70 for nearly five days, taking turns pushing Caroline in the wheelchair. Out in the plains, farther and farther from the concentrated population centers, finding motorized transportation was becoming increasingly difficult, and with Caroline in her condition, bicycles were no longer an option. But that morning, just west of Topeka, Kansas, they'd found a big Ford Expedition, the keys in the ignition but its gas gauge tickling E, and a long stretch of empty road ahead. Adam cursed their luck. This big honker, with its seven seats, could make for some easy sledding out here, if they could only find some goddamn gas. So when he saw the boxy brown truck on the side of the road, a spike of relief shot through him.

"We'll siphon the gas out," Freddie had said after they'd pulled up behind the UPS truck.

"With what?"

"I've got a hose," he said.

And he hadn't been lying. A tightly spooled green coil of garden hose in his pack. For what, Adam had no earthly idea. But he had it, and maybe they could siphon the gas out of this UPS truck, if there was any to be had. It wasn't like they had any other options. If this didn't work, the Expedition would run dry, and they'd be walking along I-70, this big, empty gorgeous stretch of road, with no wheels.

Water, water, everywhere, not a drop to drink.

As Adam stepped down to the pavement, he felt a cool breeze rustle his shirt. The rain they'd awoken to had pushed off, leaving behind a clear, sunsplashed afternoon. Fall. That first taste of it right at summer's end. Just a little taste. It was hard to picture the seasons changing with so much of his subconscious still occupied by those hot, hellish, plague-ridden days of August. But ended they had, just like summer would. The world was going to keep right on spinning, with or without them.

Adam and Sarah scouted out the UPS truck, but all they found was the desiccated corpse of the driver in the front seat, still wearing the familiar brown uniform. Here was a case study in Medusa. Guy wakes up, feeling a little off, heads off to work anyway. Delivers packages and death. A few hours later, the virus ravaging him now, he pulls off the road for a quick nap. Closes his eyes and that was that.

"Clear," Sarah called out, and Freddie got to work on the gasoline.

"How long has it been since the outbreak?" Sarah asked as she watched Freddie feed the tank of the SUV.

Adam checked his watch.

"Today's September 18," he said. "Five, six weeks."

"So call it a month since everything broke down?"

"Sounds about right," Adam said. "Why do you ask?"

"The gasoline. It's going to go over soon."

"What?" Freddie asked, looking back over his shoulder.

Adam blew out a noisy sigh.

"She's right," Adam said. "Gasoline goes bad. The stuff with ethanol, that's got a shelf life of about three months or four months."

"Jesus H. Christ," Freddie said. "Ain't we ever gonna catch a break?"

Adam rubbed his eyes and chuckled to himself.

"We'll figure something out," he said.

"Hey, check this out!" Max called out, his exuberance cutting through the sudden frost like hot steel.

Sarah followed Max's voice to the back of the UPS truck, where she found the kid climbing into the open cargo bay. She peeked around him and saw dozens of packages still in the truck.

"It's like Christmas!" Max shouted as he began digging through the boxes.

Although it seemed a bit morbid, Sarah couldn't help but smile a little as the boy pawed through the packages.

"Go on and bring them out here," Adam said. "We'll load them up and go through them when we make camp tonight."

Max jumped on his new assignment, quickly clearing the truck of sixty-five boxes and envelopes. He created three piles: small, medium and large.

"Can I open them now?" Max asked when he'd finished.

Adam checked his watch, his eyes narrowing. Sarah could tell he wanted to go, go, go, narrow the gap between him and his daughter.

"OK," he said. "We'll take an hour to go through them. It's one-twenty now. I want to be back on the road by two-thirty."

Max's face lit up.

"You open," Adam said, "and I'll keep a list. Deal?"

Sarah felt her stomach flip with excitement as Max nodded.

They found a notepad and pen in the glove compartment, and Max set to work tearing open the packages and envelopes. Before opening each one, he read the name and address of the package's intended recipient. It felt weird and awkward at the beginning, but after half a dozen or so, Sarah was glad Max was doing it. In some small way, it felt like a memorial service for these sixty-five people they'd never met, who almost certainly lay dead in a hospital or bedroom or in a shallow grave and would otherwise have been lost to history.

The names flowed through them like a dark, deep river, rich with hidden meaning and import, but rushing by too quickly to impart any truth.

"Natalie Sears. 543 Michigan Avenue. Yukon, Pennsylvania."

A prom dress.

"Russell Yang. 3231 Godfrey Street. Salem, Oregon."

A case of printer paper.

The unboxing revealed a dizzying array of treasures, from gourmet coffee to a real estate sales contract, a Polaroid camera to a purple vibrator (and hadn't *that* been a fun one to explain to Max), a cashmere scarf to a collection of dog toys. Cans of Campbell soup and a traffic cone. A set of car keys attached to a University of Missouri keychain. A jar of gourmet peanuts. A portable video game system. A hardcover novel. A sheaf of multi-colored construction paper bearing finger-paints of little hands and glued-on pipe cleaners. X-rays. DVDs of old movies. Deeper they dug into the scores of dead letters and deeper ran the fissures in Sarah's heart, until it was on the verge of breaking. America. This was America they were opening, one piece at a time, an America that had disappeared around them like a mirage.

It was well past two-thirty when they finally finished, but no one seemed to care that they'd missed their self-imposed deadline. As she wiped tears from her face, Sarah looked up to see Freddie doing the same thing. And after all that, only a handful of boxes contained anything worth taking. The soup. The garlic peanuts. A carton of cigarettes. A novel called *The Poacher's Son* that Max wanted to take.

God *damn*, this was hard, she thought. God damn.

Maybe they'd needed this. Her last memories of the old world were of it sick, dying and panicky, caught in a humiliating pose. The looting and the riots and the fear. The Bronx. She combed her memory banks for something before the plague. An early outbreak of flu, she'd heard on the news.

Before that, though, Wells, before that. Something before that.

St. Croix, back in March. She and two of her girlfriends, Keri Williams and Dawn Vann, officers like she'd been, now dead like she wasn't, had bugged out to St. Croix for three days, drank and flirted and she hooked up with one guy, an architect from San Diego, if she remembered right. A quickie in the hallway outside her room, and thank God she'd had a condom with her because she was going to bang him whether she'd had one or not. It had been a fun trip, the last fun thing she remembered doing because then she was working a lot, getting ready to ship out in September. She supposed she felt a little better and, as she looked around at the other faces, she suspected her friends might have been engaging in similar trips down memory lane.

They tossed the white elephants back in the truck and shut the cargo doors. As Sarah stepped on to the running board to slip behind the wheel of the Expedition, she caught movement in the corner of her eye. She turned toward it, toward the dead cornfields to the north, and saw a lone figure staggering toward them.

Sarah and Adam raised their weapons as the figure approached, but the straggler either didn't see them or didn't care, and collapsed at the edge of the cornfield. With Adam covering her, Sarah approached the figure, a woman, she could see now. She was olive-skinned, her eyes a fierce green color but clouded with confusion and fatigue. She was ranting, her words coming in a machine-gun spray of English and Arabic.

"My God," Caroline said to no one.

She was filthy, barefoot and dressed in tattered blue coveralls. Her arms and feet had been scratched and scraped to hell, and she was woefully thin. Her cheeks were sunken in, and her eyes were glassy. When Adam knelt to examine her, she recoiled away from him, violently, and toward Sarah. He backed away from her, his hands up in surrender. She seemed to relax, if only a hair, as Sarah tried to soothe her.

"Hey there, you're gonna be OK," Sarah said. "You're gonna be OK."

She repeated it over and over.

"Get me some water for her," Sarah ordered.

Max brought two bottles and a hunk of bread to Sarah, who handed them over to the woman. Even Max seemed to understand that Sarah would be this woman's intermediary for the time being. She guzzled both bottles of water and ate the food so quickly that Adam worried she might choke on it.

When she was done, Sarah took the woman's hand in her own.

"Sarah, look at her arm," Adam said.

Sarah gently turned the woman's wrist and gasped. Burned into the underside of her wrist was a tattoo. It was the same phoenix rising from the ashes they'd seen spray-painted on the tent earlier. The woman looked at her, the panic bubbling on her face like a pot of water left unattended.

"It's okay," Sarah said. "You're safe now. We're all together."

The woman swung her head toward Adam and then back to Sarah, as though she were trying to decide whether to believe them.

"Sarah, a word?" Adam said.

They stepped away from the group.

"She's been hurt bad," he said to Sarah. "Possibly raped. Make sure she knows it's her decision."

"What if she says no?" Sarah replied. "I won't leave her alone."

"She won't say no," Adam said, although he really had no idea what the woman would do.

Sarah and Caroline went back and sat next to the woman on the ground; Adam motioned for the men, and the three of them drifted down the highway to give the women some privacy. They stood awkwardly, shifting their weight from foot to foot. Max, who was short for his age, looked up at them like a child caught between warring parents.

He watched Sarah console the woman, who'd burst into tears once she was with Caroline and Sarah. She buried her face into Sarah's shoulder and wailed, the sound almost painful to hear. It was as though all the grief that had accumulated since the outbreak was flooding out in one fell swoop, as though she'd never had a chance to deal with what had happened. Sarah and Caroline sat with her, holding her hand as the woman slowly regained her bearings. Her voice softened, her herky-jerky movements slowed down. As they waited, he found himself hoping very much that the woman would come with them. Sure, he wanted the woman to be safe. If she could find comfort in their ragtag group, so be it. But that wasn't the whole story. He stole glances at Sarah's face, at the angled cheekbone, at the eyes that glimmered in the light. He liked the way her t-shirt fit her body, the slender sheath of muscle in each of her arms.

The kiss they'd shared hadn't been far from his mind. There had been something there, he was sure of it. They hadn't discussed it, but in the past week, he'd caught her staring at him the way she'd caught him eyeing her. But she had remained silent. And, he supposed, maybe there just wasn't any room on their plate for that kind of nonsense right now.

"I hope your daughter is still alive," Freddie said, jarring Adam from his daydream.

"Oh," Adam replied. "Thanks. I'm not kidding myself. I know it's a long shot."

"I'll be honest with you," Freddie said, his voice dropping to a whisper. "I saw both my girls die, and I don't know what's worse. Knowing they're gone forever or not knowing at all."

Adam couldn't imagine anything worse than knowing Rachel was dead, but in a perverse sort of way, he understood what Freddie meant. What if he were just setting himself up for crushing disappointment? What if he never found her? Wouldn't that be worse than just knowing that she was dead? These questions spun through his head like a hamster on a wheel, haunting him as Sarah and Caroline counseled the woman. He tried to think of something else, anything else, but out here, in the big nowhere, there was nothing else to think about.

"I'm very sorry about your family," Adam said.

"What can you do?" Freddie replied. "Some of us just draw the shitty hand."

Adam didn't know how to reply. He wasn't sure if Freddie was just firing off platitudes or if that last comment had been a dig aimed at him.

"It's a terrible thing," Adam said.

An hour later, Sarah and Caroline approached Adam, Freddie, and Max, the newcomer hanging well behind them.

"Guys, this is Nadia," Sarah said.

"Nadia, this is Adam, Freddie and Max."

Adam and Freddie nodded.

"Hi," Max said.

Nadia nodded toward Max, but she didn't make eye contact with Freddie or Adam.

"Nadia has agreed to join us," she said.

Nadia nodded again.

Caroline took Nadia's hand in her own and squeezed it. Nadia placed her hand against Caroline's swollen belly and smiled. They loaded up the Expedition, and ten minutes later, they were westbound again.

What if?

What if?

What if?

25

"Adam."

He whimpered softly.

"Adam," Freddie repeated again, this time shaking his shoulder. "Wake up, man."

He didn't want to. His head throbbed and, along with the dry, gummed-up mouth, foretold the hangover that awaited him. And being shaken awake wasn't helping. Whatever it was would have to wait. But then Freddie said the one thing that made him forget about the hangover, about the headache, the one thing that terrified him above all else.

"Baby's sick."

Adam sat up like a shot, sending his systems into massive revolt. His head swam, conspiring with his stomach to magnify the nausea tenfold, and then there was nothing he could do to stop it. He scampered out of his sleeping bag as far as he could before his insides erupted. On his hands and knees, gripping the dirt for dear life, he waited as his body violently flushed out the remains of the previous day's festivities, Freddie's terrible message pinging away in his brain.

Freddie handed him a bottle of water, and Adam drank it down. It was lukewarm, but that was fine by him. Made it go down a little faster, without the threat of brain freeze. His desiccated body absorbed the water like a new sponge. He used a bit of the water to wash out his mouth, and then he wiped his lips clean with the back of his sleeve.

Baby's sick.

The words were like bullets to the chest.

God dammit, why had he let himself get his hopes up?

After taking a deep breath, he staggered to his feet and followed Freddie toward Caroline's tent. A light but steady rain was falling from low, gray clouds, which were nestled in the kind of sky that told you you'd be better off just staying in bed and watching movies. The rain rustled the leaves, spattering the shells of their polyester tents, steady, steady, steady. They were a few miles east of Salina, Kansas, where, on September 20, they'd set up their most permanent home to date, waiting for the baby to come. Adam hated to stop their progress, but the travel was starting to wear on Caroline. Plus, his last examination of her suggested the baby had dropped and would be coming any moment.

Caroline had gone into labor early on the morning of September 26. By the early afternoon, her contractions were four minutes apart, and she couldn't wait any longer. With Sarah and Freddie working as *de facto* nurses, Adam set about the familiar work of bringing new life to the world, even if it was into a world with which he was decidedly unfamiliar. It had been a smooth delivery, given the circumstances. Caroline had told him her original birth plan had been to deliver without pain medication (and Adam couldn't help but smile, virtually all of them said that, and then virtually all of them accepted the epidural after one or two good contractions). In this case, however, Caroline had gotten her wish. Oh, she had most certainly gotten her wish.

And six hours after she started pushing, right about the time he'd started thinking about an emergency C-section, out came a healthy, howling baby boy, out the way they had come for the entire history of the human race, his skin as fair as his mother's, his head topped with a fine layer of red fuzz. He maxed out the 1-minute and 5-minute Apgar scores, pinking up and screaming his little head off. It was the most beautiful thing Adam had ever seen, and in that moment, as he handed the infant to his exhausted mother, all their problems just fell away. She named him Stephen, in honor of his father, who had succumbed in the second week of the epidemic. Their good luck continued several hours after his birth, when he began nursing like a seasoned professional.

They passed the baby around like a good joint, each taking a hit of that baby smell, and even Freddie seemed happy. He made ga-ga faces and changed diapers so Caroline could sleep in between feedings. Thirty-six hours in, Adam had started to relax, enjoying a cigar and a scotch while the others passed around a bottle of champagne Sarah had snagged during a supply run. The baby was feeding well, sleeping in two to three-hour bursts. He'd even found his thumb and was happy and alert.

One scotch became four, and on no sleep since Caroline had gone into labor, the alcohol had hit him hard and fast, precipitating the hangover he was feeling as he hurried into Caroline's tent. He found her tucked in her sleeping bag, holding the baby close to her body.

Stephen was coughing, those tiny hacks, and immediately, Adam tried to attribute it to anything but what he feared it would be. Allergies. Drool. Milk going down the wrong pipe. He always thought it funny that doctors did the same thing as their patients, their minds working the same way, to explain away the thing that you feared the most.

"When did this start?" Adam said, kneeling by her.

She looked exhausted, and the glow that had been there after Stephen's arrival had faded badly, like a once shiny penny that had been put through its paces.

"About two hours ago," she said. "And I think he's running a fever."

A soft hand to Stephen's fragile forehead confirmed Caroline's diagnosis. The tiny little boy, a wrinkly, squirmy pile of pink, was wearing nothing but a diaper, but he was still warm, very warm. Adam wrapped his hands around the boy's toothpick legs and found those uncomfortably warm as well.

Adam fought to maintain as straight a face as he could. In normal circumstances, a fever in an infant under twelve weeks of age was deadly serious, warranting immediate medical intervention. Hearing it now made him weak, dizzy, and if he hadn't had one knee firmly planted in the ground, he might have tumbled over.

"I don't want to jump to any conclusions," Adam began, "but I'm not going to lie to you. This is not what I was hoping to see."

Her jaw clenched tight, and he saw the panic bubbling there like a forgotten pot of soup, her eyes bouncing from Adam to Freddie and back again. She stared at him, and he could feel it in her stare.

"Do something!" Freddie barked.

A cough, a deeper one, exploded from Stephen's little chest, and Caroline continued to rock him as she began to cry.

"Jesus!" Freddie snapped. He pointed at Adam. "You. Outside."

Adam recoiled as a spike of fear coursed through him.

"Be right back," Freddie said, but Caroline wasn't listening. She rocked Stephen gently in her arms as the men ducked through the flaps of the tent.

Outside, the rain had intensified. Sarah and Max were lingering by the tent, anxious to hold the baby, anxious to kiss the baby, anxious to just be in the same goddamn room with the baby. They were like addicts waiting for their dealer to dish out a little more of that sweet, sweet horse.

"God dammit, ain't there anything you can do?" Freddie asked.

"What's wrong?" Sarah asked.

"Stephen's sick."

"Aw, shit."

"No, no, no!" Max said, bursting into tears.

"Is there anything you can try?" Sarah asked.

"I don't know what I can do," Adam said. "Not if he's got it."

"What the hell kind of doctor are you?" Freddie snapped. His cheeks flushed, his left eyebrow twitching.

"A realistic one," Adam said. "I don't want to get her hopes up."

"There's got to be something."

"You've seen what it does," Adam said.

Max fled back to his tent, leaving the three of them standing there in the rain. Freddie closed his eyes, his breathing shallow and ragged. He placed his massive hand on Adam's chest.

"Please," he said, his eyes closed now. "Can you just try?"

"How about we leave the doctor stuff to me? How about that?"

Freddie's face drained of color, Adam's emasculation reaching him at his very core. Adam hadn't set out to embarrass the man, but he had to take control of the situation. If his expertise, the one thing he brought to the table, was going to mean anything, he had to plant his flag now.

Freddie stormed back inside the tent. Just like that, Adam and Sarah were alone again.

"You really think he's got it?"

Adam looked down at his shoes.

"Maybe it's just a cold or something," Sarah said.

"I don't think so."

"These aren't exactly ideal conditions," she said. "Maybe he picked up something on the road. I just don't want to assume all is lost."

They stood in silence, and he watched her watching him, wondering if she now regretted hitching her wagon to his, wondering if he wasn't the man she had thought he was.

"I can try an antiviral," he said finally. "I heard some chatter it was distantly related to the influenza virus, but I have no idea if that's accurate. It's not usually indicated for infants this young, but there isn't really any other option. Maybe a combination of the medicine and any antibodies he inherited from her will make a difference."

"OK. An antiviral. Can we find it in a pharmacy?"

"Yes. Assuming there are any supplies left. Remember, I'm sure everyone and their brother tried it during the outbreak."

"You always this glass-is-half-empty?"

"Can you blame me?"

"No, I guess not."

She turned toward the tent's opening, and he grabbed her gently by the wrist.

"Seriously," he said as she turned back to face him. "Please don't get her hopes up. I'm telling you this as a doctor. This is a Hail Mary pass."

THEY POWERED WEST ALL MORNING, hitting half a dozen pharmacies, unable to find antivirals, unable to find virtually any medicine at all. At noon, they reached the outskirts of Salina, smack in the dead center of Kansas. Salina had been at the hub of the state's wheat industry, once a pleasant city of about fifty thousand souls. In the eastern suburbs, where Adam and Sarah had found a Walgreen's drug store, cookie cutter development had been in full swing when the plague had hit, giving them a sense of the familiar they'd seen in almost every town and city they'd passed through on their trek west.

The box-shaped building was at the south end of a strip mall, bordering a new residential neighborhood. The moisture barriers for half-completed homes flapped in the rain, the skeletal shells of the unfinished homes beginning to bear the scars of inattention. New saplings dotted the area, but the once-manicured common areas were starting to go to seed. An Applebee's restaurant anchored the shopping center, the words IMMEDIATE SEATING AVAILABLE still flashing in the window, a gaudy, neon red. This gave Adam the willies almost more than anything they'd seen on the road.

"Power's on here," he said, pointing toward the restaurant.

"Strange," she said.

"Backup generators?"

"I suppose."

Sarah glassed the area with a pair or binoculars, shaking her head after a moment.

"I don't know about this one," Adam said. "Maybe we should keep looking."

"Didn't you say time is of the essence?"

"Yes," he said. "Every minute counts with an antiviral. The longer we wait, the less effective it will be."

"Then we go in here. You got your piece?"

He nodded.

"You sure you're ready to use it?"

He nodded firmly, hoping it masked his terror.

He cleared the chamber and made sure the pistol was ready to fire as Sarah swung the doors open.

"Ready?"

He nodded, his face oily with sweat. It was cool out, still drizzling, but his cheeks were hot, and perspiration matted his shirt to his skin.

"Stay behind me," she said.

Adam's heart was pounding as they crossed the threshold into the store, which was silent but for the buzz of the overhead lights. Sarah motioned skyward toward a closed-circuit television mounted near the ceiling, still functioning. The picture cycled from one angle of the store to the next, giving clear views of each aisle. The store appeared empty, but Sarah maintained her position, crouched over, her hands gripped tight around her weapon.

"Stay alert," she whispered, her face taut, her jaw set like stone.

Using the long shelves for cover, they moved from aisle to aisle, poking their heads around ransacked displays of sunscreen, disposable cameras and corn chips. After they finished their sweep, Sarah led him back to the middle of the store, and they moved in tandem down the center aisle, back to back. The place was a mess, the shelves stripped bare, disheveled, toys and tchotchkes littering the linoleum floor. An issue of *People* lay face up on the floor, a pair of married celebrities adorning the cover. The headline read, *More Kids for Hollywood's Power Couple?* It was dated August 6, a harsh reminder of how quickly the world had ended. As they moved deeper into the store, Adam began to lose hope, as the place had been picked over pretty well.

The pharmacy, which was at the back of the store, was dark, the overhead lights shattered. Bits of glass littered the floor, crunching under their feet as Adam checked the shelves. There wasn't much left. Bulk containers holding pills to treat high blood pressure, high cholesterol, and erectile dysfunction lined the shelves, but the antibiotics and narcotics were gone. He was about to give up hope when two stray bottles on a nearly bare shelf caught his eye.

Please, please, he thought.

He grabbed one of the bottles and studied the label.

Oseltamivir phosphate.

The antiviral.

It was the generic form, with nothing on the label to indicate that it was an antiviral. It was in capsule form, so they'd have to crush the contents into a bottle of formula for him. He still didn't think it was going to work, but at least they were doing something. And he owed that to Caroline. To let her know he had done all he could.

"I've got it," he called out.

When Sarah didn't reply, he froze. He leaned back, staying in shadow, and peeked out toward the store proper. From his vantage point, he could just make out Sarah's profile. Behind her, a slender arm, holding a gun to the back of her head.

He looked around and saw a closed-circuit monitor mounted on the counter. The black-and-white picture flickered through two shots of the store before snapping over to the pharmacy area. In the three seconds the shot remained on screen, Adam picked out two bandits, a skinny man and a heavier-set woman, both young.

"Come out with your hands up," a gruff voice called out. "Gonna count to three. Then the bitch gets it."

Bitch.

Well, he thought, at least that told him what kind of folks he was dealing with here.

"You hear me?" the man barked, his voice screeching now.

Adam chewed on his lip, the edges of a plan taking shape in his mind. He pulled the gun from his waistband and considered his options. He stared at the gun like it was an alien artifact, beyond the powers of his puny human comprehension. One versus two. And Sarah was being held hostage. In his untrained hands, the gun would be about as useful as a ball of yarn.

"I'm coming out!" he said, setting the gun and the antiviral down. He scanned the shelves and grabbed two more bottles.

Oh, Adam, what the hell are you doing, buddy?

He eased his way around the counter and out into the aisle fronting the pharmacy, his hands sky high, the pill bottles visible in his partially clenched fist. Sarah was about six feet away, a girl close in behind her, the gun pressed firmly against her temple. The girl's face was blank, betraying not a single emotion. She was heavier set, her hair cut short. The second gunman, whose wide face and even wider-set eyes reminded Adam of an owl, stood just off their shoulder, brandishing a shotgun. Sarah's M4 hung from his shoulder. He aimed the shotgun directly at Adam's face. The twin bores, black and empty, stared at Adam like a dead-eyed monster.

"What's in your hand?" the owl said, his words marinated with a thick Southern accent.

"Medicine."

"What for?"

"You promise to let us go if I tell you?" Adam asked.

"How about you give it to me 'fore I kill you?" Owl snapped.

"If you kill me, you won't know how to use it."

"What's it for?"

The temperature seemed to be climbing with each passing moment. Adam felt rivulets of sweat channeling down his sides, and he tried to steady his breathing.

"It."

An audible gasp.

"You mean *Snake*?" the girl said.

Snake. Medusa. So many names. Adam nodded as gravely as he could.

"That shit's gone," the girl snapped, her words clipped and desperate. "Everyone left's 'mune."

"Lucy, he's just bullshitting you," the owl said.

"Yeah, we thought everyone was immune, too," Adam said, gently lowering his hands to his head. It was a calculated risk, but he thought if he kept his hands over his head, they wouldn't notice. Especially given the bomb he was about to drop on them. His arms were starting to burn; it was time to play his hand. He held his final card, holding, holding, as he watched their jaws tighten, their eyes widen with fear.

"Until she came down with it yesterday," he said, jutting his chin directly toward Sarah.

Lucy's deep-seated instinct to survive kicked in, and she shoved Sarah away from her hard, stumbling backwards as she did so. Sarah lost her own footing, crashing into Adam and sending them both to the ground. Owl was on the retreat now too, holding his hand up, as if that might stop the spread of the phantom illness. Lucy was wiping her hands down on her jeans, pulling her shirt collar up over her lips and nose.

"No, no," Owl said. He raised the gun back up and covered his mouth with his sleeve.

"No, wait!" Adam said. "If you shoot her, you'll spray blood everywhere. Then you'll definitely be exposed. There's still time. She hasn't coughed or sneezed since we came inside the store!"

"What?" Lucy said.

"I'm a doctor, trust me!" Adam said. "Medusa spreads like the common cold. You have to be exposed to droplets of the virus. You can't get it otherwise."

"You're shitting me!" Owl said.

"No, I was with a CDC team in Kansas City during the outbreak," Adam lied. "We figured out that the disease spreads easily, but not that easily. But you gotta get out of here now!"

The owl stood there, shifting his weight from foot to foot.

"Jack, let's go!" cried Lucy. "I fucking touched her!"

"Go on now," Adam said as grimly as he could. "Before it's too late. She's been coughing and sneezing a lot. I can't believe she hasn't yet in the store."

"What about you?" Jack asked.

Adam shook his head.

Jack's finger slipped in and out of the trigger guard as he swung from one choice to the other. Murder or flight.

"Please, hurry," Adam yelled. "Please, I don't want you all to get sick!"

"What about the medicine?" Owl asked. "It won't work. If it worked, everyone would still be alive."

"This medicine works," Adam said. "They just didn't have enough of it. I found some hidden in the back. This is the last of it."

"Give it to me!" he said.

Adam gingerly handed the bottles to the man, as though the very act of it pained him. As Jack took the bottles, Sarah's M4 slid off his shoulder and clattered to the tile floor. But Jack left it there and fled down the aisle.

"Jackie, wait!" shouted Lucy, pursuing her companion.

"Stay away from me!" he called out, his panic-filled voice echoing through the nearly empty drugstore. "Don't you come near me!"

Their howls continued out the door into the parking lot; eventually they drifted away, leaving Adam and Sarah alone in the store. Adam placed his hands on his knees and took some deep breaths; he felt dizzy and hot.

"Jesus Christ," he said. "I thought we were dead."

"Wow," Sarah said, retrieving her M4. "Where did you come up with that?"

"I don't know," he said. "I knew I had no chance with the gun. Then it occurred to me that if there's one thing everyone's still afraid of, it's Medusa. Wait here."

"Where are you going?"

"I gave him blood pressure medication. The antiviral is still in the back."

Sarah laughed out loud.

Adam retrieved the bottles from the pharmacy, and they left the store. The rain had stopped, but it was still cloudy and misty. He threw the truck into drive and screeched out of the parking lot.

26

They buried baby Stephen in the shade of a large pine tree on the edge of the camp.

Deep down, he'd known there was nothing they'd be able to do, that the trip he'd taken with Sarah had been nothing more than a lark and frolic, one that had nearly gotten them killed. They'd fought the good fight, administering as much medicine as they could, as often as they could. It had given Caroline a small measure of comfort, there at the end, as Stephen drew his last few breaths. But in the end, it hadn't done any good. His fever continued climbing, the cough worsening and deepening. And, as Adam expected, Medusa did to Stephen what it had done to everyone else, and he had died on the morning of September 30.

"Thank you for trying," she'd said to Adam, holding Stephen close to her, quiet and free of his suffering.

Freddie spent the afternoon digging a tiny grave for Stephen. He took great care in doing so, excavating a small but virtually perfect rectangle that faced east. Caroline liked that it looked back across the empty country toward Georgia, where, in another life, another universe, another dimension, little Stephen would have grown up.

The women stood at the foot of the grave; Caroline wept silently, her left arm linked in Sarah's, her right in Nadia's. Max stood next to Adam, shifting his weight from one foot to the other, silent, miserable. At Caroline's request, Adam held Stephen and would be the one to hand him over to Freddie for his final interment.

"Can I touch him one more time?" Caroline asked, looking over at Adam.

He didn't know why she thought she had to ask, but he looked into her pleading eyes, flowing with tears, and it seemed important to her that he bless her request.

He nodded.

Stephen's body was wrapped in a light blue baby blanket, peppered with all manner of airplanes and helicopters and spaceships, which Caroline had been carrying with her for weeks. It had become a talisman in the last days of her pregnancy, but now, instead of naptimes and comfort, this blanket would serve as his shroud. She took him into her arms, held him close and kissed him on the head. Adam wondered if she would uncover his face, and he hoped she wouldn't. See, in her mind, she was picturing the face she'd seen upon his birth, the face she'd imagined a million times as an expectant mommy. To look at his face now, in the aftermath of its terrible war with Medusa, would destroy that and remind her of all that was awful and dark and evil.

But she did.

She unwrapped the blanket and kissed his forehead and his cheeks, and she began to wail. Adam closed his eyes and waited for it to be over.

"It's time to say goodbye," he heard Sarah say.

He opened his eyes and saw Sarah holding Caroline's face, red and gaunt, in her hands. He thought she did this to discourage her from kissing the baby again.

"It's time to say goodbye," Sarah said again.

Caroline nodded and passed the baby to Freddie, who lay Stephen down on the black dirt, so tiny and small, given back to the world that hadn't given him anything, not even a chance. The big man knelt down and picked a few stray bits of dirt off the blanket, an act of kindness that Adam found almost incomprehensibly sad.

"Adam?" Caroline asked, her face still in Sarah's hands.

He looked at her.

"Would you say something?" she asked. "For Stephen."

She looked at him again, with that expectant face, the one that had once looked upon him with hope and promise and belief that it was all going to work out, because seriously, what were the odds that she'd find an obstetrician after *ALL THIS*?

"Of course," he said, his words barely a whisper.

He cleared his throat and searched for something to say, anything to give this poor woman comfort. Any of them, really. He looked down at the small figure, free of all the horrors this world had seen fit to share with them.

"Dear Lord, we gather here today to say goodbye to a very brave, very beautiful little boy."

Caroline began to sob.

"This world we live in now, it's a new world for all of us."

He paused, the words not coming easily. He didn't know if he was coming across as sincere. He didn't know if this was comforting Caroline or torturing her. They were just words. What good could these stupid words do? No matter how beautifully or eloquently he spoke, Stephen would still be dead. The world would still be a graveyard. But he pressed onward, aware of his voice, his posture, everything feeling wrong, wrong, wrong.

"And I don't know why You chose to take him back so soon after he got here. But, I suppose, that may not be for us to know. So, all we can ask is that You welcome baby Stephen into Your loving arms. That You look after him now and always. That You bring his mother comfort and solace for the difficult days ahead. That You protect us and give us the guidance and wisdom we will need going forward.

"Amen."

A ripple of *Amens* from the others.

They all looked at Caroline, who continued staring down into her son's grave.

"Thank you, Adam," she said. "That was very nice."

She said it flatly, without emotion. Adam felt like she was just going through the paces, saying the things she thought people would expect her to say.

Each of them carefully poured a shovelful of dirt into the grave, Caroline going last. She sprinkled the dirt gently over her son and handed the shovel back to Freddie. As Freddie refilled the hole with the loose dirt, Caroline drifted away from the group, away to deal with her grief however she planned to deal with it. Adam, Sarah, Nadia, and Max watched as the dirt piled up, up, up until the hole was full.

THE SCOTCH TASTED DIFFERENT.

What had been warm and inviting on the day Stephen had been born, like a roaring fire on a cold New England night, now tasted swampy and hot. It reminded Adam of all those houses under gunmetal skies in all those towns and cities they'd passed through, the air conditioning long dead, full of roasting corpses.

But Adam drank it just the same. He tipped the bottle to his mouth, feeling it scorch its way down like gasoline, and nestled the bottle between his thighs. He was seated on the floor of his tent, at the foot of his sleeping bag, exhausted but awake. It was late, after midnight. Fast-moving clouds zipped along overhead, giving a slight strobe effect to the night.

As a clinical matter, he knew he was drunk. If he'd been out driving and had been pulled over by an observant state trooper (and what he wouldn't have given to see a cruiser blow by on a busy highway, its blue lights oscillating, pulsing with tremendous urgency and importance), he'd blow right past the limit just as simple as you please. But he didn't feel drunk. He didn't feel anything. Whatever the opposite of feeling was, that's what it was. He suspected it might have been within shouting distance of what Caroline was feeling.

Sure, the world had ended, had come undone around him like a sandcastle at high tide, but even then he'd felt something. *Terror. Panic. Confusion.* Those were all full-blooded feelings. And then he'd heard the message from Rachel, and that had been another feeling. *Joy. Relief.* So there, the gamut of human emotion was still there, even at the end of all things.

But this. This was something else.

An absence of emotion. Numbness. The way your lips feel after the Novocaine.

How easy it had been to say the words at Stephen's memorial, to make them sound good. He'd never enjoyed laying down words of comfort when a patient had lost a pregnancy or the Pap smear had come back abnormal, but they seemed to work. And so he had done it, without believing the words he was saying, the way he hadn't believed the words he was uttering at Stephen's funeral.

After the memorial, each of them had retreated from the gravesite into his or her own tent, forsaking the group dinner. No one felt like eating anyway. As night had fallen, the camp had grown quieter and quieter; even Caroline's sobs had petered out to silence, a once-rushing river drying up in a salt flat. The next morning, no one had emerged from their tent, and they'd spent the day grieving for Stephen, for Caroline, for all of those lost, for all they still had to lose.

He heard a rustling outside his tent.

"Adam?"

"In here," he said.

The tent flap drew back and Sarah eased inside. Even by the weak light of the lantern, he could see the sadness etched on her lovely face.

"Have a seat," Adam said, motioning toward the ground.

Sarah took a seat, cross-legged, directly across from Adam.

"Drink?" he said, tilting the bottle toward her.

She shook her head.

"Suit yourself."

He tilted the bottle back and took a drink. The slug went down the wrong way, and he began hacking and coughing, the alcohol burning his nostrils and throat, until he was able to clear his airway.

"You OK?"

He nodded, turning his head and spitting in the corner of the tent. Then he screwed the cap back on the bottle and tossed it near his pillow.

"Sorry."

"I've seen worse."

"You're not here to tell me that I did everything I could, right?"

"Nope. Any idea how he caught it?"

"From his mother, I suppose," he said. "If I had to guess, her antibodies protected him *in utero*, but after he was born, he was on his own."

"That doesn't bode well for us," Sarah said.

"No, it doesn't."

He reached into his bag and took out two chocolate bars.

"Want one?"

"No, thank you."

"You're really turning down a lot of southern hospitality here."

He opened the first bar, snapped off a quarter of it, and popped it in his mouth. He chewed slowly, trying to enjoy the taste, but with the residue of the scotch lingering on his tongue, it tasted bitter and hot.

"You need something?" he asked.

"No need to get nasty."

He rubbed his eyes with the thumb and index finger of his left hand.

"You're right. I'm sorry."

"I thought we needed to talk," she said.

Great, he thought. A big, heaping spoonful of humiliation on top of the shit sundae.

"Nothing to talk about," he said. "I'm a big boy."

"No, I know. You don't understand."

He was too tired to argue, so he sat silently as Sarah struggled to organize her thoughts. He took another bite of the candy bar. This piece tasted a little better.

"It's just that..."

Chew, chew, chew.

He honestly had no clue where she was headed, and he figured he could only make things worse by saying anything, so he continued eating the candy bar. When he finished it, he unwrapped the second one.

This seemed to derail her, and she pointed at the chocolate in his hand.

"Really throwing caution to the wind, huh?"

"All that time, worrying about what I ate," he said. "I could be dead tomorrow. Not in the abstract sense, like people used to say. For real. Any of us could be dead tomorrow. After that thing with the fox, I'm lucky I'm not already dead. So I'm going to have two candy bars tonight. And if I'm still alive tomorrow night, I'll have two more."

Then he nodded his head at her, forcefully, demonstrably.

And that was when she started laughing. Her whole body shook, and she clapped her hand over her mouth, presumably to keep herself from making too much noise, but she couldn't stop; the giggles overwhelmed her. Tears streamed down her cheeks, but these weren't tears of sadness. Her eyes sparkled in the dim light, and for a moment, even Adam's chocolate bar tasted good.

The laughter subsided after a few seconds, and then they were back in the moment. She took a few deep breaths to settle herself down.

"The way you nodded your head at me," she said. She pressed the tip of her thumb against her teeth and closed her eyes tight. "That was just too much."

"If you're willing to share," she said, "I think I will take you up on a little of that chocolate."

He snapped off the piece he'd bitten from and handed her the rest. She took a bite and smiled, perhaps tasting the chocolate the way it was supposed to taste, the cocoa hitting her dopamine receptors. He winked at her as he chewed, and she winked back.

"So," Adam said, crumpling up the wrapper and tucking it into his duffel bag. "What was it you wanted to talk about?"

She held the remaining chocolate up.

"You know what?"

He raised his eyebrows.

"I think it can-"

A deep, primal howl exploded through the camp, shattering the night calm. Sarah dropped the candy bar as she scampered to her feet. She pulled the flap of the tent back just enough to peek out toward the center of the camp. Her heart thudded crazily, and she was relieved she'd made it a rule to not go anywhere without her M4. She glanced over at Adam, who'd retrieved his own gun and had taken post opposite her.

Ten seconds.

That's how close she'd come to telling him. Another ten seconds, and she'd have told him about the Huntington's.

Yeah, she thought. *Focus on that right now. The camp could be crawling with killers right now, but your near tell-all to the handsome doctor, that's what's important. Idiot.*

She primed her ears and listened for the telltale sounds of intruders in the camp, but she heard nothing. She looked over at Adam, who was craning his head this way and that, trying to make out what was going on, but he shrugged his shoulders upon returning her gaze.

Years of embedded training took over. Yet another drill drilled, another scenario planned for, repeated *ad nauseam* until she could execute it in her sleep. In Iraq and Afghanistan, they gamed it, a terrorist or supposedly friendly local sneaking into camp at night and looking to massacre U.S. soldiers. She ducked out into the darkness, her weapon up and ready, sweeping it from side to side. She scurried along the edge of the tents, trying to stay invisible.

"Help! Somebody help!"

Freddie.

Freddie's tent was across the way, but his voice seemed to be coming from this side of the camp, where Caroline had pitched hers. She pulled back the flap of Caroline's tent and ducked inside. The smell was what she noticed first, a thick slap of sourness hanging in the air, as though someone had been sick recently. A lantern glowed in the corner, casting the interior in a ghastly yellow light, the color of sickness and infection and jaundice. Freddie was on his knees in the corner, near Caroline's bedroll, his massive frame blocking Sarah's view of Caroline.

"No, no, no," Freddie was pleading.

"What's wrong?" Adam barked.

"I think she's dead," Freddie said softly, his words coming out in barely a whisper, more like a sigh.

A touch on Sarah's shoulder startled her, and she looked back to see Adam's face, tight and drawn, staring back at her. He had the look of a man who'd seen about all he could take and she glanced away so she wouldn't have to look into that fallen face, that face devoid of anything.

"Let me see," Adam said, curling around Sarah like smoke.

He knelt next to Freddie and felt for a pulse, first in Caroline's wrist and then in her neck. His shoulders sagged, and he rocked back on his haunches, his arms draped over his knees.

"She's dead," Adam said.

Freddie stood up, his head in his hands, grimacing like he was experiencing the world's worst migraine; he paced around the tent, muttering to himself over and over.

"Fuck, fuck, fuck!"

Sarah edged toward Adam for a closer look and saw Caroline's face. Her eyes were open, blank. Her mouth hung open, a thin film on her lips.

"What happened?" Adam asked.

"Couldn't sleep," Freddie said. "Saw her lantern was on so I came over to check on her. Found her lying here."

Adam began scouring Caroline's sleeping area while Freddie resumed his pacing.

"God dammit," Adam muttered a moment later.

"What?" Sarah asked.

He held up a small pill bottle; its amber color glinted in the light of the lantern.

"This is oxycodone," Adam said. "Did anyone know she had these?"

"Oh, no," Freddie said.

"What?"

"She said her leg was bothering her this afternoon and asked me for something," Freddie said.

"Where did you get these?"

"Before we hooked up with you guys. On the road."

"And you didn't think to check with me before prescribing these, Doctor?" Adam snapped.

Freddie stood silently, towering over Sarah and Adam, who looked like a toy action figure next to the big man's mass. Sarah didn't like where this was going at all.

"At least I thought to check on her," Freddie said.

"I'd given her a sleeping pill," Adam said. "I'm her doctor. Not you!"

Freddie's head rocked backward, like a championship boxer taking an unexpected right cross from a lightly regarded challenger. Sarah herself felt her insides drop when she heard this.

"Maybe it was an accident," Sarah offered.

"I specifically told her not to take any other painkillers for this very reason," Adam said.

He stood in the center of the tent with his hands on his hips, shaking his head. Sarah exhaled, sadness rushing in to replace the fear and terror that had gripped her when she'd first heard the scream. She slung her rifle over her shoulder and stared at the sweet woman who now lay dead before her. It had been a shitty couple of months for everyone, but Caroline's surviving Medusa only to watch her first-born perish had seemed particularly cruel.

Death. Death. Death.

It had been a routine part of her adult life, swirling around her like fog. From the first time she'd seen a fellow soldier die in battle, to her first confirmed kill, an insurgent hiding in a house who'd gotten the drop on her only to see his rifle jam, and then blooming into many fellow soldiers and many confirmed kills. She'd expected to die somewhere along the line, not because she was cloaked with an extra-strength dose of bravery in volunteering for the most dangerous missions but because how much better it would have been to die in battle than to be slowly squeezed by Huntington's.

Suicide had never been an option. She could never abandon her troops. As long as she could serve, she couldn't bear the thought of one of her soldiers dying because she hadn't been there for him or her. Even if that meant denying herself an early exit from the scourge that awaited her, the Grim Reaper, his bony arms crossed against his skeletal chest, tapping his foot impatiently. She'd always thought suicide the coward's way out, and even here, she found herself thinking that a little bit about the late Caroline Braddock; she felt bad about thinking it, but that didn't mean she didn't think it.

"I think she left a note," Adam said, derailing Sarah's train of thought.

"It's got your name on it," he said.

Sarah took the page, which had been folded neatly into a square. Sarah's name was etched in big block letters on the outside. She unfolded it and read silently.

Dear Sarah,

I'm sorry for what I've done.

But this world fucking sucks. I don't want any part of it. I don't want to live without Stephen. I don't and I won't.

Good luck.

Love,

Caroline

"What did she say?" Freddie asked.

She tucked the note into her pocket and glanced at Freddie. His eyes were wide with anticipation, and she could see how much it mattered to him to know he'd helped Caroline. She looked at Adam and saw something different, his face blank, his eyes looking somewhere else.

"She said she was sorry. And thank you."

Adam covered Caroline's body with a blanket and extinguished the lantern.

"We can bury her in the morning," he said softly. "It's too dark to do anything now."

They wrapped her body in a blanket, and at first light, Freddie dug a second grave next to Stephen's. Sarah, Nadia and Max watched as Freddie and Adam lowered Caroline into it. They refilled the hole in silence. Sarah was thankful for this; she didn't think she had it in her to hear a rote recitation of platitudes. She'd heard enough eulogies to last ten lifetimes, and at the end of the day, dead was still dead. She had a terrible fear that someone would suggest exhuming Stephen's body so they could bury him with his mother, but mercifully, no one did.

When it was over, they all began packing. No one had to say anything; everyone just seemed to understand it was time to hit the road. They'd been here for nearly two weeks, the longest any of them had spent in one place since the epidemic, but what had once borne the stirrings of home now felt dead and cold. Sarah packed quickly and then helped Max with his things. The baby's death had rattled him badly, and he was morose.

They consulted their maps before pushing out.

"We should head south out of Salina," Adam said, tapping a finger in the center of Kansas. "If we stay on I-70, we could hit snow in the Rockies. We can pick up I-40 in Oklahoma City and turn west there. That will take us south of the mountains."

Sarah found herself nodding in agreement. She sensed a decisiveness in Adam's voice, one that hadn't been there before. She sensed the same thing in the commanding officers she'd looked up to in her career, the ones who'd earned their ranks.

They hit the road in a cool drizzle, and wasn't that the most symbolic thing ever, she thought as the wipers squeaked back and forth across the thick glass. They took I-135 south out of Salina and set a course for Wichita, where they could slingshot around the city onto I-35 and chart a westerly course.

No one spoke.

27

I t was the hardest stretch on the road yet. Ninety miles from Salina to Wichita and they'd be walking nearly all of it through an astonishing automobile graveyard. It seemed that as the world had come tumbling down, the residents of each of those cities had concluded that the grass was much greener and healthier in the other. And so into their cars they'd climbed, sick, blind with panic, and in their cars they had died, along that stretch of interstate highway.

A few miles of clear road and then nothing but gridlock. Worse, the traffic jam appeared to be as wide as it was long, spreading off-road into the plains, into the grasslands, creating a sea of steel. Hundreds of thousands of vehicles glinted in the morning light, the shimmer of windshields stretching away to all horizons. They'd tried going around the jam, taking advantage of the big SUV's four-wheel drive, but after a few miles bouncing through thick grasses with no end in sight, they'd abandoned the truck on October 1. But for a short dogleg about halfway between the two cities, the highway ran straight as an arrow. And it was along that long ribbon of asphalt that Adam and the others trekked for those ten days in October.

They averaged eight to ten miles a day through the Big Jam, as they'd taken to calling it. The cars were jammed together like sardines, leaving the narrowest of openings to negotiate. In some places, they'd had to walk topside, skittering from trunk to roof to hood and then back to trunk. And in almost every car, a sad story. A body or three or six. Families. Children. Mommies and Daddies and Nanas and Papas, entombed for all eternity. The bodies dried up and brown.

They made camp early on the seventh day, agreeing that they could use some extra rest, some extra time just doing nothing. As had been their habit, they scoured the vehicles for supplies first and then pitched their tents wherever they could find enough room. The cars were treasure troves of supplies. People had packed well for their final road trips - protein bars and bottled water and medicines, as though any of that could've stopped Medusa's relentless march across the globe.

When they were settled in, Freddie walked the perimeter while the others sat around the campfire. It would be a chilly night, and Adam made a note they'd need to stop for more cold-weather gear when they made it to Wichita. God knew how long they'd be walking. Just a few feet clear of the fire's reach and the night cold gripped hard. Amazing, he thought, the logistics involved in this trek. How their forefathers had done it, without SUVs and Gore-Tex and reliable guns, he'd never know. Just cut from different cloth, he suspected. Tougher cloth.

Max sat across from Adam, the boy's face blank as he scarfed down his dinner. Adam smiled as he watched the boy eat; Max was possessed of a teenage appetite that would not be denied, apocalypse or not. Throw in the long hike they were on, and his stomach was basically a bottomless pit. He was doing reasonably well, Adam thought, given the circumstances. He'd taken a shine to Freddie, that was for sure. Freddie was big, larger than life. Adam still didn't know what the man had done for a living, but it no longer seemed appropriate to ask. That was all in the *Time Before*, when things like that might have mattered. But now they were all the same.

Sarah was making decent progress with Nadia. She was originally from Stillwater and had just turned forty-one a few weeks before the outbreak. Her husband and three teenaged sons had died on four consecutive days in August. That was as far as they'd gotten, but Adam was still impressed. Nadia slept close to Sarah, almost like a frightened child curled up with her mother, and she rarely, if ever, let her out of her sight.

But tonight, she'd had a bit of a breakthrough.

When Adam had served her the canned spaghetti, warmed over the fire, she smiled demurely and said thank you. Those were the first words she had spoken to anyone other than Sarah. It was a small victory, almost nothing, but it had made Adam feel good, an emotion in increasingly short supply. Man, he was beat. It was getting to the point he couldn't remember a world before the epidemic, a world in which he wasn't on this westward quest, his own personal manifest destiny. Sometimes he felt like he'd been on this journey his whole life, that it had no beginning, that it would have no end. A hamster on a wheel.

He reached into his pack for the photograph of Rachel he'd snatched from his bedside stand before leaving Richmond. At first, he'd felt silly taking it. But he was glad he did; he looked at it every night before retiring and every morning before setting off to remind him what was at stake, to keep his eyes on the prize. She was out there somewhere. She had to be. She had to be. He traced the outline of her face with his finger, then along the thick mane of her perpetually messy brown hair. Her eyes were deep brown, like pools of dark chocolate.

He looked up and saw Nadia staring at him, another smile on her face.

"Your family?" she asked. Her voice had a hint of a Texas twang, buried just under the still pronounced Middle Eastern accent.

"I'm sorry?" he said.

"The photograph," she said, nodding toward the picture in Adam's hand.

"Oh," he said. "Yes. My daughter. It's possible she survived."

Nadia's eyes widened at this.

"Really? That would be very unusual, no?"

"Yes. Very. And I'm not one hundred percent certain she's alive. But I have to be sure."

"Of course," Nadia said. "May I?"

Adam proudly handed over the photograph of his daughter, excited to introduce her to someone else. It was times like these he wished he hadn't missed so much of Rachel's childhood, missed the chance to brag about her.

Nadia looked at the photograph and gasped, her hand clapping hard against her mouth. She mumbled something unintelligible, possibly in

Arabic. Sarah, who'd been reading by the campfire, looked up, alarm evident on her face.

"Nadia, what's wrong?"

"*Ya Allah, ya Allah, ya Allah,*" she said over and over, staring at the photograph, as though she'd seen a ghost.

"What did you say?" Sarah barked at Adam.

"Nothing! She asked to look at the picture."

"Nadia, what is it?" Sarah said, grabbing Nadia's chin with her hand. Nadia reared back and looked up at Adam, her eyes boring directly into his.

"I know her," Nadia said, pointing at the photograph.

Adam felt his insides drop.

"What do you mean you know her?" Sarah asked.

"She was there. She was there. Rachel."

"Yes, yes!" Adam shouted. "Her name is Rachel."

Adam got up and stumbled around the camp, feeling light-headed, dizzy, almost drunk.

"She's alive?" he said to no one, his hands clasped together behind his head.

Nadia nodded and shifted away from Adam. Maybe he'd freaked her out a little. But Adam didn't care. Tears stung his eyes.

Rachel was alive. Rachel was alive. His daughter was alive.

"YEAAAAAAAAAAHHHHHHHHHH!" he howled, his bellow echoing across the empty plains like a sonic wave.

EVERGREEN

BOOK 3

We always pay dearly for chasing after what is cheap.

ALEKSANDR SOLZHENITSYN

28

Stupidity.

Sheer, unvarnished, in-the-raw stupidity. Free-range, organic stupidity.

That's what had gotten her in this mess.

Rattled by the horror that had unfolded before her, she had made decisions she never would have made in ordinary circumstances, and that's what really pissed her off - with her back against the wall, she'd failed to make the right decisions at the moments they'd mattered most. You'd never have busted Rachel Fisher for something asinine like going to the grocery store on an empty stomach, but, no, no, when the apocalypse hits, she'd run around like a goddamn fool. She'd done what *other* people did, people who let their emotions get the best of them, heat-of-passion decisions. Perhaps it could be excused, and maybe someone else would've been quicker to forgive herself.

But not Rachel Fisher.

And now here she was, stirring her bubbling pot of regret like a thick soup in winter.

Now that she was here, she was trying to keep her wits about her. Focus. Study. Learn. The others were panicky, weepy. But Rachel didn't want to be like the others. She wanted to know more about this place, find out what the hell was going on. They'd started to look to her, these women that were ten or fifteen years her senior, looking to her for answers, for reassurance, for help. She didn't know why. She'd never been particularly good at making friends, and she really hadn't had many in her life. It wasn't that she didn't want friends, it was just that she seemed to be missing some key piece of equipment that let people connect with one another in some meaningful way.

She was lying on her side, dressed in the sky-blue jumpsuit that was their standard uniform. She studied her arm, the small π etched on the inside of her left wrist. It was weird to look at the tat now, this thing she'd carried with her from the old world; in fact, it was the only thing she had left from before. Never had she thought she'd have a tattoo, but it was math, and she was a programmer, and that made it seem okay. On the opposite wrist, of course, was the tattoo these monsters had tagged her with, but she didn't bother looking at that one anymore.

The room was small and getting smaller each day, a noose tightening around her, threatening to choke off her sanity. A cot. A small banker's box, in which she kept her three jumpsuits and the few personal effects the captives were allowed. She got up and crossed over to the window, a perk of the room for which she was ever grateful. The prairie stretched on interminably, stark and endless. She thought they were in Kansas or Nebraska, but she wasn't entirely sure about that. The last few days had been relatively uneventful. No testing, no speeches or ridiculous orientation sessions. Just three relatively square meals and an hour of free time in the yard with her fellow captives.

Rachel didn't know who these people were, but there was something very off about them. Granted, she'd been a loner most of her life, happiest in the soft glow of a computer screen or with a problem set. She wasn't good at small talk, and she was even worse at big talk, and so as she'd gotten older, she'd become more and more comfortable with herself and less comfortable with the world outside her door. But when she thought about the dead world around her, the panic would rise up like a rapidly inflating balloon, taking her breath away. These people, however, seemed to have taken the end of the world in stride.

Just because she didn't play nicely with others didn't mean she'd welcomed mankind's extermination, and she would think about math and programming and remind herself that unchecked emotion wasn't going to help anything, certainly not how to solve the mess she was in.

And now she thought back to her life, and how she'd spent most of her years avoiding other people. One evening, a couple of weeks before the outbreak, she'd been at a Starbucks with her laptop; a nice guy wearing those tight jeans had started chatting with her, and she had just ignored him, trying to disappear into the glow of her MacBook. Why did she do things like that? And now, she supposed, that nice guy was almost certainly dead.

Jesus, what a cluster-fuck the end of the world had turned out to be.

She'd been getting ready to head back to CalTech when the virus hit Southern California like a meteor. By August 15, commercial air travel had been shut down, the buses and trains had stopped running, hell, all interstate travel had been banned, and it hadn't made a lick of difference. Medusa still got in, the most uninvited guest of all time, and burned through the population like a brushfire.

Her stepdad Jerry had gone totally ape-shit when things started to get bad. He'd barricaded them in the house, filled the tub with water, rationed out the food. She'd argued with him, telling him he was blowing things out of proportion (and if she was being honest with herself now, she was worried he'd mess up her upcoming move back to Pasadena). He didn't sleep, spent every waking minute in front of the television, his iPad and iPhone close by, Twitter feeds monitored. Internet access became spotty around August 15, but by then, it was spitting out the same old shit hour after hour after hour.

None of them got sick until the sixteenth, when her mom woke up with it, crying. Jerry had quarantined her in her bedroom, leaving food and water at the door, and that hadn't gone over particularly well, especially after Jerry came down with it. At first, and she was ashamed to admit it to herself, even now, two months after it had happened, she'd been fascinated by the outbreak, to be alive for such a paradigm shift. But then her mom had died on August 17, and Jerry was dead by the eighteenth. Although she hadn't been that close to her mom and Jerry was kind of an idiot, watching them die had been pretty goddamn horrible because she saw how she would die. But then a day would go by, then another, and then another, and it began to dawn on her that she wasn't going to catch it.

Then the urge to see another living person, any living person, became overwhelming, and she finally was ready to chance going outside. On the afternoon of the nineteenth, she tiptoed down the brick walk with a kitchen knife in hand, the sun shining the sky crystal clear blue, so blue it made your head hurt. And far away, she'd hear a wayward gunshot or a mournful scream, like she was hearing a television in another room. House by house in their tony subdivision she had gone, knocking on doors, looking for someone, anyone who was still alive, and every door remained pulled tight. Six doors down, her knocks had been greeted by a series of painful moans, which had scared her back down the porch steps and fleeing for the safety of her bedroom, her bladder letting go on the way back. Still wearing her soiled clothes, she hid under the bed the rest of that day and all that night, like Macauley Culkin in *Home Alone*.

By August 20, when the sirens and helicopters buzzing overhead were gone and the power was out and the silence encased the city in a thick crust, she decided it was time to take action. With her mom and Jerry lying dead in their bedroom, because she didn't know what the hell to do with their bodies, she sat at their expensive antique dining table and made a list of *Things to Do*. It was a project, one she nicknamed *Shawshank*, a little homage to her mom's favorite movie, the one with Tim Robbins spending two decades in a Maine prison for a double murder he didn't commit. It was not unlike the programming projects or computer hacks she'd undertaken. You start with a goal, and you just worked backward from the end result you wanted and then figured out the pieces you absolutely had to have to get to that outcome.

Tahoe had been a bust. She'd made it to the outskirts of town on August 28, only to find it had burned to the ground, nothing left but smoldering ruins, thick tendrils of smoke still reaching for the sky. With that gone and done with, she decided to head east, holding out hope her dad was still alive. It sounded like he'd survived deep into the second week, and well, it wasn't like she had many other options. The idea that he was still alive was grist for the mill, enough to keep her moving each day, especially as the scope of the disaster became apparent. So she had headed east, back toward the place she'd been born, for the first time since her mom had moved her out to California nearly two decades earlier.

By mid-September, she'd made it east of the Rockies, past Denver, feeling pretty good about herself. And then she'd gone and gotten herself caught by these yahoos.

At precisely seven a.m., the jiggle of the door, which, of course, only locked from the outside. She leapt out of bed to greet her guard, Ned. He was a tall, nervous fellow with a narrow face that he was constantly touching with his slender fingers. As captors went, he was about as good as one could hope for. He was almost apologetic about it. He rarely spoke and refused to make eye contact, as though he was embarrassed to be part of this.

"Good morning, Ned," she said, as warmly and cheerily as she could. The greeting had become part of their daily dance, and per their usual agreement, Ned replied with an almost imperceptible nod.

"You just don't seem like the kind of guy to get caught up in all this," she said.

Each day, she'd dug a little deeper, a little at a time. She didn't know where any of this was going, but it was a project that might one day bear fruit. An experiment you stuck in the corner of the lab and maybe it paid dividends down the road.

He let out a small sigh, one he may not have intended, and he caught himself midstream. He looked at her for a moment, scrunching up his lips as though he were deep in thought. Even though they were alone in the room, he glanced over his shoulder.

"What's it really like out there?" he whispered.

Her eyes went wide.

"Don't you know?"

"Management keeps things kind of close to the vest."

"It was bad, Ned."

She let that set for a moment before continuing.

"Every city and town in America is a rotting, stinking graveyard. It killed almost everybody."

She paused for dramatic effect and then repeated the last word slowly, emphasizing each syllable.

"Now I want to ask you a question," she said, moving in while his guard was down, while he was processing her report from the field. "What am I doing here?"

His eyes, which had been drifting, snapped into focus.

"We shouldn't be talking about this," he whispered.

Rachel's heart leapt into her throat. Not a *shut up*, but the more conspiratorial *we shouldn't*.

"Bad enough what your bosses are doing," she said. Important to start separating him from the monsters at the top. "It has to stop."

"Stop it," he snapped at her.

Enough, she told herself. That was enough for today. But the plant was starting to bear fruit, if only a small bud. A healthy bud, perhaps, but still a small bud. Too much attention now could strangle it.

They ate breakfast together every morning, to the extent it could be called breakfast. They ate protein bars and MREs. Vitamins. Water. Coffee, but shit coffee, like someone had re-brewed it through a used diaper. Part of her was surprised that they let the women commingle like sorority sisters at brunch, but she gathered it was important to their captors that they enjoy a semblance of normalcy.

After breakfast was their hour in the yard. A six-foot-high fence had been strung around their building, leaving them just a little patch of hardpack to get all the fresh air they were going to get for the day. Rachel chose to walk the perimeter, ever mindful of the guards with their automatic weapons. The complex was unlike any place she'd ever seen. Fortress like. Off in the distance, to her west and north, high walls enclosed the compound.

Sounds of activity elsewhere in the compound filled the air. Generators, trucks, tractors, revving to life on this cool but not cold morning. Life was moving on here, and for the thousandth time, she wished she knew more about this place. So many questions.

Who were these people?

What were they doing here?

Had anyone died of the plague here?

Had they really just ridden it out?

And most importantly: What was in store for her and the other women?

She'd made a full loop of the perimeter when she noticed a handful of women had gathered at the center of the yard.

This was the crying group, the ones committed to telling their sad stories of the plague over and over, in new and horrifying ways. And they were at it again this morning. Stories of how this child or that spouse had died, when they had died, what they had done after the person had died. Why relive it? She tried to listen and understand it from their point of view. Maybe the simple act of telling it flushed it out, leached the poison from their systems. The fact that all of them had experienced the same kinds of losses, she supposed, didn't make each person's individual loss any less profound. She had to remember that. Her mom had died, but she'd known lots of people who'd lost a parent and it hadn't been the end of the world (*except in her case, it had been, ha-ha, will this gallows humor ever STOP?*), and her dad might even still be alive, so who was she to judge them and their terrible fate?

Was it because she was still single and childless?

Was she just a sociopath?

Erin Thompson was telling her tale now, the tears flowing, her shoulders heaving. Rachel looked at her, she really looked at her. She was a pretty woman, down there deep, underneath the grief, underneath the hard shell that had formed in the years she had spent constructing her appropriate middle-class life. It no longer mattered whether it had made her happy or whether she had mortgaged her dreams to become a stay-at-home mom because all of it, from the endless parade of birthday parties to her husband's somewhat lackadaisical attitude toward marriage and fatherhood and family in general, was better than this hellscape in which they'd been abandoned.

"All my life, I prayed to God to protect my family," she said. Then: "God can go fuck Himself!"

A few of the other women gasped, and two crossed themselves. Undone. These women were coming undone, a little bit at a time.

She glanced around the faces that grew more familiar every day. One of the faces that had been there in the early days was still missing. The Middle Eastern woman, Nadia. A sweet lady. This would be the third or fourth day that Rachel hadn't seen her. Maybe she'd escaped. She was probably dead.

So easy, that word. Dead. Once spoken in hushed tones, never around children unless it was spelled out, and always with eternal respect, lest it be your lot sooner than later, now it was just a word. A market flooded with it, its value cheapened.

But that was the thing. While dead might have become valueless currency, life was now the gold standard. Simply by being alive, Nadia had earned some measure of respect. Undoubtedly, her very existence had been important to these people.

But why?

As sex slaves?

Given the number of female faces she'd seen, many of them quite attractive, that didn't quite add up. Dozens of beautiful women here, lean, athletic, vibrant, intelligent. And Rachel's group of twelve was, on the surface, very ordinary. She herself didn't hold a candle to most of the women here. This wasn't low self-esteem talking; it was just who she was. After a classmate's messy death from anorexia in high school, Rachel had long since made her peace with her slightly pear-shaped build.

And just like that, the hour was up, and Ned and the other guard herded them back inside. Rachel took in a lungful of fresh air, fixating on its cool sweetness, something to remember as she spent the next twenty-three hours indoors. Ned escorted her again, his face looking long and drawn. He kept looking at her, long enough for her to catch him, and then he would cut his eyes away. She wondered if she could trade what she knew about the outside for more information about what was happening here.

As they made their way down the narrow corridor back to her room, the last one on the end, she considered faking a sexual interest in him, but she dismissed the idea just as quickly. For one thing, she'd never tried anything like that before, and she didn't think she was a good enough actor to pull it off. But the most important reason was that she sensed she had the upper hand in the relationship. As a woman, she'd been a relative rarity in her chosen field. Something like ninety percent of engineers and programmers had been men, and she'd drawn her share of interest at CalTech and during her two summer internships. Even from the gross professors, who'd had years to perfect their game with the undergraduates, but still pathetic with their clumsy, one-beat-too-long invites for a programming session and "hey let's order some Chinese food and I've got this bottle of wine someone left in my office," like they were reading from a script of a romantic comedy making fun of dirty old computer geeks.

"You lose anyone?" she asked as they arrived at her room. All the other women were secured in their rooms.

"No," he said harshly.

He shoved her into her room. As he stepped back out into the hallway, he paused and looked back over his shoulder.

"My sister and her family," he whispered. "They lived outside Chicago. I don't know what happened to them."

"I'm sorry," she said.

He scraped a flake of dried paint from the doorjamb.

"Sometimes things are different in practice than in theory," he said.

"What?"

"Nothing. I'll be back at dinner," he said.

He walked away without another word.

29

A stomach bug swept through the group in the second week of October, and Adam called for a good long break from the road to let them recover and figure out their next step. Although the trip had been extremely difficult, especially in the wake of the deaths of Stephen and Caroline, and had taken its toll, Nadia's bombshell about Rachel energized the group's spirits as they recovered.

They took up residence in a dilapidated travel motel called the Cadillac Inn in South Haven, about fifty miles south of Wichita. It was the kind of place that had fallen on hard times long before Medusa, where the cheap electronic marquee always blinked VACANCY and made fancy promises of free cable and clean rooms. It sat on the access road paralleling I-35, a sad little island in the middle of nowhere. Adam couldn't imagine it had been much busier before the plague than it was now.

In the last room, Adam had found a family of five, dead long enough that the smell had either faded or they were all becoming way too used to it. He pulled the door together as quickly as he could and retreated to the other side of the motel, where the rest of the group had started establishing camp. Adam took a room with Max. Nadia had agreed to share a room with Sarah, and Freddie moved into a room at the far end of the corridor, which was fine with Adam. The less he saw of the man, the better.

Adam had taken a chance that one of the two vehicles still in the parking lot, a red Subaru Outback with nearly a full tank of gas, had belonged to the deceased family in the last room, and it had. It seemed terribly morbid, returning to ransack their room for the keys, but it was necessary. Adam didn't know whether to be happy or depressed about understanding the necessity of these things. But they'd walked nearly 130 miles in the last two weeks, and they were exhausted. Worse, having to walk limited the stock of supplies they could carry, making them more dependent on what they could find out here. The further they got away from the metropolitan areas, the harder it was to find your Walmarts and your big grocery stores. Sure, the supply of goods was far exceeding demand these days, but if you weren't able to find those goods, they didn't do you a hell of a lot of good.

And the truth was that he was having a hard time thinking about all these variables. Ever since Nadia had recognized Rachel's photograph, Adam had forgotten everything and everyone. The stolen kiss, his concern about Freddie, all these issues had evaporated under the bright light of the news of Rachel's whereabouts. But all he knew so far was that Nadia had known Rachel, that they had been held captive together, and about a week before they'd found her, Nadia had escaped. He'd bitten his tongue when he considered asking her if it would have been too much trouble to take Rachel with her, and that was probably a wise move. Even without that bit of commentary, he'd come on too strong, way too strong, peppering her with questions about who she was, where she'd been, what she'd been doing there. Within seconds of unleashing his fusillade, Nadia had closed up tight like a turtle drawing up in its shell. This had just made Adam even more desperate, his questions becoming ever sharper and more pointed, the way a fly trapped in a spider-web made things worse simply by struggling harder.

Eventually, Sarah had stepped in, draping a comforting arm around Nadia and shooting Adam an icy stare that would haunt him, and that had been that. That had been days ago, and Nadia hadn't spoken since, not even to Sarah. In the meantime, Adam and Max had ranged out in every direction gathering supplies. In addition to the basics, they each found their special treat – Nadia's tea now added to the list. Freddie, in all his stubbornness, still refused to ask for anything. Adam desperately wanted to begin a focused search for Rachel, but without help from Nadia, he knew he would be wasting his time and energy.

They started taking their meals together in the motel's reception area. Afterwards, they'd play cards or just sit around and talk. Freddie rarely joined them, choosing instead to eat in his room, which bothered Adam immensely. The more he tried to include the man in the group, the more he pulled away. He had taken Caroline's death incredibly hard; in his mind, he was oh-for-two in the protection business.

On their fourth day at the Cadillac Inn, Adam was propped up in bed, reading an old John Grisham book, when a knock on his door interrupted him. A steady rain was falling, the patter of raindrops on the rooftop comforting, as it always had been. Max napped on the other bed. Adam opened the door to find Sarah there, Nadia standing just off her left shoulder.

"Got a minute?" Sarah asked.

"Of course," he said, backing away from the door to give Nadia her space. He invited them in and then propped the door open with the table in the room. It might make her feel more comfortable, knowing the door was open.

"Nadia wants to talk."

"Great," he said, his heart racing, his body flush with shame. He held his hands out toward the two cheap chairs. "Please, have a seat."

His formality struck him as a bit ridiculous, but he was desperate not to mess this up. He couldn't have done a worse job handling Nadia's revelation about Rachel had he sat down and planned it. As they took their seats, he sat on the edge of the bed facing them, his left leg crossed over his right one, his hands laced around the knee.

God, please let this be the least offensive, least aggressive pose possible.

Jesus, his career had put him between women's thighs on a daily basis for more than a decade, and he'd become a pro at neutralizing the uncomfortable, keeping it cool, professional, as clinical and un-unsavory as possible. He kept his mouth zipped tight, waiting for Nadia to kick things off.

"Go ahead," Sarah said. "Tell him what you told me."

Nadia was sitting ramrod straight, her hands stacked neatly on her lap. She eyed him warily, the look of a child after a severe beating at the hands of an angry father.

"I met your daughter at the camp," she said. She paused, as though she were trying to figure out which way to go with the narrative.

Adam desperately wanted to unload a barrage of questions, but he bit his lip, sinking his teeth into his lower lip until his eyes welled with tears from the pain.

"There were a lot of people there. Dozens."

Even these vague descriptions set off explosions in his mind.

"After, uh..." She stopped and gently tapped her lips with a clenched fist. She cleared her throat, shoving aside the emotional roadblock, and continued. "After my family was gone, I left Stillwater. It was very scary at night, and the smell..."

Sarah placed a well-timed hand on the woman's knee, and Nadia looked over at her, nodding her head.

Yeah, I think we're all pretty goddamn familiar with the smell, Adam thought, and he felt shitty for thinking it. He hated the way such thoughts just crashed through like an unwanted party guest.

"I hated to leave my family there," she said, spreading her arms wide, "but what could I do? What could I do?"

Sarah took Nadia's small hand in between hers, enveloping it, protecting it.

"I walked for many days. It was so hot, and I felt crazy. Dead bodies everywhere. Sometimes I would hear a dog barking, and it sounded so close, but then I would walk ten miles and it sounded exactly the same."

Adam felt like he was about to burst, but he kept quiet, knowing she had to do this, that she had to unload it. It was poison cargo, and if she didn't get rid of it, slough it off like the dead skin it was, she'd have no chance to heal the terrible wound that had been inflicted on her soul.

"I ended up with a small group of people. Two men and an older woman. We were headed west. I'm not even sure why we were headed that way."

Her olive skin colored red, as though her act of self-preservation had been something to be ashamed of.

"They came for us at night," she said, her voice softening. "I woke up to the sound of screaming, horrible screaming, and then I was being pulled out of my tent. I remember the moon was very bright, and I could see them, there were four of them, so clearly even though it was the middle of the night. They marched us out to the road and they shot the men. Just shot them like they were dogs.

"Then they asked us how old we were," her voice barely a whisper, and Adam had to lean forward to hear Nadia's tale. "The other woman, she said she was fifty-one, and they shot her right in the head. So I lied and said I was thirty-four but this is a lie. I am really forty-one. And I thought they would shoot me, but they didn't. They just shoved me inside this truck and drove me to this big place where they kept us in a building."

Adam uncrossed his legs and leaned forward, his elbows propped on his knees. His mind was spinning, questions sprouting like mushrooms on a dark, damp forest floor. What was this place? Who were these people? How could there be so many still alive? They probably hadn't seen a hundred people total since leaving Richmond, let alone that many in one place. Did they have a vaccine?

"They did tests on us," she said, her voice cracking now. "They, uh..."

She jerked her hand clear of Sarah's, as if she'd touched a hot stove, and her chin dropped to her chest. They were losing her. She was headed for a dark place, one she obviously had no desire to navigate right now, and he had to steer her away from it.

"And you met Rachel?" he asked, as gently as he could.

"Yes," she said with a sigh, lifting her chin up. She seemed relieved that Adam had changed the subject, as though she'd lost control of her own narrative, a jetliner spiraling toward earth, its pilot frozen and unable to pull up.

"I met her the day after I got there," she said. "At breakfast. She's a very sweet girl."

Adam's heart thumped crazily, and he was certain they could all hear it.

"And she's OK?"

"Yes, I think so," she said.

"How did you get away?" Sarah asked.

She turned to Sarah.

Her face darkened again.

"One morning, they drove me away from the camp. Two of them. Out near the woods. They were going to kill me. So as soon as they stopped, I got out and ran as fast as I could into the trees. It was raining so hard, and the forest, it was very thick, so I think they didn't look for me for very long. I ran and ran and ran. I didn't stop until it was dark."

It occurred to Adam that this mysterious camp was likely no more than a day or two's drive from where he now sat.

"I was by myself until I found you," she said, her voice going stiff and flat, the tone of a woman who was wrapping things up.

The trio fell silent. Adam massaged his temples with the points of his index fingers, trying to decide what to say next.

"Can I ask you a couple of questions?" he asked.

Nadia looked at Sarah, who nodded.

"Okay."

"Do you remember anything about where this place was?"

"No, I really don't," she said, her face dour. "They wouldn't say."

"This place, was it like a city or a town?"

"No," she said. "It was like a ... castle. But not really. There were walls around it. There was a farm and they had electricity. They seemed very prepared for all this."

"After you left, were you on foot the whole time?"

"Yes."

"Which way were you walking?"

"I'm not really sure exactly. Mostly east, so the sun wouldn't be in my face in the afternoon. But I can't say it was due east."

"How many days before we picked you up did you escape?"

"A week," she said. "Maybe ten days. I'm sorry. I wish I could be more helpful."

He resisted the almost overwhelming urge to express his disappointment. After all, this woman was his sole link to Rachel. If they hadn't found her, he probably would have never seen Rachel again.

He smiled his best smile.

"Please. You've given me the best news I could have hoped for."

A thin smile appeared on Nadia's lips.

"I think I'd like to rest," she said.

Sarah escorted Nadia back to her room. While she was gone, he wrote down as much as he could remember on a notepad he found in the drawer of the end table by the bed.

"What do you think?" Sarah asked when she returned.

"Hard to believe," he said. "But she did know Rachel's name."

"Yeah," Sarah said. "What now?"

Adam sighed.

"We were near Topeka when we picked her up," he said. "She said she'd been on the road a week, maybe ten days?"

"More or less."

"Say she walked ten, fifteen miles a day. She probably made it a hundred miles or so on foot. So this camp she's talking about is probably within a hundred and fifty miles of here. Let's round up to two hundred miles. Hell, we may have driven by it already."

"Sounds about right, but that's a huge search radius. And that's assuming she's remembering things correctly. She had a pretty rough go."

"I don't know what other choice I have," Adam said. "I'll get some maps, lay out some search grids and start looking."

"It could take months to find this place. If you ever do."

"Months I've got," he said. "Years I've got."

A strange look crossed Sarah's face. And then it hit him.

"You guys don't have to stay," he said.

Sarah chewed on a fingernail, her eyes focused on something behind him.

"I can't thank you enough for what you've done," he said.

More silence.

"I know this is a shithole in the middle of nowhere, but I have to stay and look for her."

Sarah nodded and went back outside. She stood under the overhang and smoked a cigarette as the rain continued to fall. Adam watched her for a moment through the door and then joined her.

"I'll stay," she said, not looking at him. She held out a hand and let rainwater collect in her palm.

"Are you sure?" he asked.

"It's just sort of hitting me now," she said, shaking the water from her hand. "There's nothing out there. On the road for two months, and there's just nothing. It was easy not to think about it while we were headed west. You know? Then St. Louis was a bust, and Caroline died, and now we're here. You've found what you were looking for. Not exactly, but you know what I mean. It's like the rest of us have been supporting characters in the story of Adam."

"I didn't mean-"

"I know," she said. "I know. And that came out wrong. I was happy to be part of your story. It meant I didn't have to think about what came next. But now, next is here."

They stood silently as the rain intensified.

"You remember that night I asked you about God?"

"Yeah."

"I think I was still in shock," she said. "Like we were watching this terrible thing that had happened to all these other people. And it was a thing to talk about, like we were in some college seminar. But now, it hurts so bad. To be left here all alone. And being with you, with the others, it made it hurt a little less."

"So, I'll stay. Nadia will do whatever I do. Max will stay. And we'll just keep going like before."

She walked away.

30

He always checked the mailbox first.

No specific reason. It just seemed like the right thing to do.

Dr. James Rogers flipped open the mailbox's small metal door, which squeaked on rusty hinges, and pulled out a stack of mail, probably two or three days' worth. A greeting card postmarked August 10, right around the time everything started going to hell. A credit card solicitation. An L.L. Bean catalog. The mail was mostly intact, but the catalog was damp and swollen, the ink having run and smeared. He gently closed the box and made his way up the driveway to the front door of the small ranch house, snaking around the silver minivan still parked in the driveway. Plastic toys littered the front yard, which was choked with knee-high weeds. Dead leaves and branches clogged the streets and storm drains, leaving a thick soup sloshing along the curbside.

"I'll meet you inside," he called back toward Ned.

Ned nodded and collected the gear from the car, the cleaning supplies, water jugs, mops, the garbage bags. Rogers briefly wondered if anyone had noticed his and Ned's absence from the Citadel, but even if they had, he wasn't sure he cared all that much. The first time he'd done this, about three weeks ago, he'd been terrified. But he hadn't been able to stop himself from taking a pickup truck and making the twenty-minute drive here to Beatrice, Nebraska. In the weeks since Medusa had finished its terrible work, he hadn't been sleeping, he hadn't been eating. He'd lie down at night and picture the house he'd grown up in, a little rancher in Lansing, Michigan, not very different than this one he now stood before. Eventually, it was all he thought about. It began to eat away at him, a little bit at a time, knowing that the bodies of his brother Jeff (who'd bought out Rogers' share in the house in Lansing after their parents had died), his wife Shannon, and their three kids were almost certainly in there, rotting away, that they would lie there for all eternity, until the bones were dust.

Ashes to ashes. Dust to dust.

This was his sixth trip to Beatrice, and it was the only thing that brought him any joy anymore. Well, joy might have been too strong a word. Relief. Peace. They were entering a period of terrible danger, and for them to be effective, they would need peace. There were five others, and each had already accompanied Rogers on an excursion. It had become their sacred pilgrimage. Today, it was Ned's turn.

The front door was locked, but a swift kick at the lock took care of that. The door swung hard inward, slamming against the interior wall before bouncing back toward him. The house was a mess, as the others had been. Clothes and blankets and spoiled food lay everywhere. The stench of death had largely faded, leaving behind just a hint of mustiness and decay. The living room was dimly lit, the curtains drawn.

After setting the mail down, he did a quick loop through the house; in a back bedroom, the body of a small child lay on the floor, tucked under a pathetic-looking blue blanket. On the bed was a female body still dressed in a thin nightgown, the corpse gray, the skin drawn tight. He sat down on the bed. He always sat with the bodies.

You did this.

He cried.

The tears came harder with each successive trip he made here.

How had he let this happen?

Congratulations, Jimmy, you're gonna go down in history as the man with the worst case of regret, *ever!*

When the tears finally stopped flowing (*a minute, an hour, he didn't know...*), he got up and got to work. They started in the living room, cleaning up the trash and the junk that had piled up as this woman and her son had succumbed to Medusa. He dusted and fluffed pillows and washed dishes and scrubbed the little gas stove. He made the beds and scoured the toilet and the bathtub and stacked mail and magazines. He shined the counters and swept the floors. He carried out two trash bags and set them in the can on the side of the house.

Then they carried the bodies of the woman and her child outside and buried them in their tiny backyard. It took them the rest of the afternoon, but eventually, they were both in the ground. When he topped off the makeshift graves with the last bit of dirt, he felt better. It would be short-lived, of course, because dead was dead, and they were dead because of him, because he had been too much of a coward to stop it and there were tens of millions of other houses just like this one, and what the hell difference did it make whether he cleaned these poor people's houses anyway?

Dead was dead.

This was probably going to be the last time he did this, he realized.

He was due to leave the Citadel in a week. To leave forever.

They were waiting for him.

It had all been part of the plan, you see.

But then the plan had changed. And no one knew it but him.

When he and Ned were done, they sat on the back steps and smoked stale cigarettes. Rogers was up to a pack a day, and he prayed he would develop lung cancer. At least emphysema or COPD. He deserved it. Suicide was too good for him, he knew that. He needed to suffer. He would smoke three packs a day if that's what it took. They sat in silence for a few minutes. In the distance, a coyote howled its mournful cry.

He was scared, so scared.

"How are you feeling?" Rogers asked.

"I don't know," Ned said, his voice cracking. "A little better, I guess."

"We can't undo what has been done," Rogers said.

"I know," Ned said, his shoulders sagging.

He'd recruited Ned last. Ned's last few psychological evaluations had revealed markers of guilt and remorse about what they had done. He was growing erratic, his work performance was suffering. He'd originally been brought on for his survivalist skills, one of these apocalypse junkies, but when the shit had hit the fan, he hadn't been able to handle it. Their stupid psych evals. As if they really would have been able to tell how people would react after they murdered seven billion people. When Rogers had finally broached the subject with him, Ned had seemed almost relieved.

Ned dropped his cigarette to the brick step.

They drove back to the Citadel in silence. It was raining when Rogers made it back to his quarters on the eastern side of the compound. He fixed himself a cup of tea and sat down with the file that had brought him to this point, the file that had finally pushed him over the edge.

Rogers had debated telling the others what he had found, but he hadn't been able to form the words. Not that it mattered, really. But he should tell them. They had a right to know that they'd been lied to. Lied to from the beginning. He could barely wrap his head around it. He thought he'd known all there was to know about the project. But then they'd captured her.

He ran the tip of his finger over the name hastily written on the tab.

RACHEL – LAST NAME UNKNOWN

It was supposed to be a routine physical. Gynecological examination, fertility testing, blood, urine, the whole nine yards. The results of her tests, however, had been anything but routine. There, clear as day, flowing through her veins, was the nanovaccine. Not the one that he'd administered to Chadwick and the ninety-eight other residents of the Citadel.

It had all been part of the plan, you see.

The sterility hadn't been an unintended side effect. Rogers had programmed it into the nanotech under Gruber's orders. Miles Chadwick didn't know what the Citadel really was. Compartmentalization and all that. Gruber had desperately wanted Chadwick to succeed, but it was never guaranteed that he would. And if things had gone south, Gruber had wanted to make sure that there was no link back to him. Everything had been carefully constructed to make sure that the trail ended with Chadwick. Cut the loose thread.

Rogers thought he had known everything. But he hadn't, and he really shouldn't have been surprised. He'd made a deal with the devil, after all.

But who was this girl?

How had she gotten the vaccine?

Did Gruber know about her?

Did she know about Gruber?

He was too afraid to ask her.

When he saw the nanovaccine coursing through her blood, that's when he knew that it was all doomed to fail. It was too big. A crack here. A fissure there. It would all come apart. Nebraska. Colorado.

Colorado.

Chadwick had changed the game by bringing in these women. It was something Rogers hadn't counted on, and looking back, it was pretty goddamn stupid of them. Chadwick was brilliant. Of course he'd want to use survivors as surrogates. It made sense. It was a good idea. And the truth was Rogers was a bit curious about whether it would work. But then he'd think about Jeff and Shannon and Mikey and Jessica and the little one, the cute butterball whose name he always forgot, and he'd hate himself all over again.

Why?

Why had he agreed to it?

Had he let Gruber brainwash him?

All those years working at NanoMed, one of Penumbra's many subsidiaries, Rogers had always looked up to the man, even saw him as a bit of a father figure, where his own had been an abusive, alcoholic plumber who couldn't hold a job. And there's your Freudian link, Jimmy! Good job.

What a goddamn mess.

He closed the file and set it on his lap. The tea had cooled enough to drink, and he took a swallow. He couldn't undo what had been done. But he could help these women. And then he would disappear.

It was almost time.

31

By the evening of October 23, Adam had spent fifty-four hours looking for Nadia's camp and had nothing to show for it.

They'd been on the road since first light. Riding shotgun while Sarah drove, sipping three-day-old coffee, he studied his maps, a Sharpie in hand. A chilly rain was falling. They were still holed up in the Cadillac Inn, trying to ignore the fact the days had gotten progressively cooler and the nights were much, much colder. They'd taken to stripping the empty rooms of their bedding and loading up with blankets and quilts and towels to stay warm at night.

That would do for now, but they were approaching a come-to-Jesus moment in a couple of areas. A few more weeks, and freezing to death would become a legitimate possibility. If they didn't find Rachel by November the first, they'd probably have to pull up and head south for the winter, like a flock of Canadian geese. Second, motorized transportation was becoming increasingly hit-or-miss; a bad load of gasoline had grounded the Outback, and since then, they'd resorted to peeling vehicles off the Big Jam like fruit from an automotive tree. Some ran; others didn't.

He spent as much time as he could searching for the camp. Some days he had company; others he traveled alone. Today, Sarah had come along, and for that he was glad. As they banged around the back roads of the empty Midwest, sometimes they talked, mostly about the world gone by, and sometimes they said nothing. This afternoon, he'd been quiet, feeling particularly morose about their quest. Now darkness was setting in, earlier and earlier with each passing day. He checked his watch; it was a hair before seven o'clock. As he shaded in a map section they'd searched that afternoon, he felt the vehicle decelerate sharply.

"What is it?" he asked, looking over at Sarah.

"That light," Sarah said, slowing to a stop on the shoulder. They were up in the panhandle of Oklahoma, a couple hundred miles from their little home base in South Haven.

He followed her gaze toward a soft glow to the northwest, at his ten o'clock. The rain had pushed off to the east late in the afternoon, taking the cloud cover with it and leaving behind a dark, moonless night, very dark. This effervescence was a lighthouse in an ocean of darkness. Adam's pulse quickened.

"What do you think it is?" she asked.

"Hopefully a steakhouse."

She laughed.

"That would be good."

"We should check it out," he said. "While we can use the light as a beacon. If we wait until daylight, we might not be able to find it again."

"Agreed."

She went to shift into gear and then paused.

"Look," she said, touching Adam on the arm.

A small herd of deer crossed the road in front of them, emerging ghostlike from the tall prairie grasses at the side of the road. A large doe paused and turned her head toward the windshield, her eyes glinting in the shine of the headlights. Her head, a creamy light brown and speckled with white spots as though she were a careless painter, twitched once, and then she followed her herdmates into the prairie on the other side.

"Hunting season would be coming up soon," she said.

"Probably going to be a good one for the deer."

She laughed as she guided the truck back on the road, the glow in the distance their only guide.

"Be interesting to see what nature does without us in the way," she said.

"I've been thinking about that," Adam said. "The virus didn't seem to have much impact on animals, at least that I've seen. But nature is going to roar back in a hurry, I can promise you that. Think how fast grass and weeds grew even when we were staying right on top of it. The wild animal population, the ones usually culled by hunting, will probably explode, until the food chain stabilizes again. Oceans and rivers will start to cleanse themselves. I suppose overfishing will be a thing of the past, at least for the next few centuries."

"Think our society will ever re-form?"

"Hard to say," Adam said. "We've probably seen the last of the good ol' U.S. of A., much as it pains me to say. I could see a bunch of little communities popping up all over the place, particularly in the south, in the rural areas, where the temperatures are warmer and where there probably aren't as many bodies to deal with. Assuming that some of the babies survive, and the communities begin to sustain themselves with food, water, shelter, they'll begin to interact. Possibly violently at first."

"Violently."

"I hope not, but that's what I'm afraid of. Some of these communities, they may be headed by dictatorial types. Remember, the people who survived – they weren't selected for their ability to survive in a post-apocalyptic wasteland. They were selected for their ability to survive exposure to the Medusa virus. And that's it. All over the world, there were infants and quadriplegics and Alzheimer's patients who were immune but died within a few days because there was no one there to care for them. So you're going to have people who won the genetic lottery but who have no idea how to survive on their own. They may be more than happy to let someone else run the show. And those are the kinds of people who scare me. There's going to be a huge push to get the power turned back on, or at least some facsimile of it. People are going to start stockpiling things like weapons. In fact, we should be doing that ourselves. Even if we don't need them right away."

He paused and considered all the challenges that lay ahead and it began to make his head spin.

"And if the babies aren't immune?" Sarah asked.

"Then we turn the lights out before we leave."

The mood in the car soured. His back ached, and he wanted nothing more than to climb into his big king bed back home, in a world where none of this had happened, where he could sit in front of the TV with some old DVDs, slurping down spicy chicken tortilla soup.

"How are we on gas?" he asked, deciding to change the subject.

"Not great," she said after checking the gauge. "We can either keep going and possibly run out of gas before we find this place, or turn back and possibly run out before we get home."

"Super."

He chewed on a fingernail, trying to push emotion aside and focus on the logical choice.

"I'm up for it if you are," she said. "You're right. It may be hard to find again."

"It's risky," he said. "I want to find Rachel more than anyone, but I don't want you to do something you don't need to do."

"Fuck it," she said. "What was it the kids were saying before the virus hit? YOLO?"

"Yolo?"

"You only live once."

"Oh, YOLO."

"The kids, Doctor. The kids."

They spent the next ninety minutes zipping along back roads, cutting through fields and then back onto state highways, the ever-present glow drawing closer on the northwest horizon. Sarah forded an overgrown farm, the bodies of half a dozen horses dotting the landscape in the sweep of the headlights, dead of thirst, if Adam had to guess. At the farm's gated entrance, Sarah turned west onto Route 815, the glow dead ahead. Just then, the truck sputtered and hitched, the final warning that they were riding on fumes.

"Kill the headlights," he said.

Sarah flicked the lights off, leaving them cocooned in darkness.

"You think this is her camp?"

"I don't know," she said. "I don't see any walls."

"Well, either way, we're committed now."

He was sort of glad there was no turning back. The glow was hypnotic, drawing him in. Something different about this place. Why it felt different than the others, he didn't know. Maybe this was a destination rather than a way station. He thought often of Sarah's query about what he would do after he found Rachel. There would have to be something to make life worth living; otherwise, they could all be headed for a dark place indeed.

The problems were piling up quickly. His feelings for Sarah at the top of the pyramid, not because it was the most pressing, but it was the most familiar type of problem. Unrequited love, that was a road he'd been down before. Beneath that, Freddie's state of mind. OK, not your everyday problem, but still in the range of human experience. He was still worried about the guy. Of course, Rachel.

And the last one, of course, the foundation of all the other problems they were facing, the one that vexed him, had been baby Stephen's death. Of course, it looked like he had died of Medusa, but had his body put up any fight at all? Had he inherited any resistance from his mother? If Medusa resistance required a complete copy of the gene, meaning a baby needed to be born to two immune parents, or worse, if it wasn't hereditary at all, then they were all in a lot of trouble indeed. Even if it was hereditary, the survivors were so scattered he didn't know how enough of them would re-connect to rebuild the species. Conceivably, not enough women would become pregnant, and going forward, each successive generation would be smaller than the last, until it was too late, until the population dipped below the point of no return, and that would be that.

The engine finally quit, and the SUV rolled to a stop as Sarah guided it to the shoulder. They slipped out of the truck, grabbed their guns, and zipped up their jackets against the night's chill. A cold wind blew in off the prairie, frosting the back of Adam's neck.

They walked for another ninety minutes along Route 815, a two-lane groove slicing through the flatlands. About five miles west of where they abandoned the SUV, a sign rose up from the darkness. It read *Welcome to Evergreen, America's Greenest City!*

Just beyond the sign, the city of Evergreen rose up like the pages inside a child's pop-up book. Bright and sprawling, slapped down in the middle of the wide, empty prairie. As they drew closer, the soft white glow sharpened into the thousands of twinkling lights illuminating the town. Adam felt dizzy, sort of the way he'd felt the day he'd gone for that fateful run along the oceanfront at Holden Beach, when he'd found the beach empty and deserted. Outside normal limits.

Nothing moved.

They crept along the sidewalk at city's edge, keeping close, their weapons at the ready. A low-slung white brick building, the name NORTHSTAR stenciled along the side, fronted this block. Across the street, a post office and an ice cream shop called Ericka's.

"How can all the lights still be on?"

Adam shook his head.

He checked his watch; it was nearly eleven p.m. They were hours overdue, but there wasn't anything they could do about that. He hated to think about them worrying, knowing there was nothing they could do but sit and wait and wonder how long they should wait before deciding Adam and Sarah weren't coming back.

They moved street by street, block by block. The streets were virginal, as though they'd just been poured. Bright streetlights poured warm, inviting light across the town square. At one intersection, which bracketed the west side of the town square, they found a park starting to go to seed. At its center was a lake, its surface shimmery and still and dark. It had been a lovely park, ringed by young saplings, their leaves in full Technicolor now. Shiny late-model cars and small SUVs dotted the town.

"Notice anything about the cars?" Adam asked. Something about the place had been nagging him as they'd made their way into the town proper, and it had finally clicked.

Sarah shrugged.

"They're all electric."

A flicker of movement ahead of them, on the east side of the park. A small figure, perhaps a child or teenager, waving frantically at them.

"Help!" the figure called out. "We need help!"

"Let's go!" Sarah hissed, breaking into a run.

"Wait!"

Adam bolted across the park after her, his gun up at the ready. His legs swished against the tall grass as he knifed toward her. But she was fast, quickly widening the distance between them as she zeroed in on her target. Just ahead, just as Sarah had started to gain on her quarry, the figure slipped through the park gate, across the street toward a residential area, and around a corner.

"This way!"

"Sarah!" he yelled. He had no idea what she was thinking, what would possess her to take such a risk. He barreled through the gate and across the street (pausing to look both ways because some habits were *damn* hard to break) and around the same corner.

As he cleared the turn onto a narrow dead-end side street, finding an array of guns trained on Sarah, he realized how big a mistake they'd made.

32

I f there was one lesson Adam was learning in this post-apocalyptic wasteland, one nugget of knowledge he was really taking to heart, it was that everyone had a gun. And people thought it had been easy to get a gun *before* the plague!

Ba-dum, crash-cymbals!

He was staring at the business end of four firearms. A tightly grouped bunch, two women and two men, their faces tight and drawn, plus the rail-thin teenaged girl that had initially drawn their attention. Sarah had her gun up as well, and wasn't this just a hell of a scene?

"Whoa, whoa, whoa!" he yelled out casually, like he were warning a driver about to back into a shopping cart.

"Step back, Adam," Sarah hissed.

"Everybody calm down," he said as calmly as he could, holding up his palms.

"Put your guns down!" a voice squeaked. Adam cut his eyes toward the sound and saw its owner, a heavier-set bespectacled man of about fifty.

"Look, let's all be real careful here," Adam said. He hoped his voice sounded calm. "If we put our guns down, will you promise not to shoot us?"

As a show of good faith, Adam slowly rotated his gun in his hand, taking it by the barrel, and laid it on the ground.

"Put it down, and we'll see what's what," the teenaged girl said. She had a husky voice, coated with the smoke of illicit cigarettes. She was older than Adam had initially thought, probably closer to eighteen or nineteen.

"Sarah," Adam said. "Put the gun down."

She gave him a stare that might as well have been lined with battery acid, but she relented. Holding one palm up, she lowered the heavy gun and dropped it on the ground. It clattered ominously on the asphalt, and just like that, both of them were unarmed.

"See," Adam said, "we're not here to hurt you."

"Who are you people?" the man asked.

"We saw the lights."

"Are you with them? Are you?"

"With who?"

"Don't lie to me!"

"We're not with anyone, I swear! My name is Adam. This is Sarah."

"Let's just shoot them!" one of the women said.

"I don't want to shoot anyone," the man said, his shoulders sagging. His eyes were baggy with exhaustion. "We don't even know if they're with them. They haven't been back in weeks. Let's take them down to the cells. We'll let the mayor sort this out."

"Jeff, we don't even know if mayor is-"

"Shut up!"

The group fell silent, and their captors marched them down the main drag, named Main Street, back the way Sarah and Adam had come. They passed a diner, a law office, a dry cleaner, and a few other staples of a downtown area. There was a small-town feel to it, sure, but there was something about the place Adam couldn't quite put his finger on. One thing he was sure of: this was not Nadia's mysterious camp.

The town hall, back near the lake, was a modern looking brick building with a wide, utilitarian staircase. Adam and Sarah followed inside, where they felt the warmth of the heat blowing through the vents, which felt indescribably good. Jeff led them downstairs to a trio of jail cells. After confiscating their personal items, they put Adam in the cell on the far end and Sarah into the one closest to the door, leaving the middle one empty. Jeff had started sliding the cell door shut when the frantic footsteps of someone descending the stairs filled the air.

"Jeff!" a woman called out.

Adam craned his neck for a better view; a middle-aged woman emerged from the shadows. Her forehead was shiny with sweat and she looked to be in tears.

"What is it?" Jeff asked.

"Gwen just had a seizure!"

Adam shivered with dread. *Medusa?*

"Hey, I'm a doctor," Adam said. "Let me help."

Jeff and the woman looked up at Adam.

"I swear!" Adam said. "There's ID in my wallet."

Jeff didn't seem to be interested in the identification.

"Are you really a doctor?"

"Yes, I was an OB/GYN."

"All the doctors and nurses here died or left town," the woman said. "Will you look at Gwen?"

"If you agree to let us out."

Jeff grunted, a noise suggesting he'd known this ultimatum was coming.

"Jeff, come on, we can't let her die."

"She might die anyway," he said.

"Please, Jeff."

He sighed.

"Fine."

He opened up the cells and said, "Follow me. If you try to run, I will shoot you."

"Any idea what's wrong with her?"

"Lemme think. Today's Saturday. Friday morning, we were at breakfast. Anyway, she complained she was tired and dizzy. And hot! She said she was hot, tired and dizzy. Then she fainted."

Adam set his mind to work, running a differential diagnosis as best he could, drawing on all his medical knowledge, from medical school textbooks, through the continuing education courses, through every random ailment his patients had experienced in his sixteen years in practice.

"Go on," he said. "Every detail matters, no matter how minor you may think it is."

They went up a stairwell to the second floor, Jeff narrating the entire way. Trailing behind was the young woman they'd initially spotted coming into Evergreen. Her name was Charlotte Spencer.

"We had to wake her up for dinner that night," Charlotte said, cutting in. "She ate a little, but she was still out of it. Kind of a mess, actually."

"Fever?"

"Not that I could tell."

They moved into a large room at the end of the corridor, where they found Gwen Townsend on a couch, wrapped in blankets, sleeping. It was an ornate office, one wall lined with bookshelves. Another wall consisted entirely of glass and looked out toward the center of town. A middle-aged woman was sitting with her. The mayor was sweating, her hair matted to her face, but her forehead was cool to the touch. Her pulse was flying.

"Does she have any health problems?"

"I don't know," Jeff said. "I'm sorry."

"Don't be sorry," he said. "Not your job to know. This is her private office, right?"

"Yes.

"Does she have any medicines she keeps here?"

"I'm not really sure. Maybe her desk."

He pointed to a large antique-looking desk on the far side of the room. Adam hurried over to the desk and began pawing through the drawers. In the third one down on the left, he found a black pouch containing several vials of liquid glucagon. Behind that, several sealed syringes and hypodermic needles. He studied the label of the glucagon and was relieved to discover it was one of the newer formulas, the ones that didn't require reconstitution before use. Glucagon was notoriously unstable in solution, but the drug companies had started to figure out how to stabilize it, which allowed for quicker injection.

"She's diabetic!" he called out.

He measured out a dose quickly, tapping the syringe to clear the air bubble, and then rushed back to the mayor's side.

"Jeff," he said. "Help me get these blankets off her."

Together, they unrolled the blankets and hoisted Mayor Townsend to a seated position. He jabbed her thigh with the needle and depressed the plunger.

"Will this work?"

"Assuming she hasn't suffered any irreversible damage, it should work quickly."

Adam held his breath as he waited for the woman's blood glucose levels to recover.

Please, he thought. Please.

~

PATIENT A's name was Kelly Stoddard. She was a thirty-year-old architect expecting her first child, a boy. She'd spent every free second reading every book and pamphlet she could about pregnancy, delivery, and motherhood. She cut out all coffee and soda, even after Adam had assured her that a little caffeine posed no risk to the baby. Hell, even a glass of wine a night probably wouldn't harm the fetus, but Adam would never dare tell an expectant mother that.

Kelly's pregnancy had been unremarkable in every way until her thirty-eight week checkup had revealed a slightly elevated blood pressure reading. Adam reminded Kelly to notify him at once if she noticed any unusual symptoms. The next evening, she called and reported she was feeling a bit lightheaded at dinner, and he told her he'd meet her at the hospital.

He was pretty sure he would go ahead and induce labor at that point. The baby was full-term, measuring more than eight pounds, and there was no reason to keep him in there any longer. Adam couldn't point to any specific reason why he'd made that decision. It wasn't the result of any quantifiable analysis he'd done. It was just a decision constructed with the raw materials of ten thousand other choices he'd made in his career as an obstetrician.

The labor and delivery ward was quiet when he'd arrived at 11:21 p.m., about five minutes before Kelly and her husband Hank. It was a slow night, devoid of even a sliver of the moon or thunderstorm or anything that might have triggered a mass wave of labor across the area, which made what happened later that night all the more maddening. There was nothing else Adam could point to, no distractions, no complicated deliveries or emergency c-sections that might have explained, if not necessarily excused, whatever had constituted the first link in the chain of events that had ended with Kelly and her baby both dead long before their time. To this day, he still didn't know the moment that had constituted the point of no return, the subtle change in her condition that sent things over the cliff, irretrievably so.

Her blood pressure was normal, but her pulse was a bit elevated. The baby's heartbeat was normal. Cervix was dilated to four centimeters, the contractions intermittent and irregular. Adam administered the oxytocin, the synthetic hormone designed to induce labor, at 12:34 a.m. on November 14. Another patient, at thirty-two weeks, came in at 12:57 a.m. with what turned out to be false labor, and she spent the night resting as her contractions faded. At 1:34 a.m., Kelly, who was then dilated to eight centimeters, suddenly began complaining of a severe headache. At 1:47 a.m., her blood pressure skyrocketed to 165 over 120, sending her cart alarm into conniptions.

Adam rushed her into the operating room for a C-section and made the first incision at 1:59 a.m. The surgery proceeded normally, but Kelly's headache continued to worsen, and her blood pressure began climbing again. A neurologist scrubbed in and began monitoring Kelly's neurological condition. Her husband, who'd been friendly and chatty through his wife's pregnancy, grew quieter as he began to notice that something was amiss.

At 2:10 a.m., just as Adam had successfully opened the uterus, Kelly suffered a massive seizure. A nurse escorted Kelly's husband into the cold off-white corridor outside the operating room, where he watched his own personal apocalypse unfold through the tiny window cutout in the door.

As Adam extracted the baby from the uterus, Kelly went into full cardiac arrest. Despite extensive attempts at resuscitation, Kelly was declared dead at 2:34 a.m. The baby was alive but minimally responsive; instead of pinking up, his skin remained the color of a light bruise, and instead of crying, he gasped for air like a fish out of water. His heart rate was dangerously low. The neonatal intensive care staff rushed the baby into an incubator and placed him on 100 percent oxygen, but inexplicably, the infant passed away at 2:44 a.m., exactly seventy minutes after

Adam's patient had first complained of a headache. Adam grimly carried out both pronouncements of death.

Adam could not remember specific details of the discussions with his surgical team, but when it was over, and the machines had been turned off, he remembered bellowing "WHAT THE FUCK JUST HAPPENED?"

It was a rhetorical question, and he didn't wait for an answer. Instead, he slowly made his way to the corridor to talk to the husband, whose face had gone as pale and ashen as the cinderblock walls. Adam could barely stand to look at him, having failed him so egregiously, and so he kept his surgical mask draped across his face, hoping that it hid the shame and bewilderment he was feeling. The man crumpled to the floor, his face in his hands.

"I'm very sorry, Mr. Stoddard," Adam said. "Your wife and baby experienced significant complications during the surgery. Despite all our efforts, they did not survive."

He left it at that, namely because he didn't know what else he could say. Oh, they'd experienced complications all right, on par with a perfectly maintained jetliner plummeting into a field on a clear windless day.

"Noooooooooo!" the man bawled, his sobs mixing with his howls of grief.

Adam stood there, towering over the puddle of a man like an unforgiving god whose answer to a penitent's prayer had been not only *no*, but *fuck no*, his mind a mess of regret and shame, reminding himself not to say a word that might be construed as an admission of guilt and then hating himself for remembering to remind himself.

He waited with the husband for one of the hospital's grief counselors, and when she arrived to counsel the bereaved, Adam slithered away, feeling very much like a cockroach exposed to bright light. In the meantime, a staffer from the morgue came to collect the bodies, where they would await autopsies.

Adam worked the rest of his shift, and when he got home, he went for a long walk, replaying the episode in his head. He'd had one patient die in childbirth before, but she had had severe underlying health conditions that had put her at extreme risk for complications. Never before had a delivery unspooled so quickly and so unexpectedly.

An autopsy classified the manner of Kelly Stoddard's death as natural and the cause of death as sudden cardiac arrest. The baby had died of hypoxia. At the morbidity & mortality conference two months later, Adam sat ashamed while his colleagues armchaired his decision-making. It did not make him feel better that, but for a few minor details, the other physicians would have followed the same course of action that Adam had followed that fateful night.

A hospital investigation into the matter concluded that Adam had done nothing wrong, but in January, Kelly Stoddard's widower filed a complaint with the Virginia Board of Medicine and retained a well-known medical malpractice lawyer. The Board's investigation and the lawsuit hummed quietly in the background of Adam's life for the next seven months, up until the day he'd received the letter from the Board summoning him to appear before it.

The day, as it turned out, he'd first seen the Medusa virus in action.

GWEN TOWNSEND'S eyelids fluttered and flew open a few minutes later.

"She's awake!" Charlotte said, rushing in and taking the mayor's hand in her own. Adam eased behind her, out of the way of the reunion.

Townsend turned her head slowly toward the sound, her lips curling up in a smile when she saw Charlotte at her side.

"Hiya, sweetheart," she said.

"This doctor saved you," Charlotte said, leaning in and kissing the mayor on the cheek.

Mayor Townsend's eyes roamed around the room until she found the stranger's face.

"Ms. Mayor, how are you feeling?" Adam asked.

"Better," she said. "Please, call me Gwen."

"My name is Adam. And you still need to rest," he said. "And you're going to have to carefully monitor your diet and insulin levels."

She blew out a soft sigh.

"I know. We've just had a tough couple of weeks. I let it get away from me."

"That stops now."

"Yes, sir," she said, winking at him.

Adam asked Charlotte to gather some diabetic-friendly foods for the mayor. The others approached one at a time and gave the mayor a warm embrace.

"Can I stand up?"

"Let's wait on that," he said.

"So what's your story?" she asked after the room had emptied out and it was just him, Sarah, and Jeff.

He told her. He told her about Rachel's six-week-old voice-mail message, about their westward trek across America, about Caroline, and about Nadia and the mysterious camp. He told her the whole story, the words rushing out of him like a swollen river after a storm.

He didn't know why he felt the urge to unload his emotional cargo on this woman he'd never met, but he felt like he'd been carrying it for weeks, and, after all, she was a captive audience. There was no motivation to lie or shade or hold back. Out came the truth as best as he could remember it. Maybe the fact he didn't know her made it easier to tell it like it was. Maybe it was because he'd gotten a chance to do a little doctoring here, even if it had been nothing more than administering a simple injection.

He thought about his next move and decided that bluntness would be the best approach. There could be no sugarcoating it. Winter was on its way. Rachel was out there. And he was well on his way to becoming convinced that they all faced a dangerous enemy out there in the never-ending darkness.

"Well, I guess it's my lucky day you showed up here," Gwen said.

"What is this place?" Adam asked.

"What do you mean?" the mayor replied.

"How is all the power still on?"

"Haven't you ever heard of Evergreen, Oklahoma? *America's greenest city*?"

He shook his head. Sarah did the same.

"The town generates its own power," Gwen said. "Wind turbines and solar panels. It's not on the electrical grid."

"I didn't think that was possible on such a big scale," Adam said.

"The town was owned by NorthStar Corporation. Ever heard of them?"

"Sure," Adam said. NorthStar had been one of the nation's largest power companies, supplying electricity to much of the plains states.

"The plant is about a mile away from here. I don't know all the science behind it, but NorthStar figured out a way to make wind and solar power work on a bigger scale."

"And NorthStar owns the town?"

"They own every bit of the land and every building on it," she said. "Or they used to, at least."

"How long will the power stay on?" Sarah asked.

"They said indefinitely, as long as the plant was properly maintained," Gwen said. "Even if the nation's power grid went down."

"Who lived here?"

"Only NorthStar employees and family."

"And you all are the only ones left?"

"We think about a hundred and fifty survived the plague. About a month ago, a group of folks from down the road tried to take the town. Things got ugly. We lost another dozen or so that day. I couldn't believe how folks just turned on each other. We fought them off."

Adam glanced at Sarah, who nodded.

"Would you think about taking me and my friends in here?" Adam asked.

"You don't beat around the bush, do you?" Gwen replied.

"No, I guess not."

"You gonna be the town doc?"

"I think that would be a fair trade," Adam said. "And we can help defend the town again if need be."

She sighed, and her shoulders sagged. It seemed like what little fight she'd had in her just sluiced away.

"It's been a rough couple of months," she said. "I know it looks like we've got it made in the shade, but people are on edge with winter coming and no doctor. We got some disabled folks, I'm not sure what to do about them. One of them's a sex offender. Believe that? Luckily, he's got Alzheimer's, so he doesn't seem to remember he's a goddamned pervert."

"What's he doing here?"

"His son Jim was a big NorthStar executive. He got kicked out of his last residential facility, so his son arranged for him to come live here about a month before the outbreaks. Jim neglected to tell the Housing

Commission about Dad's proclivities. And of course, the dirty old man survives but I watch a thousand children die in the span of a week."

"It was an equal opportunity virus."

"When I woke up here a few minutes ago," she began, "I was sort of hoping I'd dreamed the whole thing and I was back in my own bed. You know that feeling when you wake up from a nightmare and it takes you a second to realize it was just a bad dream?"

He nodded.

"That's what it was like," she said. "I kept waiting for that realization, but it never came."

Her eyes spilled over with tears.

"Goddammit, look at me." She wiped her cheeks with the heel of her hand. "I'm sixty-seven years old. What good can I do, I can't keep up with my insulin? Why did this goddamn thing spare me?"

"The virus didn't spare you," Adam said. "It did what viruses do."

She waved him off with a guffaw.

Then she covered her mouth with her hands and wept.

"How many of you are there?" she asked.

"Four adults, one teenager."

"How long you been out there?"

"Two months. I started in Virginia. Sarah came from New York City."

"What's it like out there? I mean, what's it really like? I haven't left town since it happened."

"Quiet," Adam said. "You can go days without seeing another person. But there's this constant feeling of dread, death just a blink of an eye away. It just hits you more and more each day that we're all on our own. No one coming to help."

"I can relate to that."

Something else came to mind, and it felt weird. It wasn't something he'd given a lot of thought to, but there it was, all the same.

"On the other hand..."

"What?"

He scraped a fingernail against his chin.

"With all the noise of the world gone, it can be quite peaceful. When everything else is stripped away, when it's just you and the land out there..."

Shame flooded through him like the ocean intent on capsizing a boat.

"Jesus, I can't believe I'm saying this out loud."

"No, I think I understand."

"It almost sounds like I'm glad it happened."

"Whether you're glad or not," Gwen said, taking his hand in her own, "the fact of the matter is that it happened. How we deal with it, that's going to determine whether we make it or not. That'll be true for each of us. I will admit, I probably had it easier than most in this thing. I've been divorced thirty years. Never re-married, never had kids. Parents dead a decade. I had me a stepbrother in Minneapolis, but we weren't close. I tried calling him when things started getting bad, but I never heard back.

"But I'm getting off track here. The point I'm trying to make is that this is the world we've been left with. A world with its danger and this quiet beauty you talk about. You're a young man. Hell, even I've got another fifteen years coming to me according to the actuarial tables. Assuming I can remember my damn insulin, that is. And if we can't find something worth living for, if we can't find some joy in something simple, if we can't be the tiniest bit grateful we're still alive, then we might as well have died with the others."

The room was silent.

"True."

"I'll tell you all something I haven't told a soul," she said, pointing a bony, frail finger at him and Sarah.

"When it started to occur to me I wasn't going to catch it, I was over-joyed. I didn't want to die. I was so scared I could barely see straight. I can't even imagine what it must have been like to be that scared and sick to boot. I didn't think about what kind of world I'd be facing or that I'd be one of a handful of survivors or what have you. All I could think about was surviving. And each day I didn't come down with it, I was just glad to be alive, even as the world came crashing down around us. Know what I mean?"

He nodded.

"God forgive me, I know it's a terrible thing to have felt, to have been so happy as the world ended, but I was. I wanted to live."

Now Adam was the one crying. He'd thought all these things, and he'd felt guilty for thinking them. It had felt so wrong, goddamn near immoral, to have been glad to have survived. He suspected that most survivors were torn between these conflicting feelings - happy to be alive but sad to have survived such a terrible thing; it seemed like a distinction without a difference, but there was a real if not faint line there.

"So are you waiting for an invitation?" she asked.

He smiled with embarrassment.

"Maybe."

She blew out an exasperated sigh.

"So Doctor, you think you and your friends like to stay here in Evergreen?"

"Yes," he said. He felt a lightness in his chest, the sense that he'd accomplished something. There was more to be done, of course. Rachel was still out there. But finding a permanent home had also been on the to-do list, a place where they could be safe from the world beyond. It was a dangerous world out there, of that, there was no question. For so many reasons, making Evergreen home seemed like the right thing at the right time.

"Yes, I think we'd like that very much."

33

Rachel had been watching Erin Thompson for the better part of their hour in the yard. Erin had spent most of her time in the corner, her fingers interlocked with the chain link fencing, looking west toward the wall. Despite a chill in the air, Erin had come outside wearing her short-sleeved orange jumpsuit, imprinted with the words South Nebraska Women's Regional Jail, but nothing else. She wore no coat. She was trembling in the cold, Rachel could see that from where she stood, but Erin did not seem to care. It was a change in the routine, and that alone made it interesting for Rachel.

Erin was normally the chattiest of the bunch, the center of the largest clique of Rachel's fellow captives. She liked to talk to everyone, to get to know everyone, as though the very act of socialization would make things easier to deal with or perhaps forget that they'd happened at all. Rachel liked her because she was good to the other women, the women still in shock from everything that had happened.

But today was different. A few of the others, Julie and Latasha and Robin, had approached her, tried talking to her, but Erin had acted like they weren't even there. After a while, they'd given up and retreated back into their clique, forgetting, for the moment, their suddenly quiet friend.

Maybe it had all been an act, Rachel thought. Maybe Erin's good samaritan was nothing more than a quick coat of paint over a devastated landscape. Maybe the wreckage that was Erin's personal horror story was seeping back through that simple covering. It was possible that Erin's shock was finally wearing off and she was now seeing the world the way it really was.

Rachel glanced at the guards, Ned and Jeremy; they were smoking cigarettes by the door, their machine guns slung casually over their shoulders. Then she drifted slowly toward Erin, walking casually, moving toward the fence. She didn't want to come on too strong, make the woman feel like she was invading her space; she wanted it to seem natural, that she, too, saw the truth, that they were bonded. Erin needed someone now to look after her, the way she had looked after the others. And no one else was doing it.

Rachel feigned interest in the hardpack of the yard, crouching down and plucking small stones from the ground. She flung two over the fence, keeping her eye on Erin as she felt the dirt and grit embed her nails. Then she saw it. A flash, a shimmer in Erin's left hand. Rachel glanced back toward the guards, who were deep in their conversation, not paying much attention. She wondered if Ned was feeding Jeremy the info she'd given him, about what things were like outside the walls.

She cocked her head to the left, hoping to secure a better view of the object in Erin's hand. Erin's head was turned to the right, away from Rachel, but back toward the guards. Rachel stood back up and moved a little closer to Erin, a tiny alarm sounding in her head that something bad was about to happen. Erin turned away from the fence toward the yard, her eyes locked in now on Jeremy and Ned. And now Rachel had a clear line of sight toward the object in Erin's hand. It was some kind of homemade shank.

Oh, no.

Rachel picked up the pace; she was about twenty yards away from Erin. She had to get there before the guards realized that something was amiss, or Erin would be dead. She picked up the pace, as fast as she could go without running because that was something the guards would notice. Behind her, the other women continued to chatter, oblivious to the fact that death was now in the yard with them, waiting to see what would happen.

Ten yards. Then five. Then a foot. Then she clamped her hand on Erin's elbow. Erin swung her head toward Rachel, a look of total mania enveloping her face. It was a look of someone who'd somehow managed to lose something even after all was already lost. She ripped her elbow free of Rachel's grip and started to shove her aside. They tussled for a second as Rachel struggled to grab Erin's arm again. Anything to interrupt her suicide mission.

"Don't." Rachel said as firmly she could.

This stopped Erin cold. Her face loosened, her jaw sagging as though some great burden had been lifted from her.

"Put it in your pocket," Rachel hissed. "Do it now. Quickly."

Erin's breath was coming in ragged gasps, and her eye was twitching.

"But you don't know what they've done. I have to."

"Did they hurt you?" Rachel asked. Part of her dreaded the answer because if they had, she wasn't sure she could begrudge Erin her wish to exact some sort of justice on these assholes. Hell, maybe she would join in, go all *Thelma & Louise* on these yahoos. They overpower these two, get the guns. Then anything would be possible.

"No," Erin said. "Yes. No. I don't know."

Erin's legs buckled underneath her, and she dropped to the ground, sobbing. Rachel glanced over her shoulder; this had drawn the guards' notice, but they didn't seem inclined to intervene.

"What's wrong?" Rachel asked, taking a knee next to the hysterical woman.

She looked up at Rachel, her eyes red, her grimy cheeks glassy with tears.

"I'm pregnant."

The words were like a knife to the heart.

"What?"

"I think that's what we're here for," Erin said robotically, without a hint of emotion.

Her words chilled Rachel to the core. They chilled her because she knew that Erin was right. That's what all the testing was for. Prenatal testing. And she knew that Erin hadn't been raped, at least not in the traditional sense of some young thug crawling through an old lady's window at three in the morning and forcing himself on her. But it was still a violation of the highest order, done with syringes and petri dishes and blood draws. It was clean and dirty all at the same time.

She stole a glance at the guards, chatting, laughing, smoking their stupid cigarettes like they were at a post-softball-game keg party, and she hated them. Never had she thought it possible to hate something with such breadth and depth. It radiated from her core, replicating like the virus that had overcome the world, braiding itself to the thing that had once been Rachel Fisher. She understood now what it meant to give oneself over to something completely and totally, the way a late-blooming evangelical found God late in adulthood, the way a jihadist was willing to sacrifice his own life in furtherance of his cause. Her cheeks felt warm with it. If it was the last thing she did, these monsters were going to wish they'd never captured her.

She thought these things, and she came to one conclusion.

There could be no other outcome.

Miles Chadwick had to die.

SHE WAS silent as Ned escorted her back to her room, chewing on the news that Erin was pregnant, trying to read the tea leaves. Why was this happening? Who were these people? What was the endgame? But it just made her head throb. Trying to unravel the mystery of this place was beyond her powers of comprehension. She had no reference point, nothing to start from. It was like trying to solve a thorny programming issue in a language you didn't even know. She wondered how the others would react to Erin's pregnancy. Nearly all of them had been mothers, which meant that nearly all of them had experienced the singular misery of outliving their children. This could destabilize the group's tenuous calm.

Before she knew it, she was back at her door.

Ned removed the zip ties and she went inside her room. As she stood there in the center of the cell, she became aware of a presence behind her. She glanced over her shoulder and saw Ned still standing there, like a bellman waiting for a tip. He had a goofy grin on his face.

"What?" she asked. She was in no mood for him right now.

He took one step inside the room.

"Thank you for stopping her," Ned said. "That could've been ugly."

The comment caught her off guard, and she didn't know how to respond; she stood there dully, watching Ned watch her.

"Be ready," he said. Then he disappeared down the corridor.

34

It was closing in on dark on the last day of October.

At dusk, Evergreen's streetlights kicked on, bathing the town in a soft, warm glow, leaving it an illuminated oasis in a world gone dark. It was Adam's favorite time of day. The lights made things seem almost normal, the indigo sky softening the edges of their harsh world. Adam had been busy all day with his preparations, which had been complicated by the secrecy of his plans. At five-thirty, he conducted a final inventory of his supplies. When he was finished, he threw on a jacket, loaded everything into a large wheeled suitcase and headed out of his small apartment on the north end of town.

He found it hard to believe they'd been here a week. Harder still that their group had remained intact. Getting Freddie to agree to come here had been nothing short of a miracle. When he and Sarah made it back to the Cadillac Inn the morning after they'd found Evergreen, courtesy of one of Evergreen's electric cars, Max and Nadia were beside themselves with worry, and Freddie was on the warpath, packing his bags, ready to hit the road without them. And Adam would have been happy to let him go but for the fact that Max wanted to go with him. The argument had been terribly bitter.

"This could be a place we can call home," Adam had said. "I think it's the best move."

"Best for us? Or best for you?" Freddie said.

"What's that supposed to mean?"

"You act like you care about what happens to the rest of us," he said. "But you don't give a shit. All you care about is finding Rachel."

"Haven't I taken care of the group?" Adam shot back. "Haven't I made sure we've stayed safe and healthy?"

"What have you done for us?" Freddie bellowed, his voice booming across the parking lot and out into the emptiness. "Stephen's dead. Caroline's dead. Just our luck, hooking up with the shittiest doctor in America."

Adam pointed at the desolate road fronting the motel, trying not to show how much that last barb had stung.

"Well, there's the road, big guy," he said. "There's the road."

Freddie stood there, frozen.

"Well?"

"No, please!" Max begged. "I want him to stay."

Freddie stomped off, Max trailing behind him.

"Please, Freddie, can I come with you?"

The combatants retired to their rooms. An hour went by, then two, and then finally, Freddie emerged from his room. He agreed to travel to Evergreen and check things out, but he wouldn't commit to anything until he'd seen it with his own eyes.

"Fair enough," Adam had said. "For what it's worth, I think we should stay together. I think we're better off together than we are out on our own. We've all seen how dangerous it can be. If we're going to stay, I think we should all agree on it."

Freddie's barbs had stung, as much as Adam hated to admit it. He was only doing what he thought best, and yeah, that probably meant thinking about himself and finding Rachel. But if the shoe had been on the other foot, if it were Freddie's daughter out there, he wanted to believe he'd be there for the big man, that he'd be the sidekick in the story of Freddie.

The truth was that nothing was keeping them together but the promise of human companionship and the possibility of a happy ending in a world woefully short on them. Then again, although it may not have seemed like it on the surface, in this empty world, that was pretty strong glue. He'd watched Freddie stare out across the open road, wondering what, if anything else, was out there. What was the old saying? The devil you know?

And so they'd made the hour-long trek back to Evergreen, where Adam and Sarah had introduced them to the residents of the town. Freddie spent hours exploring the town, drilling the mayor about the power, about the residents, about who would be responsible for watching after the kids, about where their supplies would come from, about mounting a defense against future raids, about immigration (he'd actually called it that). They took a tour of Evergreen's mystical power facility. Finally, that evening, he'd cast his vote in favor of staying. Max, of course, voted to stay, and Nadia went along with whatever Sarah wanted.

So on his first full morning as a resident of Evergreen, Adam had gone to the town library at the north end of town to do a little research. The musty aroma of old books and dust hung in the air. He found a large map of the plains states, rolled up tight, in the reference room, and he spread it out on a long oak table. The corners insisted on curling up, so he weighed them down with encyclopedias from a dusty, forgotten shelf. In the absence of the Internet, the day of the book had returned. No more movies, no more Facebook or Twitter, no YouTube videos. What they needed was an army of librarians who could shepherd this new world through the mountain of information they'd need, information that would only be available in books.

He spent hours studying the map. Using a black Sharpie, he enclosed Evergreen in a thick square and divided the rest of the map into search-able grids, about five miles by five miles square. It had taken him all day, processing all the variables, their current location, where they had found Nadia, her own reports of her time on the road, but he wanted to do this right. He wanted to make sure he didn't spend the next month walking in circles, especially as cold weather set in.

The next day, he and Sarah had set out on their first expedition.

They were gone one night, making slow progress through the search grid. They saw nothing resembling Nadia's description of a walled compound in the middle of the plains, and that first night, as he lay in his tent in the cold, wrapped up in Gore-Tex and long johns and gloves and hat, the needle-in-a-haystack-ness of it all swirled around him. He dreamed he was wandering the plains, his hands gnarled with arthritis, unable to remember what he was looking for. He woke up, afraid he'd yelled out in his sleep.

And so it had gone since then, six trips into the empty wilds of the American plains with nothing to show for it. It was a hell of an expedition, that was for certain. They passed through empty town after empty town, south to Amarillo, north into Kansas, through border towns, all silent and still but for the trash and debris swirling through the streets. He spotted elk and antelope loping about the grasslands, venturing closer to the highways and back roads that they had long avoided as the balloon of humanity had swelled around them. At night, the sky rippled with starlight. He stayed up late watching them, the billions and billions of stars shining their ancient light on this little blue-green rock. It made him sad to think there was no longer anything down here worth shining a light on. If there was intelligent life out there, and he'd believed there was because it made scientific sense to believe it, they'd no longer have any interest in them. Unless they needed a move-in ready planet.

As for Sarah, there was no revisiting the kiss weeks earlier, but Adam still wondered about it, even as time clouded the details of the memory. It seemed like a lifetime ago. He didn't know why she had pulled away from him; he had sensed her interest, he had known it was there, but there was no answer to these things sometimes. His second year in medical school, before he'd met Rachel's mother, a girlfriend had ended things after a year-long relationship, after they'd been talking seriously about marriage and a future and children. Just like that, she'd said she didn't love him anymore. Just like that.

So they searched and searched, but those excursions had turned up nothing but the big black X through one of Adam's sixty search grids.

But today, he was putting all that aside. It was time to think about someone besides himself. These were good people he'd found here, and they deserved whatever he could give them. They had welcomed him and the others without question, and on the condition that they help out, to start transitioning to a life worth living rather than one spent looking back at what could not be undone.

He needed a break from the increasingly maddening search, the frustration of chewing up mile after mile with nothing to show for it. A break from the little voice in his mind that sometimes drowned out all the other ones and shouted at the top of its lungs that it would all be for nothing, he could search for the rest of his life, and he would never see his daughter again.

He continued wheeling the suitcase down Evergreen Boulevard, the wheels thrumming over the pristine asphalt as he made his way toward the town hall. It was a chilly, cloudy night, and the low sky threatened rain. Another few weeks, and this kind of sky might be bringing a load of the white stuff. He hated snow and pushed that out of his mind for now. He wasn't quite ready to deal with that.

When he got to the town hall, the others were already there waiting, buzzing with anticipation. Dozens of Evergreeners were present, and it looked like all the kids, about fifteen of them in total, were there. He didn't know if any of the children had an inkling of what he had planned, but he doubted it. As hard as it was for the adults to keep track of the days, the calendar had ceased to have any meaning for these kids. Probably be a long time before the day of the week mattered again.

"What's in the suitcase?" asked one child, a little girl named Madeleine. She was a precocious brunette who had attached herself to Sarah.

"That's for me to know and you to find out."

The children giggled and squealed.

"Mayor Townsend," he said turning toward Gwen, "can you take these kids inside and wait with them in the first office on the right?"

"Of course. Come along, kids."

She herded them inside like sheep. The curiosity was killing them, their little heads turning back to watch Adam even as she shuffled them inside the thick oak doors.

When they were inside and out of sight, he called the adults around and unzipped the suitcase. He showed them the dozen Halloween costumes and candy he'd been collecting during the past couple of days. The calendar on his watch had reminded him Halloween was approaching, and unless they did something about it, these kids were never going to have another Halloween or any other holiday again. He glanced up at the others and saw their eyes moisten, their lips curled upwards in sad smiles.

"They're going to love this," Nadia said.

"Where did you find this stuff?" Sarah asked.

"I've got my little secrets," he said.

He handed them each a bag of goodies and dispatched them to the various rooms of the town hall, where the excited trick-or-treaters would visit them. Then he stepped inside the office, where the kids were impatiently waiting.

"Does anyone know what day it is?" Adam asked after he was able to quiet the kids down to something resembling a dull roar.

The kids looked at each other blankly and shook their heads.

"Are you sure? Maybe this will help."

When he removed the first costume, a Spider-Man mask, the kids lost their minds. An Iron Man and a ninja costume followed, and eventually, they sorted it out. Madeleine went with the doctor's lab coat. After a few minutes, all the kids were appropriately decked out, each holding a plastic orange bag. Mayor Townsend bear-hugged Adam and planted a kiss right on his mouth.

The kids spent the next hour trick-or-treating, making loop after loop through the building until their bags bulged. Even Max got in on the fun, after watching it from the sidelines for a bit, insisting he was too old for Halloween. He dug through Adam's bag and found a werewolf mask; he pulled it on and chased the children through the building. At first, Adam thought the scare might be more than the kids could handle, but they loved it, exploding with squeals and screeches of joy as Max lumbered after them with a throaty deep growl.

When they were done, the group gathered in the mayor's office and enjoyed the spoils of war. Adam ate a bag of corn chips and drank a lukewarm fruit punch while he watched the kids absolutely ruin their dinner with junk food. Sarah gently teased Madeleine by hiding her bag of goodies from her, feigning ignorance when the little girl found her bag tucked behind Sarah's back. He caught the mayor staring at him. When their eyes met, she placed her hand across her heart and mouthed the words *thank you*.

He nodded, feeling his throat tighten, his eyes water. It had gone off just as he'd hoped. These kids were incredibly important, the most important thing this world had. Each of the adults here had a responsibility to them beyond simply housing and feeding them. If the world at large was going to have any chance at some peaceful future, these kids were going to be a big part of it. They would be the last generation to remember the old world, and for the younger ones like Madeleine, that memory would fade soon enough. They would be the last ones to teach any future generations about the good that had been present in the world and warn them about the bad.

He smiled at the mayor and hoped they would be up to the job.

SARAH TOED the welcome mat at Adam's front door, her heart pounding in her chest. She'd known for a while that she was in love with him, but for whatever reason, it had taken his little Halloween stunt to drive it home like a nail into a two-by-four. It had been an amazing thing to watch, people forming their first truly good memories since the cataclysm had befallen the world. The children, who had developed a heaviness about them, seemed light and carefree, and it had been all due to Adam.

Another memory, that of their disastrous kiss, loomed large in her mind, a thing she had to fix, a chore she kept pushing off and finding ways to avoid. She'd been in love before, but it had ended because he'd been a civilian and he'd never quite understood what it meant for her to wear the uniform. That had been before the diagnosis, when there was still a chance things would go her way and there was still the prospect of finding someone she might grow old with. Then she'd gotten the bad news, and she made a point not to get too close to anyone because even if it were meant to be, it was meant to end badly, and the thought of the stupid disease being the thing that broke it up was more than she could deal with.

But then the world had gone off and ended and left her behind in what had to be the biggest cosmic joke ever. She wondered about others like her and it came close to driving her mad. The poor quadriplegic, unable to do a single goddamn thing for himself, perfectly Medusa-free and abandoned. She pictured him (and in her mind, it was always some young guy with shaggy brown hair who'd been injured in a snow-boarding accident) slowly dying of thirst, terrified, his lips cracking, his mouth drying like a desert.

The door opened before she knocked, startling her, making her feel exposed, like she'd been snooping, a Peeping Tom. Adam was wearing a *Crosby for President* sweatshirt and blue jeans. An ambient hiss in the background, from one of those efficient space heaters they'd all agreed to use to reduce the load on the town's power supply, kicked off, leaving the apartment deathly quiet, as though waiting for someone to fill the void of silence.

"Howdy," he said.

"Can I come in?" she asked.

"Please," he replied, stepping out of her way.

They sat on the sofa, Sarah in the pool of light spilling from the lamp on the end table, Adam on the other end, shrouded in darkness. On the coffee table in front of her was a book about farming. It was a project he was working on. The center of his personal solar system might have been his search for Rachel, but he was starting to fill in the orbit with other things. She didn't know if that was a good thing or a bad thing.

Adam sat with one leg crossed over the other, his left arm draped across the back of the couch, and she almost called him on it, the way he was going out of his way to look casual, but she decided against it. She stared at the empty cushion between them and found herself wishing they were sitting closer together. Jesus, she hadn't been this lovesick since high school.

She tented her hands at her lips and lightly tapped her fingers together, cursing herself for not knowing what to say. Finally, she thought of something.

"That was a hell of a thing you did," she said. "It meant a whole lot to those kids."

"Yeah. Thanks."

Just throw yourself at him. He's a guy. He hasn't had any action other than his hand in months (neither have you, I might add), He's not going to resist.

"It really worked out."

"I love you," she said.

Blerrrrrggghhhhh.

What the fuck was THAT?

She didn't even recall forming the words before they just blew out of her mouth like they'd stolen something.

He sat there looking at her, and for a moment, she hoped she'd just imagined herself saying it, because seriously, no one could be that stupid. Right?

"But?"

"But what?" she replied, confused.

He smiled at her and slid over one cushion, into that void between them, for which she was grateful.

"You love me but..."

She couldn't hold his stare, and her eyes wandered off, looking for something else to fix on. She landed on a bookcase in the corner, lined with paperback books, the familiar names on the spines facing her. Bond. Clancy. Grisham.

"Look, I'm a pretty smart guy. I went to college for like twelve years."

Just pretend you're talking to the bookcase, she thought. Easier than looking him in the eye, right?

"I'm dying," she said finally.

"What?"

It took all she had, but she swung her head around and stared him directly in the face. Let him see this stupid woman, this dumb chick who'd just told him she loved him and would be dead in the next five years, if she was lucky enough to live that long.

"Huntington's."

She said it like she was lobbing a grenade, and she expected to see on his face the look one might express when seeing one roll up by your feet. But he just stared at her. His face didn't sink or shatter; his eyes didn't well up, and his lower lip did not begin to quiver. He simply looked at her.

"My mom had it," she said. "She died when she was forty. I had the testing done when I turned thirty. I carry the gene for it. You're a doctor, you know what that means."

"Yes, I know what that means."

"So there it is."

"There it is. I love you anyway," he said.

"You do?"

He'd moved closer to her, his arm still draped casually over the back, but their knees were touching now. She felt his hand on the back of her neck, stroking it softly; then he was drawing her toward him, and it felt warm and safe, like she was sliding into a bath, like they had done it a million times before. Their lips met, and she tasted fruit punch from the Halloween party. A light kiss at first, and then her hands were on him, peeling off his sweatshirt; she felt her shirt come up over her head, and she was wrenching her jeans off because she couldn't wait any longer. The air in the apartment was cool on her skin, but she felt heat everywhere else as his hands roamed across her body, finding her breasts, slipping between her thighs, and she pushed hard into his touch.

Their clothes shed in a pile on the floor, she pulled him down on top of her, and then he was inside her, and she was happy.

Fuck Huntington's, fuck this stupid graveyard world, she thought, as their bodies rocked together, her hands holding his face.

As she climaxed, her body quivering, she thought of the life stolen from her, the one only made possible by seven billion deaths, one where she and Adam might have grown old together in a clean, empty world. She thought of the hysterectomy, which she'd undergone when the test had come back positive because there was no way she would chance conceiving a baby into a world where there was a fifty percent chance it would contract Huntington's.

When it was over, he led her to the bedroom, where they made love again. After, she curled up alongside him, draping an arm across his bare chest, and lay there in the dark. He kissed the top of her head and fell asleep. She lay awake, staring at the cheap plaster ceiling in the blackness of the night, wishing that so many things could be different.

35

Rough hands shook her awake, and Rachel felt her throat close up with fear. This was it, she thought, the idea clear, even as her mind was foggy with sleep.

They're coming to kill me.

Or worse.

"Rachel, wake up," a voice hissed at her. "We need to go right now."

She sat up quickly, so quickly that the rush of blood to her head left her dizzy. Two figures stood at the foot of her bed, the room dark but for the ambient light. Their faces remained veiled.

"Quick, get this on and meet us outside," the second voice said. A woman.

A bundle of fabric hit her in the face, and it gave her a start. As quickly as she could, she slipped on the heavy coat they'd brought her and her shoes and then she followed her visitors into the corridor. In the dim light of the hallway, she saw Jeremy, one of the guards from the yard, and a woman she didn't recognize waiting for her.

"Hands," the woman said.

Rachel held her wrists out, and Jeremy slapped the zip ties on her, but only loosely. She looked up at him, and he winked at her, a slow, deliberate wink of conspiracy. Nothing lascivious about it. Her heart was beating so quickly it felt like a purring motor; she could barely distinguish one beat from the next.

The trio moved quickly down the corridor, Rachel in the middle. Icy sweat exploded on her skin. It was late, a moonless night greeting them outside. A car was idling in the access road, its exhaust gleaming in the red taillights like an ominous fog.

"Get in the back," the woman snapped when they reached the car's rear bumper.

Jeremy followed her into the backseat, and the woman rode shotgun. Rachel was barely in her seat before the car sped off like a sprinter breaking from the blocks. The driver's identity remained a mystery as they careened through the outer part of the grounds, paralleling the long perimeter fence surrounding the Citadel complex. Not a word was spoken as they approached the main gate.

After a minute, the car slowed to a stop, and the woman got out. She sprinted for the gate and accessed a control box at the base of the fence. The driver – her buddy Ned, she now saw – looked back at Jeremy, whose eyebrows went up. A tense moment passed; then the gate began to slide open. The woman bolted back to the car and they were moving again even before she'd had a chance to sling the door closed.

Rachel glanced at the dashboard clock as they rocketed through the gate.

It was 3:47 a.m.

～

THEY RAN SOUTHEAST FOR A WHILE, the world zipping by Rachel's window. It was the first time she'd been outside the gates since her capture, although she wasn't sure how long it had been. Even cloaked in darkness, the land overwhelmed her senses. She saw farms and billboards and feed stores. Here and there, a corpse or two.

Fifteen minutes later, Jeremy pulled into the parking lot of a warehouse on the outskirts of Beatrice, Nebraska. The quartet exited the vehicle and climbed the stairs to the office door, where a dim orange light glowed in the window. Ned rapped on the door in a series of coded knocks. The door opened, and they filed inside.

Three people were inside in the dimly lit room, seated on metal folding chairs, smoking cigarettes, their faces drawn tight with panic and fear.

"Let's get started," the man said after everyone had sat down. Rachel took the last empty seat, the one at the center of the seven, the keystone, and it made her feel very uncomfortable.

She recognized the man next to her as James Rogers, Chadwick's second in command. Jeremy and Ned sat to her left. The remaining three members of the group were women.

"Rachel, my name is Dr. Rogers."

"Yes, I know who you are."

"Do you know what the Citadel really is?"

She looked around the room and saw six faces looking back at her with longing there. As if they wanted her to forgive them for something they had done.

"No," she said.

The others exchanged nervous glances; their chairs creaked as they shifted in their seats. Rogers looked down at his lap, plucked a piece of lint from his pants and flicked it away.

"We created the Medusa virus," he said, his eyes still cast downward.

"You what?"

He didn't reply. He just sat there as Rachel processed his words, her stomach churning. She felt dizzy.

We created the Medusa virus.

She tried standing up, but her knees buckled underneath her, dropping her back into her uncomfortable seat.

"No."

No.

Not because she didn't believe him. But because it was too much to comprehend. The room seemed to shift off its axis before snapping into place again. The epidemic replayed in her mind, those terrible images of watching her mom drown on her own blood, of Jerry, curled up on the kitchen floor, naked, crying, covered in his own waste. The human race wiped out, and here she was chatting with the people who had done it. Her body felt soft, like it was filled with jam, and she was glad to be sitting down. She looked around the small office they were gathered in, still bearing the relics of a lost civilization. A wall calendar with a photograph of a monster truck, stuck on August, when the world had stopped.

Grave Digger, indeed. She zeroed in on an ashtray on the corner of the desk with its pile of cigarette butts.

"Jesus Christ, why?"

He laughed, a high-pitched giggle, laced with manic.

"Miss, is there really any answer I can give you that would make you feel better?"

A good point.

"No, I suppose not."

She closed her eyes for a moment and took a deep breath. How the hell was she supposed to deal with what they'd just told her?

She opened her eyes and looked at these six ordinary looking people sitting there with her. Crazy. So goddamn crazy. And then she started laughing. Because what else could she do? It started small, a few giggles. But then it got away from her like a housefire. She laughed harder than she ever had in her life. They waited as she laughed, waited until she laughed so hard her sides hurt.

"The reason we've brought you here is simple," he said, lighting a cigarette. "Although we cannot undo what has been done, we can put a stop to any future atrocities. You know we had a vaccine against the virus."

"Well, hell, of course you did!" she snapped, and the giggles started to make a comeback. "How else would you survive the great plague! It really wouldn't do if you all ended up like my family now, right?"

Dead silence. She eyed each of them, one at a time, but none could hold her gaze.

"Well, the vaccine had a side effect that we failed to detect during testing," Rogers said. "It rendered all the women who received it infertile."

Rachel shook her head.

"But not us," she said, the final piece falling into place.

"Correct."

"You need concubines, right?"

"In a manner of speaking."

"Jesus fucking Christ."

"Rest assured, we are all deserving of every ounce of scorn and contempt that you feel for us," Rogers said. "But that will not help us right now."

"What do you need me for?"

"We've now captured thirty-four women since the epidemic ended. We want to end the project and destroy the Citadel."

"Why? I mean, why now? Isn't it too late for your little attempt at redemption?"

"Not for your fellow captives."

Rachel leaned forward in her seat, her head spinning. She rested her elbows on her knees to regain some balance.

"Why not just kill Chadwick and let the women go?"

"Aren't you the bloodthirsty one all of a sudden?"

"Fuck you."

"Sorry," Rogers said, holding up his hands in surrender. "You're right. It's a reasonable question. I haven't seen Chadwick in a week. We communicate by walkie-talkie now. I don't know where he is half the time."

"No way to run a railroad," Rachel said.

"Dr. Chadwick has been growing increasingly unstable," Rogers said. "He won't meet with anyone directly. Has bodyguards with him all the time. They'll do anything for him. Anything. And they're not the only ones. The others, as best as we can tell, are in for the long haul. We're too scared to approach anyone else."

"Not much of a rebellion."

"It's all we've got. And the time to strike is now."

"You got me out tonight," she said. "You could just let us all go."

"We can't take that chance," Rogers said. "We're making our move tonight when we get back to the compound. You need to be ready for our signal."

"But I still don't understand what you want me for."

"When the time comes, we want you to help them get out. They look up to you."

"That's bullshit. I'm barely old enough to vote."

"And they're scared and weak. They admire you."

"Why did we have to do this out here? You could've told me all this back at h…"

She'd started to say 'home', but she stopped herself. She ran her hands through her hair, feeling a wave of nausea ripple through her. This was crazy. She should have been in her dorm room at CalTech, studying materials science or linear engineering, possibly passing around a joint with her friends. Instead, she was here, being recruited into this bizarre amalgam of mass killers. And then it hit her.

She had started to feel sorry for these six people, these rogue lines of code that had diverged from the mainframe's original programming. She had started to identify with them. The enemy-of-my-enemy-is-my-friend. Transitive property. If-then. She gave her head a hard shake and reminded herself of the women back at the compound, their numbers growing bit by bit. That's why she would do this. For them.

"There's something else," Rogers said. "Something I haven't told the others."

He looked around at his confederates, who were looking at him with confused stares.

"I'm sorry," he continued. "I should've told you all from the beginning."

He lowered his head and scratched his chin. Then the door to the warehouse office exploded off its hinges like an overcooked turkey leg ripped from its joint. A flurry of bodies rushed into the room like locusts, and then she heard the heavy *thwack* of metal and wood on flesh. Black-clad figures overwhelmed the group, which barely had time to blink, let alone raise any kind of serious defense. A few screams and grunts, and it was over.

Rachel scurried for a corner in the room, where she huddled and watched her six co-conspirators beaten and pinned facedown to the ground. Zip ties cinched around their wrists and ankles, and one by one, the rebels were carted out of the warehouse like sides of beef.

"You," the last one in the room said, pointing at Rachel. He was aiming a large handgun at her face. "Let's go."

Rachel crawled out of her sad little hiding spot and went outside, the last commando falling in line behind her. She followed the queue to the far end of the warehouse parking lot, where two black Suburbans and a Lincoln Police SWAT truck sat idling. The black-clad figures tossed Rogers and the others into the back of the SWAT truck and latched the door shut.

When she saw Miles Chadwick standing there in the glow of the truck's headlights, wearing a black duster, his hair rippling in the cold wind, her blood turned to ice.

RACHEL RODE in the backseat of the lead Suburban, her head leaning against the frosty glass of the window. Chadwick was seated next to her, stone cold silent. The rage radiated from him like heat from a charcoal grill. She was wearing zip ties now, tightly fastened, pinching and chafing her no matter how much she tried to adjust them.

"You'll forgive the restraints," Chadwick said coolly, not looking at her. "But we're in a state of emergency right now. I am very sorry you had to be part of that. I didn't realize how brazen they'd gotten.

"My mistake. It won't happen again," he said, almost apologetically and more to himself than to anyone else.

She dropped her hands into her lap and remained silent. She tilted her head just so and could make out the panel truck carrying Chadwick's new captives in the Suburban's sideview mirror. The truck's lightbar oscillated, throwing pulsing blue shadows across the dark landscape.

She couldn't imagine the fate awaiting them. Rogers had tried to undo it, all of it. Yeah, if she were Chadwick, she'd be pretty pissed too. The very thought of his brand of justice made her shiver.

By the time they reached the main gates, a bit of pre-dawn light had begun to leak into the night sky. The caravan slowed, turned onto the main access road, and then followed the road around toward the amphitheater at the north end of the compound. Rachel was surprised to see dozens of people waiting for them, sipping coffee and milling about. Rachel had seen folks out here playing catch or spreading blankets out for a picnic when the weather had been warmer.

The vehicles jerked to a stop, and a flurry of activity commenced. While Rachel, Chadwick and their driver stayed put, the others poured out of the SWAT vehicle. After a minute or two, someone rapped twice firmly on Chadwick's window and opened the door.

"It's time."

As he got out, another person opened Rachel's door and guided her by the elbow over to Chadwick. The morning was brightening fast, the sunshine gilding the field like golden paint. Everyone was here. The whole gang, she thought, shielding her eyes from the sun as it slid skyward from its invisible nest just beyond the horizon.

"Take her over with the others," Chadwick said.

The woman nodded and led Rachel to the other women, who stood deathly quiet.

"What's going on?" Latasha asked her when they were alone. "Where the hell were you? We thought you were dead."

Rachel shook her head. She wanted to say something, but she stood there, empty, frozen, unable to keep a single thought in her head save one. They had done it. They had destroyed the world.

The stage, looking south toward the growing fields, was bare but for a square wooden table and a cone-shaped object set at the center of the stage. Chadwick headed in that direction, trailed by one of his lackeys, and then hoisted himself up onto the platform. From where she stood, he looked silly and small to Rachel, like he was a little boy playing an imaginary game with his little friends.

As he strode across the stage, his heels clicking on the wood and echoing into the morning air, the crowd fell silent. He inspected the table, pressing down on the center, checking its stability. When he was done, he picked up the cone - *a megaphone* - and turned to face the crowd, which had drawn in tight, like a hive ready to listen to its queen.

"My friends, today is a dark day for our fledgling nation," he said. His voice sounded tinny and mechanical. "Perhaps the darkest we have faced.

"But, I believe that it is always darkest before the dawn. Much like the world we left behind, which was truly a wretched and dark place before the birth of this new paradise."

Heads began to nod. A few *yeses* and *mm-hmms* fluttering about like birds.

"Now," he continued, his voice starting to ramp up, "before we can see that dawn, before we can see that glorious sunrise over this new world, we have to excise the darkness. Because will the darkness fade away on its own?"

"No," the crowd murmured.

"I ask you again, will the darkness fade away on its own?" Now he was getting worked up, his voice starting to crackle and thunder.

"No!" the crowd boomed.

"Hell no!"

"Hell no!" they repeated.

"The darkness is like a cancer, and you don't sit around waiting for the cancer to shuffle off with its tail between its legs. You go in there and you cut it out."

More *yes-sirs* and *mm-hmms*, getting louder now, and Rachel began to be afraid, more so than any time since all this insanity had begun. She looked at her fellow captives; their jaws were set, their lips tight.

"You cut it out," he said again, his voice softening, his demeanor calming, a tempest dissipating.

"Bring forth the accused," he said.

A commotion from near the caravan as Rogers and the others were removed from the paddy wagon and lined up single file. Armed men marched the group toward the wing of the stage, where a large cinderblock served as a step. The six prisoners shuffled heavily along the platform, their heads down, looking defeated. Their legs were cuffed together, their hands bound behind their backs. Someone had tossed black hoods over the heads.

"James Rogers. Martha Koontz. Ned Gartner. Jeremy Daniels. Maria McCleary. Margaret Baker. Each of you stands charged with the crime of treason against the Citadel," Chadwick called out. "I hereby find each of you guilty of treason and sentence you to die."

Rachel felt a little gasp escape her lips.

Two of Chadwick's foot soldiers took Rogers by the arms and dragged him, his heels scraping the wood, toward the low-slung wooden table at the front edge of the stage. He did not make a sound, and he did not resist, but he did not assist them either. They swept his legs out from underneath, sending him to his knees. His covered face smacked soundly against the heavy wood of the table, and one of Chadwick's goons secured his head to the table with a strap of leather.

A metal *skrink* pierced the silence, and Rachel saw a black-hooded figure approaching from the edge of the stage. He carried an enormous broadsword, slick with morning dew, its blade glinting in the morning light.

"Oh, Jesus, oh, Jesus," she whispered, her breath catching in her throat. Little gasps from her fellow captives.

"James Rogers," Chadwick said, "do you have anything you wish to say before your sentence is carried out?"

"You have no idea what you're up against," Rogers said.

"Wonderful," Chadwick replied. "Anything else?"

"Yeah. How about you go fuck yourself," Rogers spat.

Chadwick stepped back and nodded to the executioner. He reared back with the sword, raising it high above his head, and Rachel found herself praying it was the sharpest goddamn blade in North America, that it would come down through his neck in one stroke, please God, don't let us have to watch him hack through it like he's chopping firewood. Her eyes were full of tears and her stomach began to heave.

The blade rang true, stopping only when it bit into the wood of the table. Rogers grunted once, just once, when the sword's edge found flesh, and then it was over. The crowd gasped, but almost guardedly so, as if no one wanted to attract too much attention to their visceral reaction to the beheading. Rogers' body slumped down to the ground; the head lolled to the side, rolling toward the edge but stopping just before tumbling off. Arterial blood, still pumping from a heart unaware that its owner was dead, sprayed crudely across the front edge like a dye pack had exploded, before slowing to a steady gush. The grass darkened as the field greedily drank the blood cascading off the stage.

Not a sound from the crowd. Nary a cough or clearing of throat. At the back of the stage, the five condemned prisoners remained quiet.

Chadwick approached the blood-soaked table and examined the head, as casually as a man studying the produce bin at the supermarket. He lifted it by Rogers' ponytail and held it up high for the crowd to see.

"This is the price of treason!" he bellowed. The draining blood ran down his palms, down his wrists, but he did not seem to care. His eyes were manic now, nearly bugging out as he held the head high.

One at a time, the other rebels took their turn at the table, either unaware of or too traumatized by what had happened to put up any resistance. Each seemed to jerk when their faces came in contact with the blood pooling on the table, but by then, the blade was already in flight, and the doomed prisoner joined those who had preceded him in death. To his credit, and to the benefit of the condemned, the executioner was a skilled swordsman, brutally and efficiently doing his assigned duty.

When it was over, Rachel felt like she was floating. She remembered thinking that she should cover her face so she wouldn't have to witness the slaughter, but she hadn't. As she looked around the faces of the crowd, she saw no one else had either. She stood there, her ability to react somehow stripped away. Perhaps it was a function of having seen the things she'd seen, that they'd all seen when the world was in the grip of the epidemic. Had she been so deadened that the executions of six people would have such little impact on her?

That they were dead meant nothing to her.

But she wanted to feel something. She wanted to feel horrified and angry and repulsed.

But all she could muster was a terrible sense of sadness, radiating out from her core and spreading like a sickness.

36

Freddie Briggs liked to run in the mornings.

Every day since they'd moved here, he was up just as the morning bled its first hints of purple across the black sky. He would pull on a pair of shorts and a t-shirt, lace on his shoes and head out into the ever-colder morning air. He didn't wear a watch anymore, as he didn't really give a shit what time it was. He had mapped out a nice loop, about five or six miles long, first along Route 815 away from Evergreen, then cutting through dead farms, sheep and horse and cattle, along a long riverbed and back to 815 and home again.

As he pounded the pavement that mid-November morning, he admitted he had been dishonest with himself about a few things. The first two were the hardest ones to admit, but didn't they say to deal with the hard stuff first or you might never get around to it?

Anyway.

Point 1.

He didn't care whether Adam ever found his daughter again. It wasn't that he wished she were dead, although he could understand how someone might see it that way. But truly, whether they had their reunion was of no consequence to Freddie Briggs. The world did not revolve around the good doctor and his sad, almost certainly futile quest. The thing Adam did not seem to understand was that just because there were fewer people around did not mean that some larger proportion of that subset would necessarily care about his problems. They didn't. He didn't.

He focused on the route ahead. Into the trees, stutter-stepping over thick, exposed roots, watching his balance on the layer of dead leaves blanketing the ground. The last thing he needed out here was to break an ankle.

Point 2.

He wished he'd gotten in that stupid truck and ignored Caroline's pleas for help. He would have drifted off into that great beyond, quietly, peacefully, and he might be with the girls again. There. He'd admitted it to himself. And yes, Caroline probably would have died at that sandwich shop, but guess what? She had died anyway. But she'd had to watch her son die first. So instead of saving her, Freddie had merely condemned her to a fate worse than death. She got to see what he'd seen back in Smyrna. She got to see her baby, the light of her life, liquefy from the inside out. Oh, one might argue that at least she got to hold her son, if only for a little while.

Bullshit. Watching his girls die had been a far worse proposition than never having gotten to hold them at all.

His mind quiet again, he sprinted across a horse pasture, climbed over the retaining fence to add a little excitement, and then zipped back out to Route 815 toward Evergreen. He picked a line down the middle of the highway, which he found liberating after years of running along the shoulder, constantly checking for the inattentive driver who would hip-check him into roadkill. A cold rain had begun falling, slicking his arms and stinging his face. Steam billowed from his overheated skin; despite the low temperatures, down in the forties, he could feel sweat pouring from his body. He must have been really pushing himself.

Point 3.

This one was sort of tied to the second point. The urge to take his own life had passed. He didn't know why, as he wasn't feeling all puppy-dogs-and-rainbows, but maybe his original plan had been an emergency response, an overreaction to what had happened. He wanted to see his girls again, but not that way. Even if he lived another fifty years in this mortal coil, barely the blink of an eye for his family, wrapped in the warm blanket of eternity.

Point 4.

He did not like Adam Fisher.

At all.

Part of it was envy. After all, this was the Hour of Honesty with your host, Freddie Briggs, right? For one, it seemed brutally unfair that Adam's daughter was still alive. Oh, sure, she was being held captive, maybe, at that compound Nadia had allegedly escaped, but of course he'd find her, because that's how things went for people like Adam Fisher. People like Freddie Briggs, they suffered catastrophic knee injuries in the prime of their careers and then they watched their families die, and if that was going to happen, then what the hell had been the point of any of it?

If there was one thing nearly all of them had in common, the unifying thread, it was that they'd all lost everything and everyone, and they would all be starting from scratch. A level playing field, if you will. But not Adam. Oh, no. He still had one foot planted firmly in the old world, and so what had he really lost? If you survived, and your family survived, then this empty new world really wasn't all that bad. Sure, it came with its own inherent risks and dangers, and it would call for a new skill set, but it wasn't all bad. This wasn't the aftermath of a nuclear war or a zombie apocalypse. They had power here. Thousands of grocery stores and millions of homes across the country stocked with food. Those wouldn't last forever, but the folks in Evergreen had been socking away seeds since late summer and would be ready to start planting in the spring.

And that wasn't all. Fisher and that bitch (*Honesty Hour!*) Sarah were playing house now, all googly-eyed for each other. So to top everything off, the big fat cherry, Adam had a warm body to cuddle up with, polish his knob, make it all better in the off-chance they didn't find Rachel.

He was sprinting now, his lungs burning, his quads vibrating into jelly.

Squish, squish, squish. He felt the cold rainwater seeping into his shoes, icing his toes, and it just propelled him faster, faster. If only those pathetic NFL scouts could have seen him now. He wondered if any other players had survived. Fifteen hundred of them, yeah, there were probably a few who'd made it.

Where was he going with all this?

He liked Evergreen, and he wanted to stay there. He liked the kids, and they would need a positive role model going forward. A role model for the new world, not for the way it had been. Who was going to fill that role? Adam? If it had been one of his daughters who'd survived rather than him, would he want Adam Fisher looking after her?

No. Hell no. He was selfish, that much was clear. And the kids were suffering for it. Just the other day, Max had had a huge meltdown when Freddie had tried to toughen him up a little while showing him a good time. Freddie had woken up that morning with the almost overwhelming urge to drive fast, way beyond what Evergreen's sorry little fleet of electric cars was capable of. He checked the white pages in his apartment and found the listing for a dealership down in Guymon. Max, who'd been living with a group of older kids since their arrival, tagged along, always up for additional time with Freddie.

They took one of the town's electric cars, its engine pathetic and flaccid. It was just depressing. And in Guymon, his spirits perked up when they saw the bright pennant flags lining the perimeter of the lot flapping bravely in the wind, the cars glinting in the morning sun. The small marquee at the front was still advertising *0% for 60 months* on all new models. Dozens of cars lined the lot; they were dusty and grimy and speckled with bird droppings.

"How about that one?" Max asked, pointing to a cherry-red Mustang.

Freddie eyed it and smiled, pleased that Max was a boy after his own heart. Maybe there was hope for them yet.

"Absolutely, my good man," Freddie had said. "Great choice."

He made a note of the VIN number and then got to work. First, he broke the glass of the dealership with the muzzle of his gun, the sound of the tinkling huge and accusatory in the silence, like a lady screaming her pocketbook had been stolen. But it didn't bother Freddie anymore because he was used to this unmooring from the old world. He could still see it in some of the others' eyes. They were still nervous about taking canned goods from grocery stores, about breaking into people's houses for water and supplies and so on. Even here in Evergreen, where they knew that their neighbors were dead and feeding the worms.

The air was musty inside the dealership, but there didn't appear to be any bodies here. Freddie had figured out that a business' relative importance in the old world revealed itself by how many bodies were still inside once the plague had burned itself off. No one had hung around Schaeffer Ford to die, that was for damn sure.

It was dim inside, but not dark. On one of the desks, he spotted a large rat, nosing in a box of crackers. He ignored it, and it ignored him. *Rat's gotta eat*, he thought. They went behind the main desk and scanned the rows of keys until Max found the one matching the Mustang. As they made their way outside, he felt electricity buzzing through him, something that he hadn't felt in a long time.

After checking the tires, Freddie unlocked the Mustang with the keyfob and climbed in. It roared, and Max squealed with glee. Freddie took a moment to feel the Mustang's power, to really feel it, to know that there would be no more Mustangs for a hundred years, if ever. He felt life coursing through him like he hadn't before, not even during his football days. He shifted into drive and raced out of the parking lot, out onto U.S. 64, a nice four-lane piece of road, stretching off to the north. They flew through a residential neighborhood, block after block of dead ranches and Cape Cods, skittering around abandoned cars. Faster he went, clearing the town limits, and still faster he went.

"This is awesome!" Max had screamed.

But Freddie barely heard him. Caroline's face hovered there in the windshield, at first the way it looked when he'd found her on the back stoop of Pastrami Dan's, under the black awning, relief and hope and answered prayers etched on her face like the happy slashes of a toddler's fingerpaint. Back when baby Stephen's fate had been unwritten, back when there'd still been a chance. But then that dissolved and bullying its way into place was her dead face, in the tent, the thin white film pasted on her lifeless lips and it had been his fault.

Ninety miles per hour.

"Yeaaahh!!!" Max shouted.

One hundred miles per hour.

One-ten, and the car still purred underneath him, as if to ask *is that all you've got, you pussy?*

By then, Max's squeals had abated, and he'd grabbed the dashboard with both hands.

"This is pretty fast," he'd said.

"You think that's fast?"

Freddie pushed the pedal down a little farther and now the land rushed by in a blur. God, this was better than sex, he thought to himself, the needle now tickling one-thirty-five. And he was screaming now, his howls filling the car as he hurtled through the countryside like a bullet looking for a target.

"No, Freddie, please slow down!"

One-forty.

Max started to cry, pleading with him to slow down, but Freddie pushed the pedal to the floor, until the Mustang was a missile slicing through the Oklahoma sunshine. He blocked out Max's pleas because this felt so goddamn good. It was an indescribable feeling, like Christmas morning combined with your first roller coaster, toss in your first kiss and that first stolen sip of beer, all rolled into this moment.

"PLEASE FREDDIE SLOW DOWN I'M SCARED!"

"It's good for you!" Freddie yelled back. "Gotta toughen you up!"

"FREDDIE PLEAAAAAASSSE!"

Then Max had totally lost it, crying and kicking and flailing his arms, his face wet with tears and snot, until finally Freddie had eased up on the accelerator, disappointed in Max, disappointed in how soft they all really were. How were they going to survive in this world if Max, who would someday be looked upon to lead, was afraid of his own shadow? And he had news for these people. Things were only going to get tougher as the months and years went by.

"I wanna go home," Max had said quietly.

"Fine," Freddie had said. "Jesus."

So they had taken the Mustang back to Guymon and driven the electric car home, the thirty-mile trip covered in silence. When Max had gotten out of the car at the apartment building he called home, his eyes were red and puffy from his pathetic little meltdown. He hadn't seen much of Max since then; in fact, he'd been seeing the kid hanging more around Adam the last couple of days.

And Adam was blind to how weak they all really were. Everything was secondary to his quest to find Rachel. Freddie didn't necessarily begrudge him that, but that didn't mean he had to make it everyone else's problem too. That focus on his own issue, his own story, meant he couldn't be The Guy. Smart, fine. Organized, fine. But the needs of the many outweigh the needs of the few, big guy. What happens if the town comes under attack, and you're out wandering the plains like Moses? Or if someone gets sick?

The more he thought about it, the angrier he got.

Squishsquishsquish.

He was flying now, the town limit less than a half-mile away. He felt the rush, that runner's high, buzzing through him, as though he were floating along the road. His body felt strong, his mind clear. He blew into town like a rocket re-entering Earth's atmosphere, decelerating, dialing back on the throttle, until he had slowed to an easy jog.

After taking a few minutes to stretch his tired muscles, he went inside and sponged his body off. They had agreed to limit showers to two a week to conserve water, and he had gotten pretty good at this method anyway. When he was clean, he pulled on jeans and a sweatshirt, grabbed a granola bar and sat down at the small dining table in the corner of the living room.

For the next two hours, he made a list of things they needed to do. He would show them. They'd fallen in behind Adam because he was a doctor, an understandable knee-jerk reaction to the situation they were in. If Freddie acted now, while things were still fluid, he could make his mark. Being a leader was something he was familiar with. His second year in the league, his teammates had elected him the defensive captain, a title he held until the knee injury. He ran the defense as a seamless unit, getting his teammates to buy into his team-first theory, pounding it into their heads until the Falcons were a perennial top-five defense.

That could be done here, too. It was really no different. These scared, tired folks were his teammates now, and they could be molded into a seamless unit too. You just picked a philosophy and worked from there. The philosophy was easy enough. Safety and security for this new community. Water. Food. Shelter.

Defense. Law and order would also be a paramount concern in establishing a long-term community. There would be dirty work, and it would be the dirty work people would blow off. *Other-guy syndrome.* They couldn't mean *me*, don't they know what I've been through out there?

Immigration. There was plenty of room for more survivors, but they'd have to watch the influx carefully as well. Should they take in anyone who wandered in from the wilderness? At some level, it bothered him to think about excluding those in need. But it was a dog-eat-dog world now.

This *was* a soft bunch. The episode with Max and the Mustang had just driven it home for him. Things were working fine now, and that meant they'd become complacent. They'd just think that things would keep working fine. Human beings didn't like change; now that these folks had lived through the biggest paradigm shift any of them would ever see, they'd assume that the winds of change had stopped blowing. That they could stick their heads in the sand here and watch old DVDs and drink scotch and paint landscapes, and the heat would keep blowing in the winter and the canned goods would last forever and they could just live that life as some kind of reward for having survived the plague.

How terribly wrong they were. If they weren't careful, things would just get worse and the world would become more dangerous. The strong would survive, the weak would perish. He revised his earlier thought. These folks, these survivors, weren't like his teammates. Not at all. From high school through college and especially in the NFL, his teammates had been driven to succeed. Sure, there were exceptions, those who skated by on talent alone, at least for a little while, when it finally caught up with them, but by and large, they were self-starters. No one had to tell them to study film, to hit the weights, to run the drills until they were as ingrained as breathing.

No, this would be different. These folks would have to be told what to do and how to do it. Probably wanted to be told. The what and the how, that was the hard part. A lot of the work ahead would be tedious and repetitive and mechanical. They would rally around the person who greased the skids, the one who made it as easy as possible. He suspected that for the most part, people wanted to pull their weight and do their fair share. Hell, maybe it was because people were fundamentally good. But Freddie suspected that it was because no one wanted to be looked at as a slacker. Shame could be a powerful motivator, especially in this new world, where you couldn't hide among the masses and get by on the herd's efforts. The herd just wasn't big enough anymore.

He worked until his brain was mush and then lay down for a nap. As he drifted off to sleep, he recounted his work so far. He had the ideas. He had a plan. He just needed a way to implement them. When he woke up at around four in the afternoon, he felt good. Refreshed. And he knew what he needed to do.

37

It took him two full days, but eventually, he tracked down nearly every citizen in Evergreen and told them he was calling a meeting on November 24. And hoo boy, had it ever become the talk of the town, to Freddie's immense delight. As he strolled down Evergreen Boulevard on the evening of the meeting, he felt a lightness like he'd felt the day he'd driven the Mustang.

Everyone had responded positively, glad that Freddie was kicking them out of the stasis they'd seemed to settle into. People were ready to move onto the next phase of things, whatever it was that happened to be. And they were more than happy to let Freddie get that train moving out of the station. He even began to hear whispers that people were ready for a change at the top. He'd gotten a few people on his side. Bill Irwin, an engineer at the plant. Chuck Danley. Peter Salomon. Kate Crawford. They'd act as his proxies in the crowd, help him run the plan through before the town would know what hit it.

Just show us where to board, Mister Conductor!

It was bitterly cold out when Freddie arrived at the town hall a little after five-thirty. There were four chairs on the dais, the tables still marked with nameplates of the mayor and the now-dead members of the Evergreen's governing council. Freddie threw them in the trashcan in the corner of the room.

Onward and upward!

He was furiously scribbling notes as the others arrived, streaming in from wherever they'd been dicking around while Freddie had been getting his ducks in a row. He felt good, ready, the way he felt after a solid week of practice and film study in his old life. When he called the meeting to order at precisely six, there were more than a hundred people present, standing room only, like it had been for the Falcons home games the year they'd finished 14-2 and nearly won it all.

The group took their seats, filling the hearing room to capacity, and he could sense their eyes on him sitting in the center chair. Good, he thought. He wanted them to take notice that there was a new sheriff in town. He saw them glance at Mayor Townsend, looking for some semblance of an objection, but she just seemed to accept it. Freddie had banked on her silence, that she'd be a little too intimidated to raise a stink about it.

He banged the gavel three times, and it stopped the incessant chatter dead.

"Let's get started."

He had considered opening with an invocation or the Pledge of Allegiance or something similar, something to remind everyone they were the same people they'd been not four months ago, but he had dispensed with the idea. He needed to bum rush the quarterback, for lack of a better analogy.

"Thank you all for coming," he said. "We've got a lot of work to do if Evergreen is going to remain our home."

Heads nodding, people exchanging surprised glances.

"Evergreen is a special place, I think we can all agree on that," he continued. "But the power plant is not going to maintain itself. How many people worked at the plant before the plague?"

For a moment, no one spoke. Then a short, stout man in the front row stood up. His hands trembled, and he kept his eyes focused on his feet.

"Uh," the man said. "My name's Irwin. Bill Irwin."

"You're gonna have to speak up," Freddie said. "We can barely hear you."

"I was an engineer at the plant," Irwin said. "We had about five hundred on any given shift."

"How many are still alive?"

"Just me."

"Just you? The plague got all the others?"

"No, two others survived. One died in the attack a few weeks ago. The other, uh, well, he sort of went crazy and took off. "

"Have you been out there?"

"Every day."

Freddie leaned back in his chair and rubbed his chin for a moment. He knew all of this. He'd been out to the plant several times with Irwin, who'd been flitting about the place, checking on things he knew how to check, replacing plugs and wire when needed. But they were living on borrowed time. Irwin, no fan of Townsend, hadn't come right out and said it, but Freddie could read between the lines. Irwin couldn't do it alone, he didn't even know how. The plant was too complex, required too much specialized knowledge to maintain and troubleshoot its various systems, wisdom that largely had gone to the grave. Sooner or later, it would fail.

"Mayor Townsend?"

"Yes?"

"Isn't it high time Mr. Irwin had some help out there at the plant?"

The sound of one hundred necks turning toward the mayor filled the room. Townsend shifted in her seat. Freddie had planned this next bit, where he'd just stare at the mayor until she said something, until she tried to say nothing by saying a lot, the way all politicians did.

"It's just that, uh..."

Her words trailed off like a revving engine disappearing in the night.

Then he pounced.

"Gwen, I don't think the good people of Evergreen are really interested in your excuses."

He allowed himself a quick glance at the crowd. A hundred sets of eyes, boring in on the mayor like lasers. Jaws tightened. Heads nodded. He caught Adam's eye and was pleased to see a look bordering on horror on the doctor's face.

That's right, Doc, Freddie thought, briefly holding Adam's gaze before turning his attention to the mayor. God, that look was priceless. He wished he could have gotten it on camera.

"They expect leadership."

He looked back down at his notes.

"What about the food and water supply?" he asked with a deliberate sigh, as though he expected to be disappointed in the answer. "We can't rely on canned goods forever. We're going to need to start making our own food."

"There's a reservoir not far from here," Townsend said. "With our small population, we should be OK with water."

"We won't always have a small population though, will we?" Freddie asked.

"No, uh-uh," a voice from the crowd call out. He thought it was Chuck Danley.

"What's the purification process?" Sarah asked, shifting in her seat. Freddie thought she sounded nervous, as though she suspected something was afoot.

"We have a small treatment facility on the north end of town," Townsend said. "It runs on wind and solar, but we did have a electrical backup in the event the other power sources failed for some reason. The backup failed when the power grids failed, but it's still operating. I'd been checking it every day before my little episode."

"And I assume it requires maintenance," Freddie said.

"It's been pretty reliable."

"Everything requires maintenance," he said. "If we don't stay on top of it, it'll fail when we need it the most."

"I'm also concerned about defending ourselves," Freddie said. "We've been lucky so far. Tell me more about this attack."

An uncomfortable silence descended on the room. Chins dropped, eyes watered.

"They came at us one evening," Charlotte said, breaking the silence. "By chance, I was with Jeff and a few others down in the police armory, taking inventory. There were only about ten of them, but they really got the jump on us. They were just shooting anyone they found. We came up behind them and killed most of them. Two escaped."

"Where's the armory?"

"In this building," she said. "Basement."

"It's going to be important for all able-bodied adults and older teenagers to become proficient with weapons," Freddie said.

"Is that really necessary?" someone asked.

"You tell me," Freddie said. "How many did you lose in the attack?"

He let that sink in for a bit. As he looked out over the crowd, something occurred to him. This wasn't your ordinary town. Many of the people who lived here were soft. Book smart, engineers and computer nerds. They'd run their power plant and the few supporting businesses. Probably had no idea how lucky they'd been to repel the first attack.

"We lost a dozen people!" Kate Crawford said.

"I grew up in rural Georgia," Freddie said. "We teach kids about guns about as soon as they can hold one. So, yes, I think it's necessary and smart. We've got to stop thinking like we used to. This isn't the same world anymore. No one is coming to protect us. And there's nothing to stop someone else from trying to take Evergreen."

The crowd was quiet now, juiced with a healthy dose of fear. Then he struck.

"Mayor Townsend, may I speak freely?" Freddie asked.

"Please," she said.

Everyone, already locked in silence, looked at him. What he was about to do was tricky on a number of levels and could backfire at any moment.

"I'm really worried by what I've heard here today," he said. "I've come to love this place and the people in it. But I'm worried we've fallen asleep at the switch. I think we're headed down a very dangerous road."

He paused again.

"I propose that we elect a new mayor."

Chatter erupted across the room, a wild mixture of gasps and whispers, cheers and a few boos, sweeping through the crowd like a wave. Freddie breathed a sigh of relief, having had no idea how this would play out and even less confidence it would work.

"Second!" a woman's voice called out.

"Second!"

"Second."

On and on the *seconds* came, little explosions. The mayor started at each one, like rabbit punches.

"Hey, wait a minute!" Adam called out. "Plague or not, she's still the mayor of this town."

But Freddie raised his voice. He might not have been as smart as

Evergreen's resident know-it-all, but he was sure as hell louder than the son of a bitch.

"Any opposed?"

"Nay," a few voices rang out, but they were small and tinny in the meeting room.

"All those in favor of electing a new mayor, say 'aye'."

The room virtually exploded.

AYE!

"All opposed?"

A few *nays* skittered about the room like lost birds.

Freddie stood, rearing up to his full height, leaving no doubt as to who was in charge of the meeting. Then he leaned over and planted both hands on the table. He made a point to flex his forearms, popping the veins, his biceps straining the fabric of his polo shirt.

"Gwen, Evergreen thanks you for your service."

Her eyes were red with tears. She scanned the crowd, as though looking for a friendly face, and Freddie was pleased to see no one making eye contact with her.

"You're making a big mistake," Adam said, standing up to face the crowd.

"Is that right?" Freddie said. "You know better than all these people?"

That shut Adam Fisher, M.D., right down.

"What do we do now?" someone called out.

"We elect a new mayor," Freddie said.

"I nominate Freddie," Chuck Danley said, pointing at Freddie. "Freddie, uh... I'm sorry, man, I just realized I don't know your last name."

Freddie smiled thinly. Even this part had been planned.

"It's Briggs."

"Briggs? The football player?"

Freddie felt himself blushing.

"Yes."

"Freddie Briggs was one of the best defensive players of the last fifty years," Chuck exclaimed to the group. "He played in the Super Bowl a couple years ago!"

This sent murmurs through the crowd. During his NFL career, Briggs had learned that Americans had always been more impressed by celebrity and athletic prowess than almost anything else. He didn't think that had changed much yet in the wake of the plague. That wouldn't always be the case, but for now, it was still packing the same punch.

"I second," Robin Swanson said, and Freddie felt warm and icy cold at the same time.

"I nominate Dr. Fisher," said a woman named Donna Tanner. She'd been married to a plant engineer and spoke with one of those precious Southern accents that reminded you of sweet tea and cucumber sandwiches and cotillions.

"I second," said Jeff, the man who'd thrown Adam and Sarah in the jail cell.

"Gentlemen," said Gwen, "do you accept the nomination as mayor?"

Fisher glanced at Sarah, who nodded, and in that moment, Freddie hated him. He knew Adam would get nominated, but he thought if the good doctor had any integrity at all, he would decline the nomination, seeing as how his focus wasn't necessarily on the town.

"Yes," Freddie said. "Yes, I do."

"I accept," Adam said.

Freddie's core burned like an overheating furnace, his growing rage its coal. Didn't they see that Adam and his search for Rachel was the way of the old world? The old world had brought nothing but plague and death and misery. It had been a weak world, run by weak men. And Adam wanted to take them down that road again. Didn't they understand they needed to stop thinking old-world thoughts, stop pretending like everything was going to be OK? Even if Adam found Rachel, no, *especially* if he found her, then they would think that everyone was entitled to a happy ending. In Rachel, in the *promise* of Rachel, they saw their own families and loved ones who had been lost to the plague. It was this pathetic hope that left them soft, that blinded them to the way the world really was.

"Are there any other nominations for the mayor of Evergreen?"

No other names were put forward, and they closed the floor to nominations. Townsend, in her last official act as mayor, picked Charlotte, Pankaj Shere, and Michael Stills, the editor of the local paper, to serve as an *ad hoc* election committee.

"Now then," Michael said. "I don't see the point of a drawn-out campaign or anything like that. Let that be our first gift to this new world."

Nervous laughter bubbled from the audience.

"I'd like to say a few words," Adam said, standing up.

"The committee just said-" Freddie said.

"No, this is too important," Adam snapped back. "If we're going to start with a new mayor, the people have a right to hear what we're all about."

Dammit, Freddie thought.

The committee huddled together briefly.

"Three minutes each," Charlotte said.

Adam stood, his hands clasped together.

"Everything Freddie said is right," Adam began. "The truth is, we've all been in a state of flux the last few months, living off the forward momentum of the world as it used to be. And trust us, Evergreen seemed so magical when we got here, a place immune from the horrors of the outside world. But that may not last. As you said, we're not the first group to find this place. We probably won't be the last.

"But the truth is that I have hope. I have hope of a bright future for all of us. That we can find new happiness, new peace together. Even if that means saying goodbye to the old world. I'm ready for it. I'm ready to go forward with each of you. Thank you."

Healthy applause filled the chamber as Freddie scrambled his thoughts together. A lesson from his father, dead a decade now, popped into his head. Keep it simple.

Fuck it, he thought. He'd done what he needed to do, said what he needed to say.

"Freddie," Charlotte said. "Three minutes."

"I think you all know my position," he said. "Think about who'll be here for you one hundred percent. Who won't be distracted by other issues. That's all I have. Thank you."

PANKAJ CUT out makeshift ballot slips from Freddie's notebook and passed them around. Adam, still reeling from the shock of what was happening, watched the others scratch out their selection. Football star Freddie Briggs. That was why his name had been so familiar to Adam when they'd met in St. Louis. A man accustomed to winning. A man accustomed to having things go his way. And Adam had been so blind to it. He felt like such an idiot!

How long had Freddie been planning this coup? There was no doubt he'd felt slighted by the deference the others had shown Adam during the last two months. Was this how he planned to rebuild his image? Did he really want to be mayor, or did he just like the idea of being mayor? He'd had some good ideas, he'd come to the meeting prepared. Maybe he should concede the election to Freddie.

Because Rachel was still out there.

Rachel.

Rachel.

The search was morphing into a desperate, pointless exercise. The search for Bigfoot. The pot of gold at the end of the rainbow. It was late November now, and they'd crossed off seven of the search grids. The odds he would find Rachel had always been slim and were now sliding toward none. It was maddening to know she was probably alive. The itch he couldn't quite scratch, growing worse with each passing day.

If only Nadia could remember anything about where she'd been. A landmark, a billboard, even a description of the terrain, a river or peak. He didn't feel bad about being mad at her because he kept it bottled up, locked away in his mind's maximum security prison. No one needed to know he hated her for making Rachel seem so close and yet so far away. He didn't even know if he was looking in the right place. He could look for the next fifty years and not come within a hundred miles of her.

Then Adam had a terrible thought, a sudden realization. It was his obsession with Rachel that had left him blind to what Freddie had been doing. Was Adam shorting these people because of it? These people were here now, and they needed someone to lead them. They needed someone to help care for them. He wasn't sure if it made him feel better or worse, but the fact of the matter was that he had the ideal rèsumè, the skills, knowledge and experience for a post-plague world. Could he in good conscience keep putting his impossible quest ahead of the others?

He suddenly remembered Holden Beach. The place hadn't crossed his mind since his desperate escape during those horrifying days in August. What did it look like now? How long before the ocean ate the beach away, before the homes began to crumble into the waves? Had sand blown across Ocean Boulevard and covered it like a blanket? If a hurricane blew ashore with no one there to see it, did it make a sound? What world did Rachel belong in? The Holden Beach he'd arrived in? Or the dying one he had escaped?

Holden Beach was two thousand miles and a lifetime away. Evergreen, this little corner of Oklahoma, was the here and now. The people in this room with him were the here and now. It went beyond simply being the right guy for the job due to his medical training. They needed to look out for each other because the very act of being alive now was so rare. And for all they knew, they were the final act in humanity's long play. If that were the case, then they should protect what life was left at all costs, go out with some class.

And that's when it hit him.

He shouldn't concede the election to Freddie.

Because Rachel was still out there.

Freddie couldn't become the mayor of Evergreen because Freddie had no Rachel.

Freddie had no hope. These people needed hope. Adam didn't know what would become of the power plant or even the human race itself, but if they didn't have a little bit of hope and love and friendship and the solidarity of breaking bread together, then what the hell were they living for? And he had hope. He believed it in his core that Rachel was still alive. And he'd keep looking for her until his dying day. It would be the fuel to power his work here. He could do it. He could give himself entirely to both missions, to lead these people while he looked for his daughter. He could do it.

He wrote his name on the sheet and handed it to Charlotte, who was collecting the ballots in her Oklahoma State baseball cap. How primitive this was, Adam thought. It was emblematic of how lost they all really were, this messy cleaving to the old ways. He didn't have the first clue if they were being faithful to the rules of parliamentary procedure, but the fact was, he didn't suspect it mattered all that much. It was the form, not the substance, guiding them along, making them feel like they were getting their lives back on track.

Then he reclaimed his seat in the second row, which, he noticed, was now empty. He glanced across the aisle and saw Freddie's row had emptied out too. Freddie's elbows were on his knees, and he was chewing a stubborn fingernail. He wanted this badly, Adam could tell, which in turn, made Adam want it badly as well. As important as he felt it was that he be elected, part of him felt it was equally important that Freddie not be.

"The committee members will, uh, move over to the mayor's office to count the votes," Charlotte said firmly. Her eyes swept across the audience, almost daring anyone to challenge her plan. She was a strong girl, very strong. As long as she was part of the town's future, perhaps things would be OK, even if Freddie became mayor.

The crowd devolved into chatter as Charlotte and the others exited the room. Adam could feel his heart slamming against his ribcage, an angry animal struggling to escape; his right leg pistoned up and down, a throwback to his days at the office, when he'd grow bored and frustrated with the mountain of government-mandated paperwork he needed to fill out. He placed a hand on his knee to stop its manic pulsing. A deep breath, a good long one, and he glanced over his shoulder at his fellow Evergreeners.

The crowd, which had drifted to the back of the room, was deliberate in its avoidance of the two candidates. They had broken up into groups of four and five, whispering, casting curious looks at Adam and Freddie, talking about the future. Adam could divine several emotions from the tone of their voices. Fear. Excitement. Curiosity. A sort of wide-eyed, can't-wait-to-see-how-THIS-turns-out-ness about it all.

Thirty minutes later, Charlotte, Pankaj and Michael returned, their faces blank and stony, the way a jury might look before sending a defendant to the gas chamber. They took their seats at the dais, Charlotte in the center chair. As they settled in, the others rushed to reclaim their seats.

"Ladies and gentlemen," Charlotte said. "We counted the votes three times. First, we counted and verified ninety-six votes were cast." She looked at her fellow committee members. "Do the other committee members agree with this report?"

"Yes," Pankaj said.

"Yes, agreed," Michael said.

"We then placed the ballots for each candidate into two separate piles and counted them individually, again counting them three times."

"Agreed," both Pankaj and Michael said simultaneously.

"The results of the election are as follows," she said, staring straight down the middle of the aisle, not making eye contact with either candidate. "Adam Fisher received fifty-one votes, and Freddie Briggs received forty-four votes. One ballot was cast blank. Adam Fisher has been elected mayor of Evergreen."

As the crowd erupted in applause and catcalls with a few boos mixed in, Adam felt a huge surge of adrenaline rush through him, like he'd touched a live wire. Part of it was relief, stemming from his lifelong aversion to losing. Adam Fisher had done very little losing in his life, and he hadn't wanted to start today. But laced in there was a tincture of regret, thrown in like a last-second spice. An hour ago, this hadn't even been on his radar, and now here he was, the duly elected leader of this ragtag group of survivors. Even in his brief tenure as the nominee, it had been a theoretical thing, big picture. But now it was crashing down on him in a very real way. But, he decided, he wouldn't have it any other way.

Someone had to do it.

And he didn't trust anyone else.

A loud noise startled him, and he looked over in time to see Freddie storm from his seat, knocking over half a dozen chairs as he did so. His jaw was clenched so tightly, Adam thought his teeth might shatter.

Without a word, Freddie burst through the hearing room doors and into the night beyond.

38

J ust once in his life, Adam wished he would follow his gut at a
time his gut was telling him something valuable. It never
seemed to go his way. Either he misjudged what his gut was
saying, and the decision backfired on him, usually in spectacular
fashion, or he'd ignore a hunch, that niggling feeling deep down that
told you you were right and end up in the very same spot. For example,
just this morning, he'd woken up feeling gloomy, cranky, out of sorts.
He'd worked seven days straight learning the ropes as mayor, and he had
planned to spend his off day searching for Rachel.

But when he'd peeked out his curtain, a sense of foreboding washed
over him. The clouds were low. A coil of sickly gray fog had snaked its
way into town overnight, clinging to the landscape like a thrush infection. It wasn't a romantic fog. It was bad fog. Trouble fog. The kind that
told you to climb back into bed and try again the next day. Maybe he
could spend a little time organizing his field notes or studying the maps.
But instead of listening to that voice, however, that little survival instinct
working so hard to keep him alive, he'd gone ahead and resumed his
patrol after breakfast. Chuck Danley had been itching to get out of
Dodge for a bit, and he decided to accompany Adam for the trip.

And now, eight hours later, they were here, at a deserted bar, his gun
locked and loaded and aimed at some random survivor whose path

they'd crossed, while across the way there, just on the other side of the long oak bar running the length of the place, said survivor was holding a gun to Chuck's head. One man lay dead on the floor, a victim of friendly fire when Chuck's captor had inadvertently shot his companion in the back. It was the shootout in St. Louis all over again, and Adam was afraid they would keep doing this over and over, a horror movie stuck on repeat, until they finally finished each other off.

They were about an hour southwest of Evergreen, passing through Duncan, Oklahoma, an old oil town in the southern part of the state. Both men were exhausted after another futile search for Rachel's camp, and Adam had suggested camping there for the night after rounding up some supplies to take back to Evergreen. Chuck suggested a drink, and Adam had thought it an excellent idea. The bar, called Branson's, was near the center of town. A few cars were still in the parking lot, but they each sat on four flat tires. After Chuck parked, they took a minute to stretch their tired legs after hours cramped in the car, bouncing through the back roads of Oklahoma.

They stepped inside the chilly bar to a sudden hail of wild gunfire, no warning whatsoever. A scream, presumably from the guy shooting his buddy, and a loud thud. Adam slid into a booth and drew his gun; Chuck dove behind the bar, where he came face to face with his captor. He'd had no time to pull his weapon, which the man had confiscated.

Despite the chill in the bar, sweat was running into Adam's eyes, and he resisted the urge to wipe his brow, lest it be construed as an offensive maneuver, or worse, give his mirror the opening he needed.

"It doesn't have to be like this," Adam said. "No one has to get hurt."

"My friend's dead 'cause of you!" he barked.

"Let's take it easy," Adam said softly, electing not to dispute the matter with the man. His gun had been up for several minutes now, and his shoulder, which had been aching, was starting to burn. "No one else needs to get hurt."

"Fuck you!"

"I swear I'm not gonna hurt you. Let my friend go, and we walk out of here."

He had to fix this. He had to. This was just some scared son of a bitch, caught in the world's biggest shitstorm. He looked lost. This man was no different than him or Chuck. Scared, panicky, the enormity of the disaster weighing heavily with each passing day.

Adam's right arm began to shake with fatigue, so he carefully cradled it with his left, keeping the gun as level as he could. He hoped the other guy couldn't see how badly he was trembling.

"What's your name?"

The man's face scrunched up in surprise, as though he couldn't believe the question he was being asked.

"What?"

"Your name. What's your name?"

"Mark. My name is Mark. No more questions!"

"Mark, I'm Adam."

"I said no more questions!"

"I didn't ask any questions. I just told you my name."

Adam held his breath, hoping he hadn't said the wrong thing. The moment stretched out like taffy, and he became aware of the sweat greasing his body despite the chill, of the way the gun seemed to be sliding in his hand, as though lightly oiled.

"OK," Mark said. "OK. But I'll ask the questions."

Adam nodded slowly, deliberately.

"What are you doing out here?"

"Just looking for supplies."

"Where you guys from?"

"We're living in a town called Evergreen," he said.

"What's that? Where is that?"

"A ways up the road," Adam said. "You're welcome to come back with us."

"You serious?"

"I am," Adam said. "But you've got to put down the gun first. You've got to trust us."

The barrel of his gun dipped down.

"But what then?"

"We just get through it," Adam replied. "We keep getting up every day. There must have been some reason we survived. There must be something to look forward to."

"What if there isn't?"

Adam paused, trying to come up with some answer that would sound genuine.

"Because I wouldn't be trying to talk you out of this otherwise."

Mark blew out a noisy sigh when he heard this.

"Why are you even doing this?" Adam asked.

"Because as soon as I let him go, you're going to kill me."

"No. I promise."

"Then put your gun down."

A smile shot across Adam's face, as though Mark had told him a moderately funny joke.

"Not sure I'm ready to do that yet, Mark."

"OK, well, I'm not letting him go."

"Guess we're going to be here for a while then. I'm gonna take a seat."

He crossed the room and climbed into a booth, where he could prop the gun on the seatback. Immediately, he felt the sweet relief of an arm unburdened by the weight of the gun. His shoulder popped deliciously.

"You had a family, didn't you?" Adam said.

Chuck's eyes went wide with disbelief, but he kept quiet. It was a risk, treading onto Mark's hallowed ground, but maybe he needed a chance to unload it. Tell someone, not about the plague, but about the family he'd lost.

"My wife, Gloria," Mark said. He chewed on his lower lip, like he was fighting back tears.

"She was a social worker. Child protective services. Fifteen years she did it. Each kid more screwed up than the next, but she went to it every day like it was the first day on the job. She cussed like a sailor."

"I'm sorry."

"My son," Mark said, his face shiny with tears. "That was the worst. He was autistic. He was fifteen years old. His whole life, I never saw him scared of anything. Anything. And when the outbreak got really bad, I couldn't get him off the computer. Even after his mom died. He was glued to the news coverage. The morning after his mom died, he came down for breakfast, and he looked scared. He'd just started showing symptoms. And that's when I became really scared, when I thought he looked scared. Now maybe he wasn't, and I was just imagining it, or maybe I was just going insane, but that's when I really lost all hope. I didn't see the look on his face again. He kept getting sicker and sicker and reporting the news to me. He died that night."

Adam didn't know what to say.

"So there it is," Mark said. "The sad story of my wife and son, lying dead in our house."

Adam sat there, the gun propped on the seatback, his trigger finger sweaty and itchy, not because he wanted to pull the trigger but because it was just itchy.

"Can I ask you a question?" Mark said.

"Sure."

"Why did this happen?"

"Oh, man, I don't know."

"You believe in God?" Mark asked.

Adam thought back to when Sarah had asked him the same question.

"No."

"I do," Mark said. "Went to church every Sunday. Every Sunday. He fucked us but good though. Guess we weren't up to snuff."

"You think this was God's judgment?"

"What else could it be?"

"Accident. Terrorism. Who knows?"

"However it happened. The Lord works in mysterious ways."

"If you're right, I doubt He'd want you to kill anyone."

"And I didn't want Him to kill my family, but I guess what I wanted didn't matter."

"I know, it's not right."

"You'd really take me back with you?"

"Of course," he said. "We need good people. We need to start rebuilding."

All the fight seemed to leak out of Mark just then, his shoulders sagging, his chin dropping. He gave Chuck a gentle shove, pushing him away, and just like that, it was over. He tossed the gun on the bar and began to sob, his hands covering his face. If Mark felt any twinge of shame in breaking down in front of two men he did not know, he didn't show it. Adam sighed, the exhale coming shallow and ragged as his heart struggled to slow down. It felt like the standoff had gone on for hours, but Adam suspected they'd only been in the bar for a few minutes.

Adam climbed out of the booth and knelt by the man who'd been shot during the standoff. There was little chance he was still alive, and even if he was, he wouldn't be for long. The man was lying on his stom-ach, his arms pinned underneath his body, which was soaked with blood. A quick pulse check told Adam all he needed to know.

Despite the loss of life, Adam felt good. The urge to stay alive deep-ened with each passing day, and he'd survived yet another test in this world. And this time, it hadn't been dumb luck or chance or a lucky shot. No, this time, he'd done it on his own. He'd been the one to dial the situ-ation back. He had talked Mark off the ledge. He looked down at the gun in his hand, really felt its weight.

Strange, this post-mortem he was conducting. It reminded him of the process he'd once utilized in his practice, after each delivery, after each c-section. He studied each chart, no matter how routine the case had been, looking for any tidbit, any nugget he could take and apply to the next case. Maybe that's what had happened here. Maybe he'd been filing things away in this new world until he needed to call on them.

As he stood up, all ready to pat himself on the back, a single gunshot shattered the fragile calm that had descended on the room. Adam froze, his mind blank, as the gun's report echoed through the bar, hanging over them like a tortured spirit. A soft thud drew Adam's attention to the bar, where he saw Mark's body slump across the bar top before sliding down onto the floor. His head hit the floor with a loud crack. Standing above him was Chuck, Mark's gun in hand.

Adam stared at him, his mouth slightly open, as though he wanted to say something but couldn't find the right words. Chuck stepped over Mark's body and emerged from behind the bar.

"Ready?" Chuck asked, wedging the gun into the front waistband of his jeans, as casual as a man returning from a trip to the bathroom.

"What did you do?"

"Man had a gun to my head," he replied. "By the way, that was a hell of a thing you did, getting him to put it down. You Jedi-mind-tricked the shit out of him, bro."

"But he let you go," Adam said, ignoring the compliment. "He let you go."

"I took care of business."

"You took care of business. Jesus."

"I'm supposed to give him a hug because he's losing his shit over the a-fucking-pocalypse? He was a fuckin' menace. We let him walk, he pulls this shit with someone else. Fucking idiot shot his own friend. Natural selection at work here."

The cold-bloodedness of it was what really scraped at Adam's insides like sandpaper. Chuck talked about executing Mark the way he might have described flushing a nasty cockroach down the toilet.

"But you murdered him," Adam said. "The threat was over, and you just murdered him."

"You're starting to get under my skin a little, Doc," he said. "I don't mind a philosophical discussion about life in a post-apocalyptic world, but you're getting dangerously close to hurting my feelings."

A new front opened up inside Adam's soul, this one labeled helplessness. Short of yelling at Chuck, telling him how disappointed he was in him, there wasn't a whole hell of a lot else Adam could do to him. And Chuck didn't seem particularly concerned with what Adam thought of him. It had been one thing out in the wilderness, when they'd been on the road, to bear witness to the evil man could do. But this guy Mark had been harmless. And Chuck was supposed to be one of them. A valued member of their fledgling community. What was Adam supposed to do now? He couldn't let this psychopath assume a leadership role. He couldn't let the kids look up to him. He couldn't let him be part of their new world.

Did Chuck think he was just going to get away with it?

"You're not coming back with me," Adam said, his voice steely and low.

"What?"

"You heard me."

"The fuck I'm not," Chuck said.

"You're out," Adam said. "No more of this shit. You do what you want, but you do it somewhere else."

"What, are you gonna tattle on me? To your little bitch girlfriend?"

"They need to know."

"My word against yours."

Adam's heart had started galloping again. *Thump-thump, thump-thump, thumpthumpthumpthump.* Not because he didn't know what to do. But because he knew precisely what he had to do. Adam held Chuck's gaze, never letting his eyes drop to the man's waist, where he'd tucked the gun, but never letting it out of his peripheral vision. Chuck stood his ground, his hands by his sides, his fingertips twitching. This was an angry man, a dangerous man. Some itch in his psyche needed scratching, and killing Mark hadn't done it. Adam replayed the last few moments of the standoff with Mark, trying to remember if he'd secured his weapon after it had ended.

He hadn't. He was one hundred percent sure he hadn't. He was ninety-five percent sure he hadn't. Chuck's arm twitched, and he knew that Chuck was going to try to kill him because Chuck did like Evergreen and he could come up with any story he damn well pleased, and they'd never know what happened here. They were ten feet apart, and it felt like his arm was encased in concrete, as slow as it was bringing the gun up to do its terrible work. Adam's eyes zeroed in on Chuck's waist, where it seemed his hands had arrived with blinding, graceful speed.

Too late, too late, and then both guns were out, and both were firing. As he emptied the clip, the guns breathing their terrible lead exhaust, Adam waited for the hot plug in his chest, the brief crackle in his forehead that would mean it was all over, that this new world had gotten the best of him, that he hadn't been fast enough or smart enough or accurate enough.

He fired until the gun was dry, its empty clicks feeling hollow and impotent. Only then did he dare open his eyes. The air was thick with smoke and the sound of desperate gasping. Adam stole a look toward the ground, where he found Chuck writhing about, his hands at his ruined throat, blood bubbling and spilling between his fingers. He'd be dead in less than a minute.

Adam wanted to hate him for making him do this, but he couldn't manage a single discrete emotion as he watched the man die on the bitterly cold floor. He felt no regret or sorrow; it was what had to be done. He hadn't asked for this world any more than anyone else had. But as he'd been told, and as was coming into sharp, jagged relief, this was the world he'd been given. In that world, things would have to be done, things he might not like to do.

As Chuck Danley bled to death, Adam turned and left the bar without a word. He shoved his hands into his coat and walked the two blocks to where he'd left the car. The wind was blowing hard out of the west, and in the air, he could smell a hint of snow.

39

"Marry me," Adam said.

They were eating dinner in the apartment they now shared. It was early December, and a light snow was falling outside. But the juice was still on, and warm air blew up through the vents. They were the luckiest sons of bitches on the planet. For now.

"What?"

"You heard me," he said.

"Are you serious?"

"Yes," he said. "Can't promise a big church wedding or honeymoon to Maui or anything like that, but I'm serious as I can be. I love you, Sarah. More than you'll ever know."

"But what about my little problem?"

"I've been thinking about that," Adam said. "Makes me think we need to do it sooner than later."

She wiped her lips with her napkin and set it down next to her bowl. She leaned across the table and took his face in her hands.

"Adam, baby, we're not going to grow old together," she said. "This thing, it's not a maybe-kinda thing. I'm going to die of Huntington's."

He felt the tears form at the corners of his eyes.

"Listen, one of the things I've learned from living through this thing is that there's no time to waste. Think of all the millions, billions of dreams that died with everyone else. We were given a second chance, a chance to start over. But that second chance comes with a price. The price is that this is a really dangerous place now. That thing with Chuck. Sometimes I sit down and play with the numbers, try and estimate how many people survived the plague. Even if just two percent survived, that leaves more than six million people in this country alone. I'm not going to lie to you. I'm not a very optimistic person generally. I don't trust a lot of folks. I think maybe that's why I was drawn to obstetrics. I saw a lot of happiness and got to deliver a lot of good news. That's not to say I didn't treat some very sick women. Every doctor does. But it was kind of a way to self-medicate my general feeling about people."

"You sure know how to charm a girl."

"I guess what I'm saying is that for the first time in a long time, I know what makes me happy, and that it makes me happy for the right reason. And it might have been a cliché to say that life is precious, but it's pretty goddamn true these days. There are precious few lives left, and if you're lucky enough to be alive, every moment is precious. I'm telling you, I'm lucky to be alive right now. You don't know how close Chuck came to killing me out there."

Sarah nodded. She knew what had happened out there; Adam had told the others that Chuck had been shot and killed by bandits. He didn't like lying, but he wasn't sure how they'd react to the story that Chuck had been a cold-blooded killer. He knew Freddie was suspicious of the story.

"You know I can't have children," she said.

"I wouldn't think-"

"No," she cut him off, lest he misinterpret her meaning, think it was a ledge he could talk her down from. She could just picture him trying to stretch his "life is precious" argument to the next step, to a place where he'd want to get busy with the business of making little Fishers. "I mean I physically cannot have them. I had a hysterectomy."

It didn't surprise him, but he said nothing. Because there was nothing to say.

"I figured the best thing I could do is make sure that any child of mine wasn't doomed to my fate. Even if that meant not having the child at all. And after watching what Caroline had to go through, I'm not sure I'd even want to chance it."

"I'm not asking you to marry me because I'm clinging to some traditional notion of family," he said. "I'm asking you to marry me because I want you to know what you mean to me. How much I love you. Thing is, this could be a transitional world for a while. Who knows how long before we figure our shit out, if we get a chance to figure it out at all. I want you to know that the way I feel about you isn't transitional. It's for keeps."

The last walls inside her broke down, and she couldn't say no. Nothing, not a goddamn thing was guaranteed for any of them. And that had been the sole basis for her resistance. She felt a smile break across her face, a lightness spread through her, as refreshing as the spray of ocean on a hot summer day.

"Yes," she said, feeling her eyes well up with tears. She felt stupid crying, but then she saw tears in Adam's eyes, and she forgave herself. She never in a million years believed she would let herself fall for anyone again, let alone follow a path as traditional as marriage, but here she was all the same. She embraced him, wrapping her arms around him tightly and covering his face in kisses.

"And how do you propose, forgive the pun, we do this? I'm not sure a marriage certificate is required anymore."

"We'll do it however we want to do it. We'll ask Gwen to perform the ceremony."

A question came to mind, and it embarrassed her to think about it, and so she asked it before she had a chance to change her mind.

"Do you want me to take your last name?"

He paused, and his lips pursed in the way that let her know he was really thinking this one through.

"What do you think?"

She clicked her tongue.

"I don't know," she said. "My name is important to me. And I get the feeling it's going to be tough for women to maintain their identity."

"What do you mean?"

"You're bigger, stronger, faster," she said. "Women are going to have a tough time in this brave new world."

"Then don't," Adam said. "We can rewrite the rules."

"You sure?"

He laughed.

"Of course I'm sure."

She smiled and kissed him.

TWO DAYS LATER, Adam and Sarah stood at the center of the park, across from town hall, before Gwen Townsend and most of the residents of Evergreen. It was a chilly day, but warm in the sun.

"Good morning," Townsend started, her hands clasped, "we gather here today to watch our two friends take their first step on a long and happy life together."

Sarah squeezed Adam's hand; the others did not know about her diagnosis. Someday, they would know, but for now, it was best to put it up on a dark shelf, out of sight, and out of mind.

"I've officiated many marriages in my day," she said. "But this one is especially special to me. We've all seen so many terrible things in the last few months, and we're liable to see many more. We've all experienced incomprehensible tragedy. The special Dateline episode about us would be a two-nighter for sure."

Laughter rippled through the crowd.

"And the future is anything but certain," she said, her voice darkening a shade. "I wish I could stand here and tell you that everything will be just fine. But I don't know that. And I think we all heard enough lies during the epidemic that for me to stand here and sugarcoat things insults you and tramples on the thing we are doing here today.

"I don't know what tomorrow holds, but I do know this: today, love has prevailed."

Claps and hollers from the audience.

"Love has shined its bright light on this dark land. It shows us that there are still beautiful things in this world, things worth fighting for."

More cheers, the sounds rolling across the plains.

"Tragedy is temporary. Pain fades away. But love endures. And as long as that is the case, we have a responsibility to keep fighting for a good and just world where love can continue to shine."

She stopped, tears in her eyes, and hugged Adam and Sarah.

Behind them, Adam heard throats clearing and noses sniffle. She could certainly lay it on thick; he supposed that's what politicians did.

Still, he couldn't help but smile as he held Sarah's hands in his own, studied every line of her mocha-colored face. She wore jeans and a thick blue sweater; he was casually dressed as well, as they had agreed to dispense with the pomp and circumstance and focus on each other and their friends. Her hair was pulled back and curled up in a bun, revealing her slender neck. He could make out a vein just under the skin, pulsing rapidly. He stroked her hand gently and as he did so, he could see her pulse slow. That's what he wanted to do for her, be a source of peace for her, be the safe harbor for her as she was for him.

He couldn't make the world's problems disappear any more than he could cure her Huntington's. But they could love each other for as long as they could. And maybe that love could make the world around them a little better. It made sense in a weird sort of way. With so few of them left, their actions had greater impact on those around them. Each act, from good to wicked, would be amplified. Life was more precious, love more rare, evil more pernicious, every death more terrible. This, he decided, would be their legacy for the generations he hoped would one day follow.

He felt her hand squeeze his, and he broke free from his trance. Sarah and the mayor were staring at him.

"Not having second thoughts, are you, cowboy?" Sarah whispered.

"You wish," he said.

She made a face, sticking her tongue out at him.

"Adam Fisher," Gwen Townsend said, "do you promise to love and cherish Sarah for as long as you both shall live?"

"I sure do."

"Sarah Wells, do you promise to love and cherish Adam for as long as you both shall live?"

"As long as I live."

"Then I pronounce you husband and wife."

As they leaned in to kiss, the crowd absolutely exploded with joy, their cheers and hoots rolling across the park, echoing through the quiet town, up and down the streets and alleys. For that briefest of moments, the pain and suffering of the previous four months faded away, like a blistering sunburn cooled by the tangy chill of aloe.

～

THEY RETIRED to the town hall for a small reception for Adam and Sarah. Two tables of snacks had been set up, courtesy of Charlotte and Donna Tanner. They'd even managed to find matching paper tablecloths peppered with the words *Congratulations* and *Good Luck!* Miriam apologized for not making a cake, but her large pyramid of sugar cookies looked lovely just the same.

A receiving line took shape, and Adam and Sarah visited with each guest, one at a time, thanking them for being there. Sarah tensed when they reached Freddie.

"Congratulations," Freddie said, shaking Adam's hand first and nodding toward Sarah.

"Thank you, Freddie," Adam said.

Freddie didn't say anything else, and a brief silence began to morph into an awkward one, so Sarah leaned in and hugged the big man. She even pecked him on the cheek for good measure, and she tried to ignore the tension in his jaw, the way his teeth were clenched together.

"Thank you, Freddie," Sarah echoed. "And thank you for all you've done for us. You helped us all get here. Helped keep us safe."

"I did what I could," Freddie said, his voice barely a whisper.

"It was a lot," Sarah said. She was starting to feel uncomfortable, so she placed her hand on Adam's elbow and gave him a slight shove toward the next guest in the line. Caroline's face hung in the silence among them like a large painting.

When the last guest had hugged the happy couple, Charlotte plugged in a boombox and music filled the autumn night. As the first song, a Fleetwood Mac tune, erupted from the speakers, the guests froze and stared at the music player as though it had come to life. In a way, it had. Sarah could see it in their eyes and in their sad smiles, the dead world that had birthed them into this new one. No one danced or spoke or even sang along; they stood there like mannequins as the song played through.

Charlotte played a slow song next, by the presumably late Alison Krauss. As Krauss' slinky voice slipped out of the speakers, Sarah felt Adam taking her hand and leading her to the center of the room. It had been cleared of chairs, now a proper spot for a couple's first dance as husband and wife. His arm snaked around her waist and she laced her hands at the back of his head. And they danced, in the center of a circle formed by their fellow citizens, their friends, these good people they hadn't known a month ago and, in a better world, would never have met at all.

As the song wound down, she found it difficult to believe that she was married (to whatever extent marriage existed now), and she found herself wishing her father had been here to see it. He had always pushed her to live her life to the fullest; he would tell her that she was only getting one life, so she might as well take chances with it. Part of her had wanted to hate him and her late mother for having her at all, for taking such a terrible risk that they would have a Huntington's baby. But she couldn't hate them. And so she had done as her father had advised. But this, even this would have surprised her old man. She thought he would have been pleasantly surprised. She thought he would have liked Adam.

When it was over, she kissed Adam hard, and he lifted her off the ground. The guests whooped and hollered again, even more loudly than they had during the ceremony.

"Speech, speech!" someone called out, but the cheers and whistles continued.

Adam stepped forward and patted the air with his hands, trying to silence the crowd.

"How about we have ourselves a party?"

The crowd roared, and that was enough.

The party continued long into the night, stretching into the wee hours of the next morning. Adam danced with every lady; Sarah took the hand of every fellow. No one wanted to leave, and so no one did. They sang songs and got drunk on cheap beer and champagne. Someone led the motley crew in a series of ever more ribald rugby chants. As night crested and rounded the turn for daybreak, they got louder and sillier. Sarah saw at least two couples pair off for drunken make-out sessions in the corners.

At dawn, they poured out of town hall and into the chilly morning, their laughs and voices growing hoarse and strained. They streamed toward the center of the park, where they huddled together and watched the sun break over the rooftops, spilling its golden light into the town. Reddish clouds striated the morning sky.

"Pretty sky," someone said.

"Red sky in morning, sailor's warning," another replied.

"That's an old wives' tale."

"Could be. But eight years in the Navy, never wrong once."

This hushed the crowd a bit, and together they looked at the red sky, the scalloped clouds, and although she'd heard the red sky admonition too, even Sarah wondered how such a lovely scene could be a harbinger of bad weather. She thought this even as she felt her right hand twitch.

It twitched a second time, spasming and locking in place for a moment as though it had a mind of its own; then the attack withered and her hand drooped back down. That was the second time in the past week she'd experienced the twitching in her hand.

Red sky at morning, sailor's warning.

As Adam pulled her close and kissed the side of her head, she covered her right hand with her left, the way a family might hide the drug-addict uncle. This had been a long time coming, since she'd gotten the positive test while she'd been stationed at Fort Lewis near Tacoma. The genetic disease specialist had given her a thick sheaf of literature on Huntington's, glossy, high production value, written in that corporate-speak that almost made it sound like she'd been granted membership in a super exclusive club. She went home and read it and cried for two days.

The Army had never known about her disease because she'd had the test done on her own dime; she didn't want to chance getting discharged, especially since she could be years away from showing symptoms. They didn't test for it on the annual physical, and so she'd served another seven years, good ones, too, during which she was awarded two Purple Hearts and the Silver Star. The Star was for a little episode in the Kandahar Province in Afghanistan, where, she well and truly hoped, that forsaken patch of useless ground, the rock formations like broken teeth jutting from a shattered jaw, was littered with the bodies of Medusa-ravaged Taliban thugs.

But now all that was in the past, really in the past, because if the plague had closed the chapter on her life as a soldier, the appearance of symptoms would serve to close the book on the life she'd once known, a life of strength and good health and not needing a damn soul for anything.

Because now, it was here. It was as if the Huntington's had simply tapped the Medusa virus on the shoulder.

I got this.

40

Freddie left the reception around one in the morning. He'd wanted to leave hours earlier, but he had to keep up appearances. He'd handled the loss to Adam badly, he knew that, and it was important to show the others there were no hard feelings. As he let himself into his apartment, he could hear the party still going strong. He lay on top of his comforter in the dark, a hand under his head, but sleep eluded him.

No matter.

Freddie himself had remained sober, nursing a beer all night so at least he wouldn't look out of place. The weight of cumulative events were beginning to press down on him, choke him, so heavy that sometimes he found it hard to breathe. He got up at three-thirty and sat at his kitchen table.

He could just leave.

That was definitely an option.

He could pack his bags and hit the open road. He could go anywhere. South to the Gulf Coast or Florida or even Mexico. Anywhere he wouldn't have to worry about cold weather. But while those destinations might work now, in December, he couldn't imagine living that close to the equator in the summer months with no air conditioning. Summers in Baton Rouge had been bad enough, even with his little window unit rattling along. It would be an oven now. And the bodies. What had the last three months done to the millions of corpses dotting the landscape down there? How bad would it smell? Eventually, it might be an option, maybe a year from now, once there was nothing left but the bones. But now? Yeesh.

Perhaps to the northwest, Oregon or Washington? He'd liked both states when his football travels had taken him there. A lot of land for a man to get lost in. No more worries about backstabbing doctors or sad-sack pregnant women or whiny kids who would never know how truly lucky they were. Just Freddie and the land. Hundreds of well-stocked cabins, isolated, minimal body count, lakes rippling with fish, woods rustling with game.

Now that did sound good.

And maybe it would be good a month or so out of the year.

But it didn't scratch his itch.

He couldn't live the rest of his days by himself. He was thirty-three years old, and decades of isolation just wasn't singing to him. He'd lived his life around people, in front of thousands of fans, in the trenches of sport with dozens of like-minded men. He could play crowds like a concert violinist; he led his teammates like a field general. As he went, so went the team.

In the end, Freddie decided to stay. Everything he wanted was here.

He left his apartment at mid-morning. He pedaled west along Route 815, not wanting to draw attention with the sound of his truck. The weather was cool, but not cold. Thin clouds ran west to east, and there was a slight breeze, as there always seemed to be. This part of Oklahoma had a far more temperate climate than he'd expected; according to the local almanac, the average daytime temperature, even in the dead of winter, climbed into the upper forties.

Evergreen was dead quiet, the citizens sleeping off what was sure to be wicked hangovers. They'd need the whole day to sleep off the effects of the piss-water beer and champagne that they'd used to fuel the wedding festivities. Duties would be shirked today, no doubt, heads under pillows, night tables stocked with bottled water and painkillers to combat the stinking headaches in their futures.

Beyond the Evergreen town limits, the land was absolutely desolate, flat and peppered with scrub brush erupting from the ground like boils.

Farther west, Freddie could make out the outline of Oklahoma's highest peak, the Black Mesa, the source of the winds that powered Evergreen's turbines. He'd been meaning to check it out, but he hadn't made the trip yet. The power plant lay a mile away.

The NorthStar Wind and Solar Plant sat on about two hundred acres of Oklahoma grassland, with about two-thirds of the land devoted to the wind turbines and the solar panel field occupying the rest. The solar field consisted of dozens of rectangular panels rippling brilliance in the morning sun, with a two-hundred-foot tower that concentrated the heat absorbed by the panels. Beyond the panels were two large salt tanks, which stored the heat, and the conduits that carried the heat into a series of generators that converted it into electricity. The wind farm was set back some, the turbines rising up majestically like a giant's handheld fans. The blades of these three-hundred-foot-tall monoliths rotated slowly, filling the air with a strange but not entirely unpleasant hum.

He pedaled onward, a little more pep in his legs as he saw his destination. He wasn't entirely sure what he wanted to do out here, but he'd decided to make the trip out here shortly after Adam and Sarah's nuptials. Their marriage was a watershed event for the town. This plant was a watershed place. There was nothing more important to the town's future than its power supply. It's what made Evergreen special and had his traveling party talking about things like fate and destiny. It all linked together.

A long perimeter fence surrounded the complex, and he saw a single sentinel standing guard at the outer gate. This duty was rotated among the townsfolk, and today, the watch was in

the hands of John Ochoa and a woman named Felicia something-or-the-other. Ochoa was pacing around the fence line, smoking a cigarette, holding a rifle and looking generally clueless. A camper was parked at the top of the access road that led into the plant.

He coasted to a stop near the main entrance and dismounted from his bike.

"Ho, there, Freddie," John said.

He greeted everyone with "ho there," and it annoyed Freddie immensely.

"What brings you out this way? How was the big weddin'?" The way he said wedding, dropping the "g" like it was optional, annoyed him too. And the way he peppered you with questions like a five-year-old.

"It was a wedding," Freddie replied. "Felicia in the camper?"

"Oh, you know her," John said, miming the act of tipping a bottle to his lips. "Half in the bag. What brings you out this way?"

"Just thought I'd take a look around," Freddie said, his eyes focused on the large plant

behind John. "I was talking to Adam, and you know he said he thought it'd be a good idea if we all started learning more about the plant."

He thought back to the tour that Townsend had given him, Adam, and Sarah shortly after their arrival in Evergreen. It had been a superficial look at the plant, one suggesting that Townsend really didn't understand the first thing about how it worked. She was able to give the brochure tour, the explanation that NorthStar had undoubtedly put in its investment materials, that explained at the very shallowest level why it had been the place for your hard-earned capital.

Ultimately, all he gleaned from her was that NorthStar had developed a process for extracting more power from lower levels of wind and sunshine. *Wave of the future*, she'd said. Evergreen was the pilot project, and before you knew it, towns and cities across America would be coming online and that would be the end of America's dependence on fossil fuels.

"Oh, you know, I'm not sure about that, Freddie," said John. "I didn't hear anything about any visitors today from the mayor."

"That right?"

The Adam's apple in John's neck bobbed visibly, and Freddie could tell the man was a bit frightened. John went to lick his lips, sending the forgotten cigarette that had been dangling from the corner of his mouth tumbling to the ground. It hissed when it hit the gravel road.

"It's just that Mayor, I mean, Doctor Fisher said we really ought not to have you, I mean, anyone walking around inside unless there was reason for people to be here."

The rifle that had been slung on his shoulder had come askew, looped around his elbow and scraping the ground. He seemed to be caught in that middle ground, unsure of whether he should sling it back on his shoulder or shoot Freddie with it.

"Me?"

"No, no!" he said, backpedaling now, still fumbling with the rifle.

"Did Fisher tell you to keep me away from the plant?"

"No," John replied.

A metallic scraping noise drew his attention, and Freddie glanced over to see the rear door of the camper swing open on its rusted hinges. Felicia climbed out, bleary eyed and gin-blossomed. The stink of gin was evident even from where Freddie was standing. Jesus, what the hell did Adam think he was doing with this protection detail?

The best he could, a little voice squeaked out.

"What the hell is going on out here?" the woman croaked.

"Nothing," John said, never taking his eye off Freddie. "Go back to sleep."

She didn't move, holding her ground at the camper's rear bumper.

Freddie felt a bit of food stuck in his teeth, and he swirled his tongue around until he jostled it free. The image of his tongue poking around his cheek must have been intimidating because it precipitated another step backward from the good John Ochoa. The act relaxed him a bit, as he processed the news that Adam had given orders to bar him from entering the power plant. As if anyone in that shitburg town could stop Freddie Briggs from doing whatever the hell he wanted.

He could just picture Adam meeting with the security crew, taking them aside all conspiratorially and saying, "Hey, Freddie, he's a bit upset about not becoming mayor, let's all keep an eye on him, m'kay?"

The rage hit him squarely in the gut, rippling around his sides in a wave of heat. Sweat beaded on his body and traced icy trails down his flanks.

That mother-*fucker*!

"Why don't you head on back home?" John said, summoning what must have been every ounce of courage he had on reserve in that skinny, underdeveloped body of his.

"Do you even know how this plant operates?" Freddie asked.

"Not my job to know."

"Not my job, he says," Freddie repeated. "There's a hundred fucking people living in that town, and you don't think it's your job to know how our most important asset works?"

"Uh."

"We should have people out here every goddamn day," he went on, "learning the ins and outs of this place. It's nothing but a giant machine. And you know what happens to machines, don't you?"

"I'm not sure what you're asking, Freddie, but I think you should-"

"They break down," Freddie said. "They break down, and then where would we be?"

"Time to go, Freddie."

Freddie looked over and saw the woman leveling her gun at him. The firearm trembled in her hand, and he knew she would no more shoot him than she would break into show tunes.

"You gonna shoot me?"

"I want you to leave," she said. "I don't know what's going on here, but this is my job."

Freddie smiled, a real smile that curled his lips upward without any chicanery on his part.

"OK, you win," Freddie said. "I just want to help the town. I want to be part of the crew that takes care of the plant. Looks like I've got some things to talk about with our good mayor."

Felicia cut her eyes toward John, who nodded. She lowered her gun, and Freddie felt a sense of relief flood through him. He hadn't handled this well at the outset, but he was getting things back under control. He was man enough, after all, to admit his mistakes, unlike a certain pig-headed doctor he knew.

With a tip of his hand, he turned to leave, and then stopped mid-turn.

"Hey, you guys want a bite to eat?" he asked, looking back over his shoulder. "I got some sandwiches in here." He tapped his backpack.

"Sure," John said without missing a beat. "Tired of the protein bars anyway."

"How about you?" Freddie said to the woman.

"Yeah, sure."

He knelt down and unzipped his pack. On top of the extra change of clothes lay his nine-millimeter pistol, which he'd picked up before they'd made it to Evergreen. It had good heft to it, felt good in his hand. He thought about the line he was about to cross, the one he could never uncross. He thought about Susan and Caroline and Heather lying in the

Georgia soil, now part of the Earth, elemental, natural. This was the way things were, the way they had to be.

Well, he was either going to do it or not.

He came up firing.

The first two rounds hit John in the stomach, and his body curled up like a roly-poly before tumbling to the hardpan. Freddie turned the gun on Felicia, whose flight instinct had kicked in a hair too late. She'd been leaning against the side of the camper, which gave Freddie a huge target to aim at. He stepped into the shot and pulled the trigger three more times. The first two rounds missed, but the third found purchase in the hollow under her neck. The impact of the round slammed her against the chassis, and her body hung upright for a minute, as though it couldn't quite believe what had happened, even as blood sprayed from her wound. Then, she collapsed to the ground, dead.

The sounds of moaning broke Freddie from his trance; he looked back toward the main gate to see John writhing around, his shaky hands fumbling with his rifle, which had landed underneath his body.

"You fucker," John hissed, blood trickling from the corners of his mouth. "You fucker."

Freddie knelt by the mortally wounded man, his mind on cruise control. It was as if the entire sequence had been pre-programmed. He really hadn't had to do anything. John rolled onto his back and pressed his hands against his ravaged abdomen. The blood seeped through at an alarming rate.

"I think I will take a look around," Freddie said.

"The next shift's on their way," John muttered between labored breaths.

Freddie smiled. "You know just as well as I do that you're on until seven tonight."

A wave of pain washed over John and his face contorted into a terrible grimace.

"Fuck, why?"

Freddie considered the question for a moment. Then he pressed the barrel of his gun against John's temple and pulled the trigger.

∾

THERE.

It was done.

It *had* to be done.

Freddie sat in the driver's seat of the camper, sipping Felicia's gin, gazing at NorthStar's crown jewel. The power plant was large, gleaming, new. A promise of a better tomorrow. It had kept its promise even after the plague. A starter kit for a new society. Around them, a land blanketed with darkness and cold, but this place was immune to all that. A sort of symbiotic relationship existed between it and the denizens of Evergreen. Without them, this place would have no purpose, no *raison d'être*. It would have dutifully continued churning out power with no one to use it until it decayed and rotted and crumbled.

He considered what he had done. There was no going back now. And he hadn't killed Felicia and John, whose bodies were now tucked in the cargo area, for the simple sake of killing them. He wasn't a psychopath. There was a reason, a justification for this act. It wasn't because John, little shit that he'd been, had hurt his feelings. No, that would be juvenile. Immature. This was simply a link in a chain.

When you got right down to it, all their hopes and dreams were wrapped up in this place. These hopes and dreams flowed from the town through the buried cables, into this place, which converted them into gorgeous electricity and sent it back to them. But not for Freddie. What were his hopes and dreams now?

The girls. His girls. Susan and Heather and Caroline.

It was a wound that wouldn't heal. The thinnest filament of scar tissue would form and then it would split open like it hadn't been there at all. How these folks had simply moved on astonished him. They had their meetings and their dinners and Kumbaya. It was like their loved ones hadn't existed at all, and they'd been dead less than four months! Didn't these people have souls, hearts? Why would he want to lead these people anyway?

They didn't *deserve* Evergreen.

And there it was.

They didn't deserve this bounty they'd been granted, whether by fate, karma, divinity or just plain dumb luck. The callousness, the total disrespect for the world gone by was horrifying.

Chewie.

The guinea pig, may he rest in peace, had had more sense than these people. Yes, Freddie thought. The guinea pig, and all of a sudden, Freddie wished he'd buried Chewie with his girls because they had loved him so much. Instead, he'd condemned him to an eternity rotting in his sad little cage in the family room. Freddie should have stayed back in Smyrna with them. He'd left because he was selfish. He'd been too much of a coward to stay where he belonged, to be the man of the house at the most critical juncture of their lives. It was all coming clear now.

Even Caroline Braddock.

Her death had been a warning, designed to teach him a lesson.

The lesson had been a painful one, but he had learned it now. Clinging to the old world would spell doom for all of them, the way it had for Caroline. Adam had gotten her hopes up with old-world thinking. If the baby had been doomed from the start, he would've handled it better than Dr. Doolittle. That's what these people needed. A swift kick in the ass about the way things really were, the way they were going to be.

This power plant wasn't going to last, that's what these people didn't understand; it was an illusion, a beautiful one perhaps, but still just an illusion. Like a crust of ice over a lake, shimmery and glinting, but underneath was cold, cold death. None of them knew how to maintain it, let alone fix it. It was already deteriorating, from the inside out. He could feel it, he could almost *hear* it.

It was their last link to the old world. He understood its allure, its siren call, but he also understood that it was already fading away, like a sailboat drifting over the horizon, out of sight. That's what the others needed to see.

And sooner than later.

He was doing it for them.

They would thank him later.

The Israelites may have been afraid to leave Egypt, may not have even wanted to, and so it had fallen to Moses to take the reins and lead them to the Promised Land. That would be his job. A world beholden to this power plant, *that* was the threat, that was the real danger to all of them. Once they were free of the shackles of this place, of the inevitably doomed quest to keep the lights on, only then could they find salvation and truly become part of this new world.

He unlocked the gates with John's keys, got back in the camper and followed the access road running around the perimeter of the facility. The windmills churned on silently; the place hummed, a deep penetrating buzz that drilled down to the very core of his mind. As he completed the circuit, he stumbled across a few bodies here and there, shift workers who hadn't made it out before succumbing to Medusa.

He opened the door, which was unlocked, and went inside, feeling the metallic chill of the building envelop him. Inside, the buzzing was even louder. The place was cavernous, much bigger than he had thought based on his views from the outside. The walls were outfitted with switches and levers and dials and touchscreens, more than he could even count. Somewhere, a compressor hissed intermittently, like a metronome.

A handful of darkened offices ringed the interior, centering on a large control booth in the middle. More bodies here, a pretty significant concentration of them. Given the chill inside the building, they hadn't deteriorated much. Freddie took the metal steps to the control room at the middle two at a time, his heavy footsteps echoing through the dead plant. The door to the control room was locked. The mummified bodies of two workers stared back at him from their chairs inside the room.

He began anticipating the imminent silence, the way a hungry dad looked forward to his porterhouse on Father's Day. It felt so good to know that the hum would soon be gone. He could scarcely contain himself. He went back out to the truck and began scouring it for ideas.

The smell of stale grease and cigarette smoke hung limply in the air of the camper's small kitchenette. As he scratched his chin, it hit him. Grease didn't smell like that unless it had been cooked. That meant there was a cooking source on-board. After a few moments of searching, he found the small propane tank under the counter, a hose snaking upward to the stovetop.

He loosened the valve, hearing the welcome hiss of gas being piped to the burner. He shut it quickly and opened his pack, looking for a lighter but coming up short. Then he remembered John had been smoking upon his arrival. A quick search of the dead man's clothes revealed a cheap lighter. Freddie snapped the metal wheel and smiled when the tiny flame erupted from its plastic depths. He held it as long as he could, releasing the button only when it began to burn his thumb.

He lugged the propane tank into the control room and then surrounded it with anything flammable he could find. Papers, manuals, clothes of the deceased shift workers, anything that would burn. Then he strung the trail of kindling toward the door, which would buy him a little time before the propane ignited. He opened the safety valve. The pressurized gas rushed out in a whoosh.

He backed away from the tank, this soon-to-become ground zero of all that Evergreen had been or would ever be. Every few feet, he paused and touched the flame from the lighter to the kindling. Clothes and papers that had been indoors for months had seasoned and went up immediately. Tongues of flame danced across the fabric, looking for more fuel to consume.

The fire moved faster than he anticipated, and he turned to run. Even as he hit the threshold of the doorway, he could feel the heat thickening behind him; he pictured one of those cartoon thermometers, the red bubble of mercury expanding comically. As he burst through the door, into the freshness of the outside air, he began to shiver uncontrollably, the sense that he was surrounded by forces he could no longer control. The camper was dead ahead, and he was flying now, the muscles of his legs rippling as he chewed up the ground between the plant and his getaway vehicle.

As he climbed into the driver's seat, he planted a hand on the roof and glanced back toward the open doorway, which was now rippling with a red-orange corona, a throat of fire. Something twisted and broken inside him, a ruined clockspring, kept him rooted there for a long moment, but he finally forced himself to the wheel, and he backed the big camper away from the security fence. The tires spun briefly, throwing up a spray of dust and gravel, before catching. He turned the wheel hard to the right, and the camper fishtailed; for a moment, he thought the whole thing would tip over, and that would be that.

Serve you right, a tiny voice screamed out.

But the camper won its battle with the forces intent on pulling it over, and he shifted into gear just as he heard the *THWOOMP* of the propane tank exploding. He pushed the accelerator to the floor, achieving his escape velocity from the rapidly maturing holocaust behind him. In his rearview mirror, he saw a thick finger of flame erupting through the doorway, reaching out as if to tap him on the shoulder. Then it retreated back inside, and that was when the roof exploded.

When he was about a hundred yards clear, he stopped and climbed out onto the camper's running board for a better view. He could hear the fire popping, crackling, almost talking to him. A small part of him, the vestigial part that still thought old-world thoughts, fully expected to hear the screams of fire engines racing to the scene, but, of course, there was nothing.

Even from this distance, he could make out a shimmery halo hovering around the building, spreading like a fog as the fire made its way deeper into the plant, feeding off all the oxygen it would want or ever need. There was nothing to stop it now.

He slipped back behind the wheel and drove east.

There was one more thing he needed to do.

41

A loud but quick pop, followed by a hiss, was the only warning Adam received that everything in Evergreen was about to change forever. He was sitting on his stoop on that unseasonably warm afternoon, a stack of binders at his feet, one lying open in his lap. Together they constituted the operations manual for the NorthStar plant, and he was doing his best to educate himself about the town's most important asset.

Solar Array, Salt Tanks, Maintenance, and so on.

The reading was dry, terrible, but absolutely necessary. He'd been reading for hours each day, deciding it would be better to construct a foundation first before poking his head into the technological lion's den that was the plant's nerve center. Crawling before walking and all that. It was how he learned. He didn't consider himself an intellectual giant by any stretch of the imagination, but he'd been blessed with an uncanny memory and an ability to make connections when none seemed apparent. That talent had helped him breeze through medical school and his clinicals. And this, he hoped, would be no different.

He'd been reading since early that morning, when he'd awoken to a smidge of a post-reception headache. Sarah slept until eleven, a rarity for her, and then set off for a meeting with the farming committee at the town hall. They had partied long enough, she'd decided, and it was time to buckle down and make this place work. He'd wanted to consummate the marriage a third time ("just to be sure," he'd told her), but she'd smacked his bottom playfully and promised there would be time for that later.

As it turned out, there wouldn't be. Not that day.

The odd noise broke his concentration for the first time in an hour, so he got up out of the chair, placed his hands in the small of his back, and stretched. His back cracked deliciously, and he sighed. As he stood there, satisfied, another pop, this one even louder, echoed across the quiet townscape. This made the hairs on his neck stand up. He ran inside to change and noticed the digital clock on the end table in the living room had winked out. He quickly laced on a pair of heavy hiking boots, his thoughts zeroing quickly on his new bride, a pit forming in his stomach. It had been a long time since he'd had someone in close proximity to worry about, and it frightened him a little.

By the time he stepped out onto the street, he could just make out the fist of black smoke rising in the west. His stomach turned to water. Fire was one of his biggest fears. The town did have a fire station, but its sole truck had been dispatched to a nearby town at the beginning of the outbreak, and it had not returned. *On a wing and a prayer*, Townsend had said. They were living on borrowed time. He'd known it all along.

And the bill was coming due.

HE RAN west along Evergreen Boulevard, yelling "Fire!" as he went, a regular Paul Revere. Despite the warmth of the day, he felt cold, icy sweat frosting his body. A few others were already moving in the same direction, having seen the smoke curling its way skyward on that December afternoon. They paused a block west of the town hall, near Evergreen High School's baseball field. He saw a figure running toward them; it was Derek Harris, a lanky man who'd taught in the elementary school.

"It's the plant!" Harris called out. "The plant's on fire!"

As Adam bent over breathing hard, his hands on his knees, suddenly aware of what had happened, not wanting to believe it. Someone noticed him pulling up.

"Come on, Adam! We've got to go!"

They piled into Derek's electric car and headed south along the ribbon of asphalt poking out from the edge of town, rising and falling over the undulating plains. Adam sat stone still, catching bits and pieces of the conversation peppering the car, but unable to focus on it for long. Then a huge explosion boomed across the plains.

"Who's out there today?"

"John and ... I can't remember the other."

"Felicia. She's out there."

"Probably passed out." This one said in a hushed tone.

Think, dammit, think.

He could see it in their faces, the panic, the fright, and he thought he might have known what all of them had looked like when the world was in the grip of the epidemic. It was a look he had never wanted to see again, but there it was all the same. And just like before, there was nothing they could do. He knew the town was lost as soon as he saw the thick bubble of smoke. Their hopes and dreams had literally gone up in it.

Sarah.

Where was she?

She was smart, she was strong, and he told himself not to worry too much right now. She'd be making sure the townsfolk were remaining calm, looking after the kids. Derek pulled to a stop in the middle of the road about a quarter mile shy of the plant, Adam's view clear across the empty grasslands.

A huge corona of fire blazed before him, gobbling the power plant like it was a warm hors d'oeuvre. Even from this distance, he had to shield his eyes from the intensity of the flames, a rippling orange and red, nearly hypnotic. The fire swirled about like a demon breaking through a doorway from another dimension. The entire plant was engulfed now. The glass in the panels of the solar array was shattering with a harmonic tinkling. Tongues of flame lapped at the base of the windmills. At first, he didn't understand how the fire was reaching the wind turbines, but then he realized the blaze was creeping through the underground tunnels and corridors, along the very conduits that carried the power created by the monolithic generators.

How had this happened?

Sarah, Sarah, Sarah.

The image of her face kept flickering in his head, the way pop-up ads had once appeared on a website you were trying to concentrate on. Maybe he kept seeing her because it was just easier to think about her than about the ruin that now lay before them. Although it seemed like they'd just barely gotten here, it really was over now. The lights, the heat, the clean water, everything that made Evergreen special, everything that made it seem like they'd found an oasis in this post-plague hell. Gone. It had been a nice ride, a little respite from the way the world really was. But gone nonetheless.

Another explosion rocked the plant, this one yellow and harsh, like a miniature sun hovering just above the plains. The tang of burning salt reached his nose, and everyone began coughing. It smelled like over-cooked meat. Tears in their eyes, people began pulling their collars up over their noses, which made them look like a collection of sad highway bandits.

"Head back to town," Adam said. "There's nothing we can do here. Anyone seen Sarah this morning?"

Shakes of the head in reply, their eyes still focused on the destruction of the plant.

"What, honeymoon over already?" Derek asked. There was some levity in the tone, but the attempt to lacquer the disappointment with some joy fell short.

Adam laughed softly.

"I'm going to go track her down, give her the bad news."

"I'll give you a ride," Derek said.

As they raced back to town, he had the sudden but certain feeling that bad news was going to be waiting for him when he found her.

A CROWD HAD FORMED at the western edge of the baseball stadium, clustered in the outfield, looking out over the short fence toward the blaze. The faces he saw as they cruised past were long indeed, their gazes fixed on the horizon, where the thick black smoke continued billowing skyward, pushed eastward by the very winds they'd relied on to bring them the electricity.

The place already seemed quieter with the power now gone, taken from them a second time. As they passed the park, he was reminded of that awful, terrible quiet in the days after the plague had burned away, when he was adrift, unsure what the hell he was supposed to do, terribly afraid that he was the last man on Earth.

Yesterday, the park had looked good. They'd been using a push mower to keep the grass trimmed, a task that had been sloughed off onto the younger teenagers. Physically, it looked exactly the same this afternoon, but it felt dead, ominous. Derek let Adam off in front of his building. Adam got out and then leaned back in the window.

"What are we gonna do now, chief?" Derek asked.

Adam ran his thumb across the edge of the door.

"I've got to take care of something."

He tapped the roof of the car and stepped back. Derek drove off.

The apartment was empty. He hadn't expected to find her here, but he wanted to be sure, dot all the *i*'s and cross all the *t*'s. He was pretty sure he knew where she was, he was pretty sure he knew who was responsible for the fire, but stopping here had given him a chance to collect his thoughts, delay the inevitable, if only for a few moments. His next stop, he strongly suspected, wasn't going to be this idyllic.

Time to go, Adam.

Fright washed over him like a salt bath, leaving him dry and bitter. He could taste metal in his mouth.

Before leaving the apartment, he took the gun they'd kept in the drawer of the nightstand.

THE TOWN HALL was just beyond the southeast corner of the park. Its windows glinted in the early afternoon sun like wide, glassy eyes. The throng from the baseball stadium had retreated to the park, chatting, pointing, unsure what to do. The air was sharp with smoke.

For a moment, the thought that Sarah was dead gripped him so tightly it took his breath away. And there was no way to know that she wasn't. He'd have to press onward. He felt very strongly that whatever the truth was, whatever the future held, lay behind the doors of this building. Glinting and sparkling at him with terrible glee.

He crept up the stairs, staying clear of the door's line of sight. The heavy door had been propped open, and he leaned his body up against it. As he curled around the edge for a peek, he drew the gun and released the safety. The cold steel felt heavy and reassuring in his hand, buttressing his emotional reserve.

Freddie.

He'd seen it coming all along, the roots buried deep in the soil of their initial meeting, the way they'd clashed about virtually every decision, every step they'd taken along their westward trek. He had hoped to the end that the chill would eventually thaw, that Freddie would see how important he would be in Evergreen, how much he would have to offer. But he'd grown angrier and testier with each passing day. In some ways, their assimilation into Evergreen had made things worse than they'd been out on the road.

Adam slid down the corridor, keeping his back to the wall. Just ahead, on the left, was the public hearing room, the site of Freddie's electoral embarrassment. That was where Sarah's meeting with the committee had been scheduled to take place. Sitting halfway down the corridor, between Adam and the room, was Mike Stills. His breathing was shallow, and his right arm, the one closest to Adam, was soaked with blood.

Shit.

Mike turned his head and saw Adam, who nodded at him. Mike returned the nod.

"What happened?" Adam whispered.

Mike mouthed the answer, but the reply was clear enough.

Briggs.

Adam edged closer, closer, until he was at Mike's flank. He dropped to a knee and began examining Mike's right arm.

"Tell me," Adam said.

"Shot me," he said, grimacing with pain. "Gwen's dead. Jeff, too. He's in there with Sarah and Charlotte." He paused and pressed a hand to his wound. "It's not as bad as it looks. The bleeding's stopped. He just nicked me."

"What the hell does he want?"

"He wants you, actually. Sent me to find you."

"Meaning?"

"He wants you dead. Palace coup and all. He said he'll trade them for you."

"You believe that?"

"No," Mike said. "He wants you all dead. He wants to run the show."

Adam massaged his forehead with the heel of his hand. Panic was swelling in him like a balloon. A coup, indeed.

"Did he really do it?" Mike asked. "The power plant?"

Adam nodded slowly.

"Yeah," Adam said. "He torched it."

"Fuck," Mike said. "I was kind of hoping he was bluffing. Going on and on about cutting all ties to the old world."

"He wasn't. It's burning like hell out there. It catches that wind, the whole town might go up. Let's get you away from the door."

Mike slung his arm around Adam's shoulder and climbed to his feet.

"Whatever you've got planned, count me in. He's gotta fucking pay for this."

"I know."

So there it was. He had to stop Freddie, even if it killed him. Even if it meant sacrificing his quest to find Rachel. Something had broken inside Freddie. Perhaps it had started as a fissure, a fault line, one that might have remained stable under perfect conditions. But these weren't perfect conditions now, were they? Maybe the fault had ruptured long ago, when Caroline had died. Maybe it was broken before that, maybe since his family had perished, and the last couple months had been nothing more than lipstick on a pig. Adam couldn't even fault him for having those feelings.

But that wasn't the whole picture, the whole ball of wax. Freddie Briggs didn't get to choose how this new world worked for everyone else. If he wanted to go savage, pretend like the old world had never existed, well, there was a hell of a lot of open ground out there for him to lay a claim to. And today he'd crossed an uncrossable line. He'd made his decision. He was going to have to deal with the consequences.

Adam could feel the anger welling up inside him, but he tamped it down, put a lid on it as best he could so he could focus on the problem at hand. Sarah and Charlotte were in terrible danger. The whole colony was in danger.

"What's it like in there?"

"I think they're holed up behind the dais. Townsend's lying by the podium. Can't remember where Jeff was when he got hit. Sorry."

"He doesn't know I'm here, does he?"

"No," he said.

"How does he plan to get out?"

"I'm not sure he does. I'm not sure he cares."

Adam's stomach flipped, and he felt cold. If what Mike said was true, the chances they all survived this standoff were virtually zero. There had to be a way, he thought. There had to be a way. As he stood there, the edges of a plan began to form in his mind. He had to take the wind out of Freddie's sails. He had to make Freddie think that he'd won.

"Tell him some folks are back from fighting the fire, and that I went missing trying to put it out. Tell him I was seen running into the control room right before a big explosion."

"What for?"

"We've got to do something to release the pressure," Adam said. "I really never thought he'd go this far. But he wants to tear everything down."

"You got that right."

Three loud booms interrupted them; Freddie was pounding on the door.

"Stills! You out there?"

Adam nodded.

"Yeah, I'm here," Stills replied. "I needed to rest."

"Any sign of Fisher?"

Adam nodded and drifted back toward the front door. He hated to leave his friends behind, but he didn't see another option if he wanted to save them.

"Not yet," Stills said. "I'm going to go look for him now. I'll be back when I can."

As he backed out of the door onto the town hall's ornate front porch, Adam pantomimed stretching out the discussion to Mike, who returned a thumbs up.

"Wait! Some folks are back from the plant, saying he's missing!"

"Whaddaya mean missing?"

Adam scanned the town square for the best vantage point while he continued to eavesdrop on the discussion. Across Main Street was the diner, its mirrored plate-glass windows reflecting the town hall. Next door to that was a dry cleaner with a large counter that Adam could hide behind.

"Trying to put out the fire! I don't know what happened. They can't find him!"

Freddie went silent.

Adam couldn't afford to wait any longer. His entire plan, rudimentary as it was, depended solely on Freddie believing that he had perished in the blaze. If he could pull that over on him, maybe he'd let the hostages go. Adam didn't think he wanted them dead. He wanted them to suffer by being *alive*. He wanted them all to see the world as he saw it, without their precious power plant, without their late-night board games, without the heat blowing up through the vents. He wanted a world that matched his soul.

That much, Adam was certain of.

But if he so much got a whiff that he was being played, that would be it for Sarah and Charlotte. Adam hustled across the street, the acrid tickle of smoke stronger in his nostrils. The wind was blowing east, all right, escorting that fire right toward them. He wondered if there was enough gas out there, enough grass and scrub, to keep the fire alive long enough to make it to their doorstep, to the good eating. All through the town, he could hear shouts and screams of Evergreeners skittering about, running around like chickens who'd been relieved of the burden of their heads.

He ducked inside the dry cleaner and took position behind the counter. From his vantage point, he could see clear across the street to the town hall's front door.

He settled in and began to wait.

42

Adam was missing.

Adam was missing.

Adam was missing.

This tiny factoid ran on a loop in her head like a Vegas billboard, those three little words, and her heart shattered over and over. It was happening again, you see. Yet again, she'd been spared, and yet again, someone she cared about had been taken.

She and Charlotte were sitting back-to-back on the floor of the public hearing room, their legs crossed, their arms bound together with shoelaces. She shed no tears, not because she didn't want to, but because she didn't want to give Freddie the satisfaction of witnessing her grief. He did not get to see that. Not one single millisecond of it. That would be in her own time.

Her mind was working, looking for a way to get out of here, but she discarded plan after plan after plan. There was no way she would risk an escape attempt, because she knew what would happen. She'd survive (again), and Charlotte would die, probably in her arms. No goddamn way was she going to let that happen.

Freddie was still pacing the room, but his movements had become smoother, more graceful, less panicked. Like a spooked horse starting to calm down, its heart rate decelerating. Was that a smirk on his face? She wondered. A smile? Was he starting to realize that he'd gotten just what he'd wanted? She'd give anything to smack the smile off that overgrown Neanderthal.

The air in the room had grown stale in the last two hours, and it was becoming uncomfortably humid.

"You got what you wanted," she said, seasoning her words with as much self-defeat as she could. "Adam's dead."

"I didn't hear anyone say he was dead," Freddie snapped.

"He went inside that building," Sarah said. "The one you set on fire."

"Trust me, you'll all be better off without it," Freddie said. "That plant was going to cause you more misery than you'd know what to do with. It was like a Band-Aid over a cut that wasn't ever going to heal. That cut, it couldn't get enough air, it stayed warm and damp, and kept re-opening, over and over. Consider this my ripping off the bandage in one fell swoop."

"I guess we'll never know now, will we?"

He laughed, a guffaw that sounded all the more terrible because it sounded genuine.

"No, I guess we won't. You're right. You'll just have to trust me on this one."

"Now what?"

"Now we begin our lives," Freddie said. "For real this time. We begin anew without the chains of the old world weighing us down."

Sarah shivered. Her right hand spasmed. Her symptoms were worsening. She rushed to cover her hand, but Freddie had seen.

"What's wrong with your arm?"

"Nothing."

Another spasm, this one more sustained, her arm flailing about like it had a mind of its own.

"Don't tell me nothing's wrong."

"It's nothing," she said, "just a muscle spasm." Even as she said it, her arm locked up, and she was unable to lower it. She didn't want to tell him. She'd rather die than tell him. This was her private grief, the thing she would share with no one but Adam until she had to.

"Tell me what's wrong with you."

"None of your business."

He raised the gun and aimed it squarely at Charlotte's head.

"Tell me, or Charlotte dies."

Charlotte's eyes widened with fright. She didn't say anything, but Sarah could just hear a tiny whimper from her, the kind of sound a puppy might make when smacked with a newspaper.

So she told him.

And he smiled.

The son of a bitch actually smiled.

ADAM SNACKED on a jar of cashews he'd found under the counter of the dry cleaner. As he ate, he felt his mind sharpen and his body stabilize. He felt almost calm. Not because he was confident of prevailing over Freddie, because he sure as hell wasn't, but because the die was now cast. He knew that he was ready to lay down his life to protect Sarah and these others. In a way, he had Freddie to thank for this little bit of self-discovery; it had been the man's unraveling that had sussed it out of Adam. He had forced Adam to become the man he needed to be in this new world.

He hated him for it.

Adam did not want to die. He wanted to survive in this new world. He wanted to keep these people as safe as he could. He wanted to live long enough to find Rachel, no matter how long it took. But Freddie had nothing to keep him going. He'd kept part of himself in the old world, and as the gulf widened between that world and this one, it had ripped him apart. The tragedy of it all was that Freddie could see what a new world might look like, what it would take to survive it. He just hadn't been able to practice what he preached. For that, Adam was truly sorry. Freddie wasn't a bad man. He was a good man who'd been overwhelmed by the new world washing over them, even as he'd been the first to understand it.

This was all his fault.

He never should have run for mayor. He knew that now. He'd done it not because he was the one with hope. He'd done it because he'd lost hope. Because he could hide from the truth he feared. He could stay here and play doctor and pass laws and he could fill his head with the rote work of rebuilding society and he wouldn't have to think about the fact that the search had been a failure. He had even started to believe his own press clippings, that his search and his leadership of the town would fuel each other.

Bullshit.

It couldn't be both because doing both meant cheating both. Rachel deserved better. Evergreen deserved better.

Hot shame flooded through him.

It ended today.

Adam had waited for nearly ninety minutes, with nary a sign of life from the town hall building. A handful of residents were scurrying about, occasionally huddling together like a clump of cells, talking, planning, pointing, and then disassembling once more. No one seemed to know what to do.

At about three o'clock, Charlotte appeared in the open doorframe of the town hall, her hands on her head. Adam's breath caught in his throat. She cleared the door and continued down the steps. Behind her followed Sarah, her hands also on her head; both looked unhurt. Freddie brought up the rear, his gun pressed to the back of Sarah's head. Mike was nowhere to be seen, and Adam hoped he'd had the good sense to hide once Freddie had emerged from the hearing room.

He said something to Charlotte, but Adam couldn't hear what it was through the glass. The girl nodded and then fled down the steps like she was on a mission. Adam was well hidden, but if he emerged from behind the counter, he would be right in Freddie's line of sight. He couldn't chance a rescue attempt here. He also couldn't chance Sarah seeing him either; knowing her, she might well sacrifice herself to give Adam a clear shot at Freddie.

Dammit!

He'd just have to wait.

And for another thirty minutes he waited, as the smoke thickened, giving the sky a grayish, washed-out pallor. As the minutes ticked by, the residents drifted in toward the town hall, presumably rounded up by Charlotte. Eventually, it looked like the majority of the town had assembled at the base of the steps, their necks craned upward at Sarah and Freddie, who looked like a man not entirely in touch with reality. He began to speak, his voice booming across the town, loud enough that Adam could hear him clearly.

"My fellow citizens!" he bellowed. "The fire at the plant was no accident!"

Murmurs from the crowd.

"Sarah set the fire! With your mayor's help!"

Adam's blood ran cold.

Wait. Everyone knew Freddie had set the fire.

Didn't they?

He thought about the chain of events that had unfolded since this morning. He met some others on the way. Surely they had discussed it. Surely everyone knew that Freddie had been on a slow boat to Crazytown. But as he lay hidden, crouched, behind the counter, he wasn't so sure.

"I know it's hard to believe," he continued. "But Sarah's not in her right mind. She's very sick."

Oh, no, Adam thought. He knew about Sarah's illness.

"That's not true!" Sarah screamed. "He killed Gwen!"

"She's terminal, and she's very angry about it," he said.

The crowd began to simmer, heads bobbing, people looking at each other, like a pan of oil starting to sizzle. They were buying it. And why wouldn't they? Who wrote the history books, if not the victors? And Freddie was writing it. He was in charge. Already, public opinion would be hardening into something resembling truth, if not necessarily fact.

Dammit, Charlotte, say something!

But in looking at her, Adam knew she wouldn't. She was frozen with fear, her eyes fixed out at some point beyond the crowd, across the park, in the direction of the burning plant.

"Fire!"

Dozens of heads turned, following the point of Charlotte's finger; everyone looked, including Sarah and Freddie, leaving Adam unexposed, if only for a moment. He scampered from behind the counter and through the door, taking cover behind a brick pillar.

Now Adam could see what the crowd was looking at.

The wind had quickened and whistled between the buildings. The entire western side of town fronted a giant wall of flame. The bubbling crowd boiled over, and several Evergreeners began to run.

Now. He had to act now.

After making sure the safety on his gun was off, he broke from his hiding spot at a full sprint, quietly, assimilating himself into the angry, frightened crowd, never taking his eyes off Freddie. As he drew near the stairs, he saw that Freddie had made a tactical error. During his speech, he'd drifted closer to the top step, letting Sarah slip just behind his right shoulder.

If he could just get there, he might get a clear shot at him.

If he could just get there.

Fifty feet. Then twenty-five. Then ten.

That was when Freddie must have picked Adam up in his peripheral vision, because he swung his arm around, and he was already firing. The first bullet missed Adam but struck an onlooker behind him. The shooting precipitated a chorus of screams as the crowd devolved into a stinking, terrified mob.

As Freddie prepared to fire again, Sarah delivered a roundhouse kick to Freddie's left flank. Her explosive pirouette wasn't enough to bring the big man down, but it knocked him off balance. He staggered to the edge of the step and just barely caught himself.

He and Adam were less than ten feet apart; Adam wasn't going to get a better shot. He steadied his hand as best he could and squeezed the trigger twice at the ample target Freddie provided. The first bullet struck him in the upper thigh, the second in the stomach. He toppled forward like a fallen sequoia.

"It was Freddie!" Charlotte screamed. "It was Freddie! He killed the mayor. He killed Jeff! He set the fire!"

Adam carefully approached Freddie, who lay unmoving. His arms were splayed out above his head, his right leg twisted at a strange angle. Adam bent down and checked for a pulse; Freddie was still alive, but only just so. His heart was beating erratically, and he was barely conscious. Adam put the gun to Freddie's head, his finger sweating on the trigger, but he couldn't do it. Even if it might have been the humane thing to do, he couldn't do it. He waited by Freddie's side, waited as the man's pulse grew fainter and fainter until it was gone completely.

Freddie Briggs was dead.

He could feel their eyes on him, the others who'd heard Charlotte's plea. They closed in around him slowly, tentatively, as though they were worried that Adam might shoot them for almost believing Freddie. He returned their nods, accepted their pats on the shoulder, the squeezes of the elbow.

Adam continued up the steps to the porch, where he and Sarah embraced like soldiers after a terrible battle. As he held her tight, he reached his hand out for Charlotte, who was sobbing.

"I'm sorry," she said between heaves of tears. "I should've said something. I thought he was going to kill me."

"Take my hand," Adam said.

She gingerly grasped his outstretched hand, which Adam squeezed reassuringly.

"It's OK," Adam said. "You have nothing to be sorry for."

"Thank God you're OK," Sarah said, brushing his face with the back of her hand. "I thought you were dead."

"I thought you were."

"If we don't get moving," Charlotte interrupted, "we might all be dead."

Adam released Sarah and looked west. The fire was feeding off that part of town like a hungry demon, taking its time now after its quick rush across the tasty grasses of the open plains.

"Listen up!" Adam called out. "We need to get out of town! Grab what you can, meet at the town limits on 815, headed east!"

His command galvanized the troops, and they began scattering across the town, plundering and scavenging what they could.

Then he remembered someone had been shot behind him, and he hurried down the steps.

Oh, no, he thought.

Donna Tanner lay dead in the street, missing most of the top of her head.

He ran his hands through his hair and wept.

FORTY OF THEM hit the road that afternoon in a caravan of six cars, the burning remains of the town at their back. They had salvaged what they could while the fire chewed across town. Not everyone was accounted for, and Adam didn't know if they'd scattered to the other points of the compass or if they'd fallen victim to the flames. Either way, he never saw many of the Evergreeners again. Derek and Jeff and Lisa and so many more.

They drove east across desolate scrubland. When it was full dark, and their backs ached and the children were in full meltdown, they stopped to make camp along the highway. Mike Stills built a fire, and they cooked what little they had, barely enough for a few spoonfuls per person. Adam worried that a fight would break out, but no one seemed to have the energy. People ate. They yawned. Then they slept in a tight cluster of bodies near the fire, relying on body heat to stave off the deepening chill. Adam and Sarah were tending to the fire with a stick when Mike Stills sat down beside them. He lit a cigarette.

"You know, I never smoked before the plague," he said, eyeing the orange filter. "Never. So I was in a 7-Eleven getting breakfast one morning after it was all over. I was still having a hard time dealing with what had happened. And I thought to myself, 'I bet this is the kind of thing cigarettes were made for.' So I took a pack. Looks like nicotine and me are just two peas in a pod."

Adam liked Mike.

"Want the old standby lecture?"

"Not really."

"Mind if I bum one then?"

As Mike lit Adam's cigarette with the tip of his own, he asked, "so what do we do now, Mr. Mayor?"

"We try and get some sleep," Adam said. "No big decisions tonight. Today was a hell of a day, and I can barely make sense of it."

They sat quietly for a while, smoking their cigarettes. Adam rubbed the back of his neck, the stress of the day settling deep inside him, in every cell, in his marrow, until he could almost taste it. Evergreen was gone. He had no idea where Rachel was. Never had the world felt so dead and buried as it did that night.

"I should've known," Adam said. He rubbed his icy nose between his finger and thumb. It was cold, but not terribly so. The sky was clear, the stars bright, like diamond dust on black velvet.

"Known what?" Sarah replied. "That he was going to go completely fucking bonkers? You're not the one at fault here, sweetie. There was nothing you could do to stop him."

"There's nothing I can do to stop anyone anymore."

The words fell out of his mouth like hot, angry coals from an over-turned grill.

"Sort of a pessimistic attitude," she said.

"Just the way it is," he said.

"I think most people are good at their core," she said. "It's the one thing that gives me hope that this won't be a terrible world to live in."

"Very Anne-Frank-ish of you," he said.

They were quiet a moment. She took his hand in hers as he considered her take on the world and balanced it against his own. Theirs now was a world without rules, without consequences. You could rape and murder and pillage to your little heart's content. Were there enough people left who were good, who'd leave the dollar in the honor bucket when taking a cold pop from the unattended cooler? If there were now, would they stay that way? Would they continue that downward slide, realize how much easier it would be to simply take what they needed?

A race to the bottom.

All in the name of survival.

He glanced at Sarah.

How close he'd come to losing her today.

Just the thought made him seize up with panic, and despite the fact they'd survived, that they were still here, he still couldn't help but think how easily it could've gone the other way. How quickly it had all unfolded, an entire universe of actions and reactions packed into just a few seconds, decisions that he'd barely been conscious of making. How close he himself had come to dying. He wondered how many chances he'd used up to get just this far.

He couldn't let these people rely on him anymore because his fate did not lie with them right now. They had their own way to go, their own trail to blaze, and he had his.

How right Freddie had been, after all that.

CITADEL

BOOK 4

When bad men combine, the good must associate; else they will fall, one by one, an unpitied sacrifice in a contemptible struggle.

EDMUND BURKE

~

43

In the end, it was the dreams that told her what to do.

She'd wake up in the middle of the night, sweating, and it would take her a moment, sometimes a long moment, to realize that the world in the dream was the imaginary one. It would hold its shape long enough to leave her straddling both worlds, unsure of where she was, before it collapsed and she'd wonder if she'd screamed as loudly as she thought she had. But she would look over at Adam, his breathing deep and even, his sleep undisturbed.

There wasn't anything mystical about her dreams. She'd obsess about a problem, and her mind would work on it the way a jeweler might polish a stone, over and over and over, until she breathed it and perspired it, until it invaded her subconscious mind and revealed itself in her dreams. Sometimes, she found the way through in the dream world, and sometimes, the roadblocks that she'd encountered while awake would find her while she slept.

She dreamed about Rachel.

Each time, the dream was the same.

Early morning. Sitting in the cafeteria of some antiseptic building, a hospital or a lab, maybe one where she'd gone for treatment of her Huntington's. A large cloth napkin was tucked in her collar. In her left hand, she held a knife, in her right, a fork. She sat alone at a two-top as the cafeteria bustled around her, dozens of people, all wearing white lab coats, eating their breakfast, chatting, laughing, all sitting together in groups of four. She stared at the empty seat opposite her, unsure if she was waiting for someone, and she would become conscious of the fact that she was sitting alone, and then she would think wasn't she a little bit old for that kind of nonsense, and then there she was. Sarah didn't know how she knew it was Rachel. It was a dream, after all, and she just knew.

Rachel wore a biohazard suit, a shimmery silver color that caught the lights in the cafeteria. In her hands was a tray of food, which she set down in front of Sarah. When Rachel reared back up to her full height, Sarah saw that everyone now lay dead on the floor, their noses and lips smeared with the blood of Medusa. Part of the breakfast varied every day. Sometimes, she'd get a plate of eggs and bacon, two triangular slices of wheat toast. Other days, it was waffles. Pancakes. A frittata. But with every breakfast, Rachel delivered her a bowl containing half a ruby red grapefruit. The fruit's flesh was a deep crimson, the color of fresh blood, and Sarah could not take her eyes off it. Every time, she'd will herself to look at Rachel, talk to her, because she never said a word, but she couldn't do it. Her gaze would be transfixed on that red iris, a bloodshot eye forever fixed open, its white center a dead pupil.

"And that's it," she said, finally telling Adam about it one morning as they ate breakfast. She hated telling people about her dreams because she never quite understood the point. Oh, you had a crazy dream? How novel. It was like telling someone you'd had a really good poop.

It had been a week since the fire. They'd found a huge abandoned horse ranch in northern Kansas and had decided to make a go of it there for the winter. No power, of course, but after the disaster in Evergreen, no one seemed in any particular hurry to deal with electricity anytime soon. The Caballero Ranch sat on hundreds of acres of Kansas scrubland, ringed by a long perimeter fence. At the center of the tract was the main house. A number of smaller houses dotted the landscape.

"Sweetie, it's just a dream," he said.

"I *know* it's just a dream," she snapped, and he recoiled.

He smiled thinly.

"We have to try and help these women," Sarah said. "I'll keep going until I can't anymore. And I know you. You may not think I do yet, but I do. You'll keep looking until you know for sure. Even after I'm gone."

Hearing her talk about her own mortality made his jaw clench. With each passing day since the Evergreen fire, her illness had become more and more a real thing. Their love may have surrounded them with its strength, but reality was pushing at the walls. Barbarians at the gate. He wondered what she would have thought of him if she knew the truth, that he'd been ready to give it up.

"Anyway, I have a plan," Sarah said. "It's crazy. It almost certainly won't work. And if you have a better idea, I'm all ears."

"Well?" he asked.

She shook her head.

"I can't believe I'm even going to suggest this."

"Well?"

"Hang on, hang on. If this is going to work, we're going to need some help."

"OK. So what's the plan?"

She told him. And she was right. It was an insane plan.

IF HE WAS GOING to ask them to do this brave thing, Adam would need to do it face-to-face. He would be placing himself in harm's way, too, of course, but he had the most to gain from the gambit.

He packed a lunch for the two women and one man who, along with him, would make up his team, and they walked out to a rock formation near the eastern border of Caballero. It was a cloudy day and a humid breeze was blowing across the prairie. A small herd of antelope was grazing upwind from them, and they could smell the pungent tang of their hide.

"I have a favor to ask of you all," he said.

"I'll do it," Mike Still said.

Adam laughed nervously.

"Haven't even said what it was," he said.

"Don't care," Mike said. "It's a big deal to you, obviously, else you wouldn't have brought us out here."

"It could be dangerous," he said. "Strike that. It will be dangerous."

"Count me in, then," Charlotte said.

Adam felt his throat tighten. These people, he was about to ask them to go into harm's way for him, for his little girl, and they hadn't even blinked an eye.

"You all mind if I tell you what it is?"

Silence. The looks on their faces were blank, steely, almost as if they couldn't wait to hear it.

"As you know, my search for Rachel has not gone well. I've been picking through a gigantic haystack, looking for one tiny needle. It's been hard to keep hope alive. And my search may have blinded me to the threat we all faced from Freddie. For that, I apologize."

"That's bullshit," Mike said. "If it wasn't for you, he'd have taken over. You should've seen him in that hearing room that day. He was going to clean house."

This made Adam shudder, but he tried to block it out of his mind as he pressed onward.

"But Rachel's not the only one there," he continued. "According to Nadia, there are at least a dozen women being held prisoner. Possibly more.

"Anyway, there are two parts to this plan," he said. "First, Sarah and Charlotte will travel together. Alone. Mike and I will be shadowing you with a GPS tracking device. You're going to make a lot of noise, you're going to build fires at night. You're going to look helpless. You're going to lay a trap. You're going to get captured by Nadia's group. And they're going to lead us to Rachel and the other women. Part two. We'll launch an assault on this camp and free everyone."

The group was silent as they considered it.

"You think this will work?" Charlotte asked.

"No idea," Sarah said. "But it's all we've got."

"What about everyone here?" Mike asked.

"I can't lead as long as I keep thinking about Rachel," Adam said. "It's not fair to them. These are good people here and they deserve better than me."

The others exchanged glances and nods, all of them coming to an agreement.

"I'm still in," Charlotte said.

"Ditto," Mike said.

"Then let's do it."

AFTER ADAM RESIGNED AS MAYOR, the group elected Diane Williams, who'd been the cook in the Evergreen diner, as their new leader. Years at the helm of busy kitchens had left her well suited to lead the ragtag group of refugees. Adam liked her well enough, even as she all but came out and told him that his search for Rachel was nothing but a wild goose chase. But it didn't bother him anymore, even if what she said was true.

"I wish you all the luck in the world," she'd told him one afternoon. "When you're ready to come home, you know where to find us."

He hoped they made it back. He knew they probably wouldn't.

"THE KEY to this whole thing is this GPS tracking device," Adam said during their first planning session, holding up the small device, about the size of a flash drive. There was a hasp and clip on the end of it. "A few years back, I dated this real outdoorsy girl, wanted to go camping all the time."

"Is that right?" Sarah cut in.

"That is right, ma'am," Adam said. "You'd be surprised how in demand a handsome doctor like me was in the old world."

"Oh, here we go," she replied, rolling her eyes.

Laughter rippled through the room, and for a moment, Adam forgot about the dangerous mission that lay ahead.

"Anyway," he said, "I was trying to keep up with her, and so I bought all this stuff I never used until the outbreak. The ladies will keep this on them at all times."

He wagged a finger at each of them.

"At all times," he said again. "I really mean that."

"We got it, chief."

"I can follow the signal with this receiver," he said, holding up a slightly larger device, about the size of a deck of cards. "Fortunately, it's battery-operated, and if there's one thing we can find a lot of, it's batteries."

"Does the GPS still work?" Charlotte asked.

"The GPS in the car navigation systems are still functioning, maybe not as good as they used to without someone to keep the satellites in line, but close enough for our needs. I think as time goes by, the GPS will become less and less reliable, without anyone to herd them back into place when they drift out of their orbit, but if we haven't found the camp by then, we probably never will."

"Guns," Mike said. "We'll need guns."

"Tents," Charlotte jumped in. "The best we can find. We may be out there for a long time."

"I have a question," Sarah asked. "What if we're attacked by someone else? Some other group that's not connected to Rachel?"

"We'll be close enough that we won't let anything happen."

"Basically, you're saying you have no idea."

"Sort of," he said.

Nervous laughter.

"I'm playing the odds here. I really believe we're within fifty to a hundred miles of the camp. I think if you make a big enough scene, they will find you. Which is why, again, I'm going to ask you, all of you, if you're sure you want to do this."

"Adam," Mike said. "Listen to me now. I think I speak for all of us here. I'm not doing this for shits and giggles. Believe me, I'm in no hurry to die. I'd just as soon stay here at the farm, learn how to raise chickens and sheep and drink lukewarm scotch for the rest of my life. But I wouldn't be able to look at myself in the mirror, knowing there was someone, a lot of someones maybe, who I could've helped and didn't."

Adam looked around the table and saw steely eyes staring back at him, heads nodding. He saw the resolve in their faces, and he vowed never to ask them again if they were sure about wanting to help him.

"If you're right, and they're that close, who's to say they don't find this place first?"

"They might," Adam said. "All the more reason to put an end to this."

He hoped he sounded more convincing than he felt.

"You can't beat yourself up," Mike said, reading him as though Adam were projecting his thoughts right up against the wall like a PowerPoint presentation. "This is the hand we've all been dealt."

"You're right," he said.

They moved on.

As Adam and the others prepared to ship out, the farm bustled with activity. Body removal, consolidation of canned goods, sorties to nearby farms to scavenge what they could. Adam hoped they made it back someday. This was a good group, one that he wouldn't mind sailing to the great unknown tomorrow with.

On his last day at the ranch, he helped clear the last of the dead. They stacked the bodies, which had decomposed badly in the humid Kansas air, in a large pile at the ranch's main gate and set the remains ablaze. Adam stood as close as he could to the fire, until he felt the invisible heat billowing against his face, never wanting to forget what had happened to these people, to their world. It was becoming harder to remember that the world hadn't always been this way, blank pages inserted at the end of a novel.

~

AFTER A SERIES of supply runs to nearby farmhouses and a dozen meetings, the team was ready to ship out. It was December 13, and although the weather had stayed mild, it had been raining almost nonstop for the past three days.

They'd followed Sarah's lead in outfitting themselves, the way she would have done it on their long-range patrols in Afghanistan or Iraq. Each carried a full pack, complete with sleeping bag, nested pots and pans, water purification tablets, a compass, a hunting knife, MREs, personal hydration system, first-aid kit, several changes of clothes, cigarettes, energy bars and handwarmers. They went light on water, counting on the abundance of supplies that were still lying around out there in the dozens of tiny towns they'd pass through. The GPS was working splendidly, accurate to within fifty feet. Adam had wanted to give them walkie-talkies, but Sarah had disavowed him of that idea. She didn't want to take the chance that their communications were picked up.

The plan was simple enough; they would trek eastward by mountain bike for three miles and then begin moving in ever-widening circles out from the point of origin. Adam and Mike would lag behind, but never following too directly, in the event the bad guys were watching them too.

Sarah and Charlotte were leaving first, just after sunrise, so that they could open up a little cushion. They'd said their goodbyes to the others the night before, and the farm was quiet but for the patter of light rain. The rain, the gloomy sky, all of it reminded Sarah of the day the Bronx quarantine had broken, the day the Apache helicopters had blown the Third Avenue bridge. It seemed like a long time ago.

There was little chit-chat, just the nervous energy of a group on a journey whose ending was unknown. Sarah felt good, though, she felt alive. Her symptoms had subsided in the past week, a development for which she was eternally grateful. They'd be back, of course, but for now, she felt strong and full of purpose.

Adam and Sarah stood by the main gate now; Charlotte and Mike had drifted east a little to give the couple some privacy. Mike checked the GPS device, making sure for the hundredth time that it was working properly.

"So this is it," Adam said. His voice was caked with anxiety.

"What you've been waiting for," she said, taking his hand in her own. "We're going to find her."

"You think so?"

"Yes," she said.

He smiled, and she kissed him.

"I'll see you soon," she said.

She leaned in and wrapped her arms around him, and they stood there, entwined in each other's arms. It was one thing to realize that they might all be living on borrowed time. It was a much different thing to know for certain that she was, that their marriage was, that his heart was. But whatever happened out there, it was far better than staying here and waiting to die. At least this way, she could thank him for giving her the life she'd always wished she could have, if only for a little while.

She was the first one to break the embrace.

"Gotta go," she said. "Stop being such a pansy. We'll see each other soon. I promise."

After one last kiss, she hoisted her pack onto her shoulders and jogged down the road. She paused to exchange a few words with Mike as he made his way back toward Adam and then joined Charlotte.

ADAM AND MIKE watched as the women's profiles drew smaller along the horizon, until they were out of view. The die was now cast. If things went according to plan, he wouldn't see her again until she was being held captive. The whole thing made his head swim. The rain intensified some, leaving him cold and feeling alone.

"What I wouldn't give for a weather report," Adam said.

"What, you want this to be easy?" Mike replied, clapping Adam on the shoulder and laughing.

Adam couldn't help but laugh. He was glad Mike was coming along. He exuded calmness, he never seemed to get rattled. Part of it stemmed from his work as a photographer for the Associated Press before coming to run the Evergreen newspaper. He'd seen some crazy shit overseas, he'd told them, from North Korean prison camps to genocide in Darfur. He'd made it back to the States less than a week before the outbreak began. He was divorced and had no children (that he knew of, he liked to joke).

"You ready to roll out?" Adam asked.

"You bet," Mike said.

THEY HIT the road an hour later, cycling east, two tiny specks of dust in a big, empty world.

44

For sixteen days, Adam and Mike trailed the women like loyal shadows, trusting the GPS signal to keep tabs on Sarah and Charlotte when they drifted beyond the reach of the field glasses. The women quickly established a routine, traveling from about nine in the morning, making camp an hour before dark, giving them just enough time to set up camp before the sun dipped below the horizon. They made large, smoky fires and played loud music from an old battery-operated boombox. Adam and Mike mirrored them, traveling when they traveled, breaking when they broke.

It was maddening for Adam to be able to see Sarah from a distance but unable to talk to her. He missed her desperately, and being able to lay eyes on her made things worse. It was as if she were already dead, and he was just watching a recording of an event gone by.

Their search field grew with each passing day, pulling them farther and farther away from the ranch he doubted he would ever see again. He missed the people there, and he hoped he'd get a chance to make up his absence to them. It was lonely out here, empty. The land was flat and desolate, miles of grassland stretching away in all directions, broken up here and there by the black asphalt veins criss-crossing the plains. It was like standing on a different world. They saw elk and antelope loping across the landscape. Flocks of birds darkened the skies. Deer were abundant, but they couldn't risk building a fire, and so a potential venison feast remained just that – potential.

The one thing they did not see was other people. It had only been four months since the fall of man, and already it felt like the natural world was wresting control back after humanity's reign had ended. It wasn't dramatic, no palace coup, more of a subtle shift that they noticed as they continued their daily patrols. On this, their seventeenth day on the road, they passed through a border town in northern Kansas called Mahaska, where kudzu had wasted little time in launching a full offensive. The vines had invaded the small Main Street corridor and were stretching their green tendrils into every doorway and window. The sign at the town limits, reading Mahaska, Population 83, was sporting a very serious kudzu infection, the long, loose vine already curling up the signposts.

"Holy Jesus," Mike said, under his breath. They'd paused in front of a general store, the one with a stoop and rocking chair out front, carpeted with the green plant.

"We come back through here a year from now," Adam said, "this town'll be gone."

"Kind of makes you wonder what kind of future we've all got."

"Makes me realize we can't fail," Adam replied. "These people that are holding Rachel, I doubt they have anybody's interest but their own in mind. If we're to have any chance, we need to start rebuilding things sooner than later. Us. The right way. Or these monsters will do it for us. The rest of us will just vanish into the shrubbery."

"I hear you."

They resumed their trek through town, stopping in the general store for supplies. As Mike wandered the aisles, Adam found himself transfixed by the sight of mushrooms sprouting from the popcorn ceiling. Dark and humid in here for months, and why wouldn't there be mushrooms growing here?

Adam found himself glancing over his shoulder as they put Mahaska behind them, as though the kudzu might reach out and grab them, pull them down into its tangled network of vines. Adam's shirt was damp with sweat and his head hurt. Neither spoke much, focusing instead all their energies on the trek. By late afternoon, they were twenty-five miles east of Mahaska.

The women stopped for the day a little after five-thirty, right near the Kansas-Nebraska border. Adam and Mike dropped their packs and lay on the ground, too wrung out from the day's travels to do much else. In the distance, the whine of a motorcycle engine revved, but it was impossible to tell how far away it was in a world absent noise pollution.

After a quick meal of cold beans, Adam took the first shift on watch while Mike slept. It was a cloudy night, and the coldest they'd had on the road. The wind blew in from the west, cutting through them. Flurries danced in the sky. Adam watched Charlotte and Sarah with his binoculars, huddled around their fire, wishing he were there with Sarah, holding her.

The girls' campfire dwindled as the hour grew late, and Adam switched to the night-vision goggles. At two a.m., he tried rousing Mike for his shift, but the man was dead to the world. Adam decided to let him be, even as his own eyelids sagged with fatigue. Desperate times called for desperate measures, he thought. He checked his bag for a little pick-me-up and settled on a handful of coffee beans from their stash.

As he chewed the beans, a few at a time, he paced the edge of their tiny little camp, the image of the women's tent appearing in sharp relief in his goggles. An hour went by, then two. A light rain began to fall. He felt himself falling asleep on his feet, the fatigue pulling him down like concrete blocks chained to a river-bound Mafia snitch. Each blink of the eyes became a short nap.

Then he saw it.

A flicker of movement in the corner of his goggles, just at the edge of the periphery. At first, he thought it was a wolf or fox, but then the blur took shape. Four figures, approaching the camp, each carrying a weapon. His eyes bounced back to the camp, which remained still. His heart was pushing on his throat now, he could feel it almost sealing off his airways. In the planning stages of this mission, he had understood the fact that these women would be risking their lives for him, for Rachel, for all the women they had never met. But seeing it in action was an entirely different matter. A single misstep, by any of them, could mean the end.

He violently shook Mike awake. Of course it would happen tonight, he thought to himself. Freezing rain, the worst possible conditions. Of course it would. Mike seemed to sense the urgency in Adam's touch, and he was awake within seconds.

"It's happening," he hissed.

As they tended to do, things began happening quickly. Mike checked the GPS receiver, which was receiving Sarah's signal beautifully, while Adam broke down their little camp. Meanwhile, the intruders surrounded the women and hustled them to their feet. The group was on the move less than a minute after the attackers first appeared. Mike and Adam could only hope the assailants had been so focused on their prey that they hadn't been spotted, and they waited until the group's backs were to them before beginning their pursuit.

"The GPS, it's working fine," Mike said. "I've got 'em."

As they edged away from the camp, the rain changed to sleet and picked up in intensity, showering the frozen grass with a creepy, rattling sound. The conditions were awful, but, Adam realized, in their favor. The bad weather helped mask their presence, and besides, Adam was betting these silent kidnappers had no more desire to be out in the elements than anyone else did. They'd be focused on getting their prey back to home base, not worrying about some one-in-a-million-chance plan unfolding behind them.

After a few minutes of cycling, Adam saw two vehicles looming in the distance, parked on the shoulder, maybe a quarter mile away. It was almost time. He held up a clenched fist, signaling Mike to stop. There was no need to draw any closer and risk being spotted. As they crouched down, among the tall grasses, Adam watched the group board the vehicles, Charlotte in the second vehicle, Sarah in the lead. It looked like their wrists were bound.

"Jesus Christ," he said. "What have I done?"

His dark vision had come alive. His reckless, stupid, suicidal, homicidal, and insane plan was underway. The two sport utility vehicles roared to life, the sound of the engines echoing in the still night air, and Adam wondered how he could've missed their approach. With their lights twinkling in the endless darkness that stretched around them, the vehicles looked like interstellar cruisers in the cold vastness of deep space. A moment later, the trucks shoved off into the frigid night. Above them, a sickly orange sky spit down sleet on them.

THEY RAN AS HARD as they could. Sarah and the others had long disappeared into the night, swallowed by the darkness like it was some ancient, mystical creature feeding on unsuspecting innocents. They could only hope that the kidnappers wouldn't find the transmitter before Adam and Mike found the compound. They followed the GPS signal as the crow flew, across the plains, through farmland, through barren tree lines.

Eventually, they tired out, and the pair took a break on a long stretch of road fronting two adjoining horse ranches. Around them, the crackle of sleet filled the dead night with sound, as though the storm was alive.

"You all right?" Adam asked.

"I'll be fine," he said.

Adam handed him a bottle of Gatorade.

"One good thing about this shitty weather?" he said.

"What's that?"

"At least it's cold," he said. "Warm Gatorade tastes like piss."

Adam laughed and brushed icy pellets from his clothes.

"Goddamn right about that. You ready to push off?"

"Let me check their position."

He tucked the bottle under his elbow and studied the receiver's small display screen.

"Son of a bitch."

"What?" Adam asked, a chill running through him. "What?"

"They've stopped. About sixteen miles northeast of here."

"You're sure?"

"Positive," Mike replied. "Well, I'm positive the transmitter has stopped moving."

"It's possible that they found it and threw it out of the car. Or worse."

Their eyes met for a moment, but Mike couldn't hold Adam's gaze.

"Yes, that's possible," he said.

"Only one way to find out."

"Wait," Mike said. "They're moving again, but much more slowly. Now they've stopped again."

"Let's go."

They pushed off again. It was still bitterly cold, and the thin sheen of ice coating the land crunched under their tires. As they moved north, Adam's mind wandered. Who were these people they were following?

Survivalists? Doomsday fanatics whose wet dreams of a world blasted by cataclysm had come true? One of those places featured on that stupid *Doomsday Preppers* show? Adam tried to picture it in his mind. These people live here for God knows how long before their dark dream comes to life. They pull up the drawbridge, isolate themselves as they watch their horrific fantasy play out on television. Did they enjoy it? Did they take satisfaction in knowing they'd been right all along, especially since the world had mocked them for their bizarre obsession?

How had they survived?

They're cut off from the rest of the world, able to avoid exposure to the virus. As devastating as Medusa had been, you couldn't catch it unless you were exposed to it, right? It was still a virus, subject to the same laws of virology as all the others. When it ran out of hosts, that would have been that. Right?

But baby Stephen had died, and he hadn't been exposed to the virus at all. Well, that wasn't entirely true. He had been exposed, just like his mother had been, during the epidemic. And perhaps he had inherited some resistance from her, but not enough. Because even a mild case of Medusa was like a bullet to the head. Plus, there was always the possibility that Medusa had mutated into a less severe illness, doing whatever it could to stay alive (to the extent a virus was, in fact, alive), after exterminating its hosts. He then had the terrifying thought, zooming through his mind, that Medusa could mutate into a *deadlier* strain, one to which he and the others *weren't* immune. He wished there had been some way to know what, in fact, had killed Stephen.

But back to these survivalists. They wait until it's all over, and then what? They chance sending someone out into the world, risk them getting infected without knowing if the virus was still percolating? Maybe desperation had driven them beyond the safety of the wall. Maybe their food supply had failed. Maybe they were experiencing their own little custom-made apocalypse.

As they trudged northward, picking their way across the ice-crusted plains, Adam began noticing a dark outline in the distance. At first, he thought he was just imagining it, but it loomed ever larger and sharper against the horizon, tinted green by his night-vision goggles. It was dark, monolithic, devoid of the visual spectacle they'd encountered upon first spotting Evergreen. He and Mike exchanged a glance. It was exactly as

Nadia had described it. A walled compound, a fortress, a citadel smack in the middle of nowhere.

He took stock of their location, there in the middle of the Nebraska plains, not far from the town of Beatrice. A light snow was falling now, which wasn't great, but better than sleet. There was a highway off to the east, identified by the outline of the utility poles lining the shoulder like sentries. The land was flat, endless, but the grasses here were tall, which might give them some cover as they approached whatever lay ahead. They hunkered down in a relative dead zone, a place that didn't seem likely to draw any interest from anyone.

Adam told Mike to catch a little shuteye while he kept the watch. Adam was too amped to worry about nodding off. As dawn approached, the compound began to come into focus, like a vision, a dream finally coming true. Was he really here? Was Rachel in there?

Take it easy, cowboy. Take it easy. You didn't come this far to just bust through the doors and get yourself killed like a sci-fi movie redshirt.

Dawn began breaking in the east, spreading its light across the land, enveloping their position and then continuing west toward the compound, which had held its dark, monolithic nature as it came into full view. It was still a ways off, probably two miles distant. A long wall, roughly eight feet in height, ran the length of the compound's perimeter. There was a heavy gate at its east entrance. From their slightly elevated position, he could make out beyond the wall a number of buildings scattered about the interior.

"Holy shit, this place is enormous," Mike exclaimed.

Adam was chewing the nail of his left thumb as he watched the place come into full view. Mike was right. It was huge. The perimeter fence ran at least a quarter mile in either direction before cutting at a right angle and running south, away from their position.

His heart beat faster with each passing moment.

They had arrived.

45

Only when his fingers scraped the oily bottom did Miles Chadwick realize that he had eaten the entire bag of barbecue potato chips. They were his weakness, the comfort food he turned to in times of stress. He extracted his fingers and licked them one at a time, savoring the salty tang of the faux barbecue, not afraid to admit, to himself at least, that he wanted another bag.

There were no other bags for now, and so he stood at his large bay window, looking west toward the fields. They were bare now, stripped. Depending on how you looked at them, you might say they were a dead place. Or you might say they were unspoiled, ready for the coming growing season. It was late December now, and they were living on the fruits of their summer labor, literally, the storehouse stocked floor to ceiling with food. Winter had finally come to these plains; a light snow had begun to fall on this, the third-to-last day of this momentous year.

Erin Thompson was twenty-one weeks along now. Last week's ultrasound had confirmed that she was carrying a boy, which delighted Chadwick to no end. The baby was his, of course, as the Citadel's first baby should be. A girl would have been fine, he supposed, but it seemed right, it seemed just, that the Citadel's first baby would be a boy.

Maybe they'd name him Adam.

Things were coming full circle now.

Fatherhood. Chadwick should have been a father in another life, decades and worlds before. But that had been taken away from him in an instant, in a moment that had become the keystone for the balance of Miles Chadwick's life. He thought back to that terrible day, that terrible phone call at work that changed everything.

This unborn son deserved a world like the one awaiting him. A carefully ordered and controlled world, where life and death wouldn't be subject to the whims of chance, subject to the evil that had stolen his family from him. Impossible, some might say. But did not the world that now lay before them speak as a testament to what man could do, what man could control? Miles Chadwick had directed the fate of the human race! He had not merely changed history, he had ended it! And now he could bring a child into a world where the strongest survived, where the gene pool wasn't diluted by those who'd depended on modern convenience to stay alive, suckling at the teat of society and never offering anything in return.

Sure, there would be complications. Like the one he now faced. But he could control it. He could control all these things now.

Outside, the snow had changed back over to sleet, and he found himself enjoying the reassuring tinkle of frozen rain against the windows. He loved nighttime storms; they comforted him, providing another buffer from the outside. It helped him forget that there was anyone else in the world.

He thought back to the night he'd signed onto the project. What if he'd said no? Gruber probably would have had him killed. No, not probably. He'd be dead. Perhaps there were other worlds, other universes in which Miles Chadwick had heard Gruber's pitch under clear skies and recoiled in horror and run screaming from the compound.

But he hadn't said no.

Because the world was ready to go.

That's what it all came down to.

The world had been sick, not just sick, but terminally ill, and Chadwick had done it a favor. You had your racists and your religious extremists and your corporate greed, and your never-ending war, a battle for money and power dressed up as a fight for democracy. You had overfished oceans and climate change that you ignored even though the facts, the goddamn facts had been there in front of your fat, pre-diabetic faces. You had a population no more enlightened about science than their ancestors had been two centuries earlier; somehow, the more scientists had discovered about the natural world, the less inclined the world had been to believe them. You had more than a billion people who didn't even have access to clean water.

And you had your family-slaying drug addicts.

Yes, the world had been very, very sick.

You didn't let a sick dog that you loved suffer, did you?

No, you made him a big juicy rare steak, you let him sleep one last time on his favorite pillow, or maybe on your bed, before you packed him up into the back of the station wagon and drove on down to the vet's office for the last time. You tried not to think about the basket of stuffed toys and the half-full bag of dog food still in the pantry. And when you got home, you ignored the puddle of water by the bowl that he'd splashed in getting his final, sloppy laps.

Despite the progress they'd made, despite exposing the rebellion before any damage was done, Chadwick felt uneasy, like the control was starting to slip away. The executions continued to loom large in his mind. There was no second-guessing, no regret in having dealt with the traitors in the manner he had. He had ninety-three other people to deal with, not even counting the captive women, and he couldn't let them think, not for a millisecond, that such treachery would be tolerated.

He was unable to sleep. He poured a scotch, which strangely didn't taste all that out of place with the residue of the barbecue chips in his mouth, and pulled a chair up near the wall-length window of his quarters.

The rebellion had been a bit of a surprise; he'd had his suspicions, of course, that nagging feeling in his mind that told you something just wasn't right, but he hadn't wanted to believe them. So he'd managed to place a mole inside Rogers' group, a young survivalist who was skilled but impressionable. If Rogers had formed a breakaway group, Chadwick thought he might try to recruit the kid. He had, and the kid performed beautifully. He was a big, simple, effective machine that you simply had to know how to program.

Now, Miles couldn't help but wonder if the roots of the rebellion were still in place, lurking just beneath the surface, but ready to grow back, stronger than before. What if it were a bigger group next time?

What if he'd simply made martyrs out of Rogers and the others? What if this burst of conscience was as contagious as the Medusa virus had been? It could be out there *right now*, spreading from person to person, one at a time. Incubating. Waiting to burst forth.

He went back into his private office, where he kept the Citadel's personnel files locked in a safe. He grabbed a handful at random, began leafing through them, reading through the psychological profiles, wondering if in these pages lay some hint of trouble, some harbinger of betrayal. As he scanned the documents, doubt about many of the recruits crept into his mind like a thief in the night. He moved from one to the next, unsure of what he was looking for. He paused at one, a red folder containing the dossier on one of his earlier recruits.

Eldon Washington. A thirty-seven-year-old agronomist from Idaho. A foster child who'd never found a permanent home, he held a Ph.D. in agricultural science and was one of the key players in the development of the Citadel's food supply. He was brilliant, but troubled. Six years before the Medusa outbreak, he'd been Colin Barton, a professor at the University of Idaho. Then his wife had left him, and he had turned to booze for solace. One night, after downing half a bottle of tequila, he had gotten behind the wheel of his F-150 pickup and plowed into a family of three on their way home, killing the mother and the couple's infant daughter. Chadwick found Barton while he was out on bond and offered him the deal of a lifetime. A new identity and a life free of the Idaho Department of Corrections, in exchange for his absolute loyalty to the project. They faked the death of Colin Barton, and Eldon Washington was born.

This was the kind of man Chadwick needed. Someone who owed Chadwick his very life. How many like those were in these files? Certainly not ninety-three. A thought took root in his mind and began to grow. Like so many businesses that had failed in the old world, he'd over-capitalized, grown too quickly. What did he have, really? Loyal, committed soldiers? Or a large, complex system that was the thing he feared above all else – impossible to control? After all, the more moving pieces a machine had, the more likely it was that it would break down.

And it wasn't just the original group he had to worry about. They'd captured more than two dozen women. All carried antibodies to Medusa, which was good, but had he needed so goddamn many? A decision was made, right there. There would be no more captives this winter; the roads would be treacherous, and the survivors would be taking up shelter indoors, which would make it all that much harder to find them. The first big cut was coming; a million could perish out there as winter tightened its grip on the land.

A pruning.

The Citadel had gotten too big, too quickly. A lot of dead weight now. No, not *dead* weight. *Dangerous* weight. The kind of weight that could destabilize the entire community, upset the apple cart he'd spent so many years constructing. No, no, no, it just wouldn't do.

The edges of a plan began to form in his mind.

He made a list of his twelve most loyal lieutenants, all male, all men who owed Chadwick everything. Men like Eldon Washington. Men like Lewis Hoover, the mole he'd placed inside Rogers' group of traitors. The list came together quickly. It was like he'd known all along the ones he could trust.

Each would select one of the women from the group of captives. He didn't care. They were to be a means to an end. Either way, they'd have to be broken.

The rest would be purged.

It was time to evolve.

EARLY THE NEXT MORNING, Chadwick nursed another scotch, which had chased down a pain pill, while he waited for the men to arrive. There weren't enough seats for everyone, and so his shock troops lined the walls like kindergartners waiting for direction from their teacher. Chadwick scanned the faces of these good, loyal men and felt good about what he saw. It reminded him of a lean fighter after months spent in a hole-in-the-wall gym, stripped of the accoutrements of fame and wealth and pomp and circumstance. A fighter built in the crucible of hard work and sweat and blood. The rest of the Citadel, the women, they were nothing but fat that needed to be trimmed. And you trimmed it by being relentless, merciless.

Chadwick's quarters were on the top floor of the main building, near the center of the compound, just west of the lab and the clinic. Beyond that lay the east housing units, separated from the wall by a thick copse of pine trees. The three other barracks were scattered to the other points of the compass.

The men had taken the news in stride. There had been no gasps, no nervous glances at one another, no sense they were wondering whether the old man had simply lost it. They stood silent, ramrod straight, as Chadwick had explained the plan to them. Charlie Gale stepped forward and approached Chadwick's desk. He was a big, strapping man, Nordic, his hair platinum, his eyes blue like glacial ice. He took the heavy bottle of scotch and poured a finger's worth into each of the two tumblers on the desk.

After a moment of silence, he took his place back in line and raised the tumbler skyward.

"To Dr. Miles Chadwick!" Gale called out, his voice firm but proud.

"To Dr. Miles Chadwick!" the other eleven echoed in unison.

Warmth spread from Chadwick's core to his extremities. He felt light-headed, almost dizzy with joy. He couldn't remember the last time he'd felt this good. It seemed that the entire project had been snakebitten since Rogers had sat down with him and told him that the women were infertile.

His stomach dropped; he held the smile on his face, as he wanted to know how much he truly appreciated the men's loyalty. Because he did, well and truly so. But he didn't want them to see the sudden panic on his face, even as the room filled with the stench of his flop sweat.

Since Rogers had told him the women were infertile.

Rogers had been the one to tell him. Had Chadwick ever verified Rogers' report that the women were, in fact, infertile?

He must have. Certainly, Rogers must have shown him charts, lab reports, *something* that documented his testing and findings. Chadwick felt the rage swell up inside him, and he knew that he was doing the right thing. At this point, it didn't even matter. Rogers was dead. They were taking fertile women, the kind who'd trigger positives on home pregnancy tests simply by walking by them in the store. He packed away his rage as best as he could and focused on the moment at hand. He joined Gale in raising his glass.

"To you, my warrior poets," he said gravely. "To all of us. To a new beginning."

He put away the scotch with one pull and wiped his mouth with the back of his hand.

"Let's get to work," he said. "We have much to do, and not much time to do it. But by this time tomorrow night, the Citadel's future will be secure."

The twelve scattered to the winds, each bearing his own task, each holding his own unique piece of the puzzle.

46

Rachel picked at her breakfast, moving the food around her plate like a government bureaucrat intent on showing that she'd done something productive with her day. Again, she hadn't slept well.

The atmosphere reminded her of the CalTech student cafeteria on the rare occasion she'd managed to make it there for a meal. She'd normally been so busy that she often took her meals at her desk, a protein bar here, a slice of cold pizza there. The old tape in her mind unwound. It made her sad to think about the empty hallways and grave-yard campus. She'd spent most of the summer there, having gone home for a two-week break just before the outbreak had begun. Had her friends, her teachers, her advisors died there? Were their bodies still dotting the campus, the quad, the dorms? Guilt spiked through her like a burst of static electricity.

She forced herself to eat, focusing on function rather than form, chewing the peanut-butter-smeared English muffin a little bit at a time. She wished she had something hot to drink. It was cloudy and the dorm was dank and cold. She despised cold weather, the way it got into you, how it was almost impossible to snuff out once it had set into your bones. Growing up in San Diego had ruined her on cold weather, just ruined her. To stay warm now, she wore her heaviest sweatshirt, a gray Dallas Cowboys hoodie she'd found on the grounds.

Now she was thinking about home again, about how her stepdad Jerry had dragged her to dozens, no *thousands*, of Padres games over the years. How she complained about it during the thirty-five-minute drive there and how he would threaten, no, promise her that he was never taking her to another game. And then she'd get there and have a corn dog and an ice cream cone, and she'd be happy. What she wouldn't give to be at a Padres game in the middle of May when the city absolutely exploded with its sharp lines downtown and its green parks and, of course, the shimmery silver of the Pacific.

The exhaustion was wrapped around every fiber of her being, down to the roots of her hair. A mental exhaustion, the byproduct of the strain from being trapped in this hellhole. They were nothing more than slaves, concubines. She hadn't been inseminated yet, but she suspected it was only a matter of time. A few of the girls had been raped, she knew that, but so far, she'd been spared that atrocity. At least three were now pregnant. They were being incredibly careful with the program, taking their time, not rushing, making sure that each pregnancy was viable. Their blood was tested weekly for Medusa, and she could see in the way they skittered around the lab that she and the other women scared them, as though there was something mystical about their genetic makeup.

A commotion at the table drew her attention. A rumor was sweeping among the women that a couple of new girls had come in overnight and were currently being processed in the lab, undergoing the humiliating medical tests that bonded them together, creating a sisterhood.

"You stole my biscuit!" It was Julie, a heavier set woman with thin black hair.

"Why would I steal your goddamn biscuit?" replied a fiery Erin Thompson, now halfway through her pregnancy and dealing with a hell of a case of heartburn.

Rachel watched for a moment, embarrassed to admit she was fascinated by the conflagration because it was a break in their awful routine. It was something that fired up the synapses, and all of a sudden she understood the psychology of prison riots.

"Because you're pregnant and all you can think about is your stupid baby!"

Erin exploded into sobs; Julie reached across the table and plucked the allegedly purloined biscuit from Erin's plate. Then she shoved it into her mouth all at once.

"You disgusting cow!" yelled Patricia, who was sitting next to Erin. They'd become close friends, probably as close as any of the women in the group.

They were all getting a bit flaky. Fuses were getting short. Despair was growing long. It wouldn't be too much longer before Chadwick and his band of psychopaths would have exactly what they wanted – a group of broken women, capable of reproducing and little else.

"Hey, knock that shit off!" Rachel bellowed, surprised by the power of her voice. The other women fell silent.

"Don't you let them do this to us," she went on. "Don't you let them!"

Patricia burst into tears.

"Can't you see they just want to break us?" Rachel said, looking squarely at Patricia. "They want us to give up. They want us to quit."

She glanced over her shoulder and saw one of Chadwick's lackeys approaching their table.

"You bitches shut the hell up."

Patricia helped Erin out of her seat and escorted her away from the dining area. Rachel lost interest in her muffin like it was a boring book that she had to read for school. She set it back down on her plate and gave up. The fight concluded, the remaining women at the table began chattering away again, their voices on edge, probably not far from another eruption.

She wondered if it would be possible to see San Diego again.

She wondered if there was a way for all of them to escape.

She wondered whether she would be willing to die trying.

She thought that she would be.

THE MORNING PASSED by in a haze, Rachel stretched out on her bunk, her mind singularly focused on the idea of escape. She lay on top of the itchy woolen blanket these assholes provided, the one that barely covered her toes at night but that she dreaded losing. Now that she knew the lay of the land and had absorbed the routines and the rhythms, she knew she could get out of the compound on her own.

But that wouldn't do. If she left the others behind, Chadwick's retribution would be swift and terrible. He'd kill the others like he was throwing out a batch of burned brownies and start again. She'd done the math; even if the epidemic had been as bad as she feared, there were still a couple of million women out there, hundreds of thousands that would meet his needs. He'd slaughter her fellow captives.

No, if this were to work, she had to get them all out. No matter how much it ratcheted up the danger. It had to be this way or not at all.

At noon, a knock on her door. There was no need to get up, as it was a courtesy knock, and the door swung open a second later.

"Get up."

She swung her legs over the side of the bed and sat up to greet her visitor. It was one of Chadwick's men, one of the inner circle that she frequently saw by his side. A kind of caste system had come into play since the executions. Some had better access to Chadwick than others, and some seemed to barely be in the mix at all.

"Pack your things," the man said, tossing a pair of plastic grocery bags at her feet.

"Why? We going on vacation?"

The retort earned her a hard smack to the side of the head, enough to fill her field of vision with a flash of white light.

"Get your stuff," he snapped. "Don't make me ask again. You've got thirty seconds."

She packed quickly, sticking to the essentials as she stuffed the plastic bags, scolding herself for the pointless, illogical decision to give this guy lip. This was something a child would do, or someone capable of only child-like thinking. If she was going to lead these women out of here, she was going to have to start thinking like a grownup. No, she would have to think like a machine, a thing incapable of making irrational decisions, incapable of saying stupid things because they felt good to say.

She would have to inoculate herself against being human.

Outside, the sky was gray, the air cold and damp. The chill stung her nose, and she thought it might snow soon. Since Chadwick had cut their outdoor excursions, this was her first time outdoors in days, and she couldn't even manage to draw a little sunshine. She climbed in the idling SUV, which zipped away before she even had a chance to buckle her seatbelt. The driver rambled east, away from the lake and toward the road that bisected the compound into two rectangles. Then he turned south toward the group's nerve center.

A short drive brought them to a cluster of buildings just east of the road; the driver let Rachel and her escort out in front of a boxy building, slate gray. Nerves pulsed through her like lightning bolts. She twirled the plastic bags containing her meager belongings; the way they spun in her hands and unspooled again gave her a measure of comfort.

"Follow me," he said.

He paused to punch a code into a keypad at the door, which unlocked with a satisfying click. He held the door open and motioned her through it. They were in a narrow foyer now, empty and hollow. She half-expected to see one of those directories mounted on the wall identifying the occupants of an office building, telling you which floor the accountant was on, where you'd find the physical therapist. She followed him through a door on the left side of the corridor to a stairwell, gray and metal. Again, he yielded her the right of way and trailed up the stairs behind her. They came to a heavy metal door on the second floor, which he knocked on.

Her heart was throbbing now, so fiercely that it took her breath away.

The door opened.

Miles Chadwick stood before her.

He had a wild grin on his face, the look of a man who'd just heard a very funny joke.

"Rachel," he said. "Welcome to your new home."

CHADWICK and his man spoke briefly while Rachel scanned Chadwick's living quarters. It was spartan, to say the least. She counted at least three rooms – a large living room, a small kitchen, and two smaller rooms, just off the main corridor. There was a cheap-looking bookcase in the corner, stuffed to the gills with all manner of tomes. She was too far away to make out the titles.

Until now, she had not known where Chadwick lived. Truth be told, she had not recognized him as a person who needed a place to live, to sleep, to take a well and good shit in the morning. He was the boogeyman, a phantom, a monster who transformed into some terrible winged creature and flew back to his cave at the end of each day. But no, he was a man like any other. He ate and drank and had bad dreams and checked the stove before going to bed at night.

A man had rendered this terrible fate on the world.

A man.

A single, solitary man.

Behind her, the door opened and then clicked shut again. They were alone now.

"My dearest Rachel," he said.

She noticed that he still wore that terrible smile, like the Joker from the Batman comic books. A cosmetic procedure gone terribly wrong.

"I suppose you're wondering what's going on," he said.

She shifted her weight from one foot to the other and stared at the floor. She did it deliberately and slowly, because she wanted him to think that she was frightened. A scared little lamb. It wasn't that she didn't think he was dangerous. Oh no. Miles Chadwick was probably the most dangerous man who had ever lived. A million Adolf Hitlers rolled into one. It was just that she had forgotten that he was still just a man.

A man who could be killed.

"You're very special," he said. "Very special indeed."

"Thank you," she said demurely. She wanted him to feel in charge. Now was not the time to show aggression. It was time to play a little bit possum, a little bit geisha.

"Well, you're all special," he said. "You and your friends."

As he spoke, he drew closer to her.

"But I must confess," he said. Now he was uncomfortably close, and the metallic stink of his body odor hit her in the face. It must have been days since he'd bathed.

"I find you a little more special than the others."

Her eyes watered from the stench, and it took every ounce of willpower not to gag right there in front of him. He reached out and brushed a tear from the corner of her eye with a thumb.

"No need to cry, my darling," he said. "You're safe now."

She looked up at him and smiled her biggest smile.

He gestured toward the couch, inviting her to sit down.

"May I pour you a drink?"

"Sure," she said.

He went to the bar and fixed two scotches. As he made the drinks, she took a seat on the far edge of the couch and took in more of the residence. There was a small kitchenette opposite her, and she wondered how many knives he might have tucked away in its cheap prefabricated drawers. A portrait of a strange-looking older man hung over a gas fireplace. His wiry gray hair seemed to explode from his head, and his narrow features made him look like a wild-eyed bird; his cold blue eyes were empty of life. A small brass plate mounted at the base of the portrait read Leon Gruber, Father of The Citadel.

She tugged her eyes away from the portrait as Chadwick came up on her. He handed her the tumbler and sat down next to her. She took a long drink of the scotch, an alcohol she'd never tasted. It felt hot, like drain cleaner, and it scorched its way down her throat. Her gaze kept drifting back to the portrait, which seemed to be staring at her.

"I've brought you here because I've been so terribly rude to you," he said.

Another soft smile as she looked away. The shy little schoolgirl.

"I don't feel like you've been rude."

He flashed his own smile.

"You're too kind," he said. "But having you over there with the others, packed in like cattle. It's unacceptable, and for that I apologize."

"We have a warm place to sleep," she replied. "We have food, fresh water. Things could be worse. A lot worse."

"Again, you flatter me," he said. "And that might be fine for the others. But not for you."

A shiver ran up her spine, as though Chadwick had run a shard of ice along the bare skin, along each one of her vertebrae.

"The others, you see, they're just a means to an end."

"Mm-hmm."

"You, on the other hand."

"What about me?"

"You're part of the Citadel's future. Part of my future."

She paused, processing what he was telling her. She didn't like where this was headed at all. Bunking in with the ladies might not have been ideal, but it sure beat the hell out of this debutante role he seemed to have in mind for her.

"It's a big empty country out there," he said. "And it's waiting for us. We're not going to be inside these walls forever. If we're going to rebuild this world, we're going to have to spread our wings. A new world. With you as its queen."

Her head rocked back at this. She was growing more uncomfortable by the minute, but she had to hold it together. She had to make him think that she was broken. Because that was the point of all this, right? To break them?

"I want you to take your place at my side," he said. "Together, we can make the Citadel everything that the old world never was. A perfect world."

Jesus.

"You really think that's possible?"

"I do," he said. "I really do."

"Is that why this all happened in the first place?" she asked. She bit her lip and waited for an eruption.

"My dear, this happened because it was meant to be."

"It was?"

"I know that's hard to understand," he said. "Do you believe in God?"

She had, once upon a time. When they first moved to San Diego, her mom had taken her to church every Sunday, when it was just the two of them, before Jerry. They went to a nice little Methodist church where things didn't seem as religious as she thought they would, and for a while she considered herself one of the faithful. But then she started learning about science and math and evolution. And she couldn't reconcile one with the other, and so when it had come down to it, she had chosen the one that could be proven empirically. Then the plague had hit, and it seemed biblical in nature, a terrible judgment for man, if you believed in that. But she didn't. And she was right. This wasn't God's judgment. This was the work of man. As evil as anything that man had wrought, by his own free will.

"No."

"That's good," he said. "I appreciate your honesty. It's very rare. Very rare indeed."

He took a long drink from his scotch.

"We lived in an evil world, Rachel. I hesitate to even call it a sinful world, because I think that sugarcoats it too much. Sin. It's such a pathetic little word. Thou shalt not steal? Well, you pop a grape in your mouth at the supermarket before paying for it, that's sin right there. And the idea you could just repent at the end, and it would all be okay, well that didn't seem right to me. You could blow up a commuter bus or molest little children or, uh, murder a young wife at an ATM machine and all would be forgiven if you just accepted Jesus Christ as your Lord and savior? Does that seem right to you?"

She shook her head. "No, I suppose not."

"Of course not," he said, swirling the tumbler of scotch now. "It was a story we told ourselves to minimize the impact that these terrible acts had on us. To protect us from the idea that there was true evil in the world, evil that no God could ever stop. The truth is that we are the gods of our own existence. We can control what happens. Which is why the plague had to happen."

"But won't you have evil in this new world? People will still do bad things."

"We're going to do it correctly this time."

"What about the people out there? Beyond the walls?"

He smiled and placed his hand on her knee. She wanted to chop his fingers off. For a moment, she considered shattering her tumbler and stabbing him in the neck with a shard of glass, but she dismissed the idea as quickly as it had occurred to her.

"All in good time," he said. "All in good time."

You're goddamn right about that, she thought.

47

It took every bit of willpower Adam had, but he was finally able to convince himself of the old adage that time spent on reconnaissance was never wasted. They needed to watch the place, study the activity, look for patterns, get a sense of its rhythms. Nadia's tale of this place was proof enough that caution should be their watchword.

And so that was what they had done. They retreated from their position, back across the highway, and surveilled the compound with their field glasses. In the first day on watch, Adam worried the place would remain a cipher, a mystery, that it would never disclose any of its secrets, and they would have to launch a blind assault on the place, the type of frontal attack that would almost certainly end in disaster. But eventually, a bit of useful intelligence revealed itself. At nine a.m. on the second day, the gate opened, and a dark red pickup truck emerged from the interior. It rolled along the access road and then turned west along the main highway. The windows were dark, but not completely tinted, and Adam could make out two figures inside the cab. The bed of the pickup looked empty. As the truck zoomed out of sight, Adam made a note of the time and resumed watching the compound.

At ten o'clock, they split a meager breakfast. Then Adam dozed while Mike kept the watch. He didn't think he'd be able to fall asleep, but sure enough, he'd been out as soon as he closed his eyes. When he woke, it was nearly noon. He was cold but refreshed, and he had to pee. He crept deeper into the grasses for some privacy, away from the compound. As he began to relieve himself, he heard Mike hissing for him.

"Adam! The truck's back!"

Of course.

Mid-stream, and something important happens. As he prepared to zip up and leave himself with a half-empty bladder, he primed his ears and sliced through the aural clutter, focusing on the sound of an engine. He did hear it, a throaty whine, and he reminded himself that sounds carried a lot farther than they used to, and he told himself to finish. He couldn't panic about every little thing. If he wanted his body to perform at its peak, he needed to let it do what it needed to do. He waited until his bladder was empty, and then he zipped up and resumed his post with a clear mind. A small but important sign he was evolving.

He glassed the horizon and spotted the pickup on its inbound trip. When it was within about two hundred yards, he lowered the binoculars. The truck slowed as it neared the intersection with the access road, and then it turned north toward the gate. Adam checked his watch as the gate slid open and the truck disappeared inside the compound. It was noon on the nose. It paused long enough for Adam to note that it was carrying cargo. The tarp was stretched out across the top of the pick-up bed, the load secured with bungee cords.

Out at nine. Back at noon.

The tedium of the stakeout built through the early afternoon. He looked for signs of activity near the wall but saw none. At three o'clock, again, squarely at the top of the hour, the pickup truck headed back out for another sortie. Again, it was gone three hours, returning at six o'clock. Again, there was cargo in the bed area, tucked away under the beige-colored tarp, its corner flapping in the wind.

The pattern repeated itself the next day, and by the third day, the outline of a plan had formed in Adam's mind. There would be a very small window of time in which to execute the plan, almost impossibly small, but there really weren't any other options. They had to get inside the compound, and the main gate seemed like the only way in.

It was a dank day, chilly. The clouds hung low in the sky, a thick, gray blanket over the world. Around five-thirty, about ten minutes before launch, it began to rain heavily, in sheets, relentless and pounding. With the world so quiet, with nothing to absorb the sound, the rain roared across the plains, washing across the roadway in waves, as though the world was trying to clean itself of some hidden shame.

At twenty to six, they made their move. They stayed low, knifing through the grasses like jungle cats. Their packs were light, relieved of all their contents but the bare essentials. The closer they got to the wall, the tighter Adam's throat felt, as though the place had a psychic grip on his windpipe.

It took ten minutes to cover the two hundred yards, but they made it with a little time to spare. They took cover in the grasses about ten yards from the main gate. At three minutes past six, the tardiness owing perhaps to the terrible weather conditions, the pickup truck made the turn for home. A creepy gray darkness had fallen, and the truck's headlights shined like UFOs floating in the ether.

"This isn't going to work," Mike said. "We can't both do it. We'll be spotted."

Adam grunted through clenched teeth, pained to admit that Mike was correct. The entire operation was dancing on a razor's edge as it was. Getting one of them inside the gates, at least the way they'd mapped it out, was going to be hard enough; completing the feat in duplicate would be expecting to win the lottery two weeks in a row. It was a terrible tactical blunder.

"Yeah," he said. "You're right."

"I've got an idea," Mike said. "Stay low."

"Wait, what?"

Before Adam could blink, Mike burst out of the grasses, his arms waving over his head like a driver stranded by the side of the road.

Goddammit!

Panic flooded Adam's insides like water overcoming a sinking boat, and he froze, wondering what the fuck had possessed Mike to reveal himself like this. The truck rolled to a stop as the driver waited for the gate to slide open. As it idled there, the rain plinked the truck's rooftop, adding a strange hollow twang to the deluge. Mike approached the driver and banged on the window.

"How ya doing?" he yelled out over the rain, loud enough for Adam to hear. To Adam's right, the gate began to open, sliding from left to right, revealing the interior of the compound like some game-show door prize.

Muffled voices from the cab.

"I'm lost, can you guys help me?"

From his vantage point, Adam saw Mike blanch and turn his body away, but it wasn't fast enough. The gunshot roared over the rain, and Mike collapsed to the ground. The men emerged from the vehicle and tossed Mike's lifeless body under the tarp; then they climbed back in the cab.

The man's sacrifice galvanized Adam; he stayed low, shuffling from the cover of the grasses onto the roadway, praying the driver's blind spot was big enough to hide him long enough to do what he had to do. He stayed low, right at the muffler, the stench of the exhaust blistering his nostrils, even in the rain. The truck continued to idle, and there was no indication he'd been spotted. Yet.

The timing would have to be perfect.

The gate thudded home as it finished sliding into its groove. Adam remained crouched, his muscles burning as he kept them coiled, ready to pounce. When the truck shifted back into gear, Adam leapt, grabbing the edge of the tailgate, and rolling over its edge as the truck began moving. He could only hope that Mike's diversion and the truck's acceleration had masked the subtle shift in the payload, surreptitiously increased by about one hundred and seventy pounds. He eased himself down into the truck bed and covered himself with the tarp.

SHOCKWAVES OF GRIEF rippled through Adam as the truck motored its way inside the compound. Adam wanted to smack Mike's blank face for his stupid, selfless act.

Later, he thought.

There would be time to grieve later.

Don't piss away what Mike just did for you.

Behind him, Adam could hear the gate grinding along its track again, slamming home with a hollow thud. The truck continued to roll; he had to move now, before the truck picked up too much speed.

He poked his head out from under the tarp and quickly scanned the area as the truck turned right onto a narrow access road. A drainage ditch ran parallel to the road and a line of pine trees just beyond. No other signs of life, vehicular or otherwise. The rain was easing up but changing over to snow.

Now, he told himself.

It had to be now.

He touched Mike's cheek one last time. Then he grabbed the lip of the truck bed and pulled himself up from the cover of the tarp. Without taking a breath, he pitched his weight toward the back edge of the lift-gate and waited for it to happen. For a moment, he felt weightless, like a feather caught on a breeze, and then the ground came up on him all at once. His left flank hit first, the impact with the ground stealing his breath away, and then he was rolling, rolling, rolling.

His ankle became caught up underneath his spinning body, and he felt it wrench in the wrong direction. The pain shot from foot to waist, but there was nothing he could do but wait until his body came to rest.

A body in motion...

Finally, friction and gravity won out, and he lay in a heap at the side of the road. The truck trundled along, blissfully ignorant of its now-unloaded stowaway. He remained still as the truck's taillights faded into the snow, curling out of view as the road turned north. He wasn't far from the ditch, and so he crawled to its edge and rolled down into it. From his hiding spot, he scanned his new surroundings.

The place seemed even bigger from the inside than it had from beyond the wall. To the northwest, maybe a hundred yards clear of the opposite shoulder, Adam saw a large tract of undeveloped land, marked off by wire fencing; it was barren, but it bore a certain kind of symmetry. He swung his gaze northeast, where he saw the faint glimmer of light. But for the hoot of a snow owl, the place was silent.

He could scarcely believe it. He'd made it.

That stupid bastard Mike had pushed him over the goal line, giving all he had to give, just so Adam would have a chance to find Rachel. His bravery, his total lack of hesitation was almost more than Adam could believe. The mission was all but doomed, that much was clear, so he had done the only thing he could do, no matter the price.

Despite the fact that Adam was in more peril than ever, or perhaps because of it, it seemed important to acknowledge how far he'd come. He thought about all they'd seen and lived through in their nearly five months on the road. All to bring him to this point. Just to give him a chance to rescue his daughter. He thought about something Sarah had said, not long after they'd met. That she'd be doing something and forget that the world hadn't always been this way. But as the days had cascaded along like tumbleweed, stretching into weeks and months, that seemed less and less apropos.

A strange sense of the familiar had begun to pervade his life. From the constant scavenging for supplies to ensuring the water was safe to drink to burying his own waste, it had all become routine. This was neither a good thing nor a bad thing. It simply just *was*. Perhaps the key to all this had been simply finding a way through, a way that, after a while, simply became the new normal. The less time spent looking slack-jawed at yet another urban ghost town, stopping to look at each cluster of corpses that dotted the landscape, reliving the past, the better. And it had become clear that he wasn't trying to find Rachel because she was his past. He was trying to find her because she was his future.

He was stiff and sore from his truck dive, but it appeared he'd pulled through without too much damage. The ankle he'd been certain was broken was mildly sprained and would likely loosen up with continued work. After the systems check, he slithered out of the back of the ditch and disappeared into the trees. Fortunately, these were evergreens, full with needles, like a green wall. The air was thick with the scent of pine, and he was reminded of the smell of Christmas tree lots.

He trekked eastward through the trees, toward the lights, slowly, slowly, as though each step might find a land mine. A thick layer of pine needles muted his footsteps. It was cold, but his Gore-Tex jacket was doing what it was supposed to be doing, keeping him dry and warm enough that he wasn't excessively worried about how cold it was. It took forty minutes to reach the eastern edge of the compound, each one soaked in fear of stumbling across a late-night patrol sweeping the grounds or setting off some invisible alarm. After a quarter mile, the tree cover began to thin, and so he was left to slink along in the shadows, almost trying to melt into the wall.

He paused for a short break at the wall and ate a protein bar. As he snacked, he glassed the terrain ahead. A cluster of development awaited him to the north, starting with a row of nondescript buildings, shadowy monoliths in the night. This chilled him and made him hot with rage all at the same time, this human presence, the people holding Rachel captive.He gave himself five minutes to rest and then set off again, mentally cataloging each landmark he came across. A long rectangular building fronting on a cut-through access road. Across the way, a fenced-off generator field, the machines lined up like silent soldiers. A low hum filled his ears.

Beyond that, he spotted two more nondescript buildings, also inside the fence line. He studied each carefully, but he was unable to identify either structure's purpose. That was when he heard the rustle of activity just around the bend, possibly coming from the intersecting road just north of his position. He froze as the conspiratorial whispers of men on a mission drew closer, scanning their surroundings. A row of bushes lined the road, perhaps ornamental by design, but lifesaving by function. He ducked down behind the hedges as a group of three men came by. They walked briskly and with purpose.

They continued past his position, and as the gulf between them grew, he felt his heart rate decelerate. They hadn't seen him. He maintained a northerly course, torn between competing desires to tread carefully and to finish his sweep as quickly as possible. As he continued, the development seemed to thin out, and he began to hear a strange sound, coupled with the tickle in his nose of an earthy, fecund smell. Not mechanical, but not human, either. The sound of livestock. The grunts and braying emanating from the animal pens pushed him along. He had no desire to find out if these animals served some early-warning function, alerting their masters that an intruder was present.

As he ventured farther north, the odor intensified, and the snorts and chortles grew clearer. A pig here. A chicken there. In the ever-faint ambient light, Adam could just make out the edge of a barn. Again, he found himself wondering who these people really were. This kind of installation would have required an astonishing amount of capital. Some eccentric billionaire? Perhaps a secret government project?

And how had they survived?

The flash of approaching headlights derailed his train of thought, sent his testicles up into his stomach. There was very little cover along the wall, so he had drifted to the inside shoulder, toward the middle of the complex. Ahead, there was a copse of bare tree trunks, toward which he bolted, hopefully covering him before the oncoming vehicle lit him up like a Christmas tree. He slipped between the trees, like a flea burrowing into a dog's thick coat.

The treeline was shallower than he expected, and a moment later, he burst through the other side. The terrain dropped away sharply, and Adam went tumbling downward like a runaway snowball. He waited for the white-hot pain of a snapped leg or torn knee ligament to light up his body, but he came to rest in an unscathed heap on a damp patch of ground. His mind went immediately to the gun, which had come off his shoulder as he barreled to the bottom of the hill. His hands scoured the immediate area around him, scraping and clawing against damp, cold earth, and he nearly let out a sigh of relief when his fingers clamped around the cold steel of the barrel.

He primed his ears and listened for the sounds of pursuit, of a car door slamming shut, of footsteps closing in, and waited to be discovered or not. Seconds ticked by, then minutes, then fifteen minutes, and no one came through the tree line behind him. When he was confident that he'd avoided detection again, he took a moment to run a quick systems check.

He rose to a crouch and was surprised to see a large lake shimmering before him, the night babbling and gurgling, the plink of fish splashing about the rippling surface. The sight of the large body of water stopped him cold; discounting the quick traverse of the Mississippi River in St. Louis, it was the first he'd seen since his terrifying exit from Holden Beach so many months ago.

Seeing the lake scared him; it reminded him how little he knew about this place, and how powerful a foe he was dealing with. He took a deep breath and let it out, enjoying for a brief moment the cold, briny tang of the lake in his nasal passages. He got up and brushed the grit from his pants. He staked out a position just under the lip of the rise and lifted the glasses to his eyes again, back toward the lake.

To his right, a large plot of land, and Adam recognized the long, even rows of a crop field. Several acres' worth. Scarred, barren columns of earth for now, but, he suspected, part of this place's lifeblood. It would be up and running sooner than later. To his left, more of the development he'd seen during his northern passage along the east wall.

Frustration lacquered his mind. He felt almost as lost as he'd been before they'd found the place. It seemed as though he'd seen too much of this strange place to keep it all straight but not enough to make any informed decisions about how to proceed next. And fatigue was starting to become a problem. His thinking was becoming soft, disjointed. How long before he made a fatal misstep because his mind was too cloudy to function?

He checked his watch; it was already after four in the morning. The sun would be up soon, meaning he'd have to be safely out of sight by then. Perhaps tucked into the deep woods he'd seen just inside the main gate. With a deep sigh, he abandoned his post and trekked west along another access road, back toward the main road that seemed to encircle the compound. There was a thick cluster of trees across the way and just a hair south, which he set as his target for the night.

He scampered across the highway like an errant possum and dove back into the trees. Thick evergreens here, swallowing him whole. When he looked back, he couldn't even see the roadway, and the darkness was almost total. There was just enough light by which he could make out the outline of his hand.

It was unnerving, being this deep in the most unknowable spot of an already mysterious land. But he had no choice. And on the plus side, the trees were so thick here, the needle-laden branches so overgrown and interlaced that very little precipitation was making it to the forest floor. Adam set out his bedroll and covered it with a layer of pine needles.

As he slid into the sleeping bag, he was certain that he'd be too consumed with the knowledge that Rachel was right here, so close by, to sleep, but within seconds, he was asleep deep in the bowels of the Citadel.

48

Something was happening, Rachel thought. Something fundamental had changed.

Wearing a black dress that Chadwick had selected for her, she looked out across the darkened grounds of the Citadel, her eyes bouncing from landmark to landmark. The fields. The amphitheater. Barely in her line of sight, the lake, near the women's dormitory. The sun had dipped low over the plains and was close to dropping out of sight for the last time this year.

It was New Year's Eve. Nearly six o'clock. And Rachel Fisher had her dancing shoes on, which was a somewhat remarkable development for her. In the handful of years that she'd been old enough to go out on New Year's Eve, she never had. She had never wanted to. She liked to stay in with her few friends and eat Chinese food and watch Will Ferrell movies. She wasn't one of these types that had bragged about not going out on New Year's Eve, as though doing nothing had become the cool, hipster thing to do. And she wasn't one of these types that fell asleep at ten o'clock, either, because she rarely went to bed before one or two in the morning anyway. And if the world had continued along its track rather than derailing, its cars piling up on one another, that's probably what she would be doing right now.

But now she stood here at a window in the middle of the great empty nowhere, wearing a cocktail dress and waiting on her date for the evening.

It had been a weird few days. She had planned to kill Chadwick that first night. She had fully expected him to take her into his bed, have his way with her. In fact, she was counting on it, and she was going to *let* him do it, so help her God, praise Jesus, Hallelujah, she was going to let him do whatever he wanted, because when he was done, when he was sleeping the sleep of a man with empty balls, she was going to take the knife she had hidden under the mattress and turn that genocidal son of a bitch into shish kabob.

But he hadn't done anything she had expected.

Any fears that she'd have to submit to his sexual desires had been totally unfounded. Not only had he not touched her, he had barely even looked at her, so preoccupied he'd been with his work. The first night, she'd stayed up until nearly four in the morning, certain that he'd be back for his prize. He was a man, after all. But eventually, her eyes had drooped shut, and when they'd opened again, sunlight was streaming into Chadwick's sparsely furnished bedroom, and she was still alone.

Yesterday morning, Chadwick had brought a stack of files home with him. She'd gotten the briefest of peeks at them when he'd stepped inside the bathroom and he'd left them on the table. There were two files, each bearing a woman's name written in thick black marker. Rachel didn't recognize the names – Sarah and Charlotte – which seemed to confirm the rumor that there were two newcomers to the women's camp. But before she'd been able to dig into them at all, he'd rushed out of the bathroom and snatched the files off the table before heading out again. He didn't seem to care whether she'd seen them or not.

At noon today, he'd returned with the dress and told her to get ready for a very special party. A New Year's Eve party. He was in the bathroom now, primping for tonight's event. She'd debated trying to take him in the bathroom, naked, his face dusted with baby powder, but she froze. She didn't know if she would really go through with it. Could she kill a man, even a monster like Miles Chadwick, in cold blood? What if she hesitated? What if she screwed it up? He would skin her alive. And if she did manage to pull it off, would that bring about the desired result? Or would it accelerate her demise and that of the other women? And Rachel cared for these women, so much so that she couldn't bear to put their lives at risk.

But what if it did work? What if she stabbed him in the neck, what if she exacted justice for the dead world around her, what if he was the proverbial head of the snake, that without which the Citadel could not survive? They would be free.

Free to pursue whatever life they could cobble together in this new world.

She became aware of a presence behind her, but she acted as if she hadn't noticed him.

"Is the lady ready?" he said.

"I am," she replied, finally turning to face him. He was wearing a tuxedo, his skin pink and fresh from a decent scrubbing. His first one in a couple of days, if her nose was serving her well. The sweet stinging scent of Old Spice tickled her nose, and it reminded her of her father, when she used to give him the courtesy hug at the end of their semi-annual visits, wrapping her arms around him just long enough for it to qualify as a hug, and she could smell it on his clothes. She tried to recall the last time she'd seen him, and she tried to remember the length of the hug.

She didn't think about him much anymore. Not as much as she used to. And she thought that there'd been a chance when she'd finally gotten through to his voicemail. But day after day, the cell phone signal had sluiced away, like a slow drip from a faucet, until it was gone completely, and that had been that.

He was as dead to her as the world gone by.

COCKTAIL HOUR STARTED PROMPTLY at six.

They had walked to the party in almost total silence. As they'd exited the apartment, he had complimented her on her appearance, but it seemed forced, as though he were working through a checklist for a night on the town. She thanked him, and they remained quiet until they arrived at the party. Others were streaming in as they arrived, beautiful men and women dressed to the nines in what was likely the only New Year's Eve party on the face of the Earth. Before she could stop herself, her mind conjured up images of empty hotel ballrooms across the country, from sea to shining sea, and it made her sad.

Everyone was there, of course. This was a landmark moment for the Citadel, she supposed, closing the book on what had been a most eventful year for them. She imagined there would be speeches and glad-handing, and a lot of patting themselves on the back for a job well done this year. Oh, sure, the executions had been a messy affair, but all new businesses had challenges to face in their first year.

Look how far we've come. Look how many people we killed! Cross last year's resolution off the list because that mission had been mother-fucking accomplished. In Jesus' name, amen!

People seemed eager to interact with Chadwick, lining up two and three at a time for a chance to speak to the great man, issue good tidings, tell him how proud they were to be part of the Citadel, blah, blah, blah. She remained quiet, nodding a greeting when she was acknowledged by the others. As she glided through the party, she looked for other captives, but there were none. Chadwick was keeping her close, his arm clamped around her waist, making her feel very much the captive she'd been for these past few months.

He chatted with the others, but it was all surface work, one canned statement after another. *Doing great, really pleased with how things have gone, you've done terrific work.* It sounded like the words of a losing politician comforting his staff after he'd made the concessionary telephone call to his opponent. Complete with the fake smile, twin rows of pearly whites flashing every few seconds. He was charming, effusive, and terrifying.

Traffic at the bar was light. A few guests nursed strong drinks, but most stayed away. No one wanted to be falling-down drunk in front of the boss, she supposed. There was chit-chat, but it was muted. From the bits and pieces of conversation Rachel was able to distill from the other attendees, this was the first many of them had seen of Chadwick in some time.

At precisely seven o'clock, a bell tinkled, and the groups began to dissolve as everyone made their way to their seats. The room was set up for a formal dinner, but it was a very utilitarian design, lacking any levity or manufactured glee, the feel of a party thrown together at the last second. She had a seat on the dais, and she could feel the scorn, the heat from her captors who must have been wondering where exactly she fit in the pecking order, now that she was shacking up with the big kahuna.

There were twelve seats on the dais, six on each side of the podium. Two new faces joined her, replacing the pair of now-headless traitors from Chadwick's high command. She thought often of the sad little rebellion, wishing it had gone a different way, if only to buy her enough time to get herself and the other women out of here. She still wondered what secret Rogers had been preparing to divulge before Chadwick's men had stormed the warehouse.

Chadwick popped down to the bar and brought back two drinks, one for each of them. This seemed to open the floodgates, and before she could blink, the line at the bar was ten deep.

She accepted the scotch, neat, a double. She took a long drink, and it made her head swim, but it helped calm her nerves. He sat next to her, and they drank together for a few minutes in silence.

"Look at these people," he said, so softly, she wasn't sure she'd heard him correctly.

"What about them?" she asked.

"Never mind," he said. He lifted his glass, and his smile was back. This one seemed genuine, the grin of a man who was truly pleased with things.

"Where were you from?" he asked.

"I grew up in San Diego. Born in Richmond, Virginia."

"Ahh, the capital of the Confederacy," he said. "I'll drink to that. And your family?"

"They're dead, remember?"

He scrunched up his mouth, and his cheeks flushed. At first, she thought it was from rage, and that he might simply kill her there on the spot, but he simply looked away from her and down at his drink.

"That was insensitive of me," he said. "I apologize."

She looked back over the crowd, many of them armed now with their own tumblers of liquid courage.

"Well, I suppose it's time to address the troops."

He polished off his scotch and wiped his lips with his fingers. Before he got up, he reached under the table, just over her lap, and for a moment, her breath caught, as she feared that he might simply cop a feel right here in front of everyone, let her know that she was simply his property, that he could do with her as he pleased, whenever he goddamn well felt like it. She vowed that if he touched her she would plunge the butter knife lying next to her plate into some vital organ, an eye, his neck, whatever, the consequences of it all be damned. At least she would die knowing she'd gone down fighting.

She tensed as his hand rooted around under the table. It could only have been a few seconds, but the moment stretched out interminably as she waited for his cold, sweaty hand on her thigh or worse.

But again, he didn't touch her. He fiddled with something under the table, directly underneath her plate, before stepping over to the podium. She let out a quick sigh, her heart galloping, slamming against her rib cage as he approached the podium, her body icy with sweat. She trembled, and her breath came in shallow, ragged gasps.

She wondered what was under the table.

He tapped the microphone and immediately, the buzz of conversation died away. At a table near the front, Rachel could hear the crackle of ice cubes in a tumbler, sweaty as though with anticipation. A light clearing of the throat from somewhere in the back.

"Good evening, my fellow citizens," Chadwick said.

A long pause, long enough that the partygoers began exchanging glances. The moment drifted past oddity and into awkwardness, until even Rachel found herself shifting in her seat.

"What a year it has been," he said.

Chadwick began to clap, slowly, methodically, the pop of his hands echoing through the dining room like a metronome. A few moments later, the others on the dais joined in, and the applause spread across the room like the virus that had brought them all to this point in their lives. It was robust yet reserved. The way you might clap when hearing the name of the colostomy bag salesman of the year. Applause wearing its Sunday best.

He began to speak, issuing a series of platitudes. As he spoke, her curiosity got the better of her, and her hands drifted under the table. Her fingers danced along the grain of the cheap particle wood until she felt it. A bulky plastic bag, taped to the underside of the table. Whatever was inside the bag was irregularly shaped, about the size of a football. It was hard, smooth in the middle, with two protrusions on either side. She was careful not to dislodge it or make any sudden movements as Chadwick spoke.

She glanced up at him as he plowed through his speech, but he either hadn't noticed or didn't care about her exploratory mission. Her hands returned to her lap, but her thoughts remained fixated on the mysterious object under the table. She glanced to her left, toward the four other men on her side of the table. They, too, either hadn't noticed what she was doing or were uninterested in her reconnaissance. She wondered if there were plastic bags taped under their place settings as well.

Chadwick kept speaking, and she re-focused her attention on his speech, the way she might have watched the President deliver the State of the Union address in the old days. Paying attention at first, ooh, a bag of microwave popcorn sounds good, think I'll check my e-mail, and then coming back to the speech, and it sounding more or less the same than when she had tuned out.

"Now then," Chadwick was saying, "perhaps the blame lies with me."

A low murmur from the crowd now.

"Perhaps I didn't do this the right way."

He paused, and she stole a glance at him. A tear had broken loose from the corner of his eye, and he wiped it away with a finger before it had a chance to stream down his cheek. Rachel was on full alert now, the pit in her stomach growing deeper as the seconds ticked by.

"And that's why tonight, we begin anew."

He lifted a hand to his forehead and delivered a bizarre half-salute.

Then everything began to happen very fast.

Rachel detected movement from the corner of her eye. Four of the guests had gotten up from their seats, each streaming to a different corner of the room, where decorative pieces had been set up, topped with some kind of ornate covering. In one fluid, almost choreographed maneuver, the men yanked the covers clear like magicians and reached around to the back of the pieces.

Then Rachel realized what the item taped under her table was.

"Rachel!" Chadwick barked. "Under the table. Put it on right now!"

The room filled with a loud hissing noise, as though someone had dropped in a crateful of snakes, and when she blinked again, each of the men was wearing a gas mask. Her hands dove under the table, and she

wrenched the bag free. The room erupted into screams as people realized what was happening.

Ohshit, ohshit, ohshit!

She fumbled with the mask as the hissing continued. She fitted the
straps around the back of her head and tugged the faceplate down
around her nose and mouth. She reminded herself to breathe normally,
that the filter was taking care of whatever poison that Chadwick had just
unleashed on his people.

Once it was on, she froze, unsure of what to do. She glanced over at
Chadwick, now sporting his own mask, his hands clenched tight on
the sides of the podium. The lower half of his face was a cipher, virtually blank. No smile, no frown. She briefly considered attacking him
with the knife, but she dismissed the idea, as she couldn't risk the
mask being knocked from her face. So she simply watched the scene
before her unfold. To her right, the others on the dais also were
wearing masks, a police lineup of futuristic-looking bugs sitting calmly
at their seats as the scene unfolded before them. They sat there,
watching.

A cloud of gas filled the room as the terrified guests leapt from their
seats. Plates slid off tables, shattering on the floor with symphonic
crashes. A group at the back sprinted for the back door, which was
locked. A man desperately rattled the door handles, and for a moment, it
looked like his adrenaline might give him the edge he needed to rip it
open. But then the mob was upon him, dozens of people attacking the
door. Too many chefs in the kitchen. Just a mass of weight against a door
that opened toward them rather than away.

Rachel's eyes swung toward one of the corners, where a canister
continued unloading its poisonous cargo. Half a dozen people lay
writhing on the floor, overcome by the gas, their hands clawing at their
necks and faces. One of them, a woman that Rachel recognized, had a
smart idea to try and deactivate the canister, but she'd come up short
and she lay still at its base, her hand slapping gently at the metal.

Back at the door, screams and yelps of pain and panic amid the mass
of writhing, desperate bodies, as the gas continued to do its work. Some
gave up and staggered back toward the center of the room, trying something, anything to escape. One covered his face with a cloth napkin, but
it only bought him a few moments, nothing more. Gripped by a terrible

coughing fit, he dropped first to a knee, then to both knees, and then lay down and curled up into a fetal position.

A gunshot rang out, its roar inside the room deafening. Rachel dove to the floor as a squeal of pain erupted near her.

"Shoot them! Shoot them!" she heard someone call out.

She stayed low on the ground, between the podium and the dais, which gave her a tiny sliver of a view toward the mob at the door. One of the doomed guests had come to the party armed, and was doing his level best to take revenge on his would-be executioners. He was down on a knee, firing blindly, his face buried in the crook of his arm.

"Kill them all!" another voice screeched. Sounded like Chadwick, his voice coated with panic.

The air filled with the staccato whisper of machine-gun fire. Two men who'd been stationed at the corners drew toward the pulsing mass of humanity and raked the mob with their machine pistols. The screams ramped up in intensity as the shooters continued the slaughter, cutting down every last person trying to escape.

Rachel shut her eyes tight and tried to block out the screams of the dying; it was like watching the plague's march through humanity concentrated into a few seconds. Eventually, the guns fell silent, and her sobs were the only sound in the room.

"Stand up," Chadwick said.

She was on her hands and knees, her face toward the ground. She couldn't bear to look at him.

"Fuck you," she croaked.

He kicked her in her side, not hard enough to do damage, but sharply enough to sting, and she dissolved back into the floor. After taking a moment to catch her breath, she climbed to her feet, afraid his next reaction would be to strip the mask from her face.

"You're going to treat me with some goddamn respect," Chadwick hissed at her. "Or I'll make you suffer like you've never known."

Her shoulders sagged. She felt broken, finally, as though Chadwick had reached inside her and snapped her will to fight clean in half. If he was willing to do this to his own people, his own kind, what did he have in store for her? For the others? And, of course, his inattention toward her in the past few days now made perfect sense.

She felt the presence of the other survivors around her. A hand at her back, and she fell in line with the others as they made their way off the dais. She kept her eyes down, in no rush to view the carnage before her. She heard a moan to her left, which was greeted by a quick burst of gunfire that silenced it forever.

She stood by Chadwick's side as his soldiers cleared the doorway of the bodies. It was as bad as anything she'd seen during the plague. The heavy-caliber bullets had done so much damage that it was difficult to tell where one body ended and another began. They worked silently and quickly, some of them slipping in the pools of blood, then getting right back up and dragging the victims out of their way. By the time they were done, they were shiny with it, their clothes sticky and glistening.

They lined up in front of their leader like a group of butcher's apprentices.

"Let's go," he said. "It's time for phase two."

49

dam Fisher spied on the building from a distance, trying to wrap his head around the formally dressed partiers arriving for what, unbeknownst to him and them, would be their very last meal, their very last anything. He'd been inside the walls for more than twenty-four hours now. He'd spent most of the evening slinking in between and around the buildings like fog, concluding that he was going to have to start taking bigger chances if he wanted to get anywhere. Otherwise, he ran the risk of running out of supplies, out of water, or just stumbling into a patrol and getting himself captured or killed before he accomplished anything. At dark, he'd made his move toward the developed sections of the compound.

No pain, no gain, as his father had used to say. His father had had a lot of sayings, most of them angry bullshit, but that one Adam had agreed with.

No pain. No gain.

He was in the east-central section of the compound again, near the security fencing ringing the array of generators that powered the Citadel. It was dark, the night gripping him tight with its chill as the snow continued to fall. He had deduced that there weren't that many people who lived here. Oh, he was vastly outnumbered, of course; of that he had no doubt. But based on the ambient noise, the number of patrols, the general aura of the place, he thought the population numbered in the dozens, a couple of hundred at the most.

He wasn't sure if this helped him or not. The larger the population, the better the odds would have been that he could simply blend in with the citizenry at large. But the smaller population made it more likely he'd be identified as an intruder.

As evening had leached the last weak light from the sky, he'd spotted a man and woman approaching his position behind an empty storage shed that he'd found the night before. They walked casually. The man wore a tuxedo, the woman a long blue dress.

He prepared to follow them, but just as they passed his hiding spot, he'd noticed a slightly larger group approaching from the same direction. They, too, were dressed to the nines, and Adam felt his heart begin to race. He didn't know why he was getting excited; just the idea that he might be witnessing something important unfolding was fuel enough for his flagging engine of hope.

Over the course of the next quarter hour, he counted no less than fifty people, all migrating west toward the center of the complex. When the coast had finally cleared, he fell in behind them, marking their progress as he slipped down alleyways and through clusters of trees. About a quarter mile west, the smaller groups began clumping together into a larger mass in front of a low-slung building near the intersection with the road that cut through the middle of the complex. They filed inside, their chatter growing in intensity as it did when crowds began to gather, and a thought took hold in his mind. He checked his watch again, looking at the date rather than the time.

31 DEC

New Year's Eve.

A New Year's Eve party.

A wave of rage swept through him. Killers and kidnappers and God knew what else, and they were going to put on their Sunday best and dance the night away. The last five months had been a post-apocalyptic wet dream for these psychopaths, their dark fantasies fulfilled beyond anything they could have hoped for.

He kept his eyes peeled, but he didn't expect to see his companions. He tried not to let them dominate his thoughts, but he couldn't help but wonder if Rachel and Sarah had met. What would they think of each other? How would Rachel react to the news that he was still alive, that he had used Sarah and Charlotte as bait? Did they regret coming on this mission? Had it seemed a much better idea in theory, from the safety of their camp?

Adam had a nice line of sight toward the main door. He didn't know what he would learn by maintaining this stakeout, but at least he'd gotten a sense of their overall numbers. Maybe he'd wait until they were all good and sloshed, walk in and party along with them.

Maybe they'd just tell him where the women were being held!

This wishful thinking buoyed him as he bobbed slowly along the river of time, every second and minute stretching out into an eternity. It was cold, perhaps the coldest night he'd experienced yet this season, and as he huddled between the drum and the exterior wall, the chill burrowed into his bones until he couldn't feel anything, pushing his outerwear to their limits. A cold wind was blowing in from the west, and the snow continued to pile up. Another night of precipitation, and he'd probably die of exposure.

A few minutes past seven, the howl of the wind spiked in intensity, but, oddly, it wasn't blowing any harder. He primed his ears, cupping his hands around them. It wasn't wind. The howls were coming from inside the building. Screams.

Terror gripped him like a vise, the fear of not knowing what the hell was going on. Perhaps they'd brought in the captives from another entrance and were executing them as part of the festivities. What if Rachel was in there, dying right now?

Then gunfire. Multiple shots, one after the other. That was followed by the steady chatter of automatic weapon fire. It was over before Adam could crack the shell of terror that had hardened around him. The screams died away, as though someone had pulled the plug on the speakers during a horror movie, and Adam was left with the ghostly echoes of the howls.

He was afraid.

He was afraid of whatever had happened inside that building, he was afraid of what had happened to the world, of what the world would become. He was afraid that the world had already become a dead place inhabited by dead souls. People immune to the virus but susceptible to the horrors man was capable of without the watchful eye of civilization. The thing that had inoculated mankind from the evil inherent in itself.

That's what civilization was, really.

Mankind's immune system, creating antibodies that protected the people. Law. Order. Community. The thing that let kids grow up and play with trucks and dolls and have first dates and go to movies and become interior designers or bus drivers or surgeons or soccer players. The thing that let them devote their leisure time not to primitive survival but to strengthening the body and the mind. And now that membrane of protection was gone, erased, ironically enough, by a plague, leaving the patient sick and vulnerable.

Few subjects had fascinated Adam in his life more than the human immune system. The idea that the human body could adapt, on its own or with the assistance of vaccinations, to virtually any pathogen had been nothing short of revelatory, a single point of focus that had hustled him along a path toward a life in medicine. What really took his breath away, the thing that made his mind spin like a top, was that the body protected itself against microscopic invaders with a version of the invader itself. Much like civilization. Controlled chaos, in an organized world where there were rules and freedoms alike, where people were even free to kill one another as long as they were willing to pay the price, kept the civilization healthy. That's what immunity was, really. Controlled chaos. And when you had a Hitler or Osama bin Laden, the immune system kicked in, strafing the malignancy until it was destroyed.

That's what these doomsday nuts didn't understand. They probably envisioned some perfect society that they controlled, where thoughts and actions were homogenous. But it didn't work that way. To stay healthy, the human body required exposure to a variety of pathogens, both naturally and via vaccination. Civilization needed the same. You'd always have your sexual predators and suicide bombers. It kept civilization strong, on its toes.

But without civilization, you had children slaughtered with impunity and Freddie Briggs destroying an entire future with no way to undo it. And he was afraid that it would continue this way, that they'd all toddle along until there was no way back. And these last few months, struggling to survive, his desperate search for Rachel, would be nothing more than epilogue. That's why he couldn't fail here. He had to find Rachel and whomever else was here. As stupid as it sounded, the good guys had to win.

The door to the building swung open, pushing Adam deeper into the shadows of the storage shed. A small group emerged, about a dozen in total. All, or nearly all, were men. There were a few shorter people at the center of the throng. He looked for Rachel, but it was too dark to make out faces. Adam closed his eyes and primed his ears to pick up on the discussion that was underway. The chatter was heavy and animated, the tone of people who'd just experienced something dramatic. As the seconds ticked by, the noise softened and a single voice rose up over the others.

"You, take five with you to the dorm," a voice said. "Bring the ones we talked about to the lab. Kill the rest."

Adam's brain lit up like a pinball machine.

"You mean to do the procedures tonight?" a voice asked.

"Yes," the leader said. "Tonight. The time is right for our re-birth. After all, it is a new year, and there's no New Year's show on ABC tonight."

A small ripple of laughs.

The group split like a mitotic cell; about half staked a westward course, the rest, including the leader, followed a pathway behind the building, back toward the generator field. That must have been where the lab was. Adam had no choice; he had to follow the group en route to the dorm, where many women faced certain slaughter, including, very possibly, the women he loved best in the world.

His hands shook as he checked his weapon; Sarah's M4 was locked and loaded, and the spare magazines were secure in the inside pocket of his coat. Again, he was dancing on a razor's edge. His only decent card was the element of surprise. He couldn't act too soon, lest he blow his chance to find where the women were being held. But the longer he waited, the closer to doom the dial of fate would spin.

Adam emerged from the cover of the shed and followed the dorm-bound killers.

～

HE KEPT a safe distance as they moved north across the compound, his heart beating so fiercely he felt like the main character from the Edgar Allan Poe story. They made no effort to travel silently, and so the sounds of their passage easily swallowed up his own. For the most part. About a quarter mile into the trip, Adam stepped on a large branch hidden under a layer of snow, which snapped with a sharp crack. The man at the back, trailing just behind the main group, paused for a minute, and Adam froze, silently cursing his stupidity, his dumb luck, what he hoped was not his destiny. To come so close to his goal and to die just before the end.

But after a quick glance over his shoulder, the man resumed his trek and jogged to catch up with the others. Adam let out an inaudible sigh, tears of relief welling in his eyes. As he continued the pursuit, his eyes bounced from ground to group, carefully scanning for any wayward tree branches or piles of leaves.

A sense of familiarity began edging its way into him, like a tide just coming in and darkening the hot sands. The hours he'd spent combing the compound had been worth it, he realized. A tree. A curvature of the land. He was becoming familiar with it the way you got to know the city you'd just moved to for that new job. You got out there in it and wandered around and got lost and found your way home again. You found the little Chinese restaurant with the good cashew chicken and the place that did your laundry just right.

Half a mile up the road, the group angled to the northwest, back toward where Adam remembered spotting the lake. They were on a path ringing the lake now, looping around the southwestern edge of the shore. There was a building up ahead, one he hadn't seen during his previous incursion in the lake's vicinity. It was as forgettable a structure as he'd ever laid eyes on, very little else besides four walls and a roof. The building was protected by a square of industrial chain-link fencing. A portable spotlight, powered by a buzzing generator, kept the building illuminated. One of the men unlocked the gate and the group streamed inside, leaving the gate open behind them.

"Bring them out here," one said grimly. It was very quiet on this side of the compound and their voices carried a long way in the darkness. "We'll do this outside. Less mess to clean up."

Adam's stomach churned.

Five of the men went in the building, leaving one behind. Adam weighed his options; if he struck now, he could eliminate one of the threats against him, but if it went bad, then he may hasten the women's demise. He decided to wait.

He crept closer toward the gate, but held his ground near a row of bushes just beyond the fencing. It was as close as he could get and remain hidden. He was about twenty yards from the entrance of the building. Close, but he'd have to move very quickly to maintain the element of surprise when the time came to strike. He crouched down and kept his eyes fixed on the lone guard, passing the time by imagining what it would feel like to kill the man.

He didn't have to wait long. Not ten minutes later, the door to the building opened, and women began streaming outside, their hands on their heads. His heart was in overdrive now, as he desperately scanned their faces, looking for the ones he'd begun to fear he'd never see again. Out they came, one after another, some bearing fresh injuries, their eyes hollow with shock and fear.

After another half dozen or so, Sarah.

His breath caught in his throat. In the harsh bone-white luminosity of the spotlight, he could see the swollen cheek, the spot of blood above her right eyebrow.

She was working, he could tell, surveying the scene, eyes sliding from side to side. By now, he supposed, she'd given up hope that he'd be coming for her. As was her wont, she was going to take matters into her own hands. Part of that came from her awareness of her own mortality. And that frightened him. But she looked okay. She didn't look like she was too badly hurt. Her eyes sat hard in her head, like two bits of steel.

Charlotte came out two behind Sarah, her head down, her gait slow and tentative, and Adam wanted to die for letting her put herself at risk like this. He turned his attention back to the door, waiting for the thing that would have made their risk worth it. After all, he'd asked them to give their lives for her. And Mike already had. For him. True, they'd volunteered, but he could have rejected their offer. Had Rachel's one life been worth their three?

He thought about this as he waited for Rachel to emerge.

But no one followed Charlotte out.

Maybe a group of stragglers was still on its way.

Thirty seconds passed. Then sixty.

No Rachel.

Dread wormed its way through his insides like a colony of termites chewing their way through hidden floor joists.

Had he been wrong all along?

Was Rachel not here?

Focus, he told himself. Focus. Sarah *was* here. Charlotte *was* here.

And if he didn't do something soon, they'd all be dead.

One of the men barked at the women, and although Adam couldn't quite make out the words, the meaning was clear enough. His admonition drew whimpers and screams from several of them. The other men grabbed the women by their elbows and shoved them toward the wall of the building.

A captive turned and fled; she made it a few steps before her feet got tangled underneath her, and she tumbled to the ground in a heap. She lay there weeping. A man walked up behind her and fired a single bullet into her head. Then he fired another round into the air.

"Shut the fuck up!"

The remaining women fell silent as they stood at the wall. Some of them had dropped their heads, paralyzed by fear. There were dozens of them, upwards of fifty in all. The men lined them up ten across; it reminded Adam of the old Miss America pageants, fifty young women lined up, bearing satin sashes emblazoned with the name of the state they so proudly represented. But there was no talent show, no swimsuit competition here. One of the men stepped forward and, after some preliminary instructions, called out six names. The six women stepped forward and were led like sheep to the edge of the yard. They huddled together, hugging, whispering, some of them crying. One of the men watched them like a hawk, his machine gun up and twitchy.

Then each of the men took his turn, roaming through the lines, examining each captive before making a selection. Adam found he could barely breathe as he watched this bizarre recruitment unfold. He noticed that the chosen women tended to be younger, fitter, more attractive. As it always had been with men and women.

Three women were selected, including Charlotte, leaving three men to choose. The first was a tall, thin man, his face angular, his hair cropped close to the head. He took his time, studying each one closely before shaking his head and moving on. Adam's jaw clenched tight when he reached Sarah. He rubbed her face with the back of his hand, a sign of affection that earned him a vicious fist to the chest and a trip to the ground.

The other men laughed, and Adam was certain Sarah had just signed her death warrant. But the man got up and dusted himself off. He took Sarah by the elbow and yanked her out of line. He looked over his shoulder and said something to the others, but Adam could not hear what it was.

Sarah joined the other women who'd been selected by the gate. They held hands, forming a chain of women who stood in solidarity with one another. The draft continued, like children selecting kickball teams at recess, until each of the men had selected a captive. But that still left nearly forty women, and Adam had a pretty good idea what was about to happen to them.

He couldn't wait any longer.

Adam burst from the cover of the bushes and rushed the shooters at an angle. He came in low, which he hoped would buy him a few seconds before they spotted him. He raised the M4 but held his fire until he had a clear shot at the men. It had been a while since Sarah had taught him to use it, and he had to remind himself to account for the recoil. It didn't help that his hands were shaking badly. Sarah's handgun was tucked safely into his waistband; he just hoped he'd be able to get it to her so he could even the odds.

A singular, terrible thought zoomed through his mind as he kept his finger on the trigger.

Haphazardly firing this gun was the only chance these women had.

He fired at the two shooters nearest him, who fell as the bullets sliced into their flanks; screams erupted as things began to happen very quickly.

50

Sarah closed her eyes and prepared to die.

She squeezed Alison Willis' hand twice, to make sure the woman understood. They looked at each other, and Alison nodded. Alison repeated the signal down the line, and one by one, the women nodded, ever so slightly. They had come to the end, and here, in the dark, in the cold, at the end of the world, they would make their stand. She wasn't going to let these men slaughter forty innocent women. Not without a fight. She would almost certainly die, but death here was better than what awaited her. And she would finally win her sweet release.

I win, Huntington's. I win.

She felt sick to her stomach; Adam would never know how close he'd come to finding his daughter. To her great regret, she hadn't met Rachel. But the other women spoke about her like a beloved friend who'd moved out of the neighborhood. About her strength and courage, about her quiet manner. She'd tended to the sick ones, she'd kept their spirits up when they descended into despair. But all Sarah knew of her whereabouts was that the group's leader had taken a liking to her, and perhaps had moved her to his quarters. Somewhere deep in the compound.

She'd known all along that this was a suicide mission. She was glad she'd done it, though. It had been a pretty good idea to use them as bait, she had to admit to herself, and she'd been right. But there had been too many unknowns beyond that to believe that this was anything other than a one-way trip.

The other women being held here, they'd really been something. They'd taken her and Charlotte in as one of their own; they were thrilled to learn that Nadia was still alive. And now, they stood here, watching these men finish up their impromptu draft. It had been worth it, though. Just knowing what Rachel had done for these women had made it all worthwhile. She wished desperately there was some way that Adam would know about her work here.

The leader of the group called for the other men to join him and they spread out, lining up in a firing formation, not ten feet from the terrified women. Would they just stand there as the men prepared to fire, she wondered. Would they try to run? Were they so paralyzed by fear that the fight-flight connection had been severed like a power line in a storm?

Now.

It had to be now.

She let out a primal scream, deep from the depths of her soul and together, she and the others launched their suicidal attack on their would-be killers. They were a swarm, a single entity, a whole greater than the sum of its parts. *E pluribus unum* and all that. She hoped they could take out a couple of them before they were overwhelmed by the guns. As they ran, hand in hand, chewing up the ground between herself and the shooters, she heard the staccato burst of small-arms fire, that familiar rat-tat-tat that clicked in her brain like a key sliding home into its lock. It was an M4A1, and not just any; it was her M4A1.

Adam was here.

Across the way, she saw him running toward the group, the tongue of flame from the M4 bright like a meteor in the night sky. Two of the shooters went down before they realized what was happening; the other four turned their focus toward this unexpected assailant and ignored the doomed women.

"Adam!" she screamed.

He flung something toward her, and she watched it arc, end over end, through the night sky. It glinted in the harsh sodium light illuminating the cold steel. She reached up as it descended toward her, a runaway satellite that might save them all. It hit her hand awkwardly, the buzz of pain shooting up the length of her arm, and toppled to the ground. She dropped down and retrieved the gun.

When she came back up, ready to fire, the scene had dissolved into chaos, reagents swirling together to form some new unknown solution. She found a target, dead ahead, one of the bastards firing indiscriminately at a group of women running for the edge of the building. She fired once; the bullet slammed into the man's back and he seized up like he'd touched a live wire. His gun clattered to the ground, and his lifeless body followed a moment later.

Sarah scampered for the dead man's gun, her body buzzing. A chance. That's all she'd wanted. A chance. No guarantees. No promises. Just a chance. She scooped up the rifle and found cover behind the southwest corner of the building. From there, she fired a burst, dropping another shooter with a shot to the head.

The air was metallic as the surviving killers began exterminating the women, many of whom were pinned near the building. Screams of pain and horror filled the night. From the other side of the building, she heard the M4 firing again, and she was hopeful they had the shooters pinned in.

"Run!" she screamed. "Run, girls, run!"

She paused again to wipe sweat from her eyes. After clearing her vision, she took stock of the scene. One of the shooters remained upright and had retreated away from the building; she cut him down with a burst from the M4. Some of the women began streaming indoors, drawing pursuit from two more surviving shooters.

She hugged the wall and picked her way toward the door.

Movement. Across the way. She looked over and saw Adam approaching the building. His gun was up, but his eyes were focused on the ground, which was littered with bodies. At least a dozen women lay dead, including Alison. She looked at them and reminded herself that these women were doomed from the start. They'd never have been able to save them all.

But there were still more they could save.

Adam nodded toward the building; she responded with her own nod. She wanted to grab him, hold him tightly. He looked exhausted, gaunt, his eyes shiny.

"You OK?" he asked.

"Fine."

They kissed lightly and continued inside. Two short bursts of gunfire echoed through the building. The barracks were wide open; there would be no place for the women to hide. It would be easy pickings. But then she cleared the short foyer and saw something amazing. Both shooters were on the ground, dead. Pools of blood spread out from their heads. Erin Thompson held one of the guns, the barrel still smoking. The look in her eyes was one of rage. Justice for these women, for all the women that lay dead outside. Another woman, whose name Sarah did not know, held the other gun propped on her shoulder.

Erin looked at Sarah and smiled. But the smile disappeared a moment later, and the gun was now pointed directly at her.

"Whoa, whoa!" she said.

"Behind you," Erin said, the words like smoking coals.

She glanced up and realized that Adam was just off her shoulder.

"No!" she said. "This is Rachel's father."

Erin's face fell, and a ripple of gasps echoed through the room.

"Her father?"

Adam nodded.

Charlotte broke loose of the pack and threw her arms around Adam. She didn't say anything; she didn't shed a tear. She simply held him tight for a moment.

"Do you know where she is?" he asked.

Erin burst into tears, and Adam expected to get the news he'd been dreading.

"I don't," she said. "They came and took her two days ago. We haven't seen her since."

Sarah turned and hugged Adam tightly. He wrapped his arms around her, and for a moment, for just a brief moment, equilibrium had returned to her life. It was fleeting, the way a broken wall clock could give the correct time twice a day, but for that moment, everything felt right.

When they released the embrace, she saw the women had filled in around them in a semi-circle, two and three deep. They murmured their thanks, but they appeared to be in shock from their ordeal, from the long captivity to the sudden spasm of violence that had set them free.

"How many of them are there?" Adam asked.

"We're not sure," Erin said. "Somewhere between a hundred and one fifty. My name's Erin by the way."

"Adam," he replied.

"Rachel's father," she marveled.

"First let's check the others," Adam said. "There may be some wounded out there."

"What if the others come?"

"I don't think that's going to happen," Adam said, flashing back to the sounds of pain and dying inside the building he'd scouted earlier.

Adam led them back through the foyer and outside, where they found a killing field. Bodies were scattered across the hardscrabble, blood soaking the snow like a cherry snowcone, the work of a sick impressionistic painter. They spread out in twos and threes, looking for signs of life, for anyone that might be within the scope of saving. But the killers' weapons had been too powerful, too devastating. The heavy-caliber bullets had ground their victims into slabs of meat.

His eyes fixed on one of the dead women. She lay on her back, her eyes open wide but empty of life. She'd caught a burst in the upper chest, the bullets stitching their way along the right side of her neck, shredding her carotid artery and destroying her jaw. If she'd suffered, it hadn't been for very long. He took her hand in his own and stroked it gently. This brave woman had deserved far better than she'd gotten. All of them had. It hadn't been enough for them to watch the world disintegrate, to watch their families die horrible deaths in front of them; no, they'd had to end up here.

He felt Sarah's hand on his shoulder. He glanced up as she took a knee next to him.

"You sure you're OK?" he asked.

"Fine," she said. "Truth be told, it was pretty uneventful until tonight. They drew some blood, that kind of thing. Where's Mike?"

Adam shook his head.

"Damn," Sarah whispered.

"So what is this place?"

Sarah shook her head and looked away. The look on her face scared him.

"What? Did they do something to you?"

"No," she said. "Like I said, pretty routine stuff."

"Then what?"

"Something one of the women said," Sarah said. "Rachel told her."

"Rachel told her what?"

She opened her mouth to speak and then closed it again, delivering instead a sad, wan smile. She cocked her head to the side as she searched for the words.

"That they started it."

Adam heard the words as they tumbled from her mouth. He felt his knees buckle, and he eased backwards down to his bottom. He felt dizzy and hot, despite the cold that was socked in around them.

"It," he repeated.

Sarah nodded and Adam was up on his feet.

It.

The plague. The mother-fucking plague. The end of all things. The mommies and daddies and babies and poets and Thanksgiving and pizza delivery guys and accountants and interpreters and jazz music and whomever had invented French fries and 200,000 years of human progress from the discovery of fire through putting a man in goddamned outer space, all wiped out in the blink of an eye. The empty houses and restaurants and schools and churches, riddled with the wasted bodies of the dead in every city and town and village in the world. It hadn't been a bad evolutionary break, an eff-you from Mother Nature for digging too deep into some tropical jungle in the pursuit of more land for a new resort. It had been a war against humanity, one declared and waged and won before they'd even had the first chance to defend themselves.

He felt dizzy again and he bent over, placed his hands on his knees.

"Is that possible?" she asked. "That someone did this on purpose?"

"I never thought it would be possible on such a big scale," he said in between deep breaths. "But I just don't know."

He scanned the bodies for one of the shooters and stalked across the field toward the dead man; then he reared back and kicked it as hard as he could. He kicked it again, and again, and again. The rage coursed through his veins like hot lead as the magnitude of what Sarah had told him settled in on him. It all came rushing back, from the moment that Kate Sanders from Annapolis had knocked on his door at Holden Beach through his surreal bike ride through the city streets to his anger at the goddamned good guys for not catching them before it was too late.

All those years we'd spent worried about little bottles of shampoo and taking our shoes off in the security line, Adam thought, and here, in secret, these guys had been as busy as bees, building their dark dream.

"Did Rachel ever say how she knew?"

"A few weeks ago, there was some kind of uprising," Sarah said. "A breakaway group tried to recruit Rachel, and they confessed to her. But this Chadwick guy, he sniffed it out, executed everyone but Rachel. He seemed to have taken a shine to her."

Adam felt a chill ripple through his sweat-soaked body. A thought began to scratch at him like a puppy pawing at a door.

"Did she spend a lot of time with him?" he asked.

"That's what the other women said," she replied. "They think he took her to his quarters."

The thought broke through, the puppy clearing the fence and running free, and all of a sudden, he knew where he had to go.

"I know where they are."

51

Eighteen women, including Sarah and Charlotte, had survived the massacre at the barracks. Sixteen had died. No matter how many times he reminded himself that they would all have died without his rescue attempt, he felt like he'd made a terrible mistake, and their deaths haunted Adam Fisher for the rest of his days. But as the surviving women gathered together, he saw no blame in their worn, weathered faces.

"Do you mind if I say something?" one of the women asked. She was a short, stout woman, sturdy through and through. She looked so tired.

Adam shook his head.

"Ladies," she said. "We've become a family these last few months. And our family has suffered a terrible loss. But I want to tell you something. When we rushed the shooters, I was ready to die. I was fucking terrified, but it would've been worth it to try. To get these SOB's and rip their balls off."

Muted laughter.

"So we mourn our fallen friends," she said. "But know that they died fighting. They died on their feet. They died for the rest of us. But we're still inside these shitty walls. So we owe it to them to keep fighting until we're free."

A chorus of savage cheers went up with the force of fireworks.

"I need to find Rachel," Adam said as the cheers died out. "The rest of you need to go, get out of here. There's a group of us on a farm. There's room there for all of you. We're trying to rebuild. I can't promise a lot of amenities, but it's safe. Or as safe as anything is these days."

"You know I'm with you," Sarah said.

"Like Chewbacca and Han Solo," he said.

"Who's Chewbacca in this little scenario?" she asked.

"Well, obviously, I'm Han," Adam said, for which he earned a stiff punch in the shoulder.

"I'm in, too," Charlotte said.

"No," Adam said. "You've done enough. I've already asked too much of you."

"But-"

"No buts," Adam said. "Besides, I want you to lead everyone back to the farm. We'll meet up with you after we get Rachel."

"But-"

He waved Charlotte to the side for a private discussion. She followed, her arms crossed, a look of pain on her face. Sarah joined them.

"I need you to go back to the farm," Adam said. "This thing Sarah and I are doing, we have do it alone. By all rights, you should probably be dead by now. It would've been my fault. And the world is going to need you in it. You're going to have to lead."

She looked at Sarah, her eyes wide with longing.

"No, sweetie," Sarah said. "He's right. Adam is right. You're too important."

Charlotte's eyes filled with tears as the finality of the decision slammed home.

"W-what if I never see you again?"

Adam and Sarah glanced at each other, but they had no response to her question.

"Promise me you'll make it back," she said.

Sarah again didn't reply, instead wrapping the girl up in a fierce hug. They both cried silent tears, and Adam felt his own throat catch.

"I know," Charlotte said, her words thick with grief and tears, "that's a dumb thing to say. I can't make you promise."

"Go on now," Adam said. "Load up these trucks and get the hell out of here. You know the way back to the farm?"

She nodded, wiping her face clear with her hands.

Fifteen minutes later, the women had loaded into three of the Suburbans parked near the barracks. It took a while to find the keys, which had been scattered among their would-be killers' bodies, but they had finally tracked them down. The women were packed in tight, like a crowded city bus, but they didn't seem to mind. Not a bit. There were a few laughs, and the nervous chatter of a group on an exciting new journey. The engines roared to life and the trucks pulled away one by one, following Adam's directions to get back to the main gate. With any luck, they'd be at the farm before midnight.

Adam and Sarah watched the taillights wink out of view. As the trailing vehicle disappeared around the bend, Sarah took his hand in hers. A few moments later, the sound of the engines faded away, leaving them alone in the dark graveyard that the Citadel had become. He looked down at her, his jaw set tight.

"Let's finish this goddamn thing," she said.

He squeezed her hand.

THEY TREKKED EAST-SOUTHEAST, cutting across the north-south road and behind the generator field. It hummed along, powering a community coming apart at the seams. There was a wide dirt pathway running alongside the fence line, well worn with tire tracks. At the end of the fencing, they passed a locked gate, which seemed to be the primary maintenance access to the generator field. It looked like the fence surrounding Evergreen's power plant. He realized with some sadness that it would be a long time before the world could rely on electricity again.

Electricity had been a feature of a technologically advanced society, which they no longer were. In many ways, society had regressed to infancy. And that meant re-learning everything. Starting over. It had been folly to think that they could just continue on the way they had simply by dint of finding Evergreen. Food and water, shelter, everything would have to be done anew. They'd have to adapt. It made him sad, but it was good to be free of the false promise of a fallen world.

"How are you feeling?" he whispered as they drew closer to their destination.

"It's fine," she said, but her answer lacked conviction.

He didn't have to inquire any further. Her disease had begun to make itself known. Well, he thought. That was just another thing they would adapt to.

"Where are we headed?"

"I saw two groups tonight," Adam said. "The one that came to you, and another smaller group that went inside a building near this development. I think Rachel was in that group."

"Any idea what they were up to?"

"No. But I think that something very bad happened. Some kind of slaughter."

"Maybe they turned on each other," she said.

"Maybe."

They curled around the eastern edge of the generator array and moved south, toward the road that led back to his storage shed. Their eyes swept the landscape for threats, but nothing was moving but the swirl and dance of snowflakes, peppering their eyelashes and stinging their cheeks with icy kisses. No words were exchanged, as there was no telling how far their voices would carry across the snowpack.

They reached the shed unmolested and paused to survey the scene. There were two sets of sloppy tracks in the thin layer of snow. Sarah pointed at them, and Adam nodded. She checked her weapon and started to move across the street; Adam grabbed her by the elbow and turned her toward him. He held her face in between his gloved hands.

"Wait," he whispered.

"What?"

"Happy new year."

She leaned in and kissed him hard.

"Never forget how much I love you," she said.

She didn't wait for a reply; she turned back and scampered across the silent, windswept road. Adam fell in behind her as she tracked the messy footprints cutting north between the building from which the group had emerged and another building just to its west.

Their pace slowed as they moved deeper into the shadows, approaching a boxy, one-story building that Adam hadn't seen before. A single sentry was posted at the door, clumsily smoking a cigarette through heavily gloved hands. He was armed, but his rifle was slung over his shoulder. They watched for a quarter of an hour as he maintained his lonely watch. No one else entered or exited the building.

"I have an idea," she whispered into his ear. "Stick your gun in my back and follow my lead."

She bounced out of the shadows, her hands on her head, overcome with a bout of sad tears. Adam understood and followed, pushing the barrel of the rifle into her back.

"Who's there?" the sentry called out.

"This one's being a bit difficult," Adam said, hoping his voice wasn't as shaky as it felt.

"Where are the others?" he asked.

With each snippet of conversation, Adam and Sarah drew closer to their prey.

"They're coming," Adam replied. "This one caused quite the ruckus."

"Nothing's ever eas- hey, who the hell are you?"

The guard's eyes went wide and his hands clambered for the rifle, but the gloves made for difficult work. Sarah was on him like a tiger. She crippled him with a devastating kick to the knee, buckling it in a direction it wasn't meant to turn. He dropped to the ground, where Sarah snapped his neck with a vicious corkscrew twist. His body twitched, once, and fell to the ground.

Together, they pulled his body away from the door and deposited him on the side of the building, out of view. Sarah searched his pockets and removed his walkie-talkie. After combing through the channels, hearing nothing but static, she pocketed it. The gun she threw into the snow. Keeping their backs to the wall, they slinked back around toward the front door.

"Inside?" she asked.

Adam toyed with the idea of waiting for the group to come back out, but there was no telling what might happen to Rachel if they didn't attempt a rescue now. They would soon know that something had gone terribly wrong with the executions, and then all bets would be off. He pointed firmly at the door, and Sarah nodded her assent.

Adam reached out for the door, wondering what they would do if they found it locked. But the knob turned easily, as though the building couldn't wait for them to enter. He opened it slowly, an inch at a time. The door opened onto a darkened corridor, silent and dim.

The air was redolent with the clean, sharp smell of disinfectant. Some kind of medical facility, perhaps their famous clinic. There was something disquieting about the place, knowing that Rachel was in here, now, under cover of night. Something that whispered suffering or experimentation. They continued down the hallway, Adam's heart slamming against his ribs like a jackhammer, his mouth dry.

They passed by a few small offices, all of them dark and locked. The building was larger than it looked outside; the structure must have stretched up to the southern edge of the generator field. Ahead of them, the darkness abated a bit. They came to the end of the corridor, the mouth of which opened onto a large control room, also quiet and abandoned. There were three rows of individual workstations, and large monitors hung on the walls of the rectangular room.

Here, a dark voice in his mind whispered.

It happened here.

The apocalypse had been midwifed into the world in this building.

He felt Sarah's hand tapping him on the shoulder, directing his chin upward to the near wall. The front pages of a dozen newspapers had been mounted behind glass, a bizarre, twisted museum-like display. They bore the familiar headlines, their oversized fonts virtually screaming the terrible events of the previous August.

CDC: "No Progress" On Cure

Report: China Launches Nuke Attack On Iran, Russia

MASS BURIALS UNDERWAY

And so on. Adam felt sick to his stomach and looked away; he couldn't bear to read another headline from the world in its death throes.

In the dim light, Adam could just make out splotches of water, leading toward the far edge of the room. Sarah followed his gaze and picked up the trail there. The puddles led to a small door, nestled just under the darkened screen. Adam crossed the room, his gun up and ready. Sarah trailed close behind, keeping an eye on the rear flank.

The door was stark white and bore the universal symbol for biohazard, three connected rings superimposed over the center of a fourth. Underneath that, the following words were stenciled: BIOSAFETY LEVELS 0, 1, 2, 3, 4. An alphanumeric keypad was mounted on the wall, its red lamp shining red.

"What's that mean?" Sarah asked.

"More labs," he replied. "Where they handle infectious agents. Four is the most dangerous."

"Is it safe in there?"

"Probably," he said. "I assume they've got the various levels compartmentalized. If they created Medusa, they had to be very careful in handling it."

"You think they've got her in there?"

He scrunched up his mouth as he considered the question.

"I don't know. You guard the door while I check the rest of this area. If they're down there, we may have to wait them out. Assuming they follow standard protocols, this will be the only way in or out."

Sarah kept her gun trained on the door as Adam scouted the rest of the floor. There were no other offices, no keycodes, no keys anywhere, and he rejoined his bride by the door. Thirty minutes went by, then sixty, and he began to worry that they'd missed something. That Rachel's captors had slipped past them somehow.

But after eighty minutes, a noise, the first of any kind they'd heard. The keypad on the wall beeped, and the light toggled to green. Adam studied the door briefly and was thrilled to see the hinges on their side; the door would open into the room, giving them a place to hide. They crouched low against the wall as the door swung open toward them.

Two men emerged, both armed. Adam and Sarah slipped in behind them and disappeared behind the door. As the door swung closed, Adam could just make out the men marching down the corridor. They'd find the sentry missing in a minute at the most. They were just about out of time.

The door clicked shut behind them, and he heard the magnetic lock engage with a ominous thud. They were in a stairwell now, on the top landing. Opposite them was another door, marked with the numeral 0.

Adam peered down the middle of the staircase, which swirled down out of sight. Level 4, he presumed, would be at the bottom. The end of the line. The entire lab appeared to be buried in the earth.

A quick check revealed that the 0 door was unlocked. Adam cracked it open just a sliver and heard voices. His vantage point didn't give him much of a view, but it was a hospital-like setting, a number of beds lining the walls, similar to a hospital's emergency department. If Rachel were in this building, she'd have to be on this floor. There would be no rational reason for her captors to take her to the other levels, unless they planned to use her as some kind of guinea pig. And that didn't necessarily comport with the previous reports, that this man had taken a liking to her.

He paused there, the door cracked ever so slightly open by the barrel of his rifle, and he realized he was waiting for something. The right time, perhaps? He felt a gentle squeeze on his shoulder, and it was as if Sarah could read his mind.

"Now."

He opened the door and slipped inside Level 0.

The floor was dark but for a small corner at the far end of the corridor. There was a bed there, two men standing beside it, their backs to them. They appeared to be tending to someone in the bed.

Could it be her?

He pushed those thoughts aside as he crossed the linoleum floor, slinking along in the dark. Thirty feet away. Then twenty. Then a sudden clang behind him. He turned his head in time to see Sarah draw her arm tight against her body. She must have bumped into something. The sound drew the attention of the men, who began rotating toward them. As they did so, a gap opened up between them, giving Adam a clear look at the person in the bed.

Rachel.

hit.

S A goddamned tremor had wrested her arm from her control, slamming it into the metal rail of one of the empty beds just as they passed it. Another second, and she would have been clear. A lesson from one of her sergeants, way back during Officer Candidate School, snapped into focus.

"You cannot change the past," he'd said. *"You can only deal with the consequences."*

She grabbed Adam and yanked him down between two of the beds as the men opened fire on them. They took cover behind a telemetry machine that was pushed up against the wall.

"That's Rachel!" he gushed. "It's her!"

"Okay," she said as calmly as she could. "Let's keep our heads. If we fire now, we might hit her."

He nodded, his face lit up and panic-stricken. He was in shock, or something akin to it, and she had to bring him back to the reality of the situation. The room filled with the staccato pulse of gunfire. They needed a plan, or they'd be dead within seconds, and this whole trip would've been for nothing.

She had to draw them away from Rachel's bedside. Across the aisle was another row of beds, a dozen or so. If she could create a diversion, she might be able to give Adam an opening to slide in and grab his daughter.

"Listen to me," she said. "I'm going to buy you a few seconds to slide across the aisle and hide. On three."

"Two."

"One."

She pointed her gun skyward and squeezed off three short bursts; the ceiling above the men crumbled, showering them with dust and pulverized drywall and briefly distracting them.

"Go, go, go!"

Adam scampered across the open floor, and her heart stopped until he had resumed cover behind a bed. Behind her, the door to the stairwell opened, revealing the silhouette of another armed soldier. She turned and fired at him, a clip of bullets stitching the wall but missing her target. The fusillade was enough to push him back toward safer pastures, though, and the door swung closed again.

Now they had two fronts open on them. Ahead, the two shooters crept toward them, using the beds for cover. Adam was pinned against the wall, drawing heavy fire. Goddamn it, she'd forgotten how fast combat could spin out of control, especially this kind of close-quarters fighting like she'd experienced overseas. She scanned the room for inspiration, looking for anything that might help their cause.

She unplugged the telemetry machine and gave it a light shove; it rolled smoothly on its wheels, but it had real heft to it. She ran the same test on the bed behind her. Compared to the telemetry machine, it was as light as a feather.

She crouched down close behind the machine and started pushing it across the floor, picking up speed as she did so. The machine crashed into one bed, then another, then a third, and the room became a disco floor of spinning hospital beds. When she felt like she'd accelerated enough, she let go and dropped to the ground in a prone firing position. The shooters popped up to avoid the runaway machine, exposing themselves just long enough for Sarah. From less than ten feet, she fired two more bursts from the gun, striking both men in the upper legs.

They went down in a heap, dropping their weapons and writhing in pain on the ground. Sarah moved in and shot each of them in the head. With those two out of the way, she turned her attention back to the door.

It was propped open, ever so slightly, a strip of light from the stairwell cutting an angle across the floor. A black barrel was poking through, a cold, steel snake looking for prey. She fired again, but it was just a diversion. There was no other escape route; they could simply wait them out. She turned back toward Rachel, who had climbed out of the bed and was hunkered down between it and the wall. The look on her face appeared to be one of disbelief.

"Adam, grab her and let's go!"

She hunkered down and prayed they'd be able to find a way out.

That's what it had come down to.

Prayer.

ADAM STEPPED GINGERLY toward his daughter, who looked at him like he was a ghost. He wanted to scoop her up and hold her tight, the way he had the first time he'd laid eyes on her, the day she was born. Much like he'd been unable to fathom ever seeing her while Nina had been pregnant with her, it had been almost impossible these last few months to visualize an actual reunion with her. He thought about it, he dreamed about it, but it seemed nothing more than idle fantasy.

"Dad?"

"Hey, chicken wing."

She smiled and clambered to her feet. They hugged, a quick, fierce embrace. He never wanted to let her go, but he knew he had to. The road out of here was going to be harder than the one in. In fact, this rescue attempt may have done nothing but significantly shorten all their life expectancies.

"How the hell did you find me?" she asked.

"It's a long story," he said. "We gotta get you out of here."

"There are others," she said. "Other women-"

"I know," Adam said. "We saved as many as we could. But we have to go now. Sarah!"

"We've got a problem," Sarah said. "They've got the door blocked."

"Shit."

"How you doing on ammo?"

He checked.

"Half a clip, one spare."

"Drop your weapons!" called out a stern voice.

Adam turned to find three men standing there. All wore tuxes, all splattered with blood, and all were armed. The man in the center appeared to be the leader. He was a big man, broad in chest, silver-haired. One of the other men spoke into a headset.

A moment later, the door to the stairwell opened, and two more armed men entered the room. Sarah seemed to understand that the battle was over, and although she kept her weapon trained on the new arrivals, the ones she'd tried desperately to pin down, she did not fire.

She screamed, a deep, plaintive howl that told Adam that their goose was all but cooked.

Adam expected a smile, perhaps an evil smirk from the man. The look of a man who knew he'd won. The master villain, his devious plan preserved. But instead, he began the discussion with an introduction and a crude question, one that suggested he was totally befuddled by this bizarre turn of events.

"My name is Miles Chadwick," the man said. "Who the fuck are you?"

Adam considered the query for a moment and then replied with the only answer he could think of.

"It doesn't matter," Adam said.

"It does to me," Chadwick said.

Adam didn't care anymore. If they were dead, so be it. He'd done it. He'd found his little girl. Rachel knew he'd never given up on her. Maybe it wasn't going to finish with the happy ending, but that was OK. Just seeing her, even if it was just for a few minutes, had been better than years of stumbling around a plague-scarred world, wondering what had become of her, replaying her last voicemail to him over and over again, even long after he'd forgotten the details.

"So it really was you," Adam said.

"What was me?"

Adam glared at him.

"Yes. It was me."

"Jesus fucking Christ, why?"

The two newcomers filled in behind them, the proverbial noose tightening around their necks.

"I don't think I need to explain myself to a trespasser."

"Fine," he said. "I guess it doesn't even matter."

"I must say, though, I'm terribly intrigued by you," Chadwick said.

"I'm an intriguing kind of guy."

"Oh, you're a cowboy type," Chadwick said. "Mouthing off. Disrespectful when the only thing that might save you is some goddamned respect. See, the world is already better off without your kind. Again, I have to ask, who are you?"

Adam held Chadwick's gaze, careful not to look at Rachel.

"Were you here for her?" he said, nodding toward Rachel. "Do you know her?"

"No," Adam said. "Just looking for a place to stay warm for the winter."

"Really," Chadwick said. "Well, I would very much like to believe you, my friend, but I'm unfortunately cursed with this obscenely high IQ. It prevents me from buying bullshit stories like this one you're selling."

"Sorry you feel that way," he said.

Keep the conversation going, Adam thought.

"What was it like?"

"What was what like?"

"Killing everyone."

"You think I enjoyed it?" he asked, his voice cutting now, as though he'd run it across a knife sharpener.

A nerve. He'd touched a nerve.

"You didn't?"

"I'm not saying the outcome wasn't what we'd planned."

"Again, to what end?"

Chadwick ignored him, instead turning to one of his confederates.

"Bring me the girls," he said.

The man to his right, to Adam's left, stepped forward and grabbed Rachel by the elbow. As he did so, Sarah made her move. Taking advantage of this odd intermission, she turned and cut down the two soldiers behind her with a final burst from her machine pistol. Rachel howled and wrenched her arm free from the other man, who began scrambling for his own weapon. Rachel lost her balance, spinning around to her left, crashing into Chadwick's midsection, and the pair crashed to the ground.

Adam fired a burst, but the fusillade flew wild, burying into the wall beyond. He fired again, but the clip had run dry, and the trigger snapped impotently against the guard. The surviving guard was moving now, faster than Adam could decide what to do in light of his empty weapon. The man squeezed a burst from his gun, which missed. He held the barrel like a baseball bat and swung it at the shooter's head. The stock clocked solidly against the man's temple, the sickening sound of his skull cracking making Adam's skin crawl. He crumpled to the ground in a heap.

"Take another step, and she dies!"

This froze the room.

From the corner of his eye, Adam saw Chadwick's arm securely under Rachel's neck, the Uzi against her skull. He stumbled backwards, his hands up in surrender.

"Guns on the floor," Chadwick said. "Slide them toward me."

Adam looked at Sarah, whose gun was still up.

"You hurt one hair on her head," Sarah said, "and I'll splatter your fucking brains all over this room."

"Yes, that does appear to be the case, doesn't it? Except..."

"Except what?" Sarah asked.

"I doubt dear old dad wants it to come to that," Chadwick said, nodding toward Adam.

Adam's jaw clenched; he could feel his teeth squeezing together.

"It just hit me," Chadwick said. "The resemblance, I must say, is remarkable."

Again, Adam said nothing, his eyes locked on Rachel's.

"And both of you, immune to the virus," he continued. "Incredible. You're the first blood relatives I've encountered who survived."

Adam had been curious about this. So it had just been dumb luck that had brought them to this point. If he had succumbed to the plague, Rachel would have simply disappeared into this new world, subject to the whims of this madman for however long her life lasted. And if she had died, or if he'd never gotten her message, he'd have wandered aimlessly about the empty world. He never would have met Sarah.

That was the nature of the world. Events, lives, civilizations, turning on random chance. A guy forgets to set his alarm and misses the plane that crashes into the Atlantic Ocean. They stop to loot a UPS truck and they cross paths with Nadia. Roll the dice on humanity a hundred times, and Chadwick never brings the Medusa virus to market on ninety-nine of those rolls. But this one time, it had hit. And in this empty world, where connections were simultaneously fragile and profound, you'd need to be able to deal with the randomness of events. Who lived. Who died. Who suffered. Who thrived. Even bad guys had to deal with it. After all, random chance had brought this monster to the brink of ruin.

And when you accepted that, you realized there was nothing to be afraid of.

He lifted his gun back up.

"I'll kill her," Chadwick said.

"I don't think you will," Adam said.

Chadwick backed away from them, edging closer toward the door to the stairwell. Adam and Sarah followed as the situation reached a certain kind of stasis. There was an endgame here, Adam was certain of it. There was no way Chadwick would get out of this alive. But he wouldn't want anyone else to escape either. And they were in the one place where he could make sure that happened.

It all seemed choreographed now, the four of them moving in tandem, Chadwick's head bobbing from side to side as he continued using Rachel as a human shield. There was no way to draw a clear shot on Chadwick, so Adam stayed focused on his daughter. Her face was like stone, her eyes sharp. She had to be afraid; hell, he was. He hated that there was nothing he could do about it. He hated that he'd been the one to put her in this predicament, noble as his motivation might have been.

Random rolls of the dice.

They were in the stairwell now, descending into the bowels of the Citadel. Down past Level 1, the stairs echoing with their footfalls but nothing else. No one spoke. There was nothing either Adam or Sarah could do but follow, wait until Chadwick had delivered them to the last stop on this crazy ride.

Another minute brought them to Biosafety Level 2, where things began to get interesting. Here you had your influenza, your Lyme disease, your antibiotic-resistant bacteria. The descent was adding fuel to his already overheated heart, the steps carrying them down into a pathologic hellhole. Downward to Level 3. Yellow fever, SARS, tuberculosis. Scary stuff.

Then Level 4.

The big boys.

The major leagues.

Ebola. Marburg. Lassa. Smallpox. Hemorrhagic fever.

And their spiritual leader.

Medusa.

Adam was the last one on the platform, the big red 4 painted on the door virtually screaming at him. This was Medusa's dark birthplace. He could almost feel its presence, its shadow over them. This might as well have been the gate of hell, because hell was what had spewed forth from that door.

"It's not every day you get to witness something so momentous," Chadwick said. "What did you do before?"

"I was a doctor," Adam said, his eyes locked on Rachel.

"A man of science. Splendid! Specialty?"

"OB/GYN."

"How appropriate," Chadwick said.

"How do you figure?"

"You shepherded life into the old world. I shepherded the new world into existence. We're like mirror images of each other. Two sides of the same coin."

Adam was dumbfounded.

"Are you really giving me the 'we're not so different, you and me' speech?"

Chadwick laughed a little.

"Yes, that does seem a bit clichéd. But then again, how does a cliché become a cliché?"

Adam ignored him, his attention now focused on the door separating them from Level 4.

"Rachel, be a dear and type in the following code for me," Chadwick said.

"Go to hell," she said.

"Type the numbers I say, or I will shoot you."

"Then you'll die too, you piece of shit," Rachel said.

"Do what he says, Rachel!" Adam snapped.

Rachel sighed and dropped her head as Chadwick ticked off the code.

"Five. Nine. One. Six. One. Seven. Two. Four. Four. Three."

Rachel mouthed *I'm sorry* to her father and then typed in the code. The locks disengaged with a muffled thump, and the door slid open.

"Do come in, won't you?" Chadwick asked, with the verve of a proud dinner host.

dam followed them inside Level 4, Sarah trailing close behind. He heard her curse under her breath. He knew she was thinking the same thing he was. If they could just get a clean shot at him, this could all be over. But Chadwick was being careful with his positioning. The risk was too great. They'd have to continue this stalemate until an opportunity presented itself.

Level 4's anteroom was unremarkable in every way; there was nothing to suggest that death itself resided here, that there was no more dangerous place on the planet. There were two lockers, a bench and a sink. They followed through to the next room, the door sticking a little thanks to the negative air pressure, which drew air into the room. You always wanted air flowing *into* a Level 4 hot zone, not the other way around.

Blue light swirled about the room; this was ultraviolet light, a defensive measure that killed any viruses escaping from the lab, shattering them at a subatomic level. A second door stood on the other side of the small foyer. The room contained a decontamination shower, a bar of soap, a bottle of shampoo. Deeper into the lab Chadwick drew them, into the third room, the last safe room before entering the lab itself. Adam and Sarah followed, their guns up and ready, but Chadwick was still using Rachel as a shield.

The third room was the staging area. There was a desk and a computer mounted on the wall near the curved door on the far side of the room. That would be the airlock, the last checkpoint before death by organ liquefaction or hemorrhaging. There, men like Chadwick could dream up things like Medusa. There, mankind had destroyed itself.

"So this is where you built it," Adam said.

"Indeed," Chadwick replied.

"How did you get away with it?" Adam asked. "How did you never get caught?"

"You want me to explain my evil plan? Really?"

"Have you taken a good look out there?" Adam snapped. "I think it's a bit late to foil your plot."

"Fair enough," he said. "The truth is very simple. How did you get anything done in the old world?"

Adam considered the question for a moment.

"Money, I'm guessing."

"Precisely. The very thing that would have no use in this world was the very thing that helped bring it about. This was all made possible by money. The lab, the equipment, recruitment of the staff, the safety protocols."

"Dangerous work. And you were willing to die for it?" he said.

"Any good pathologist, any good scientist, really, must be willing to pay the ultimate price."

"Don't suppose you thought about using all your intellect and your resources for the greater good, did you? The CDC probably could've used a guy like you."

"Where the hell do you think I started my career?"

Adam blew a noisy sigh through his lips. He wanted to keep asking questions, both to delay the inevitable and to satisfy his own curiosity. For a moment, he couldn't think of anything to ask, and then one question roared to the forefront.

"You must have had a couple of close calls," Adam said. "You ever come close to getting busted?"

Chadwick laughed softly.

"A couple of times, actually," he said.

That was hard for Adam to hear. To hear that there'd been a chance to stop Chadwick's nightmarish vision from coming to life. To know that opportunities had been missed. To know that the clock could not be unwound, no matter how close they'd come to stopping him. The die was cast. This was the world now, forever and ever, amen.

"Once, I nearly had to activate the fail-safe."

He said it with the verve of a man at a barbecue recounting an old fishing trip.

"Fail-safe?"

"This lab is sitting on top of a thermobaric bomb," he said.

"Jesus," Sarah said, shifting her weight from one foot to the other, as though she were afraid she might detonate it.

"What's a thermobaric bomb?" Adam asked.

"It's the most powerful non-nuclear bomb in the U.S. military," she said, looking at Adam. "It would vaporize ten city blocks. It burns at four thousand degrees. But I don't understand something. It's an air-burst bomb. It won't work if it's buried underground."

"Very good," Chadwick said. "We had some modifications made. It's a one-of-a-kind piece. Amazing what you can accomplish when you're a military contractor."

"And it would've vaporized any evidence of what went on here."

"Exactly," he said.

"And how would one detonate this bomb?" Adam asked.

"I think our conversation is over," Chadwick said. "But I have enjoyed this little discussion."

It was worth a shot, Adam thought. He'd gotten the man rolling a little bit. Worth a shot.

"What do you think you're going to do now?" Adam asked. "There's nowhere else to go. We've got you."

Chadwick grinned.

"You know what they call the guy who graduates last in his med school class?" Chadwick asked.

It was an old joke, a good one, and Adam knew the answer, but he didn't want to engage in this banter. So he remained silent.

"What?" Sarah asked.

"Doctor," Adam said quickly, not wanting to give Chadwick the pleasure of delivering the punchline.

Chadwick laughed.

"What's your point?"

"Your doctor friend here hasn't thought this through," Chadwick said. "You think you've got me pinned down. My back to the wall. But it's not like that. It's not like that *at all*."

Adam was numb. At the moment he needed to be at his sharpest, he found himself dull and slow. All he could think of was Chadwick sending Rachel into a fog of disease as some kind of revenge for having his plans derailed. The man continued to hold his gun to Rachel's back.

Adam had seen enough; he took a step forward with killing on his mind. But as he prepared to make his move, he felt Sarah's hand on his elbow, giving him a squeeze. She squeezed it again, this time for a long second, and he realized she was trying to tell him something. Dread poured into Adam's heart like fresh concrete. Chadwick drifted over to the far side of the airlock, pulling Rachel along, where a touch-screen computer was mounted, and typed a series of commands into the monitor.

"What the hell are you doing?" Adam asked.

"Tying off all my loose ends," Chadwick replied.

He racked his brain for a solution that saved the three of them until it finally dawned on him. There wasn't one. All he could do was destroy the pathogen. They would have to be humanity's immune system, the antibody, the killer T-cell that finally rose up and snuffed out this terrible infection.

The airlock door whooshed open, revealing the small cylinder inside, the purgatory between the heaven of this safe room and the hell of the hot lab beyond.

"Inside," he barked at Rachel.

Her eyes widened in terror, and she began squirming like a chicken headed to slaughter.

"Don'tworry," he hissed, tightening the crook of his elbow around her throat. "All the goodies are locked up in the biosafety cabinets. Just don't break anything."

Together, they backed into the airlock. The door whooshed shut, sealing them off. A moment later, the far door slid open, and Chadwick and Rachel stepped into the Level 4 lab.

"What the hell is he doing?" Sarah asked when they were alone.

"He knows we'll follow them all the way," Adam said. "All the way."

The safety glass distorted their figures, giving the appearance of two apparitions floating about the lab. Chadwick puttered around the lab for a minute, checking a few items, before settling in at a computer workstation on the back wall. He continued to hold the gun on Rachel, but she looked frozen, too terrified to move or breathe.

"He's not trying to escape, is he?" Sarah asked.

"No," Adam said. "I don't think so. He knows it's over for him. We have to stop him from setting off the bomb."

"Into the breach, then," she said.

"Into the breach."

Adam pressed the button that unlocked the airlock and stepped inside, Sarah trailing close behind. The door sealed shut behind them. The room was very tight; he held Sarah close, and he breathed her in, knowing that it was probably for the last time. Her body felt warm against his. He could smell the cold in her hair, the hint of vanilla that always seemed present. It was over for them, but holding Sarah, being there with Rachel, managed to take the sting away a little. If they could stop Chadwick, he'd be okay with dying. He'd lived a lifetime in the past five months, and he was tired. So tired.

The airlock door opened with a hiss. The lab shimmered in a soft blue light, reflected in the glass from the UV room. Adam stepped in, his gun up. Chadwick turned to face them, but didn't seem fazed by the gun aimed at his head. He wasn't even holding one anymore.

Adam steadied the gun, but he couldn't find the resolve to pull the trigger inside the lab.

"Too scared to pull the trigger?" Chadwick asked. "I would be too, with all these scary vials in here. It doesn't matter anyway. You're too late. I've already triggered the shutdown of the generators. When the power goes, the security protocols will go. And one of us will become a new Patient Zero."

Adam's head swam with confusion.

"What are you talking about?"

"We didn't know for sure that Medusa would work. So we had a Plan B."

Rage swelled inside Adam; he sensed that time was of the essence, and here he was dealing in riddles and vague threats.

"What was Plan B?" Sarah snapped.

"Look around you!" Chadwick snapped back. "This lab houses the deadliest airborne pathogens known to man. Weaponized viruses and bacteria. When the power goes, the biosafety cabinets will be compromised. They'll disperse out of the lab, into the ventilation system, out into the air beyond. They'll infect wildlife, birds, other survivors. Who knows what'll happen then?"

"Shut it down," Adam barked at him.

"I can't!"

"Goddammit," Adam whispered. "God *dammit*."

"Oh, he did," Chadwick said. "God did damn us."

"Why do this?" Adam screamed, his voice tinged with panic now. "You've gotten everything you wanted. What possible good would come from starting another plague? Let the world have a chance."

"The world doesn't deserve a chance," Chadwick said with a terrifying finality in his voice. "Don't you get it? The world was a shitty place before the plague, and it's a shitty world now."

"Then you should've just eaten a bullet like any other psycho fed up with the world," Adam said, his rage pushing his needle into the red.

"And not make my mark on history? I couldn't have that. I simply could not have that."

"How much longer?" Adam asked. "How much longer till the viruses are released?"

"Twelve minutes," Chadwick said, looking at the monitor. "And then they'll spread for miles, infecting every living organism. You might be immune to Medusa, but you won't be immune to all of them."

Rachel, who'd backed up toward them, took Adam's hand in hers. Despite everything, Adam couldn't help but feel good about having found her. If nothing else, he'd kept his promise to her. That insane promise he'd made on his porch, drunk on Jack Daniels, listening to her desperate voice-mail message. He'd found her. He could die in peace.

That was when Chadwick went for his gun.

"No!" Sarah screamed, diving in front of Rachel and Adam just as the gun roared. The round struck her in the shoulder, and she tumbled to the ground in a heap.

"You son of a bitch!" Adam bellowed. As Chadwick prepared to fire again, Adam rushed him like a bull, slamming into him like an open-field tackler. The collision lifted the men off their feet, and they crashed to the ground. Chadwick grunted hard as his back hit the ground, absorbing much of the impact. He delivered a hard right hand to Adam's head; Adam's field of vision exploded into whiteness, and he rolled off the big man's chest.

"That's for ruining my plan," Chadwick snapped.

His head swimming, Adam launched himself at Chadwick, and how strange it was that this was now being resolved via a glorified bar fight. The greatest crime in human history, perhaps humanity's extinction, and justice was being delivered via fisticuffs.

Maybe we never did learn.

He delivered a swift shot to Chadwick's kidneys, then another, and then another. Chadwick responded with another swooping fist, and that one connected purely with Adam's ribcage, stealing his breath like a thief. He dropped to a knee, and he gasped for air, a grouper flopping about the deck of a fishing charter. This was it; Chadwick had the upper hand.

He tried to get up, but Chadwick stunned him with a knee to the chin; Adam's teeth clicked together, his jaw snapping shut before he could get his tongue out of the way. A burst of blood filled his mouth, and he toppled backwards onto his seat. His consciousness began to fade and the world began to recede from view, made opaque by a dark curtain.

Chadwick had the gun again, and he pressed it to Adam's forehead.

Sorry, world, he thought. *I tried.*

The gun roared, but Adam felt nothing. He wasn't sure if he would feel pain or if the lights would simply go out on him, but he was still there, staring at a red stain blooming on Chadwick's stomach. Adam gingerly turned his head to the left, a punch-drunk boxer on his stool looking for a loved one in the stands, and saw Rachel. And a gun in her hand. Chadwick dropped to one knee, then to both. He grasped at his midsection; blood seeped through his shirt, coating his hands, spilling onto the ground.

Adam slapped the gun out of Chadwick's hands and brought a fist down on the back of Chadwick's neck as hard as he could. The impact of the blow sent Chadwick flat on the ground. Adam reared back for a second blow, but before he could, Chadwick delivered a heavy elbow to Adam's midsection. Adam rolled away, gasping for air, his lungs burning.

Now. It had to be now. They were running out of time.

The men struggled to get off the ground; Adam focused his whole existence, every microgram of energy on beating Chadwick to his feet. He dialed back through his personal hard drive through every mile he'd run, every weight he'd lifted, every sit-up he'd done. Every power song, the anthem from the Rocky movies, anything that might get his ass off the ground before this monster.

"Dad, move!" Rachel screamed. "I can shoot him!"

"No!" Adam called out as he struggled to win this most elemental battle. His voice sounded thick and muffled. "We need to know how to stop the viruses! Check on Sarah!"

"I'm fine," she called out weakly. "The bullet grazed me."

And then he was up. As Chadwick began pushing up off his knee, Adam reared back and drove his foot square into the killer's chest. The crunch of rib bones was audible, and Chadwick flew backwards, back to the ground, emitting a desperate screech of pain that Adam worried might shatter the safety cabinets. Adam was on him like a hyena, grabbing him by the collar and pulling his head off the ground.

"Tell me how to stop it!" Adam pleaded. "There has to be a way."

Despite the stomach wound, despite the shattered ribs, Chadwick managed to smile. As he did so, a trickle of blood bubbled from his lips. "They're in final shutdown mode now."

"I know that!" Adam said. "Tell me how to stop it."

"There's only one way to stop it," Chadwick said.

"How?"

"The bomb."

Adam's heart fluttered.

"Shit!"

Chadwick giggled like a toddler who'd found a cookie.

"And you're running out of time," Chadwick added. "No more than eight minutes now."

"Tell me how to detonate it," Adam said.

"No," he said. "You can go fuck yourself."

Adam hesitated for a moment, just a split second, and then he pressed down hard on Chadwick's bullet wound. The screams of pain echoed through the lab. Adam looked into Chadwick's eyes as he tortured the man, and he realized he didn't feel bad about it. Not one bit.

This wasn't a man he was dealing with here. This was hell personified. Satan's imp. God's fallen angel. Sent to earth to destroy all things.

But then he did the most human thing possible.

"Oh, GAWWWWWD!" Chadwick howled. "STAWWWWWPP!!"

Adam released the pressure. His hand was damp and sticky with Chadwick's blood.

"The biometric sensor," Chadwick gasped. "It will read my right thumbprint and open the program that controls the security protocols. Look for an icon called Fail-Safe."

He paused, grimacing as another wave of pain washed over him.

"The detonation will be instantaneous."

He closed his eyes.

Adam had heard all he needed to hear, and he rushed back to Sarah's side.

"Rachel, keep an eye on him."

"I got him," Rachel said.

"Let me see it," he said to Sarah.

Her face was pale, and her eyes a bit cloudy. He pulled up the side of her shirt, which was thick and cold with blood.

"Aw, fuck," he said.

"You sugarcoat bad news like that with all your patients?" she asked.

"Shit, I'm a terrible liar."

Rachel stepped toward Chadwick and delivered a wicked boot to his groin; he could never be certain, but Adam thought he heard the man's testicles rupture. A final layer of pain over the walls of his mortal wounds. Chadwick moaned, his hands covering his battered genitals.

"That's for all the women who died here, you asshole."

A few seconds later, the moans faded away, and Miles Chadwick died on the floor of his laboratory, amid the ethereal afterbirth of his soulless creation.

"You need to get out of here now," Sarah said.

"We'll never make it," Adam said. "The viruses will spread in every direction."

"The bomb," Sarah said. "I'll do it."

"No," Adam said, and he felt silly saying it. It was a knee-jerk reaction, the ideal, the easy way out. Of course she wouldn't stay to detonate the bomb. They'd figure a way out, and all of them would survive.

Jesus, the human mind was an optimistic little shit sometimes.

"Someone has to stay and detonate the bomb," she said softly.

"Look, it may not be that bad," Adam said, looking for a way, any way, out. "If there's no one left to infect, the viruses will die off."

"But you and Rachel will be exposed."

This Adam had no response to.

"Sweetie, there's no other way. And you're running out of time."

Adam shut his eyes tightly and tried to silence the clinician that was always inside him. *She's right,* the voice was saying. *Either she dies, or we all die. And she's going to die anyway.* His stomach churned as he thought it, and he felt his mouth water. It was not unlike the sensation he'd experienced the day the fox had bitten him.

"The bomb will destroy everything, right?" she asked.

"If it's as powerful as you say it is, the heat will vaporize everything."

"Then someone has to stay."

Adam had to remind himself to breathe; the only thing he was aware of was a ripping sensation in his chest, as though someone had reached in and torn his heart straight out.

"You kept me going when I'd given up," Adam said behind a curtain of tears. "And now I'm supposed to leave you here to die?"

She took his face in her hands.

"Yes," she said. "That's exactly what you're going to do. This way, I don't have to die of Huntington's, and I can save you and Rachel. You won't have to watch me fall apart a little bit at a time. You won't have to watch me suffer. And I know you wouldn't do what had to be done."

"I would, I would, I promise."

"No, sweetie, you wouldn't," she said. "And I wouldn't want you to."

He held a clenched fist to his lips as Sarah turned to Rachel. For a brief, terrible moment, he found himself wishing he'd died in the plague, thinking about detonating the bomb himself so he wouldn't have to feel the pain of losing Sarah. But that wouldn't be right. It wouldn't be fair to Rachel.

"You get your dad out of here now, okay?" Sarah said.

Rachel nodded.

"Dad, he kept a truck parked in the back of this building," Rachel said. "He always kept a spare key in a little box in the wheel well."

Rachel stepped forward and hugged Sarah hard.

"I'm sorry we won't get to know each other," Sarah said. "I think I would've liked that."

"Me too," Rachel said, her words coming on a canvas of light sobs.

"Let's get his body over to the computer," Adam said.

Adam slid his arms under Chadwick's armpits and slid him across the room. There was nothing graceful about it; he dragged him like a side of beef. All he cared about was getting his thumb near the sensor. He'd bite the asshole's thumb off if he had to. It took about a minute, leaving them precious few.

Sarah tottered over, a bit more alert now, her hand holding her shoulder. Adam pressed Chadwick's stiff finger against the sensor, and the computer beeped loudly. A screen titled *Security Protocols* popped up, sporting a series of icons. The icon in the bottom lower screen was tagged FAIL-SAFE.

"You'd better go," Sarah said.

"God, I fucking hate this," Adam said. "I love you so much."

"I know. Now go."

"Dad."

Adam looked up toward the sound of the forceful summons, a bit amazed it had come from his little girl. From his chicken wing. He'd missed so much of her life. He vowed he would spend the rest of his days making sure he didn't miss anymore of it. He owed that to her. And to Sarah.

He turned back to Sarah and wrapped her tightly in his arms. He kissed her hard.

"Remember how much I love you," she said. "Now get the hell out of here. You've got five minutes."

"Dad. It's time to go," Rachel said. Tears streamed down her cheeks, but her face was hard and full of resolve. She'd accepted Sarah's gift, and she'd be damned if she was going to blow it.

"I love you," Adam said as he felt Rachel's hand take his. Then she was pulling him, back through the anteroom of Level 4 and into the stairwell. Simply being outside that horrible place galvanized him, and now they were both hauling ass up the stairs. Their footfalls echoed through the silent stairwell.

The Citadel was a dead place now.

Up four flights of stairs and then through the empty control room.

Tears blurred his vision as he thought about Sarah, Sarah, Sarah, down there, with that red fail-safe trigger, the holocaust that would consume her and bring a storm of fire and ash on this place, this terrible place. And after that storm had passed, Sarah Wells would be gone from this earth forever, an earth that might be a bit better because of what she had done.

They ran and ran, back down the corridor, past the encased newspapers of a world that no longer existed, down the hall and out into the cold New Year's morning. Being out there now, that's what drove it home that Sarah was gone now, and he froze there in the doorway.

"Dad!" Rachel screamed. "We have to go. Or it was all for nothing!"

They snaked their way around the building, where they found the Suburban waiting for them. The keys were right where Rachel promised.

"I'll drive," Rachel barked.

She climbed into the driver's seat and started the car. Adam got in the passenger seat, and they drove away.

"Thank you for coming after me."

"Thank Sarah and Charlotte."

~

So, Sarah thought.

This is what it's like to die.

She stood at the terminal, her finger hovering over the icon, watching the clock wind down toward zero. She wanted to give Adam and Rachel as much time as she could.

1:03

It would be like no death that she had ever envisioned.

Since her diagnosis, death had consumed her every waking thought, the obsession itself a virus that had infected her. And when she'd survived the plague, she couldn't think of a crueler fate to have befallen her. To be left alone in a world of the dead while her Huntington's took its goddamn sweet time. That was, at least, until she met Adam. For a short time, at least, he had protected her from her own darkest thoughts. He had inoculated her with love.

0:48

She wasn't afraid of dying. You think about something often enough, and it becomes familiar. It becomes the cranky neighbor next door that freaked you out at first, but that you eventually got used to, even when he stumbled in to your living room drunk and naked and claiming he thought he was in his own house. She wasn't looking forward to it exactly, any more than you looked forward to the drunk neighbor's antics. But she wasn't afraid. She wished she'd had more time with Adam. She wished she'd had time to get to know Rachel. And Adam had been right. There was a certain demented beauty to this post-plague world, where you'd been able to think clearly for one goddamned second without worrying about e-mail or Facebook or this new political scandal or that potential carcinogen in your pantry.

OK, she told herself. Enough pontificating.

Time to go.

:10

She held her breath and pressed the Fail-Safe icon, waiting for the flash of light, the boom, whatever it was that would be her last sensation in this mortal coil. But nothing happened.

A single window popped up on the dark screen.

ERROR

Oh no.

:07

She tapped the X in the corner of the window, which returned her to the screen of icons.

Now she was pissed, a bolt of anger spiking through her. This wasn't how it was supposed to go. They were entitled to this happy ending, as shitty as it was. She tapped the icon again.

:03

This had better work. This had better work. This had better goddamn-

A bright, terrible light filled the room.

54

dam told her to turn east at the main highway. She drove a
mile, and then stopped at a forty-five degree angle in the
middle of the lonely road. Her father sat in the back seat,
looking west toward the Citadel, awaiting the fiery holocaust that would
mean the end of this brave woman. He'd barely said a word since they'd
pulled away from the lab. But he was here. That was something she was
still trying to wrap her head around. It seemed to be an improbability of
the highest order.

She looked at the outline of the walls, distant and shadowy now, the
residue of a bad dream. How often had she dreamed about being clear of
them? It was the oddest sensation. Being outside the walls was making
her jittery, as though she'd downed one too many cups of coffee. She'd
become used to them over the long weeks and months; it had become a
shell from the world beyond, a way not to deal with the thing that had
happened. But now she was here, outside, free of the Citadel forever.
Snow continued to fall on this virgin morning of the new year, jaundiced
in the harsh glow of the Suburban's headlights.

"How did you find me?" she asked. The question popped loose like a
fart, but the truth was, she had to know. She didn't like uncertainties,
loose ends. She liked closed systems, where everything matched up.

"Nadia," he said, shifting slightly in his seat. "We met her on the road. She saw a picture I had of you."

"How is she?"

"She's safe," Adam said.

"You had my picture?"

"Yeah."

He had my picture.

She wondered what their relationship would have been like if the plague had never happened. If she were being honest with herself, and what the hell was the point of lying to yourself anymore, their relationship hadn't been going anywhere fast. She wasn't quite at the stage where she addressed her father by his first name, but on the continuum from Dad to Adam, she figured she'd been closer to the latter. They were always pleasant, to a fault, splashing around in the shallow end of the relationship pool, where no real damage could be done. She'd felt no real connection to him, and only when the world was literally ending around them had she thought to call him. Absence had not made the heart grow fonder. Absence wiped away connection like a pencil eraser, leaving nothing but a faint residue behind.

"I'm sorry," Adam said.

"What?"

"I blew it. From the moment your mom and I split up, I blew it. I should've been there for you. I should've been where you were. You ended up here, in this place, because of stupid, selfish decisions I made twenty years ago. If I'd been nearby, like any good father with a lick of sense, you wouldn't have had to go through that."

"But then you would've missed out on your exciting cross-country adventure."

He laughed at that. A definite chuckle.

"And I wouldn't have met the women I met," she said. "And Chadwick would've gotten away with his little plan."

It was hard to argue with her logic. They'd have survived, and Chadwick would be here, building his empire a little bit at a time.

"When did they take you?" he asked.

"Mid-September, I think," she said. "I was headed toward St. Louis."

"You heard about that too?"

"Yeah."

"Don't feel bad. There was nothing there."

"I couldn't get your message out of my head," she said. "I kept thinking there was a chance you were still alive. And until I knew one way or the other, there was no reason to stop. It wasn't like I had anything else to do."

"On your own for a month," Adam said, mostly to himself. "Hey, I'm sorry about your mom and Jerry."

"Yeah," she said. "Hey, thanks for the flowers."

"What?"

"You sent me flowers."

"I forgot all about that."

"I got them the day I first heard the news about the flu outbreak back east."

Silence descended on the passenger cabin once more. One way or another, whatever time they had left was running out. Because if Sarah couldn't detonate the bomb, another bomb was ready to take its place. An invisible bomb that could take them all down. The waiting became a rapidly expanding balloon, the stress fracturing the thin membrane keeping them sane.

They didn't have to wait much longer.

A pinprick of light told them it was happening. Like a supernova, the tiny dot of crimson inflated exponentially into a star of fire, followed by the sonic boom of the explosion. No words were exchanged, but they both got out of the car at the same time. Rachel shielded her eyes; even from this distance, the explosion had hastened an early if temporary dawn. Despite the deep chill, the blast wave blew its warm breath across the plains as it turned the Citadel into a memory. Maybe they should come back here one day and put up a sign, she thought. To remind the world what could happen in secret labs when no one was paying attention.

The fireball continued through its lifecycle, narrowing at the throat, expanding at the top into the familiar mushroom cloud shape. It lit up the night, the air filled with the strange sound of snowflakes hissing as they were extinguished by the gigantic blaze. They watched until the fire began to recede, having gorged itself on its fuel supply and now quickly running out of gas.

Rachel glanced over at her father, his face illuminated by the orange glow of the blaze. Tears cut through the grime caked on his face.

FIFTEEN MINUTES LATER, they were back in the truck, making their way east toward the farm. Adam was driving, puttering along at less than fifteen miles an hour. Snow had begun to sweep across the blacktop, making it difficult to distinguish between highway and the rough terrain of the plains. The sparse road signs and billboards served as lane markers, but even then, he drifted onto the shoulder a couple of times and then had to pray the four-wheel drive had the *oomph* to get them back on the road. The whole drive, he was consumed by the image of the fireball erupting in the snow-laden sky.

She had done it.

Part of him was glad for her. Nothing had scared her more than the prospect of a slow death by Huntington's. And the idea that he would watch her die, a process that could've taken months or years, was too horrible to contemplate. Especially in a world where access to modern medicine was limited at best. That was the mature part of him, and it had been a small one at that. No, the selfish side of him, the greedy chief executive officer of Adam Fisher, Incorporated, was sick with grief because the woman he'd searched for his whole life had been delivered to him tied in a bow of cataclysm and then taken away from him just as cruelly.

What had been the point of all this then?

What had been the point of heaping pain upon pain, sorrow upon sorrow?

He felt Rachel take his hand in her own.

"Dad, I'm sorry about your friend."

He squeezed her hand.

"You would've liked her, I think."

He chewed on that for a moment.

"Or not. Hell, maybe you would've fought like cats and dogs. But I would've been okay with that. Because it would've meant that I had both of you around."

"How did you meet her?"

Adam told her, starting with the fox, continuing through Freddie and Caroline to meeting Nadia in Kansas to Evergreen and Freddie's betrayal, and finally through Sarah's sacrificial plan to find the camp. He told her about Sarah's confession about Huntington's and he saved the best part of the story, their wedding, for the end. His words came in a flood, the discussion with his daughter watering a part of him that had been left dry long ago. It began filling a hole inside him, one that he'd barely been aware was there, one that may have remained empty if the plague had never happened.

That was a hell of a thing to wrap his mind around.

These great and pure things that had filled his life in the past few months. This reunion with Rachel, his relationship with Sarah. They'd only been possible in the face of humanity's near-extinction.

When he was done, he felt a little better.

They made it to the farm a little after four in the morning. Adam carefully navigated the narrow road servicing the main house, his heart in his throat as he scanned the scene for the vehicles carrying Charlotte and the other women. Then he saw it. Lanterns bobbing about in the dark. As he got closer, the outlines of the other survivors began to take shape in the dim light cast by the lanterns.

"They made it," Rachel said excitedly. "They made it."

A smile stole across Adam's face.

"Welcome home, Rachel."

55

Spring.

Adam stepped outside the guesthouse he shared with three other men, his back aching but otherwise not feeling too bad. It had been one thing to be a forty-two-year old man in the world before the plague; it was another thing entirely for that man to be thrust into a pre-Industrial Revolution world. They'd spent the day before sowing the fields with the early-season vegetables, the seeds harvested from the stores of farms around the area. A check of the local almanacs had given them the data on when to plant what, and they were following the intelligence they'd uncovered to the letter. None of the survivors were farmers, and so it was a lot of trial and error. But it was something they had to get right if they had any hope of establishing a permanent settlement here in northern Kansas.

Adam sat on the old weather-beaten rocking chair and looked out over the farm. It was early, the sun just poking over the horizon. The air was sticky with humidity, promising the first real warm day that year. The feel of the thick air on his skin reminded him of those terrible days when Medusa had carved its initials into the world. It was Sunday, and the farm was quiet, the sole day off from working in the fields that the group had agreed upon.

He missed Sarah terribly. Once the rush of finding Rachel had passed, her death had hit him hard. Someone organized a memorial service for all those who had died at the Citadel, including Mike Stills, whose crazy-ass sacrifice had proven perhaps more important than anything Adam himself had done. The service was nice, those lost memorialized by wooden crosses at a sunny end of the farm.

The winter had been long and harsh. Temperatures struggled to climb out of the thirties for most of January and February, and each thick, gray front that moved in brought with it the threat of heavy snow. Most of the time, the clouds brought with them flurries or no moisture at all, but a few times, they found themselves socked in with a heavy snow-fall. It was during this time that everyone wished they'd never spoken a bad word about meteorologists in the pre-plague world because a some-what accurate forecast, it turned out, was far better than no forecast at all.

The cold-weather months had been spent living day to day, foraging for food and clean water. There was no shortage of cold-weather gear or woodstoves, so the low temperatures had not been much of a problem. Two residents, both on the north side of sixty, had died during the winter. One succumbed to a massive heart attack, or at least, that had been Adam's guess. A second had developed pneumonia and had not responded to treatment.

With the addition of the Citadel refugees, the population of their collective rose to seventy-three souls. Twenty-four men, thirty-five women and fourteen children. There weren't enough beds at this farm to accommodate everyone, and so they'd spread out to five neighboring farms. Each farm elected its own representative, and together, the repre-sentatives formed a governing body of sorts. The women from the Citadel had clung together, occupying the farm closest to the central compound and selecting Rachel Fisher as their representative. Diane Williams, the chef who'd stepped up in Adam's absence, was elected to serve a four-year term as mayor of the collective. The group had decided that a single leader was necessary, but the five-member board carried an override power to ensure that no single person amassed too much power.

Fresh water was a priority. Each of the farms sported its own well, which had been a good start, and they taught themselves the basics of well maintenance with books from the library in a nearby town. To be extra safe, Adam directed that all water used for drinking and cooking be filtered through charcoal, sand and gravel and then boiled for two minutes. That had seemed to do the trick, as no one became ill from drinking water.

There was no shortage of things to worry about. Security of the farm was never far from his mind. They hadn't seen many others, which didn't surprise Adam given the remoteness of the farm. But, he suspected, that wouldn't last forever. He worried about bandits and warlords and rapists and folks who'd been bad guys in the old world, now living in a world without any filters at all. And it wasn't just bad guys they'd have to worry about. At some point, they'd have to interact with other people for trade or for the far more basic need of pairing people off for procreation.

Adam's greatest concern was for the welfare of one Erin Thompson. She wasn't the only pregnant woman in the collective, but she was the first one due to give birth. The baby's fate might well be all theirs. There was no way to know whether all babies born to immune mothers would die, or whether baby Stephen had just drawn a shitty hand. There was no way to know what fate awaited Erin's baby, the progeny of a naturally immune mother and a vaccinated father. Adam hated Miles Chadwick, but he found himself praying on a daily basis that the monster's vaccine was as good as advertised. He had a recurring nightmare in which he was the only one left on the planet.

He was so lost in thought he didn't notice Max toddling up the steps.

"Hi, Doc," he said.

"Hey, Maxie," Adam replied. "Have a seat."

Max sat in the other chair, and they rocked in silence for a while. He seemed like he wanted to say something, but Adam didn't force the issue, lest he scare the boy off like a frightened puppy. He had shot up over the past few months, looking less like the scared boy they'd found in the chip aisle of that grocery store so many months ago. His resilience had surprised Adam; these were heady times he was living through, and a sudden change might knock him on his ass for a bit, but he was always back up on his feet in no time. Maybe it was because kids weren't as set in their ways as adults; they were more malleable, more adaptable to change.

"Can I ask you a question?" Max finally said.

"Shoot."

"Why did he do it?"

Adam's chair stopped rocking. Max was asking about Freddie. Freddie, who Max had worshipped. Freddie, who had destroyed so much.

"Well," he began, and then he paused.

He thought about Freddie and Caroline and Sarah. He thought about how much Freddie had lost when so much had already been taken from him. He had died because he had no hope, much like Caroline had. Sarah, on the other hand, had died for precisely the opposite reason.

"I'm not entirely sure about this," Adam said gently, "but I think it was because he didn't think things would ever be good again."

"What do you think?" Max asked. "Do you think they will be?"

Adam considered the question for a long moment.

"I do."

ERIN THOMPSON WENT into labor on the fourth day of June. She toddled up to his house as the sun was going down, just as he'd sat down to enjoy his evening whisky and cigarette. He allowed himself one of each every day, but no more. There were no other nurses or doctors in residence at the farm, and so Adam had to be on call twenty-four hours a day. Rachel and Max had expressed interest in learning medicine, and so Adam was doing his level best to teach what he knew. How inadequate it all seemed compared to his own medical training, but what choice did they have? No more medical schools meant doing it this way or not at all.

"How far apart are the contractions?" he said.

"About five to six minutes," she said.

On the porch with him was Harry Maynard, another refugee from Evergreen.

"Harry, run and find Rachel and Max for me, please."

Harry was a big man, but he bolted off the porch like a cheetah. Adam saw the terror in his eyes. Everyone had been anxiously awaiting the baby's arrival, as they all wanted to know the same thing as Adam.

Would the baby live or die?

He escorted Erin over to the makeshift clinic he'd set up on the first floor of one of the guest houses, where he'd cobbled together instruments and supplies as best as he could. No one had needed major surgery yet, but their luck would run out at some point. He could only do what he could do, he told himself over and over. Frontier medicine would be all they had. Part of him wondered if they should try and relocate to one of the smaller cities, where they'd have access to a hospital, but then he would think about the avalanche of corpses or roving gangs and the fact that a hospital with no electricity was no better than the clinic he'd set up here.

Rachel and Max were already at the clinic when he and Erin arrived. They were busy setting up the gurney and the stirrups and all the supplies for what would hopefully be a routine delivery. Based on his weekly check-ups, they should be in good shape, but he didn't have to wander too far down his mental corridors to find that dark room marked Patient A.

After Erin was settled in the bed, Adam pulled on a pair of latex gloves, fresh with powder, and palpated her abdomen. A test he'd done a thousand times, ten thousand times, so often that it was like breathing. His stomach flipped when he realized that the baby had turned breech since he'd last examined her a few days earlier. Naturally, he thought. Nothing was going to be easy. Erin was in a fair amount of pain, but holding up well. She needed to know what was going on, but he didn't want her to panic.

"Erin," he said, using his most doctorly voice. "The baby's flipped, but it's going to be okay."

Huge droplets of sweat had beaded on her head, and she paled at the news.

"Breech? It's breech?"

"Yes, but I know what to do." He was terrified, but he kept his voice calm. So much was riding on this baby, and that bet wouldn't even kick in unless he got it out of her womb and into this world.

"Anything," she said. "Do anything you have to do to get the baby out."

Adam couldn't help but smile a little; he was reminded of the Crusading Mom-to-Be he'd occasionally encounter in his practice, the ones hell-bent on executing a specific birth plan, cleaving to it like it was some religion. He worried about these women, those who lost sight of the big picture, the only picture that mattered – getting the baby out safely. That was all that mattered. Not whether the baby was born in a loud hospital or underwater or with a doula or on the back of a circus elephant. He was thrilled to see that Erin was on board.

"I'm going to manipulate the baby a little," he said. "That can often work. He may just need a little encouragement to flip back around."

"OK," she said, her voice small and quiet.

It was all on him now; Erin had done all she could do. Now was the time that he earned that honorary at the end of his name, the respect accorded him since the day he'd been able to call himself Dr. Fisher.

He began a procedure called the external cephalic version, carefully moving his hands around her swollen belly, poking and prodding the little one along. It was painstaking and risky work, especially without an ultrasound machine, ensuring that he was putting the right amount of pressure here, easing up there. But he didn't want to do a C-section unless it was absolutely necessary. His mind had cleared out all the clutter that he'd once allowed to distract his thinking. Then he let an image of the hidden fetus fill his brain, and he could see in his mind's eye the baby rolling, rolling, rolling. He didn't let himself think about the happy outcome he was hoping for or the devastating outcome he feared. He worked solely in each moment, in each centimeter that he moved the baby's head downward.

He paused and wiped his brow with his forearm, and then went back to work. Everything had fallen away around him. Rachel and Max, even Erin herself seemed very far away. This was Adam and the baby, Adam and the future of their little community, perhaps the world beyond.

Then it was done.

He checked again and felt the baby's head oriented in the proper position. He exhaled loudly; if it hadn't worked, he would have had no choice but to perform an emergency C-section.

Then he let the world back in; he found Erin eyeing him like a hawk, trying to read his face for any nugget she could interpret and obsess over as he conducted his work.

"It's going to be OK," he said. "His head is in the right position now."

She cupped a hand at her lips and began to weep.

EIGHT HOURS LATER, and the time was drawing near.

"One more big push," Adam said. "Wait for the next contraction and then really bear down."

"I can't," Erin Thompson said. She was red-faced and sweaty. Her hair was matted down on her face. She was at the end of her rope. Thoughts that she wasn't going to make it began to creep around the edges of his mind, and plans were being made for a C-section. They were equipped for it. Sort of. Adam had performed a few hundred of them, but it wouldn't be the relative piece of cake it had used to be. Without proper equipment and infection control protocols, so many things could go wrong. And yes, the day would come where he'd have to perform one. He just didn't want it to be today.

"Yes, you can, Erin," he said. Gentle but firm. "You lived through the last year. You can damn well make it through this."

"No! Please. I want to rest."

Rachel, who'd been at the bedside, watching, learning, leaned over and whispered into Erin's ear. Erin listened, rapt, her eyes wide and unblinking. As Rachel spoke, Erin nodded a few times. Adam couldn't say under oath that she'd smiled, but a look of peace came over her face. He didn't know what Rachel had told her, and he didn't much care, because the patient was back in the game now. They were getting to the end now; they'd survived the final crisis.

"You ready, Erin?"

"Hell yes," she said. "Let's get this baby out."

He heard her taking some deep breaths as he kept his eyes on her baby's head, now crowning. One more push, and the baby would be out, and the clock would start all over again. He'd been dreading this day as much as he'd been looking forward to it. Again and again, his mind returned to the variables at play here. A naturally immune mother, a vaccinated father. Would the baby's blood carry the necessary antibodies to fend off Medusa? Miles Chadwick had seemed to think so. Then Erin gave one mighty push, and all modesty was lost. A deep, manic howl of pain and effort, a small bowel movement, and then the shoulders were clear.

"One more!"

Another push, and out came baby Thompson, shining, glistening with viscera, and a little bit blue. Adam guided the little boy into the cleanest towel they had, one they'd been holding for this very moment;

as he cleaned the baby off and checked his mouth and nostrils for any obstructions, he began marking the seconds on his watch, his old friend, the watch that now marked the way forward. At eight seconds, the baby whimpered once and then screamed. The blue skin tinge began to fade as the pink hue of health began seeping in like a morning sunrise. At one minute, he ran through the Apgar testing. Heart rate and breathing were good. Arms and legs flailing about. At five minutes, he repeated the testing, and the baby passed with flying colors.

"Great job, mom," he said to Erin. Rachel was leaned over, hugging the new mother. Both were crying. Max was looking down at his feet, his hand shielding his eyes. Even Adam felt a few tears well up.

Erin Thompson held her swaddled baby close to her chest, and nuzzled the little boy's forehead with the tip of her nose.

"Thank you," she said. "Thank you, thank you, thank you."

～

IT WAS AFTER MIDNIGHT. A full moon hung in the sky, fat and happy and bright. Adam was far too jazzed up to sleep, and so he sat outside the clinic, smoking a cigar. He'd spent the last two hours monitoring Erin and her baby, but she seemed to be recovering quickly. Max and Rachel were tending to Erin now.

The others were celebrating the news of the birth. It was a bit of a hollow celebration, given that they'd be on pins and needles for the next week to see if the baby would come down with Medusa. You didn't need a medical degree to know which way the wind was blowing. But until then, they would have themselves a party. Someone had built a bonfire out in one of the fields, and they drank warm beer and toasted to the group's good fortune. Several had come to congratulate Adam and invite him to the party, but he declined. He wanted to be near Erin.

He heard the door behind him, and Rachel stepped outside the clinic and onto the porch with him.

"How is it in there?" he asked.

"Both asleep," she said. "She tried nursing, but he didn't seem terribly hungry."

"At this point, it's more important that she goes through the motions, establishes a routine," Adam said. "Babies usually aren't super hungry the day they're born. By tomorrow or the next day, that's when he'll start chowing down."

"Oh," Rachel said. "And if the baby doesn't nurse?"

"We'll go with formula."

"And, uh, if the baby gets sick?"

"Then we'll deal with that, too."

Rachel began to weep.

"I don't want that baby to die," she said behind a curtain of tears.

Adam plugged the cigar into the ashtray and got up from his chair. Rachel threw her arms around her father and buried her face into his shoulder. He held her tightly, letting her cry it out. He tried to remember the last time he'd held his daughter to console her, but he could not. He wasn't sure he had ever done it.

"There's no way to know what's going to happen," Adam said.

"I just wish there was something we could do," she said.

"I know," Adam replied. "Me too. But all we can really do is wait. How about you wait with me?"

Rachel nodded and sat down in one of the chairs. Adam reclaimed his cigar and sat down as well. The air was warm and redolent with the smells of summer. The cicadas chirped loudly and the fireflies pinged the farm with their warm yellow light.

Together, they began to wait.

≈

≈

≈

ABOUT THE AUTHOR

David lives in Virginia, where he works as a lawyer and novelist. His short comedy films about law and publishing have amassed more than 2.5 million hits on YouTube and have been featured in *The Washington Post*, *The Huffington Post*, and *The Wall Street Journal*.

Visit him at his website.

ALSO BY DAVID KAZZIE